Angela Jackson is an English historian and writer now living in Catalonia. Her doctoral thesis, *British Women and the Spanish Civil War*, was published by Routledge in 2002, after five years of research that also provided the historical background for *Warm Earth*, her first novel. In 2003, she won the Jocs Florals in Torroja del Priorat for a study that was published first in Catalan, then in English as *Beyond the Battlefield: Testimony, Memory and Remembrance of a Cave Hospital in the Spanish Civil War*, by Warren & Pell, 2005.

The focus of her recent research has been on the period shortly before the Battle of the Ebro. Based on interviews with local people and the memories of International Brigadiers, this new book is to be published in 2007. As president of the Catalan association, 'No Jubilem la Memòria', she works to promote research and education on the subject of the civil war.

See www.nojubilemlamemoria.tk

WARM EARTH

ANGELA JACKSON

WARM EARTH

Pegasus

PEGASUS PAPERBACK

© Copyright 2007
Angela Jackson

The right of Angela Jackson to be identified as author of
this work has been asserted by her in accordance with the
Copyright, Designs and Patents Act 1988.

All Rights Reserved

**Whilst many of the stories in this book are true,
the characters are fictional and are not portrayals of real
individuals, either living or dead.**

No reproduction, copy or transmission of this publication
may be made without written permission.
No paragraph of this publication may be reproduced,
copied or transmitted save with the written permission of the publisher,
or in accordance with the provisions
of the Copyright Act 1956 (as amended).

Any person who commits any unauthorised act in relation to
this publication may be liable to criminal
prosecution and civil claims for damages.

Cover illustrations: Nuria Estapé
Courtesy of D.O. Montsant & Josep María Llorens

A CIP catalogue record for this title is
available from the British Library.

ISBN 978 1 90349 031 0

*Pegasus is an imprint of
Pegasus Elliot MacKenzie Publishers Ltd.*
www.pegasuspublishers.com

First Published in 2007
**Pegasus
Sheraton House Castle Park
Cambridge England**
Printed & Bound in Great Britain

In memory of Frida Knight

CONTENTS

1.	Bright Hopes	13
2.	Warm Earth	52
3.	Golden Threads	103
4.	Eager Hearts	134
5.	Winds of Change	184
6.	Gathering Clouds	224
7.	Lost Dreams	267
8.	Worlds Apart	304
9.	Twilight Fires	338

CHAPTER 1

Bright Hopes

I

Richmond, London, Summer 1996

The chill waters of the Thames enfolded her. She suddenly felt the weariness of her eighty years, an aching to be still, to surrender, but the patterns of a lifetime are not so easily overcome. Constance Courtney had learned how to struggle against exhaustion in the past and now her reaction was almost involuntary. A gentle touch from a memory of swimming in another place, in a sunlit long ago, brought life to her motionless limbs. As her head broke the surface and she took a first, rasping breath, she could see the small upturned boat a few yards away, the bone thin arms of her old friend, Addie, clasping the hull with determination. Nearby, the balding heads of Max and Sam popped up like white blisters in the water. She could hear their cries. Addie was calling for help in her clear strong voice that still bore the unmistakeable trace of an American accent. Max joined in, his shouts reedy and thin from too many years of smoking. Soon, above all, Constance could hear Sam calling her name, thinking of her before anything else as always, his harsh, deep bellow still powerful after years of street-corner speeches. Voices from the bank were crying out, 'Hold on, hold on.' The only words that came to Constance's mind and then fought their way from her lips with increasing frenzy were 'My handbag! My handbag!'

Afterwards, in the hospital, Constance had still not regained the long-practised grip she maintained over her emotions, and the sobs kept rising inexorably to the surface. The photograph, a fragile sepia reminder of days when happiness could unexpectedly light her life in vivid warm colours, was now irretrievably lost in the cold and gloomy waters of the river. The glimmer of brightness she had been able to recapture when looking at the picture, so many times during the years that had passed by, might now be impossible to grasp without his image, caught and held in her hand. Memory could be so elusive. You thought you would never forget, but things kept on slipping into the shadows, out of reach. She had always carried the photograph in her handbag, and had transferred it with care to the zipped pocket inside each new bag when the old one was worn out. She could have had the original copied, but that wouldn't have been the same. This was the one that he had given to her; this was the one he had touched.

Her son was aghast at her unaccustomed display of despair. He ran long fingers nervously through his thinning fair hair and made a minute and unnecessary adjustment to the position of his glasses, a habit that tended to annoy anyone who troubled to watch him for any length of time.

'What ever is the matter, mother? You'll be out of hospital tomorrow. It was only an old handbag. We can replace anything missing. There's no need to get in such a state about it. And the others are fine – just a bit shaken up.'

What ever had made the four of them take a boat out anyway? They just never would behave, he thought, with a momentary resurgence of the embarrassment that had built up over the years at most things connected with his mother and her friends. She was more often than not in the forefront of some fracas or other. Although, he thought as he looked at her in the unaccustomed role of 'the patient', the shock of the day's events had made her seem uncharacteristically helpless. Or, he asked himself, was this just the first time that he was truly aware of the fact that his mother was now an old woman? Even, he thought with a shiver of apprehension, verging on doddery?

Constance was by now grasping the edges of a degree of

composure. She had begun to wonder why she had never shown the photograph to her son. Perhaps, she thought, if she had a daughter..? But a son was less likely to be interested in old loves, and hers in particular would have squirmed in discomfort to hear of her youthful passion, long before she made the mistake of marrying Harold. For a moment, a few frames from the category 'Before' flickered across her closed eyes. Usually, when someone else was present, she would quickly snap shut her mind on these images. When talking about the war in Spain she could direct her thoughts into carefully constructed channels. Lately, journalists and historians had come to her for interviews with increasing frequency, and, as a remnant of living history – a role she embraced with amusement and more than a little pride – she had been asked to talk to several groups of college students. Her narrative would flow through the days and nights of her work as a nurse near the front lines, conveying an impression of those turbulent times; the hopes and the horrors, but steering clear of the maelstrom of her deepest feelings, always fearing an uncontrollable public plunge into the past. By keeping silent on the most precious things, inextricably bound up with the most hurtful things, she could keep them for herself, to nurse like wounds. Despite this need for hoarded secrets, she had chosen to call her son Charles, although her husband would have preferred something more in keeping with his family tradition. At least she had passed on Karl's name, if not his genes. So few remained who knew anything about those days she cherished.

Perhaps as a result of the sedative she had been given, she was finding it more difficult than usual to keep the memories safely buried, even though she was still aware of her son in the room, seeing him hovering uncomfortably by the bed through the fringes of her eyelashes. But Charles could tell that she was, at last, growing calmer. Her eyelids quivered but stayed shut, and no new tears added to those that remained in the wrinkles at each side of her decidedly idiosyncratic nose – a nose that had been so elegant in her youth, till she had sailed from her seat by the driver through the windscreen of the lorry. Only a gnarled old olive tree had saved them from plunging into the depths of the valley below. She had never blamed the exhausted Spaniard for nodding off after so many hours driving on the twisting mountain roads, though her collision with the bonnet had left an indelible imprint - a marked diversion in her formerly aristocratic profile.

Charles found himself feeling undeniably perturbed by his mother's dishevelled hair, usually captured securely in a variety of styles involving coiled plaits, but now escaping to unaccustomed freedom. Surely someone would come and sort that out for her. Trying to sound sympathetic to compensate for his former impatience, he said more softly, 'I'll leave you to rest now Mother, and come back later,' but traces of his eagerness to be gone were easily detectable to someone who had heard a million visitors escape from hospital bedsides with platitudes, duty done. He slid out with a small sigh of relief.

'But he couldn't be expected to understand,' she thought without bitterness, 'no-one does who wasn't there.'

A familiar face peeped round the door. 'Here you are,' said Addie in a stage whisper. 'They didn't want you to have more visitors, but we couldn't leave without seeing that you were alright.' All three friends shuffled in, trying to be quiet but not succeeding very well. Sam's round frame seemed to collide with various pieces of equipment in the room and Max, whose hearing aid had been ruined by the unplanned immersion, greeted her in a voice several decibels louder than he realised. Addie perched on the edge of the bed, taking Constance's hand. The depressing atmosphere of the hospital room seemed to brighten a little with the energy she radiated. The abundant creases on her face deepened with the addition of a crinkled smile. Anyone looking into her ever-alert eyes discovered a strength within them which more than compensated for the impression of frailty given by her small frame.

'We'll only stay a minute,' said Sam, anxious not to tire Constance too much. His large white upswept moustache stood out against his rather florid complexion. He pulled at it, as he usually did in moments of thoughtfulness or stress. Max, head always full of plans, of ways to fix things and make them work, could see that Constance needed cheering up. His methods for raising the spirits of those around him, honed during a long period of incarceration in a Spanish prison camp, were simple but effective. East-end London humour was one of the mainstays, a wry comment being his response to even the most dire situation. Getting people to talk about their favourite meals usually produced good results too, even if the food itself was not likely to be available for some time. The last approach, one he felt was suitable on this occasion, was to look to the future, to better days ahead. Enthusiastically he began to speak of the trip they were planning to Spain later in the year with a large group of old friends.

Max moved to the head of the bed and bent down towards Constance, his face breaking into its customary grin, 'Connie,' he whispered loudly into her ear. He was the only person who dared to shorten her name in this way, somehow getting away with it when all others failed. 'What'll you say to the Spanish prime minister when you meet him? Will you tell him he looks like Charlie Chaplin?' There was, without doubt, a distinct similarity between Prime Minister Aznar and Chaplin, particularly on the moustache front, though definitely no common ground as regards sense of humour. 'Will you give him a kiss on both cheeks?' continued Max, warming to his theme.

'I shall give him exactly what he deserves,' was Constance's ambiguous reply, delivered with mock decorum.

'Ah,' thought Sam, 'she's perking up a bit.'

Seeing Constance's mouth regain a little of its usual

resolve, Addie joined in the speculation about the invitation they had all received to return to Madrid. The honorary citizenship that the Spanish government was now offering them had been earned sixty years before.

'Think of the old friends we may meet there,' said Addie, squeezing Constance's hand a little too tightly, 'people we haven't seen for years.' Constance pulled her hand from Addie's grasp and patted her arm affectionately. She had avoided going to Spain for all the sixty intervening years – there were too many ghosts for her there. Now, however, she realised that she actually was looking forward to going back, just this once. As Constance's eyelids began to droop, her friends said their goodbyes and left as quietly as they could, relieved that she was not as bad as they had feared.

A faint smile crept to the corners of Constance's mouth as she heard a shrill burst of birdsong outside the window. 'That sounds like a wren,' she thought as she drifted into sleep.

II

East London, Summer 1936

Yet another bedspring had worked its way upwards through the layer of newspapers. Constance had spread the pages over the sagging frame of the double bed, not wishing to deliver the baby onto the pile of old coats that served as a substitute for the missing mattress. The coats varied in degree of disintegration, but were uniformly filthy. As she knelt on the edge of the bed, attempting to lift the woman into a more comfortable position, she could feel the escaping spring dig sharply into her knee, catching on the black wool stocking. 'Another darn!' she thought with annoyance. But on seeing the pathetically grateful smile of her patient, she found it impossible to be angry about it for more than a moment.

Constance, freshly qualified as a midwife, had found a position at the London Hospital for Mothers and Babies. She was now enjoying the independence of working 'on the district', away from the confines of the hospital, but the disciplines relating to hygiene and asepsis she had absorbed during her training had done little to prepare her for the conditions she was to encounter away from the wards. This time, she had arrived to find her patient about to give birth to her fifth child. Like many of the mothers she saw these days, this one was weak and worn out from pregnancies following in close succession, from lack of food and from bringing up her children in a tenement block that was clearly unfit for human habitation. Constance had immediately taken charge of the situation, shooing most of the gathered neighbours away, giving the least desperate looking one a penny for the meter to heat water on the shared gas stove that lurked in the shadows on the landing, and asking the least harassed of them to care for the woman's other small children who had been sitting wide-eyed and uncertain, close to their mother.

It was not just the nurse's uniform, crisply contrasting with the drab and slightly greasy surroundings, that had produced obedience to these instructions without protest. Although for many years her family had been living in what were commonly referred to as 'greatly reduced circumstances', early years spent in relative comfort had left her the legacy of an upper-class accent and an authoritative manner. Even junior doctors, normally hard to deter as far as attractive nurses were concerned, soon lost confidence when they encountered the dark-eyed gaze of the distant and disdainful Constance. This did not endear her to many of the nurses at the hospital, who would have welcomed such admiring attentions. Amongst others however, she was grudgingly respected for the way in which she always undertook more than her fair share of unpleasant tasks. She had also proved useful when a spokeswoman was needed to put forward complaints about the inedible meals they had endured for weeks in the nurses' home. A slight improvement had resulted from her competent handling of the interview with Matron. Constance had based her argument firmly on the need for the nurses to have adequate nourishment in order to fulfil their duties to the patients. This approach was the only one that could have brought a favourable response. During this brief confrontation, despite the gap in their ages and positions in the nursing hierarchy, each had recognised a kindred spirit. Both were aware that they shared a deep commitment to nursing, and were prepared to make the sacrifices that the work demanded.

Now, as Constance waited to help bring yet another infant into the world, she couldn't help thinking how this would increase the already insupportable burdens carried on the scrawny shoulders of the woman who lay before her, clammy with cold sweat after hours of labour. Only the charity of philanthropists on the hospital board had prevented her from giving birth with no medical care at all. With a husband in prison and the few shillings she was allocated after the Means Test, there was little hope that things would improve for her in the future. The baby, limp and blue, eventually emerged, and Constance had to work quickly to induce a first breath from the tiny inert form. As her hands moved expertly to carry out the needed rituals, an icy shard of thought crystallised in her mind.

'Why add to this poor woman's sufferings?' she asked herself miserably, then immediately flushed hotly at the idea of abandoning both her newly born patient and her principles.

Later, returning to the hospital on the bus, her mind kept returning to that moment of doubt. Fatigue made her feel as if she would never escape from the whirling circle of thoughts that always led her back to the same inevitable conclusions. She was a nurse; she was supposed to help to relieve suffering; instead, she seemed to be adding to it. She had wanted to be a nurse for so long. Even in childhood she had hated to see creatures in pain. Soon she no longer found comfort in the church sermons she attended with her mother and sisters. It became impossible to believe in a God that allowed little birds to die in the winter cold. As she grew up, she clung fervently to the belief that nursing would give her the chance to do something for the poorest people who needed help most. Now, she felt that all she was doing was prolonging their pain. The grinding notes of the bus engine seemed to go on interminably, like the monotony of the poverty she saw around her.

The bus was making little progress through the traffic and Constance sought something to distract her from the painful recognition that the image she had held of herself as a sort of angelic figure ministering to the poor now seemed risibly pretentious. The persistent and disturbing voice of her conscience, mocking her former naiveté, was silenced by the sight of a growing puddle of blood, slowly leaking from the bag on the floor at her feet.

'Afterbirths are such a problem,' Constance thought with irritation, 'when they don't appear there are dire complications, and when they do, there's nowhere to put them.'

The disgusting sanitary provisions in the tenements, down several flights of stairs and across the communal courtyard, were less than adequate for their disposal, and the piled-up rubbish was subject to the constant attentions of rats and cats. Constance usually chose what for her was the lesser of evils, taking them back to the hospital for incineration, preferring not to venture closer to the overpowering smells of the accumulated waste and sewage.

She looked about her for something to reinforce her inadequate attempts at wrapping and located a tattered newspaper on the unoccupied seat behind her. As she returned to her seat with haste to stem the increasing flow of leaking fluid on the floor, her eye was caught by the photograph on the front page, a young woman, smiling, with some sort of unwieldy-looking gun resting on her shoulder.

'Women Take Up Arms to Defend Democracy in Spain' ran the headline. Constance had been too exhausted of late to follow events taking place abroad, and was not much interested in the popular news topic of the romance between the future King and an American divorcée. She normally had little time for reading the papers, and certainly no spare money to buy them herself. But the cheerful face of the girl in the photograph, surprising when considered in the context of war, made Constance preserve the outer pages of the newspaper for closer examination. The rest, fortunately bulky, a day full of newsworthy events, she either folded and stuffed around the parcel in her bag, or used to cover the unsightly pool. She then turned her attention to the article accompanying the photograph, initially intending to skim through the facts but becoming more engrossed as she read on. Phrases such as 'legally elected Republican Government' and 'right-wing insurgents' and words like 'Reds' and 'Fascists', needed further consideration to be fully understood. Nevertheless, she soon gleaned enough information to know that the Spanish people had voted for a government with a programme of radical reforms to help the poor and illiterate, and that now all these plans were under threat because the rich and powerful were mobilising forces to recapture their traditional authority.

Constance read with great care the report on how women had actually taken to the streets to fight with the men to defeat the rebellion, and were now marching with the militias to the front lines. Assailed by her own doubts, she was envious of their apparent certainty, risking everything to fight for a better future. 'They're really trying to *do* something in Spain,' she thought, 'whilst here we all just put up with it.'

She saw with sudden clarity the striking contrast between the numb resignation on the face of the mother she had just left and the determined optimism of the girl in the newspaper portrait. Her eyes drifted down to a printed box at the bottom of the page, 'Volunteer nurses wanted for Spain'. A sharp intake of breath was followed by a tense pause during which she read the details of the advertisement. Then a look of relief spread slowly across her face as she realised, 'I'm a nurse. I can go to help them,' and an unaccustomed expression of happiness began to light up her solemn brown eyes.

All the next week, Constance's mind incessantly revolved around the idea of nursing in Spain. She decided not to tell anyone. They would only try to dissuade her, and although she was certain that their attempts would be in vain, she felt she would be unable to summon up reasonable replies to counter even the most obvious arguments against volunteering. Of course it would be dangerous, and people would say that she was foolhardy to go. They could also point out that she was ill-informed as to the causes of the war and ask if it was right to interfere in someone else's business. In response to such logic, all she would be able to say was that her instincts told her to go, that this particular struggle went straight to the heart of all that was wrong with the way people were living.

An outbreak of sickness amongst the nurses and midwives at the hospital meant that several weeks passed before she could plan a day off duty to go to the address given in the newspaper for the recruitment of nurses by the Spanish Medical Aid Committee. She hoped that it would not be too late. Perhaps hundreds of nurses would have already applied, she thought, a flutter of vexation in her mind at having had to wait. Firstly however, there was a visit home to endure. Her rare days off on Sundays were usually spent with her parents, listlessly helping her mother with the housework and cooking in the small, cluttered house where they now lived. Her father had never recovered from an ignominious bankruptcy following the collapse of the family book publishing firm. Jessica, Constance's mother, had never been able to adapt to the harsh realities of living without servants.

Meals especially, were a source of vague perplexity to her. Sometimes the potatoes were served with abundant hard lumps in the mash. Occasionally they disintegrated into the water and appeared in the tureen like soup. Constance could not understand why basic culinary principles seemed to be beyond her mother's grasp. Her father didn't seem to care one way or the other, as he sank ever deeper into his own failure. Her younger brothers, inured to gastronomic disasters, complained only when the meal was totally inedible.

This particular Sunday however, was even more trying than normal for Constance. The desultory process of preparing vegetables in the cramped and dark kitchen seemed interminable, and the squabbles of her brothers at the table during lunch began to grate even more than usual on her taut nerves. During the meal, the growing longing to break the boredom of the day eventually proved irresistible.

'I shall probably be going away for a while,' she said in a brief pause between bouts of her brothers' bickering. 'I'm going to volunteer to nurse in Spain.'

Much to her surprise, the statement did not explode like a bombshell over the table, but instead, was immediately greeted with approval by her mother.

'But darling, how exciting! What a coincidence. Only yesterday I was talking to Nancy Cunningham at our bazaar – I hadn't seen her for ages. Well, her daughter – you do remember Diana, don't you? You used to play together so nicely – she is going to Spain to work as a nurse there too.'

Constance had distant memories of Lady Cunningham, and of playing with Diana in the big nursery with the dapple-grey rocking horse. Their close friendship had been terminated, quite kindly but firmly, with her parents' sudden loss of financial security and social status. Jessica no longer moved in the same circles as Nancy, but church bazaars were always considered neutral territory, where even those from the upper echelons of society would mingle with lesser mortals.

Constance, in watching a worried frown spread over her father's face, had lost the thread of her mother's enthusiastic dialogue. As a child, she had loved her father dearly, and still remembered the hours they had spent together, engrossed in the books he would bring home specially for her; the children's encyclopaedias with illustrations of far away places and strange-looking animals, and the adventure stories of castaways and heroes. These books had laid the foundations for a lasting delight in literature. But she had grown ever more angered by her father's lack of fighting spirit in the face of adversity, by his resigned acceptance of disappointment. Somewhat guiltily, she realised that she hadn't given his reaction to her plans even a moment's thought. She grasped her mother's flowing train of conversation again at the point where her name was being mentioned.

'So, Constance dear, we can *both* go to the manor house this afternoon when I go to ask Nancy if she will help with the 'Distressed Women and Children's Appeal', and then you will have the chance to talk to Diana about Spain. What a good idea it would be to travel together.'

Constance was immediately aware of her mother's blatant strategy to re-establish a friendship with Lady Cunningham through their daughters' shared adventures. Jessica, struck by a sudden ray of optimism, envisaged a renewed intimacy between the girls that would improve her daughter's chances of meeting a 'suitable' young man. 'Though heaven knows,' she sighed inwardly as her hopeful anticipation faded, 'Constance will be a difficult girl to place in a good marriage, despite her looks - just too serious.'

That afternoon, Constance reluctantly acquiesced in her mother's designs and accompanied her to the manor. At her mother's insistence, she had tried to 'make herself look nice', sewing a missing button on her blouse, polishing her shoes and tidying her hair, sticking even more grips into the coiled bun at the back of her neck. Curiosity at the prospect of revisiting her childhood haunts and seeing Diana again was combined with a certain degree of pleasure at the idea of travelling to Spain with a friend rather than alone. After all, it was a far away country, full of unknown challenges.

Lady Cunningham's welcome was, as to be expected, gracious, without a hint of obvious condescension. Constance realised with shock how unfashionable and dowdy her own mother now appeared in comparison with the slim elegance of Nancy.

'You must stay for tea,' Lady Cunningham insisted, when Jessica mentioned Constance's intention to go to Spain. 'Diana will be back shortly and you can discuss your plans. How adventurous you girls are today!'

In the spacious drawing room, with beams of afternoon sunlight streaming through the tall, draped windows facing the gardens, Constance's mother began to relate her own adventures as a young woman, when she had travelled to the wilds of Canada to live with her brothers for several months as they tamed new territories.

'The pioneering spirit, you see,' she said delightedly, 'it runs in the family. The snow was so deep we had to travel by sleigh and we couldn't get through to the town for weeks.'

Nancy was soon speaking of her journeys in India as a girl, of Rajahs and elephants. Constance sat stiffly on the settee, surreptitiously glancing around her, attempting to look as if she were accustomed to be in a room that exuded the unmistakable aura of wealth. With horror, her eyes strayed from the silk carpet at her feet to the newly acquired ladder marching from the foot of her stocking, prominently ascending the side of her calf to disappear beneath her skirt. She tucked her legs beneath her in a vain attempt to hide this damning sign of lack of grooming. The sensible lace-ups that she wore for work unfortunately left traces of polish on the carpet as she moved. The offending shoes suddenly reminded her of the large black coal barges on the canal, closely coupled side by side to be pulled by the horse on the towpath.

Diana's entrance startled her from these meanderings. Still in cavalry-twill jodhpurs from her ride, Diana nevertheless looked unmistakeably sophisticated. Her sleekly bobbed hair swung across her cheeks as she reached out for the bell pull.

'Shall I ring for tea, mother?' she asked brightly, before coming forward to be introduced to the guests.

'Yes dear. Do you remember Jessica and Constance – it's so long since you last met.' Diana's eyes glanced briefly over the visitors, needing little time to assess their social position. 'How absurd the impoverished upper-middle classes seem when they hang on so pathetically to the vestiges of gentility,' she reflected, scathingly. Meanwhile, her small, well-painted lips formed an empty welcoming smile as she dropped into the chair beside Constance.

'Hullo,' she said listlessly, then, as she glimpsed a memory from her past in Constance's solemn expression, she added with more interest, 'I remember you – you always got to ride the rocking horse.' Constance also vividly recalled the battles between them in which the loser, usually Diana, ended up with the dilapidated hobby horse.

A large silver tea service encircled by bone china cups appeared as if by magic, discreetly placed before them on an ornately engraved heavy tray. Jessica and Nancy were discussing fund-raising for the 'Distressed Women and Children'.

'Of course,' Nancy was saying, 'I'm sure we could make sacrifices and raise quite a good sum if we rally round. We could all go without a fish course at breakfast for a month, as a sort of gesture of solidarity with those poor mothers. Contributions from that should amount to a nice donation.'

Constance wondered how she was remaining demurely on the settee in the face of such injustice. Only yesterday she had been helping yet another malnourished mother with a difficult delivery, passing the intervening hours by counting cockroaches. The chair on which she had been sitting had been one of the few remaining pieces of furniture, not even worth pawning. Now, as her fingers dug into the rich fabric on the arm of the sofa, it seemed preposterous to be listening to talk of 'going without'. Those like Nancy knew nothing about what the words really meant, she thought with impotent rage. She longed to shake Nancy's complacency with an angry tirade on the subject of poverty, but knew her mother would be deeply hurt by such a social gaffe. With sadness, she realised that the sheer immensity of the gulf between those who expected a fish course every day and people who were lucky to get a small portion of cod and chips once a week was certainly too wide a chasm to ever be bridged by politely restrained reasoning.

Jessica noticed that the sporadic conversation between her daughter and Diana had faltered. Without responding to Nancy's offer of a fish course embargo, Jessica said hurriedly, 'I hear you are going to nurse in Spain, Diana. Constance is going too.'

'Oh, really!' Diana seemed most surprised. 'I had such trouble arranging to go – they're hardly accepting any volunteers from abroad. I only got my chance because Princess Cristina, the Infanta, is a friend of mother's and she has arranged for me to stay with the Duquesa de Montemar in Jérez and take a nursing course so I can work at the front. Much better than spending another boring season in London.' She turned to Constance.

'How are you getting there?'

A slow tide of apprehension was rising to Constance's throat. 'Through the Spanish Medical Aid Committee,' she replied very quietly.

This time her words did fall like a bombshell, causing a sudden silence in the room.

'But,' said Diana at last, amusement mixed with derision clearly evident in the pursing of her lips, 'those people are helping the Reds!'

Jessica felt her heart descending to the pit of her

stomach. Although unaware of the meaning of most political jargon, she did know that the 'Reds' were the communists and their allies – a godless assortment of rabble rousers, murderous anarchists and revolutionaries who threatened decent society. How could her daughter be thinking of becoming involved with them?

As Constance had suspected, Diana would be on 'the other side' with General Franco who was leading a military uprising to overthrow the Republican government. The Catholic Church and the landed classes were firmly behind him. 'A Christian gentleman', Franco was called by the rich and powerful, 'the Saviour of Spain.' She tried to murmur something about the rights of the ordinary people who had voted the Republic into power, and the need to defend democracy, but having little knowledge of the details, her confidence quickly failed and she fell silent. From her flawed stocking to her outmoded hairdo, from her social inadequacy to her suspect political affiliations, she felt herself to be an interloper in the drawing room. 'They would like to excise me,' she said to herself, thinking of the cancerous growths that the surgeons sometimes removed with such relish.

Jessica was attempting to gloss over the awful discovery that the two girls would not be likely to form a bosom friendship. She returned to the safer subject of the charity appeal. Nancy, now determined to bring the awkward encounter to a close, was guiding them towards the door. Their progress was delayed by Diana, who drew attention to a particular framed photograph on the bureau. It showed the Infanta with her husband, Prince Alfonso, and their three sons, two of them in air force uniform. Diana's eyes instantly alighted on the face of one of these aristocratic looking young men. She pointed to him with unconcealed joy.

'This is Freddy,' she told Constance. 'He's flying with the German Condor Legion in Spain. I shall be able to see him more often when I'm over there and....' Her fixed gaze on the figure in the photograph and the words she left unspoken left no room for doubt as to where her hopes lay. Constance noticed that the rather soft features of Diana's beloved were marked by a small but prominent scar beneath the right eye.

'The scar's from duelling,' said Diana excitedly, seeing Constance's curious stare, 'he's half German, and it's a tradition, you know.' She was eager to continue talking about Prince Alfredo, always referring to him as Freddy, in what to Constance seemed like a tone more suitable for small furry pets.

'His father is a cousin of the King of Spain and his mother is a German Princess, that's why he's with flying with the Condors,' she explained proudly. 'His brother's with them too. We've all known each other for ages because our families always spent the summer together when we were children. We had such fun.'

Diana obviously could have continued on this theme for hours, if not for the interruption of her mother who ushered the visitors out into the hall, her impeccable politeness marred somewhat by her haste in running through the ritual phrases. The disappointment Jessica felt at the outcome of the meeting as far as her daughter was concerned was hidden behind a forced smile as she thanked Nancy for her promise of donations to the appeal. Despite her initial reservations, Constance had felt herself warm a little to Diana as she talked of Freddy with what seemed to be a genuine deep affection. Though no longer the tomboyish friend that Constance remembered, Diana at least seemed willing to risk the hazards of going to Spain to do something useful, rather than drifting through the endless round of parties that were normally the staple interest of her set. This was certainly a point in her favour in Constance's view.

'Well,' said Diana turning again to Constance, 'I don't expect our paths will cross in Spain if you are really going to nurse the Reds.' 'But,' she added rather more generously, 'the best of luck anyway'. Constance managed to smile in return.

'Will being on opposite sides mean that we become enemies absolutely for ever?' she wondered as she walked with her mother down the long gravelled drive to the bus stop.

III

Autumn came crisply to Cambridge in 1936. Adelaide Eglantine Maclaurin, driving her Austin Seven along the Backs by the river, blinked as her glance was caught by the sunlight flickering low between the leaves. She was, as always, amazed by their yellows and reds, and like a child, took great pleasure in kicking their rustling colours into the air whenever she walked across the windblown open greens. She hummed the melody that for several days she had been struggling in vain to capture on the violin. Loving music utterly was not enough to make one an inspirational performer it seemed. Nevertheless, the tune suited her buoyant mood as she swung round the corner and over the bridge into town. Several years before, her family had come to England from the United States to live in her mother's home town of Cambridge. Her father, one of the most respected American scientists in his field, had accepted the prestigious Rouse Ball Lectureship at Cambridge University, but when the year of tenure was over he had been loath to leave the project he was working on with colleagues in the research department. Rather than return to Boston, they had stayed, a move that Addie didn't mind at all. She loved the university city, though her upbringing in the States had given her an openness and lack of respect for convention that sometimes caused problems in the traditional, somewhat rarefied atmosphere that prevailed in Cambridge.

The porter at Trinity College greeted her with a smile, quite willing to extend one of the special concessions due to a research professor to his amiable daughter. 'Alright, Miss

Addie,' he said with a nod, once again allowing her the privilege of parking on the cobbled forecourt. Nobody who knew her called her 'Adelaide', and she hated 'Eglantine', although its meaning, derived in part from the Latin for needle, sharp and keen, rather suited her nature. Her younger brother had taunted her with it when they were children. 'Addie-layed-an-egg-and-Tina-ate-it' he would chant over and over, rapidly and monotonously, till she was forced to beat him into howling submission for his lack of wit and annoyingly relentless repetition. Now she was twenty-one, such battles were beneath her, but relations with her brother still tended to be fraught. Not that she really had much in common with her two elder sisters either. From the lofty heights of their academic achievement, she felt that they had regarded her lurching progress through educational establishments with more than a little disdain. School had bored her to distraction and she was more likely to be found paddling in streams catching sticklebacks than attempting to complete long overdue homework. She had also broken with the hard-won tradition, begun by her mother, of studying in Cambridge at Newnham College. When they had arrived in England, her sisters had followed in their mother's footsteps, even to the extent of living in the straight-laced atmosphere of the women's Hall of Residence so that they could fully experience university life. Though Cambridge University still did not deign to give degrees to women students, it did give them a certificate to prove they had taken the same exams as the men, and sometimes beaten them too. Addie was certainly stubborn enough to overcome the derision that the women faced on many occasions as 'blue stockings', but formal studies and the restricted life led in the women's colleges were not for her.

Thinking of an alternative however, was proving more difficult than she had expected. There was so much to be done, so much to change in the world, the problem was where to begin. Helping with her mother's philanthropic causes didn't seem to be at all satisfying. On the scale of things that should be put right, such charitable efforts would hardly register. She impatiently pushed her thick, dark, unruly curls behind her ears yet again, and her rather plain face took on its customary determined air, illuminating her features with energy. This vitality was difficult to resist. For anyone in Addie's radius, life became unmistakably more exciting. Anything might happen, and usually did - bastions fell when Addie set her mind to something.

At the moment, one unwary moth in particular seemed to be drawn to the flame. It had slowly begun to dawn on Addie that the attention being paid to her by a certain Professor was not only because she could enliven the conversation at dreary college functions. She saw in retrospect that her intense interest in Professor Burchill's brilliant mind might possibly have caused him to suppose that her interest extended to his less than exciting body. Lately she had pondered on whether, if she were to keep her eyes firmly closed, the revulsion she felt on imagining herself with him in some sort of undefined sexual embrace could be consumed by the incandescent fires of a union of their minds. Despite the gentle pleading of his (undeniably myopic) eyes, she was as yet undecided about attempting the experiment. Her current choice between the eager and insensitive gropings of male contemporaries at college balls, or the hesitant pressings of the Professor's less than firm flesh, was one that she preferred to postpone as long as possible.

As she got out of the car, she recognised a few people she vaguely knew amongst the small group of students who walked out through the college gateway. They were weighed down with boxes and bags, and an awkward looking collection of poles. On seeing her, they broke off their animated conversation. A wide smile broke out across the face of the dishevelled and slightly grubby looking young man she remembered having met once before. He was a distant cousin of the Gardener family, an earnest undergraduate with political aspirations who had seemed a little overawed by his slightly bohemian relations. Addie, having got to know the Gardeners well since coming to Cambridge, felt herself totally at ease amongst the casual jumble of manuscripts and half-finished artistic endeavours in their home. Surrounded by an assortment of musical instruments, and sitting by the fire on the faded patterned rug with her legs tucked beneath her, she had often thought that this was her idea of heaven. Clive and Frances Gardener continued to invite her to join their musical evenings from time to time, even though their own children were hardly ever in Cambridge nowadays. 'Both certain to make a stupendously brilliant mark in the world,' Addie thought with more than a touch of envy. Helen was already recognised as a rising star on the concert stage and John had just been awarded a double first from Cambridge. They had lost touch lately, and Addie wondered if their gawky cousin, now approaching her, had any recent news of them. She was also curious to know where he and his friends were taking all the paraphernalia they had with them, and what its purpose would be. Whatever it was, it must be more stimulating than being stuck here, as she was, attempting and failing to win music scholarships abroad.

The young man called out to her excitedly, forgetting the preamble of polite social introductions, 'Hello, have you heard?'

Not having heard anything that would warrant such animation, Addie hesitated and was about to answer when he continued, all in one enthusiastic breath, 'John's joined the International Brigade and gone to Spain to fight the Fascists and we're off to tell everyone that they've got to help support the Republicans.'

Addie's sharp mind tried to grapple with all the implications of this information, but kept returning to the image of John, idiosyncratic and disorganised, attempting to become part of any sort of military unit. He was the antithesis of the model soldier. His hair usually formed tangles above his wide forehead, his high cheek-boned face hardly ever without a thoughtful, earnest expression. The same worn, sage green, knitted jumper was an almost permanent feature beneath his crumpled tweed jacket. She knew he had become more fervently committed to his political ideals during recent months, and had herself been on the receiving end of some of his early attempts to explain the theories that he was convinced would reshape society. Now she realised with a jolt that all the seemingly endless dialogue could lead to other things, noble deeds perhaps, but also the possibility of a messy and miserable death, or something worse.

Practicalities soon interrupted this train of thought. 'How about coming along too?' the earnest young man was asking hopefully, 'We could cover lots of the villages round here if we could use your car. We're collecting money for medical supplies and an ambulance to send to help the Republic.' One of the girls had a megaphone, another had collecting tins with 'Medical Aid for Spain' painted on them in drippy letters. A frisson of excitement touched Addie's heart at the prospect of being involved in something with such a dramatic and urgent purpose as saving the world from fascism and, at the same time, she thought, suppressing a small shudder of anxiety, doing something that might at some point be of help to John.

An exhilarating day had followed, a whirl of heartfelt speeches, interspersed with earnest conversations. They had met others working for the same ends; people from the Young Liberals, the Young Communist League, and some that had at first seemed unlikely to be involved, such as the members of the Clarion Cycling Club, who were actually all keen socialists. The group from the Left Book Club seemed to know all about the war from their avid consumption of literature on the subject of Spain. Addie eagerly took the books they offered to lend her. All that she read, she reiterated to her father, Hugh, during their long conversations. They had always been close, ever since she was ten years old and a childhood illness had confined her to bed for several months. From the start, he had spared a few minutes to visit her each day, visits that she awaited with anticipation as she loved to hear him talk. He would tell her about all sorts of different things, but particularly about scientific discoveries and world current events. She soon found out that he could be persuaded to stay longer if she asked questions, the more informed the better. As her health improved she would spend hours pouring over the newspaper, struggling to understand the long words in the scientific articles and the difficult concepts relating to political affairs. Their conversations grew longer and longer. Proud of her ability to grasp the essentials of quite complex issues, Hugh had encouraged his daughter by bringing curiosities to show her and books to read. His other children had all followed firmly in their mother's footsteps, preferring Classics to Science.

'What a strange little girl she is,' he would sometimes think when he arrived to find her propped up by pillows, engrossed in some weighty volume, or lying down almost hidden by sheets of newspaper that she could never quite refold properly. Her real education had begun in this way, and their conversations continued to bring great pleasure to them both. Sometimes now they would argue fiercely, enjoying the debate.

The reasons for the war in Spain and its ramifications soon became the dominant subject for discussion. Hugh, perhaps partly as a result of his more detached American perspective on European affairs, was strongly in favour of non-intervention in the conflict. He sympathised entirely with the attempts of the British and French governments to contain the war and prevent its escalation. Addie was outraged by their lack of support for the Republic and particularly by their policy of turning a blind eye to the help that Franco was getting from Italy and Germany.

'It's not fair,' she would cry with exasperation, 'if Franco has all these weapons and soldiers from the Fascists, then the Republicans should at least be able to buy the arms they need to defend themselves.'

As the weeks passed, Addie became more and more caught up in the drama enveloping Spain. 'Aid Spain' committees were springing up everywhere in the towns and villages and Addie helped to start one in Cambridge. Hours were spent planning how to raise funds, demonstrating against non-intervention, and trudging round endless streets making door to door collections of tinned food and milk. The feeling of being part of a growing movement, of sharing an important cause with other young people, filled her days with purpose. The experience was elating. If only she could go there too, she thought restlessly as she bade farewell to yet another group of men who were leaving to join the International Brigades. The only women who got the chance to go to Spain were trained nurses. She asked everyone on all the committees she knew to think of her should any opportunity arise. As the weeks passed, her hopes faded.

'Oh, well,' she thought, trying to suppress her frustration, 'I'll just have to be content to do what I can here.' Even as she spoke the words, she knew that, in her heart, she would never be content until she found a way to go to Spain.

IV

As she peeled the pungent sock away from the grubby foot to which it had become firmly attached by a mixture of blood and seepage from the blisters, Rose Baker felt a surge of unwelcome anger. Not anger directed towards the weary man sitting before her, who had marched for a week already in his ill-fitting boots. She was angry because the carefully constructed wall she had built around herself was suddenly under threat of collapse, rocked to the foundations by nothing more than a pair of festering feet. She was now bitterly regretting that she had allowed her new friend at the hospital to persuade her to come. But, thought Rose, Betty was the type of nurse who could never resist the chance to rush to minister to the suffering, and Rose, eager to keep up the blossoming friendship, had no excuse ready to put her off.

The hunger marchers were in the nearby town of Hertford, and the long column of unemployed men on their way to London from the north would be staying overnight in the church hall. A request had been sent out for off-duty nurses to give first aid treatment to some of the marchers. It would have been much too difficult to explain to an enthusiastic Betty why she was so averse to the idea of simply sparing an hour or two to help these unfortunates. The truth was that she had chosen to work in a select private nursing hospital for the express purpose of distancing herself as far as possible from men like these, from the ugliness that accompanied their poverty; the dirt, the smells, the diseases. Divulging such truths would inevitably make her sound selfish, and she supposed, rightly so. She was barely aware on a conscious level of the fact that she had been attracted to nursing as a way of waging war on her past. She just knew that she loved the white starched cap and apron of her uniform and that, unlike most of the other young nurses, she never resented the Sisters' constant emphasis on cleanliness and hygiene.

She dropped the coarsely knitted sock on the floor with distaste, horribly familiar with the pattern of darns in the heels and toes, and the darns on the darns. Mending her brothers' socks had featured highly on the list she used to repeat like a mantra – all the things she was never going to do again if she ever fought her way out of the back streets of London where she had grown up. A cesspool, she always thought, lower than the gutter - at least gutters had running water sometimes - or a stagnant mire. As a girl of fifteen, she had felt it pulling her back when she struggled to go to evening classes to make up for her lost years at school. She didn't care if her family thought she was stuck up because she was studying for meagre secretarial qualifications and trying to speak nicely and dress neatly. Such spiteful remarks were nothing to the taunts she had endured in her childhood. What, she would ask herself, could compare with the indignity of having to take turns in sharing the one pair of available knickers with your younger sister?

Her mother meanwhile struggled with other people's washing and fits of depression during which she would announce her intention to kill herself and walk out, leaving her children fearful and tearful. When Rose was small, she remembered how her father could tell a joke to make his friends laugh and slap him on the back, and how he could throw her in the air and make her scream with delight. But faced with a diminishing number of casual labouring jobs, his sense of humour had faded. Rose had hated her life with a frightening intensity - the frequent 'flits' to abandoned houses where the bugs were hungrily awaiting new arrivals, the weekly trips to the pawn shop – another task high on the list of embarrassments she endured. Worst of all was the sight of her parents emerging noisily, sometimes belligerently, from the local public house, after having enjoyed a few hours of drunken escape.

Her patient jerked his foot away with an impolite exclamation. Her cleaning of his suppurating toes had become less than gentle as she fought with her conscience. She had managed to make a new life for herself, she didn't want to think about the poor and their problems. But she knew that the loathsome blistered foot confronting her would remain imprinted on her mind, an image that would not allow her to forget that her nursing skills were needed most by the very people she wished to avoid. Trying to regain her concentration on the task before her, she gently eased the foot into a bowl of water, only momentarily distracted by the flash of a camera nearby. She was unaware that her image at that moment had been captured by the photographer for the *News Chronicle*. He knew a good shot when he saw one, and the expression on her face, a look he mistook for justifiable anger at the plight of the suffering man before her, would be sure to get a prime place in tomorrow's edition. The contrast between the pretty blonde girl, well rounded and neat in her uniform, and the gaunt grey figure with his unshaven, malnourished face and dishevelled clothes was striking. 'Beauty and the Beast' - always a real winner, he thought with satisfaction.

Matron was not amused when she opened her newspaper to see Rose Baker, one of her nurses, tending someone who would be regarded by her clientele as a member of the 'great unwashed'. She had taken Rose on with some reservations. A determined girl, Matron had judged, but one whose chin fleetingly lifted in response to any criticism in a manner which hinted at a strongly rebellious streak. Good qualifications had initially outweighed the shadows of a dubious family background, but here she was, for all to see, plainly in sympathy with a rabble that were set on causing trouble. Matron was firmly of the view that those who no longer had work in the midlands and the north would be better employed trying to find jobs elsewhere in the country, rather than marching about and living in idleness on the handouts they were given by the government. She had little time to spare to consider how it would feel to face the stringent Means Test, to have everything you owned removed, except the barest essentials, in order to qualify for a little money to buy food for the family. Matron's foremost concern was the respectability of her nursing staff. Rose Baker's behaviour certainly would not 'do'.

Rose entered Matron's office nervously, but in ignorance of the crime she had committed. Matron, always a formidable force, today seemed to have an even more monumental presence than usual.

'What,' she asked in sonorous tones, 'is the meaning of

this?' She had almost made up her mind to dismiss this girl before more trouble occurred – a face as pretty as hers was always likely to cause problems. Nevertheless, good nurses were hard to find, and perhaps, on the demonstration of a suitable amount of contrition, a second chance could be allowed. Rose cast her eyes downwards to the newspaper, and felt the plummeting of her soul to somewhere in the region of her highly polished shoes. She wondered for a moment if she should be penitent, if pleading would soften Matron's heart enough to let her keep her job. But somehow, the words wouldn't rise from the leaden lump in her chest. Matron saw from the tilt of the chin and the compressed lips that no excuses were forthcoming. She paused and then somewhat reluctantly, drew breath to bring the interview to a close. The apology remained unspoken, Rose had made a choice.

As she walked back through the hospital grounds to the back regions where the nurses' quarters were hidden, Rose was determined not to cry. Once in her room however, the angry tears began, flowing down her cheeks like the salty broth that used to boil over the rim of the blackened pot onto the fire. Rose recited the same curses her mother had used then. Clenching her fists she threw herself on the bed to beat the pillow as she had done as a little girl. She hadn't let them win then and they weren't going to do so now. As a small and unrepentant child of about eight years old, Rose had stood before her mother, Annie, accused of leaving the younger ones unattended when she had been given strict instructions to 'mind' them. Rose had succumbed to the temptation of following an organ grinder with a monkey. The cheerful music and the amusing antics of the monkey in his pillar-box hat had drawn her like a magnet and she forgot all about her irksome responsibilities. When the music stopped some while later, the joy of escape was replaced by fear at finding herself in unknown streets. She had eventually found her way home, fearing the beating she would be given on her return almost as much as remaining lost.

'Why should I always have to look after them?' she had screamed at her mother when the inevitable scolding was underway. Annie, exhausted from delivering the heavy washing back to her clients, had only energy enough to wallop Rose once or twice before shutting her in the upstairs room where they all slept.

'I shan't ever look after them again,' Rose had said through clenched teeth. She hated having to push the huge pram around the streets with her two baby brothers at the far end and her younger sister at the front. Negotiating the kerbs took all her strength, once or twice it had tipped up and the babies had rolled out like soft damp skittles. As nappies were in short supply they always seemed to be wet, and more often than not extremely smelly too. She was always the odd one out. Children of her own age had made themselves scarce when they saw she was encumbered by a string of snotty siblings, stickily clinging to her skirts. She was never allowed to join in their street games, or go with them to play on the scrubland near the railway lines.

But, Rose had thought wistfully as she sat hugging her knees in the dreary bedroom, even ice cream, deliciously sweet as she imagined it to be, couldn't be better than the feeling of freedom she had enjoyed that afternoon. And just like ice cream, it had melted away. Her gaze roamed the room, and she noted with distaste the piles of old clothes, the sagging mattresses, the peeling walls. At night, she would kick her brothers and sisters beside her in bed, trying to gain a little more space for herself. Then she would lie awake, trying to cover her ears when her parents argued or worse, heaved and groaned together in the bed they shared with the babies. She was beginning to know that room for what it was, a prison, trapping her whole future within its miserable walls.

The small kerosene stove they used on the coldest nights stood in the corner. Rose had an idea she thought perfect. Still not old enough to understand the full implications of her plan, she jumped up to examine the stove.

'I'll drink the kerosene and die,' she said to herself, adding out loud, 'That will show them! They'll be sorry then. They won't be able to treat me this way anymore.'

The kerosene tasted foul. Rose tried to taste ice cream instead, but her imagination failed her as she gagged on the oily substance she was trying to swallow. Instead of peacefully expiring to be found lying like a lovely fairytale princess on the bed, she began to be sick, retching repeatedly till her whole body hurt. The greasy stew from their mid-day meal was regurgitated, partly digested, the soggy lumps of carrot and turnip becoming entangled in her hair. As she smelled the acid reek of vomit on her clothes, another spasm gripped her stomach, but there was nothing left. Hearing her daughter fall to the thin floorboards above her head, Annie climbed the stairs wearily to investigate. Rose lay in a small, crumpled heap, semi-conscious, the spilled kerosene at her side telling its story.

Using the corner of her apron, Annie made ineffectual efforts to wipe the ghastly mixture of food and fuel from Rose's damp, pallid skin. She knew this could probably be just the first of many similar incidents. Her own mismanaged or threatened suicide attempts stretched out behind and before her in an endless chain, like the rosary beads that no longer served to console her. The older children had at first trailed after her like ducklings when she had announced that she was going to the Regent's Canal to throw herself in. But after a while they learned that she usually stopped at the pub for a little Dutch courage first, and that it was not necessary for them to sit waiting on the pavement outside for hours till she came out. She would find her way back somehow, forgetting her earlier destination - the Hackney Mortuary - till next time.

Rose's blue eyes opened again to see her mother looking at her sadly. For a moment, they shared an understanding of their common misfortune. This fleeting experience was soon replaced by their usual feelings towards each other. Rose already despised her mother, and for Annie, Rose was a growing burden, certainly the most difficult and rebellious child of her unruly brood.

A timid knock at the door brought Rose back to the reality of her present predicament. News of her dismissal had spread rapidly and Betty had sacrificed her lunch break to find out what was happening to her friend. When Rose told her the reason why she had lost her job, she felt a twinge of guilt at having asked Rose to help the marchers. Surprised at the severity of the punishment, and anxious for her friend's future, she said with conviction, 'Surely, if you plead with Matron, she'll give you your job back. We are so short-staffed at the moment.'

'I'm not going to beg her, or anyone,' replied Rose stiffly, though she realised with a flutter of panic that finding a new job without references was going to be hard. Private nursing work always required impeccable testimonials and she dreaded to think that she might end up working on the poor wards. Betty then came up with an alternative that at first seemed ridiculous, but which gradually appealed to Rose more and more.

'Oh, Rose,' she said excitedly, 'you could go to nurse the wounded in Spain. There's a war on there, and I know Mrs Manning is on a committee to send medical supplies. I'd like to go myself but I can't, not while my mother is so ill.'

Whilst Rose packed her things, they discussed the possibility of volunteering.

'Mrs Manning is a Labour MP,' the more politically knowledgeable Betty said, 'When I went to her last meeting, she definitely said something about needing nurses there.'

As Rose looked thoughtfully at her, she added, 'Think of all the experience you would get in treating casualties. It would be so interesting, and you'd be helping such a good cause.'

Rose wasn't so sure about the cause, but could see

advantages in the plan. A committee with a socialist MP as a leading member would be unlikely to criticize her for losing her job helping the hunger marchers. After all, even Rose knew that one of the Labour MPs, the fiery Ellen Wilkinson, had actually marched with them. And not only would she be able to get good nursing experience in Spain, it would also be 'one in the eye' for her family if she became a nurse at the front like Florence Nightingale. Her brothers and sisters had always belittled her attempts to 'better herself'. They'd mocked her struggles to pass exams at evening classes. When she began nursing training by taking the only position she could get, in a fever hospital, they all thought she would be too fearful of the risks to stay for long. After years of striving, she had qualified at last. Now she was furious at having lost her first 'decent' nursing post. She couldn't bear the thought of giving her family the chance to say that after all, she was no better off than them - jobless. 'I'll show them,' she thought with resolve, her mind almost made up.

When Betty left, Rose sat for a while on the bed, looking at the scrap of paper Betty had given her with Mrs Manning's address scribbled hastily in pencil. Daydreams had always been a comfort for her as a little girl, escaping into magical realms like those she had seen in picture books on rare occasions. Now she drifted into a world where she was a heroine, welcomed back by everyone from duty at the frontlines. The dangers and the reality of the work she would have to do were, for the moment, firmly pushed to the back of her mind.

A few days later, Rose found herself sitting in a shabby waiting room, ankles neatly crossed, her small handbag clutched in her gloved hands on her knee. Leah Manning had been kindness itself, quickly taking Rose under her wing when she had heard the sad tale of dismissal and the plan to volunteer. Just the presence of her comfortable maternal figure had helped to lift Rose's spirits, and her enthusiastic support for the Spanish Republic was infectious, even for someone as uninterested in politics as Rose. Leah had arranged an overnight stay in the nearby YWCA hostel, and a train ticket to London the following day. She had even given her the money for the bus to the offices of the Spanish Medical Aid Committee where Rose now awaited her interview. Looking around her, Rose observed several other girls waiting their turn who, judging by their appearance, were almost certainly nurses. One by one they entered the inner office, not to pass through again on their way out after the interview. This gave the sinister impression that they were whisked off to the front in Spain immediately. It also gave the remaining girls no chance to satisfy their growing curiosity about the interviews.

Eventually, only one other applicant remained. Rose smiled nervously at her, in the hopes of being able to ease the tension that was building during the long wait, but the other girl barely acknowledged her. Despite feeling rebuffed by this seemingly haughty treatment, Rose decided to try again. She always felt the need to try to form friendships, however transient they might be. In truth, she had never had a really close friend. She had no desire to keep in contact with the girls she had known in her childhood, or for that matter, those she had met at evening classes. They had seemed content to remain typists for ever, Rose was much more ambitious than that.

Rose looked again at the other girl, thinking her pale and interesting, like an unhappy heroine locked in a tower, waiting for a prince to come.

'Are you here to volunteer for Spain?' Rose asked her, speaking in her best accent.

The suppressed working-class vowels were immediately obvious to Constance, skilled in detecting social background as revealed by the spoken word. Years of listening to her mother's comments on each new acquaintance had made such an accomplishment inevitable. Until Rose had spoken, her thoughts had been miles away, thinking of the newsreel about Spain she had seen in the cinema the night before. It had featured the small, rounded figure of Franco, strutting along in his cavalry boots. It was incredible how one little man could acquire such power. She turned her head and for the first time looked at Rose properly. Her blonde curls appeared at strategic points around a small, velvet hat, jauntily placed on her head at the most flattering angle. Her clothes, though rather worn, were immaculately clean and pressed, but too fussy to be fashionable. 'She must spend hours in front of the mirror,' thought Constance disparagingly.

'I think we're all here for that reason,' replied Constance after what seemed to Rose an impolite pause. 'For fools rush in where angels fear to tread,' she added almost to herself, quoting a line she remembered from Alexander Pope that seemed particularly appropriate. Rose knew that it must be a quotation, but had read very little poetry and wasn't quite sure what it meant. Constance, she thought, was clearly one of those stuck-up girls who believed herself better than anyone else. She seemed to be looking down her nose at Rose's hat, one she had saved up for weeks to buy. With a rush of remorse, Constance realised that her distracted response to Rose's friendly overtures must have seemed insufferably rude. She was about to attempt to make amends when the secretary put her head round the door and called her name. An apologetic smile was all she could offer as a reconciliatory gesture.

Rose sat alone. The walls were almost bare. There were no magazines to read and nothing of interest to be seen from the window. She began to have serious doubts as to whether or not she was doing the right thing. She knew she was a good nurse, that she was popular with the patients and had no difficulty in charming the doctors. Perhaps, though, when faced with danger, she might do something cowardly and everyone would know. A chill shiver ran down her spine at the thought. Maybe she wasn't going to be brave enough.

'Humph!' she snorted suddenly, her chin lifting and her blue eyes narrowing a little, 'If *that* girl can do it, then I certainly can.'

V

When she was asked to be one of the drivers delivering an ambulance to a children's hospital in southern Spain, Addie couldn't believe her luck. The vehicle, a converted van, paid for and filled with medical supplies by Scottish miners, was to be shipped to France from London the following week and driven all the way. Her name had been put forward by the Duchess of Atholl who chaired the National Joint Committee for Spanish Relief. The Committee was functioning as a sort of umbrella group, co-ordinating the work of all the hundreds of Spanish Aid committees that were now operating all over the country. Addie had written to the Duchess, an old friend of her mother's, when she had been helping to set up the Medical Aid Committee in Cambridge. This had given her the opportunity to stress her availability to go to Spain if the need arose for a willing volunteer. Now her chance had come. She was to go to London where someone would meet her at the docks to share the driving.

Addie spent the next few days making frantic preparations and saying her goodbyes. The response from friends and relations to the news varied from incredulity to envy. Her mother, Virginia, already drawn into the organisation of fund raising for Spanish refugee children, knew there would be little point in trying to dissuade her headstrong daughter. Hugh showed his support by offering to leave pro-Republican publications in prominent places in the staff common room. Quite a concession, thought Addie, in view of his support for non-intervention. She was more affected than she had expected when she bumped into Professor Burchill striding along Trinity Lane behind

Gonville and Caius College, his gown billowing behind him. The street was too narrow to avoid him, and anyway, it was probably better to get it over with and tell him, thought Addie with resignation, rather than continue to postpone this particular goodbye any longer. His face betrayed his dejection when she told him of her imminent departure.

'But, so soon,' he stuttered in surprise. 'I had thought we might go to the Chorale at Kings together next week.' He extended his hand to cover his sadness with a formal gesture of goodbye, but once she had given him her hand, he seemed unwilling to let go.

'I'll write to you if you can let me have your address,' he said hopefully.

'That might be difficult as I'll be moving round a lot,' Addie said gaily, softening her reply when she saw him flinch by adding, 'but I'll certainly try.'

The ambulance parked on the dockside looked to Addie like a big white elephant. She had learned the expression from her mother, who from time to time amassed an odd variety of discarded items to be sold on the 'white elephant' stalls at her charity bazaars. The ambulance was indeed gleaming white, seemed as big as an elephant and was also probably no longer wanted by its former owners, being both ancient and battered. But the new coat of white paint could not hide the scars of past collisions, although the large letters emblazoned on the sides did lend it a certain air of pride. 'From the Workers of Cambuslang to the People of the Republic', proclaimed the slightly unevenly-spaced red letters.

The docks, uniformly grey in the weak winter light, were a new experience for Addie – the noise, screeching winches, shouting dockers, and all the continual bustle of loading and unloading. Her stomach fluttered a little at the thought of the adventures ahead as she waited impatiently for the ambulance to be put on board for Dieppe. A small sandy-haired man approached her, a duffel bag over his shoulder and a heavy tool bag in one hand.

'I'm Max,' he told her with a wide smile, 'you must be Addie Maclaurin.' His well-scrubbed skin still retained a few vestiges of ingrained grease and a vaguely oily aroma emanated from the lumpy canvas tool bag. 'I see you've come prepared then,' he added, looking with longing at Addie's small picnic hamper, carefully packed with sandwiches and a thermos by her mother.

'We can share these now if you like, while we wait for the ambulance to be loaded,' offered Addie, opening the hamper straight away.

'Thanks, love,' he answered. Perplexed by her accent, he tilted his head and wrinkled his face, concluding 'You're not from round here, are you?'

Addie's slight American inflection was not easy to identify, diminished by the presence of her English mother's voice throughout her childhood.

'I was born in the States,' she told him, 'but I've been living here for a while now.'

They sat companionably on the dockside together. Max hungrily munched his way through his share, explaining, 'Didn't 'ave time for me breakfast this morning – had to organise the tools.' He indicated the bag at his feet.

This was the first of many times Addie would hear this word, its meaning significantly altered from accepted usage. In Spain she would come to understand it more fully. To Max, and to many others, 'organise' implied a mixture of find, acquire, or borrow without asking. He told her of his family in the East End, about his work as a mechanic, and a little bit about why he had volunteered.

The meal finished, Max passed Addie his copy of *The Daily Worker*.

'There's quite a bit about the war in it today,' he said, 'not all good news. Do you want to 'ave a butcher's?' Addie knew that *The Daily Worker* was the Communist Party paper, sold on many street corners by party members. She hadn't seen a copy for a few days so was keen to catch up on the latest left-wing news. The paper was already well-thumbed and had been handed to her with the centre pages folded to the outside. She looked carefully at several large photographs showing International Brigaders, mostly with arms raised in their clenched fist salute, just in case she could see anyone she knew. An article caught her attention.

'Aid for Spain: women of Rhondda send help.' She read on.

> In spite of widespread unemployment and dire poverty in the Rhondda Valley, the women have determined to give all the help they can to the Spanish democrats. 'We in this district,' writes a member of the Tonypandy Working Women's Guild, 'know what fascism stands for. At this moment we have 36 workers waiting their trial at the Assizes for putting up a fight against Mosley and his Blackshirts.'

Addie knew something about Mosley, the British fascist leader whose anti-Semitic propaganda was rising to fever pitch. She was about to ask Max if he had been to any of the huge demonstrations against Mosley in London, but as she turned to the front page, her heart stopped.

'John Gardener killed in Spain'. A small paragraph in the stop press cited the bare details of date and place, nothing more.

'What's up, love? asked Max, concerned to see Addie's face drain of all colour. He peered at the section she was reading, 'Was it someone you knew?'

'A good friend,' said Addie. Her former exhilaration at the thought of going to Spain now seemed childish. Of course people would die, she had known that all along, but when it was someone you knew, someone who had been so bright and alive, well, that was a whole different ball game.

CHAPTER 2

Warm Earth

I

Constance was amazed by the colours of Valencia. She kept glancing upwards to see if the sky really was so densely blue. It seemed to her as if she were walking within a child's painting. Colour was everywhere; oranges so brilliantly orange that they shone like suns, greens that were bursting with life. She could smell the warm earth of the civic gardens, and the flowers that were starting to bloom - red, violet and yellow - three vibrant hues that were echoed in the colours of the fluttering Republican flags. Perhaps best of all was the sea, glinting so brightly that it hurt her eyes, and so wide, offering endless horizons of possibility.

Her interview with the doctor in charge of recruitment at the Spanish Medical Aid offices in London had been brief. She had given details of her qualifications and references, and, without further delay, she had been accepted. A little bemused, she stood on the street outside the office, knowing that her life had taken a new direction. It was as if someone had opened a sluice gate and diverted her future into a waterway that would pass through an entirely different landscape.

But then, instead of a continuing momentum building to departure for Spain, Constance had to endure a disheartening period of anti-climax. The first two medical teams had already left, and she had to wait for the next group to be organised. Even more annoyingly, several other nurses who had been recruited after her were sent out. This, she was told, was because they had specific training and experience in theatre work, and these skills were needed urgently. The little extra time off work that Constance had over Christmas and New Year were spent reading newspapers to find out what was happening in Spain and trying to suppress her feelings of discontent with everything around her. A few weeks later, she heard from the Committee at last. The waiting would soon be over.

Within a few days she had been kitted out with a nurse's uniform; smart blue dresses and starched white hats. 'Ridiculously unsuitable,' she thought with perfect foresight. Those on the committee who ran the organisation seemed unaware of the limited means of their nurses. Volunteers would not be receiving any pay in Spain and Constance had amassed no savings from the paltry sum she earned in addition to her board and lodging in the nurses' home. She wondered how she would replace her shoes and underwear, almost worn out already. Pre-made sanitary towels would be out of the question. How would she be able to afford stamps to write home?

She was hoping to find answers to the ever-growing list of questions when suddenly, the pace accelerated. She was told that the commander of the British Battalion in the International Brigades was gravely ill in a hospital in Valencia, probably dying. He had been diagnosed as suffering from typhoid and his distraught wife was going to pay the costs of sending a trained British nurse to care for him. On learning that she had been selected for this task, Constance had at first wanted to say no. Nursing just one, rather wealthy, British officer was far from what she had in mind when she volunteered. But when the anxious Mrs Upward telephoned and spoke to her in person, she was unable to refuse. Instead, she consoled herself with the thought that at least she would be there, in Spain, ready to be transferred to the front as soon as her patient was recovering. In what seemed to be a whirlwind of activity, rushing from one office to another, a passport and visa were obtained for her and arrangements made for her journey to Spain. She reviewed the ironic implications of her situation with amusement when she was told that the bus that would take her to the private airport at Croydon would be leaving from the Dorchester Hotel. With her half-empty, threadbare bag of possessions, she would be travelling to Spain in a manner normally enjoyed only by the rich and powerful, the very people who, as likely as not, feared and despised those that Constance was flying to support.

The next day, Constance found herself in a small plane, soaring for the first time in her life up through the grey clouds, leaving England's overcast skies behind her. The journey was a confusing turmoil of train stations, airstrips, strange sights and smells, and French spoken so fast that she could only catch the odd word. It seemed a bewildering jumble of un-sortable impressions for someone who had never been abroad before. Eventually, the plane crossed the Pyrenees into Spain, and she peered through the small window to see the giant snow-covered mountains spreading out below her, tinged rose pink in the sunrise. 'It can't be real. I must be dreaming,' she thought for a moment. But then, unbidden to her mind, came the memory of the all too real scene when she had handed in her notice. Matron had been unexpectedly angry. Constance knew that long ago, she had fought tooth and nail to found the much needed maternity hospital. It had since earned well-deserved acclaim for its high standards and treatment of the poor. Matron would surely sympathise, thought Constance, with the aims of the Republicans to bring social reforms. She had entered the well-ordered office, fully expecting to be praised for her decision to go to Spain, even admired a little for facing unknown dangers in such a good cause.

'An emotional indulgence,' Matron had called it curtly. A crestfallen Constance had then been given a lecture on putting duty to patients in England first, not jaunting off to foreign parts. There was plenty to be done here. Matron was exasperated. She hated to lose a good midwife, especially one in whom she had placed such high hopes. To leave on these terms saddened Constance, but she was not to be dissuaded.

As she slowly unfolded her cramped limbs in the sunshine of Valencia, Constance wondered if she was far from the hospital. A bus had taken her from the small airport where the plane had landed to the city centre, but now she was unsure what to do next. As a crowded tram approached she rummaged in her pocket for the address of the hospital to show to the driver. The sight of the name on the paper combined with her nurse's uniform, produced an instant flurry of excitement. The driver and the passengers, all talking at once and pointing at her, began smiling and cheering, slapping her on the back in a most familiar way.

'Americana?' they asked, 'No, English,' she replied.

'Inglesa, inglesa', they shouted delightedly.

There had seemed to be far too many people at the stop ever to fit into the tram, but this, Constance realised, was a limitation that was not going to be observed. Those who couldn't squeeze inside, all piled on round the outside, holding on to the tram by whatever means they could, and to each other. Her small case was passed to someone through the window as she was encouraged to climb up alongside the remaining passengers. Then, with her toes resting on a small rail and her arms held firmly, they careered off down the tracks, rattling and swaying round the corners. When at last her stop was reached, the tram waited whilst passers-by were accosted and her destination and nationality explained to them. She was passed like a parcel to these new friends who talked non-stop and repeatedly patted her arms. She had no idea what they were saying but the welcome in their voices was unmistakeable. One of them had recovered her suitcase from the turmoil within the tram, and dismissed with an airy wave of his arm her attempt to carry it herself. She was deposited at the hospital entrance, stunned by the rain of kisses on her cheeks from perfect strangers.

The building was large and squat, an old fever hospital

now in general use and also taking casualties transported to the rearguard from the front. No one was at the desk by the doorway. There was only the overwhelming smell of carbolic to greet her. Constance walked along seemingly endless corridors, repeating the name of her patient, Tom Upward, with a questioning lilt, at every opportunity. Despite the number of people she saw, chances for enquiries were few and far between. Everyone seemed to be rushing somewhere, usually deep in animated conversation, and she didn't like to interrupt. Each ward she glimpsed had the usual rows of patients, but was also full to bursting with their relatives and friends. Peace and quiet was not the rule in Spanish hospitals apparently. 'Where are all the nurses?' wondered Constance, exasperated after several more failed attempts to locate her charge.

The main corridors were arranged round a large courtyard. Turning a corner she found herself in a different part of the hospital. Her footsteps echoed in these quieter passageways, and a musty smell gave the impression of abandonment and neglect. Suddenly, as she passed a half open door, she caught a few murmured words spoken in English. This at last, could be her patient. He was trying to say something to a pale young woman sitting by his side, but could barely speak. Unshaven, unwashed, the man lay listlessly on the bed, the sharp prominences of his bones elevating the stained sheet that covered a loose, now sadly wasted body. Although it was still only early in the year, the room seemed oppressively hot and small flies incessantly attempted to congregate on his sweating face. They were discouraged from landing there by the attentive girl, who fanned the air round his head with a magazine.

'Is this Tom Upward?' asked Constance, trying not to betray the anxiety she felt at the likely imminent demise of the man before her.

'Oh yes,' cried the girl with relief. 'You must be the nurse they've sent out. I'm Kitty.'

She smiled, a wide American smile, showing her large, even, white teeth. Constance, accustomed to the gaps and discolorations in the mouths of the poor, found this demonstration of American dental care quite remarkable. Kitty looked very young, apart from the clearly evident signs of exhaustion and worry in her eyes. Knowing nothing about nursing, she had nonetheless done her best over the long weeks of Tom's illness. Now that Constance had arrived and was prepared to take charge of the situation, she was more than willing to do just as she was told.

Kitty related the story of Tom's illness in a rush of emotion at having someone to talk to in English. He had been wounded by flying shrapnel and at first, after an operation, he had begun to recover. But since then he had been on a roller coaster of relapses, growing weaker and weaker. Somewhere along the way, a doctor had diagnosed typhoid. Constance was beginning to have doubts – she had seen typhoid many times and this was not the normal pattern of the disease. Perforated intestines, intestinal poisoning and death could occur within two weeks. If no perforation had taken place by the second week, that phase was over. Food could then be given without risk. Kitty told her that Tom had been given nothing but milk and water for five weeks. Whatever was wrong with Tom, Constance concluded, it wasn't typhoid; if it had been, he would either be better or dead by now.

Lowering his raging temperature was the first priority, she decided, as she removed the annoying white cuffs from her uniform and undid the little rounded collar at her neck. She picked up an enamel bowl and set off to find the nearest tap. At the far end of the corridor, an unpleasant odour grew ever stronger. A trickle of water on the tiled floor indicated the presence of a washroom. As she pushed open the door, the sickening smell of stale faeces made Constance stagger backwards. 'How do people manage to defecate so high up the walls?' she wondered, disgusted at the lack of cleanliness. Holding her breath, she rushed in to use the tap, wishing fervently that the water would do more than dribble slowly into her bowl.

Kitty was nervously fussing around when Constance returned to the room, anxious to help but not knowing what to do. 'We must feed him up,' Constance declared, and despatched her off to buy whatever light food she could, and to find something to put up in the window to keep out the flies. She had just begun sponging her patient with the water to cool him down a little, when the doctor arrived. Constance turned to greet him, but knew that things would not go well the moment she saw him, officious and unsmiling, opening the door wide with a flourish. 'Still wet behind the ears,' she thought with disappointment.

The doctor had been told that an English nurse had arrived to take care of Upward. He had heard about this foreign system of training women to care for patients, even allowing them to administer injections, but he did not approve. Better to use nuns, or females from the patient's family who would do what they were told. With furious gestures he indicated that the sponging must stop – washing such a sick man could be lethal. Constance was limited to arguing in broken French, but the doctor understood well enough that his treatment was being challenged. Tired and hot, Constance was nevertheless not going to back down. Newly qualified medical students and housemen in England were often inordinately bossy when they first came onto the wards. Constance had dealt with many of them. Usually, they quickly came to rely on the more experienced nurses. This one however, with his blustering bravado, was going to lose the patient if she didn't stick to her guns.

Kitty came back in time to make sense of the paper that the irate doctor was now waving at Constance. The limited Spanish she had picked up allowed her to work out that it was a type of disclaimer. Constance must sign it, taking all responsibility for killing Tom through her disregard of the doctor's orders. He had decided that these foreigners were to be left to their own devices. There was no way that he was going to tolerate being defied by an insufferably arrogant, dishevelled young English woman. Almost too weary to be apprehensive, Constance signed.

Over the next two days, the food that Kitty managed to find for Tom began to take effect and he gained strength. But Constance was still worried by his wildly swinging temperature. In the evenings he would sink into delirium. As he lay semi-conscious on the third evening, she decided she must change his wound dressings. No other doctors had been near his room, so it seemed that the responsibility for this too was now hers alone. As she peeled away the gauze pads, she could see that the wounds were not healing. The stitches were still there, too tight, cutting deeply into the angry flesh. The whole area was swollen and inflamed. Could his high temperatures be the result of a septicaemia from infected wounds? If so, realised Constance, he clearly would not improve any more till something was done about it. She sterilised her scissors with alcohol and hesitantly began to cut the stitches on the most uncomfortable looking wound. A fountain of yellow and red pus shot out in a most satisfying manner. The deeper she dug, the more purulent the discharge became. With relief, she repeated the procedure, finding deep abscesses in each of his wounds. Cleanliness and drainage were the only methods of treatment available, but the infection had not yet reached the bone so the chances were good.

The two women took turns in sleeping on the empty bed in the hospital room. Constance was used to being awake during long night hours on duty so didn't mind if Kitty used the bed more during the night. She needed her strength for the daily trips into Valencia to find the right sort of nourishing food for Tom. Sometimes Kitty would manage to buy cigarettes too, which she insisted on sharing between them. Constance, always constrained by lack of money from buying cigarettes herself, soon learned to crave the wash of wellbeing that followed the deep inhalation of tobacco smoke. As Tom improved, Kitty's delight was plain to see. Constance watched as her patient's eyes followed the pale, delicate-looking American girl round the room, and knew that he was deeply in love. She couldn't help feeling sympathy for Tom's wife, but decided that the love affairs of her patients were really none of her business.

When, after a while, Tom was able to sit up in bed, Constance offered to shave him to make him more comfortable. He soon wished he had waited for the hospital barber.

'Can't you keep still?' she asked him impatiently. 'I'm not very good at this. I've only ever shaved a dead man before.'

Tom managed to laugh, despite the nick she had made in his neck. Kitty had made him well aware of the fact that, but for this tetchy nurse, he could have been as dead as the earlier beneficiary of her barbering ministrations.

To pass the hours in the cramped room, Tom had undertaken the task of beginning Constance's political education. On this occasion, he had been trying to explain to her why the war was not as straightforward as it might appear to people abroad. They saw it as a simple fight between left and right, but the reality was much more complex. His animation over the disputes between the various factions of the left was asking for trouble whilst being shaved with a cut-throat razor. Constance found his description of the anarchists particularly interesting. Their belief that people were basically good and were capable of working together without anyone governing them or ordering them about was wonderful. But, with Franco's well-equipped army to fight, was that approach ever going to work? What about the communists? They wanted a disciplined, strictly regimented army to counter Franco's forces, and perhaps this was the best plan. But, as she had learned from Tom, some people feared that if the power of the communists grew too great, the influence of the Soviet Union might overpower the more moderate alliance that made up the Republic.

All this new information buzzed round in Constance's head. It was intriguing but so infuriating. Why did they keep falling out with each other when they should all be uniting to fight Franco? When official visitors began to arrive to see Tom, Constance would pick up snippets of their conversation, or in some cases, listen to their heated arguments. These clashes were seemingly always about politics. One visitor who treated her with exceptional kindness and consideration was a round and friendly man called Harry Pollitt; she discovered afterwards that he was the leader of the Communist Party in Britain. Perhaps, thought Constance with interest, Tom might be someone quite high up in the Party to warrant a visit from him.

But Constance's main concern, becoming more urgent as the days passed, was to get to the front. Every day her nursing duties for Tom lessened, so she began to escape from the hospital for a while each day to go into the city. Valencia seemed a long way from the front. It was almost impossible to imagine that terrible battles were being fought at that very moment that would decide the future of the whole country. Constance could understand the need for the huge poster dominating the central square of the city emblazoned with the slogan, 'Valencians, remember that the front is only 150 kilometres away.' An air raid warning provided an additional reminder from time to time, but no one took any notice. Bombs were a rarity here and life carried on much as usual. In the early months of the war, the Republican Government had left Madrid, believing that its fall was imminent. They had been based in Valencia since then, and it was plain to see that the city was full of bureaucrats and minor officials, cramming the cafés, their neatly clothed figures outnumbering the somewhat haphazard uniforms of the militiamen. When she learned that someone from the Medical Aid Committee was staying in a Valencia hotel, Constance called round every day to pester him for a new posting. Her incessant badgering at last produced results. With glee, she clutched the papers transferring her to a hospital on the Aragon front and rushed off to tell Tom and Kitty. At last she could really *do* something.

II

Revolutionary fever raised hopes instead of temperatures, thought Addie, unable to suppress a smile at the sight of the women, arm in arm, marching down the Ramblas in Barcelona with banners flying. Early spring sunshine played on the patchwork bark of the plane trees that lined the wide, paved walkway. At each side, the trams and other vehicles sounded their horns noisily at pedestrians who were crossing the cobbled roads. Some sort of parade was going on, though Addie couldn't work out what it was about. Posters and flags festooned the walls and balconies of the adjacent buildings but the various acronyms, blazoned in capital letters on most of them, meant little to her. For a few moments, she caught the sound of the music that was blaring raucously from loudspeakers. The same large letters that featured prominently on the posters – CNT, FAI, UGT, POUM – had also been painted on the lorries that hurtled everywhere, proclaiming their allegiances. Many people, even some of the women, were dressed in blue all-in-one workmen's overalls, their constant bustling activity giving Addie the impression that they were all engaged on important business.

She was pleased that Max was now driving, giving her more time to absorb the scene that surrounded her. He had proved a dependable companion, his only apparent vice being his addiction to a particularly pungent type of tobacco in his cigarettes, rolled skilfully with one hand when he was driving. He told her about the Battle of Cable Street, how he had been one of the thousands in the East End who had blocked the roads to stop Mosley and his fascist Blackshirts marching through. He pointed to the scar on his forehead where he had been batoned by the mounted police who were trying to clear a pathway through the crowd. He had been arrested along with hundreds of others. Since then, he had been spending all his spare time delivering the tinned milk and other food collected by the various small committees in London to a collecting point for shipment to Spain. His best friend had joined the Brigades but Max had been turned down. 'Bastards wouldn't let me in,' he grumbled, 'rheumatic fever when I were a nipper.'

The journey across France had been long and tiring in the old ambulance, but Addie's flagging energies were instantly revived by the atmosphere in the city – deep breaths of emancipation laced with a gut-fluttering tension. She fervently hoped they would be able to spend a few days there before continuing on the journey south. Some of the boxes of basic medical supplies they had brought were to be delivered to Quakers who were running canteens for refugee mothers and children, and Addie and Max had been offered beds there for the night. However, the strange noises emanating from the engine of their ambulance indicated that Max could need more time for repairs before they left.

The ambulance began a slow climb, rumbling past the residential villas that lined the slopes of Mount Tibidabo on the outskirts of the city. At last, with oily black smoke pouring from the exhaust, they arrived at the address they had been given. The Quakers had been allocated lodgings in a huge empty villa overlooking the sea and the city. The owners, along with many others from this wealthy part of Barcelona, had left hurriedly when the fighting started, moving to the regions of Spain occupied by Franco. Addie was enchanted by the gardens – orange and lemon trees, figs and palms. The entrance hall, with marble tiles, high ceilings and sweeping staircase, gave everything a decidedly palatial air. A young woman rushed down the stairs to greet them.

She certainly didn't fit the image Addie had in her mind of serious, quiet Quakers, devoted to service in the Society of Friends. She knew some of the Cambridge Friends, middle-aged to elderly, softly spoken and earnest. This girl seemed to bound across the hall, long legs striding out in men's trousers and her pony tail swinging behind her. Max took a step back in surprise as she approached them at top speed, grabbing their hands in turn to shake them vigorously.

'How wonderful! You've arrived safely. We've been expecting you. Have you brought the medicines? Have you had a difficult journey? You must be exhausted. Would you like me to take you to your rooms now? What do you think of Barcelona? We're always pleased to have visitors, but I'm afraid the food we can offer you is pretty limited.'

There seemed to be no spaces in the flow of welcoming phrases that allowed time to answer her questions, but eventually, Addie managed to convey that it would be pleasant to sit in the garden for a few minutes. Max went to offload their bags and to take the ambulance round to the garages at the back of the villa.

Celia, as Addie discovered she was called, was not actually a 'Friend' herself. 'Oh, I'm a friend of the Friends,' she explained. 'I was studying sculpture before all this started,' she added, waving her arms expansively. 'Do you know Henry Moore? He taught me for a while, then I went to the Slade.'

Addie was always envious of those with artistic talent, whatever form it took. She knew little about sculpture, but once seen, the impressive curves of Henry Moore's women and the empty voids of their abdomens were unforgettable. Studying in a prestigious London Art College was something Addie would have loved to do, but unfortunately, her talents in that direction only extended as far as the insipid water colours expected of young ladies on their travels abroad. Celia began to tell her about the work they were doing in Barcelona - a dozen or so foreigners living in the villa and twice as many Spanish women running canteens to distribute milk to children under ten, most of them refugees - but stopped in mid flow. 'You can come and see for yourself in the morning, you don't have to set off first thing, do you?'

Addie told her about the problems they were having with the ambulance.

'Well then,' said Celia, 'you can come and help me with the breakfast shift.'

Addie woke hungry. The previous night's dinner had indeed been a frugal affair. The staff all lived on meagre rations. Seeing so many hungry children each day had deadened their appetites, they said, because anything the staff ate from the stores meant that there was less to give away. Addie found herself getting rather heated in a discussion with one of the American Quakers about giving out food to children of the families who supported Franco.

'Surely,' she had asked when she learned that the Friends' policy was to give to all without discrimination, 'these families could be evacuated to Franco's side. Why should we feed their children when we haven't got enough for the Republicans?'

'No matter how much we may sympathise personally with the Republic, we have to stay non-political as an organisation. That's what we believe is right.' There was no doubting the sincerity of the serious looking girl, but Addie still thought it would be more practical to put certain families on a train for Franco to feed.

The scanty breakfast was interrupted by a group of hungry-looking refugees begging for food. Celia sighed in resignation. 'It happens all the time,' she said sadly, 'they know we've got stores of oatmeal and cocoa and milk powder in the cellar but we have to turn them away because it's just for the children. We have to stick to a rota for that job because it's one of the hardest to do.'

Addie was taken down to the town in a rattling old van, the back crammed full of supplies of milk powder and tins of cocoa. As they approached the dock area where the canteen was sited, Addie began to see just what damage a bombardment could do. The villas of Tibidabo had been spared, leaving them ready for their owners' return, but the slum dwellings of the working-classes were a prime target for shells fired from warships just off the coast. A few houses stood in ruins, interiors exposed like the entrails of corpses undergoing autopsies. Entire walls had collapsed into rubble, in some places blocking the streets completely. Addie had seen newsreels in England that showed this new horror of warfare – the bombardment of civilian areas. But newsreels did not include the smells, the sickly stench of leaking sewage, and the acrid odour arising from the ashes of people's lives. In several places, women were forming long queues to buy food. But those who had no money formed the longest of queue of all, outside the Quaker canteen. The refugee women waited patiently, toddlers clinging to skirts and babies in arms.

Addie spent several hours helping to replenish the three great tanks of warm milk which emptied faster than they could be refilled. The milk powder had to be mixed with hot water and as the gas pressure was often low, the water had to be boiled on wood fires in the courtyard at the back of the house. Sometimes the assorted old pans and tins they used for this burned through and burst, putting out the fire or scalding an unwary assistant. Addie began to realise why someone like Celia, with her tremendous energy, was an invaluable asset in refugee work. The sight of so many small hungry faces triggered a reflex action that was almost impossible to ignore and, like birds responding to the open mouths of their young, the staff seemed prepared to carry on till they dropped.

When, at last, the queue began to shorten, Celia said kindly to Addie, 'Why don't you go out for a while for a look round? We'll clear up here as usual. I'll be going to take something to a few of the sick children who can't come out.

We could meet again here in the evening to dole out the cocoa.' Addie looked around at the long trestle tables where children were eating their oatmeal, and thought with dismay of what it must be like repeating this routine day after day - always more refugees arriving and never enough food. Her attention was caught by a small, bone-thin boy sitting at one end of the table, spoon-feeding a toddler. 'Why isn't that boy eating anything?' she asked Celia. 'Oh, he's over ten so he counts as too old, I'm afraid.' she replied. As the tears welled up in Addie's eyes, she felt that she must get outside – it was all too heartbreaking to bear.

She headed back towards the centre of the city, passing several deserted looking churches on her way. Their doors were boarded up and many of the windows were no longer glazed, their rose windows like round eyes that were now only empty sockets. She peered in through a crack in one of the doorways to see the gutted interior, occupied only by pigeons instead of sinners. Her spirits lifted a little when she arrived at the Ramblas and could amble amongst the stalls of the street vendors. The book stalls were fascinating. Political theory abounded – books by Marx and Bukharin featured prominently, the novels of Zola and Rolland appeared amongst the best-sellers. Addie picked up a small booklet from one of the piles at the front of the stall and was startled to find explicit illustrations within on the subject of childbirth and sexual hygiene. The Republicans had modern ideas on such things it seemed.

Resting on a stone bench, she watched the passing crowds, noticing that although there were many men carrying guns, none shared anything approaching what could be called a proper uniform. Some had similar jackets, but their caps and the way in which they were worn seemed mainly a matter of individual choice. Neck scarves of red or red and black were the only universal piece of apparel. Addie began to decipher the colour code and the meaning of some of the initials on the posters. The red and black flags of the anarchist CNT adorned many balconies, and even the taxis were painted red and black. Certain doorways had notices posted on them followed by the same initials. Using a small Spanish dictionary she had brought with her, Addie worked out that they were announcing, 'This business is under the workers' control'.

Drifting away from the Ramblas, Addie found herself walking in a quieter part of the city where tall, balconied houses looked down onto tree-lined streets. A commotion nearby captured her attention. In the small gardened square a group of people had gathered and, as she drew closer, she overheard snatches of English. Two women were commenting on the events taking place in the square. One of them, whose round wire-framed spectacles gave her the air of a schoolmistress, was scribbling rapidly in a notebook whilst simultaneously expounding on the subject of the iniquities of the Catholic Church to the other, a tall girl with very short hair and a once smart tweedy jacket, now out of shape where hands had been thrust deeply into the pockets. Her long, slim ballet-dancer's neck emerged incongruously from a shirt collar that was much too big, gathered loosely by a carelessly knotted tie. She gazed intently at the scene taking place before them.

Two stocky men began to wield heavy hammers, swinging with all their strength in long arcs, slowly shattering a stone plaque that had lain, partly covered, amongst the bushes. They were working methodically; without anger and with an air of detachment, not only towards the object they were destroying, but also towards the tense crowd. Amongst the on-lookers was a young Spanish girl, her eyes wide with fear and her hands covering her mouth with horror. Silence descended on the audience, only the hammer blows resounded in the air, echoing between the tall buildings in the square. Addie's curiosity was so strong that she approached the English women. She waited until the blows ceased and the fragments of stone were being collected for removal before saying quietly, 'Excuse me, do you know what's been happening here?'

The woman wearing glasses looked up from her notebook. There was something familiar about her face but Addie couldn't remember where she had seen it before.

'Ha!' she replied with relish, 'the decontamination officers have been striking another blow for freedom from superstition.' Apparently, she explained, someone had reported seeing a former servant girl from one of the nearby houses – the same girl who had been watching in the crowd - praying at the plaque in the square. It was dedicated to some Saint or other but had been overlooked in the early days of the war when the churches and shrines had become the focus for an uneducated population bent on vengeance. Hundreds of years of oppression had brought its rewards, bonfires of religious artefacts and even the buildings themselves in some cases. Fortunately, there had been plenty of people in the Republic who wanted to rescue and preserve the items of artistic value from the churches, but this plaque was not going to be amongst them. 'Not being able to read or write is the crux of the matter,' the woman added emphatically. 'That young girl in the crowd was totally illiterate. She had been brought up to believe that the church always knows best. No wonder she was scared. I think she was waiting for a thunderbolt of divine retribution to strike us all down. I'm Geraldine Rees Jones by the way.'

Addie was pleased at last to be able to remember where she had seen Geraldine's angular features before, but without her glasses. Geraldine Rees Jones was becoming quite a well known writer and her picture had appeared in conjunction with the launch of her latest book – something about revolutionary Paris, Addie seemed to recall.

Geraldine's companion did not seem to welcome Addie's presence at all. She glowered a little and her long face took on a rather sulky expression.

'Are we going now, Gerry?' she asked impatiently.

'This is Vivien Erroll,' said Geraldine, 'we've both come here to see the situation at first hand and report on what's going on when we get back to England. We're just off to the Medical Aid office. Want to come along?'

Addie was reluctant to antagonise the hostile Vivien further, but on the other hand, she really did want to visit the Medical Aid office, and she found Geraldine very interesting. Perhaps, she thought hopefully, Vivien's temper would improve on acquaintance. As they walked on together, Addie told them about her journey to Spain and pointed out where she was staying with the Quakers.

'Well, you've got a superb view up there,' said Geraldine, 'but have you seen the ghastly half-finished Catholic monstrosity on the top, a mixture of bad gothic and worse baroque – we hear it's being preserved as a monument to poor taste.' Geraldine had strong views about lots of things, Addie soon discovered. She was passionate in her support of the Republic and the valiant spirit of the Spanish, but highly critical of the British government and of some of the English working in Barcelona. 'They don't even bother to learn Spanish,' she complained contemptuously, 'they have the same dreadful attitude as the British in India.' Addie felt ashamed not to have made more effort to learn the language herself and resolved to correct this failing as soon as she could.

As they walked past the trailing bread queues, Addie told them about the heart-rending work in the canteens, 'Ten year olds with the faces of ancients,' she sighed.

Vivien at last spoke out vehemently, 'Continual poverty takes all the joy out of life - it takes the very flesh off the bones more cruelly than starvation.' She became more animated, a burning light in her eyes. 'Danger brings exhilaration. You can laugh in the face of it – it's life. But the constant deadening weight of poverty – that's death.'

This speech was delivered with the intensity of a soliloquy in a Shakespearean tragedy. Addie wasn't sure if

Vivien was reciting something or voicing her own thoughts. She lapsed back again into silence, watching Geraldine almost constantly. Addie wondered why Vivien seemed to regard her as an enemy, though she hadn't done anything that could be considered offensive – as far as she knew. 'Perhaps it's because she dislikes Americans,' was the only conclusion Addie could reach for the moment.

The office was up several flights of stairs in a cluttered room, all available surfaces piled high with papers. An irate young man dominated the small space in the centre of the office, amidst the assorted desks and tables. In a stream of French, which Addie could follow with a fair degree of accuracy, he was insisting that a safe conduct pass should be obtained for him and transport provided as quickly as possible to take him to his destination in Murcia. Despite his display of bad temper, it would have been difficult not to notice his remarkable good looks. Addie couldn't help regarding him as a work of art, perhaps a sculpture in the style of Michelangelo's 'David', though with soft, light-brown hair poetically sweeping his brow, rather than Grecian curls. 'And more clothes, unfortunately,' Addie thought with a secret smile, fondly remembering the five minutes she had spent in Florence outside the Palazzo Vecchio, admiring the marble buttocks looming above her.

The secretary, only able to speak French with a cringingly bad English accent, was struggling to follow what the young man was saying, but he made no concessions to her ineptitude. Finally, losing patience altogether, he swept up his large white hat from the desk and, arranging it stylishly on his head with a practised air, he turned on his heel, and walked out. 'We'll be in touch as soon as we can, Doctor Boulestin,' the flustered secretary called after him.

Geraldine and Vivien obviously knew the secretary quite well, and Addie had seen them discreetly raising eyebrows and pursing lips in a shared communication taking place, unobserved by the doctor, during his tirade. They all burst out laughing when the drama had been concluded by his sweeping exit through the door.

'Who on earth was that?' Geraldine asked.

'Oh, that's Marcel Boulestin, a doctor from Narbonne who arrived yesterday. He says a friend who runs a hospital in Murcia has asked him to go there to help out with the extra patients they are getting – lots of wounded soldiers and refugees too.'

Addie was introduced to Sybil, and pleasantries were exchanged before Geraldine and Vivien made ready to leave, taking a package of photographs for propaganda purposes with them.

'We're going back to England tomorrow,' Geraldine told Addie, 'but we'll be back. Nice to have met you. Good luck.' Vivien gave Addie a curt nod as they departed.

'They're an odd pair,' said the secretary with a smile after the door had closed.

'What do you mean?' asked Addie.

'Well, dear,' she explained in hushed tones, 'they're - you know - lesbians.'

Addie, though having read about such things in Greek literature, hadn't encountered real-life lesbians before, or at least, none she had recognised as such. She began to review Vivien's baleful glares in her direction in a new light. Could it have been jealousy that had made her so resentful? With growing awareness, Addie remembered Geraldine's reassuring touches on her companion's arm in moments when the scowls had become particularly evident. She wished that she'd taken more notice of everything about them. She resolved that next time she met a woman wearing a man's shirt and tie, she would be more observant. Everyone talked so much about politics these days, but they didn't say much about sex, at least not within range of her sharp ears.

Sybil listened eagerly to the news that Addie and Max had arrived with an ambulance, and that after Max had finished repairs, they were intending to travel further south.

'Oh, that could work out beautifully,' she exclaimed. 'You could give Doctor Boulestin a lift. We should be able to get him a pass by then.'

As Addie hesitated, a little reluctant to spend too much time confined in close quarters with the irascible Doctor, Sybil had another bright idea.

'And we're desperate for mechanics to work on vehicles for the medical units. I wonder if there's any chance that your Max could stay with us? Everything grinds to a halt if the supply lorries and the ambulances break down. Do you think he would consider it? You could share the driving on your journey to Murcia with the doctor.'

Addie knew immediately that Max would jump at the chance to stay and work there. She consoled herself with the thought that at least she could practise her French, hoping that the gorgeous Marcel might be so grateful for the lift that he would be in a slightly better mood during the journey.

Setting off again in the ambulance, Addie was in some ways sad to be leaving Barcelona, and also rather sorry to be saying goodbye to Max. He was working on the old van that the Quakers were using whilst waiting for his new instructions. Addie had helped with the cocoa at the canteen and had found time to explore the city a little more. Although a feeling of revolutionary excitement still prevailed, her keen senses had detected a wariness in the air. Propaganda posters and large stencilled slogans on the walls promoting the new 'Popular Army', were often given disparaging looks by the independently-minded militia soldiers who were taking time off from their assorted units. She tried to read the newspaper, and with the help of her dictionary and her reasonable French, she could understand that the militia groups – especially those of the anarchists and Trotskyists – were being criticised strongly for their inefficiency and poor discipline. 'They have saved the day though, up until now,' thought Addie, not quite understanding how anyone could really expect ordinary men and women volunteers to do any better in an emergency situation.

Her interest in the novelty of all that lay ahead soon replaced any regrets at leaving Barcelona. She also discovered that Marcel could indeed be a charming fellow traveller. When he drove, she could sneak sideways glances at his profile, the light tan of his face and neck contrasting nicely with his creamy-white, hand-stitched shirt. Slim hands with elegant fingers and neatly trimmed nails rested lightly on the steering wheel with a sure touch. Addie wondered what that touch would feel like. They talked of French literature and philosophy, or rather, because her French was far from perfect, he talked and she made occasional comments. He told her that he was hoping to improve his surgical techniques in Murcia. He had left his previous position, he said, because there had not been sufficient opportunity for career advancement. When they took a break for a meal, he was a perfect gentleman, holding open doors for her and taking her elbow to cross the street. Addie was aware that she would have been quite happy for the road to be a mile wide. When she was driving, at one point he leaned forward to wipe the inside of the windscreen, placing his other hand alongside her trousered thigh, barely in contact until they rounded a corner, after which, she could feel a light pressure and a warmth from its continued presence. It distracted her somewhat from her driving while he related amusing stories from his medical college days. He smiled warmly at her whenever she laughed.

Arrangements had been made for them to break the journey at a convalescent hospital for International Brigaders at Benicasim, a small town on the coast. Several large villas had been taken over for this purpose, and they were to stay in the one mainly occupied by British Brigaders. Convalescent men sat on the terrace overlooking the sea, or lay on their iron beds in the pleasantly airy rooms. But Addie was dismayed when she saw their horrendous mutilations. As a child, she had, of course, seen many of the casualties returning from the First World War, but their amputations were neatly encased by sleeves or trousers, folded and pinned. These were fresh and raw, the stitch marks still clear and often irregular, like badly sewn children's samplers, unpicked and ready to be done again with more care. She chatted light-heartedly to some of them, giving them the latest news from England, trying to ignore truncated limbs and in one case, a livid scar crossing the empty eye socket of a stoic Liverpudlian. He joked in an off-hand manner about everyone's disability with a black humour that appealed greatly to his enfeebled friends, all desperately determined not to feel sorry for themselves. One man remained apart, never smiling, staring into space or at the wall most of the time. Seeing Addie watching the man's impassive face, a Yorkshire Brigader whispered to her, 'He got wounded early on. The rest of his lot went on to Boadilla – they were all killed and the things that were done to them by them bleeding Moors - it don't bear thinking about. It's no good trying to cheer him up, Miss,' he added sadly, as she rose and moved in the direction of the immobile figure in the corner.

Marcel was leaning against the wall overlooking the sea when Addie eventually emerged from the villa. Despite everything, the determination of the Brigaders to carry on their fight against fascism had left her feeling uplifted rather than depressed. As she walked with Marcel next to the beach, she found that she didn't object at all when he put his arm round her shoulders. As evening fell and the setting sun made the sky blaze with vivid vermillion reds and pinks, for a short while Addie forgot about the war, her breathing slowing to a pace in time with the small waves breaking on the shore. She was not really aware of the fact that her mind was busily attempting to construct a personality for Marcel that would coincide with her own vision of the ideal man. She could excuse his bad manners in the office in Barcelona if she tried very hard. Perhaps he was so desperate to be able to help the wounded that he had momentarily let the frustration of inaction overcome him. But, when she had raised the subject of politics, he certainly hadn't wanted to talk about it. Maybe he thought that she wouldn't understand, or perhaps he was an important member of a particular political party and didn't trust her enough yet to tell her about it. She was also beginning to wonder whether or not she was going to be kissed. Their pace was slowing and his arm seemed to be encouraging her to turn towards him.

Marcel cursed as he stumbled on the path in the rapidly fading light. The tranquil mood of the evening disappeared as suddenly as the white rabbit in Alice in Wonderland, leaving Addie embarrassed at the memory of the scenes that had been surging through her imagination. She looked at him in surprise, but was unable to decipher the strange, restless look in his eyes. Had he perhaps suddenly remembered a wife and children at home in France?

'We must get back now,' said Marcel, making no effort to encircle her shoulders again. 'It's getting late.' He set off at a rapid march, and soon she had to repeatedly run several paces to keep up with him. He said 'goodnight' to her in a cursory fashion when they reached the villa, attempted a weak smile, then tripped over the steps leading up to the door. 'Well,' thought Addie, 'he doesn't have to fall over himself in his hurry to escape my clutches.'

Next morning, Addie rather dreaded meeting Marcel again. She had slept poorly; thoughts of the previous night's events circling endlessly in her mind like midges in the Cambridgeshire fens. Marcel seemed to have forgotten all about the abrupt end to their walk. He was just as attentive and charming as the day before. Addie even began to think that she had imagined the whole episode. The scenery changed as they drove ever southwards; the mountains, stark and imposing, rising from the more fertile plains. They made slow progress, repeatedly having to stop at road checks for their papers to be examined, a process that could involve lengthy consultations and debates before they were allowed to proceed. Sometimes marching troops or slow moving lorries delayed their progress. By nightfall they were both exhausted and glad to find rooms for the night in a seedy hostel in one of the villages, indistinguishable to them from countless others through which they had passed.

Addie awoke with a start when Marcel came into her room in the morning, knocking but not waiting for a reply. He greeted her with exhilarated enthusiasm and, not wishing to deflate his buoyant mood, Addie found it impossible to reprimand him for his uninvited entry. He sat down beside her on the bed, talking of the day's plans, stroking her arm lightly as he spoke in a way that Addie found delightful. Still only half awake, Addie had no time to anticipate the even greater pleasure she experienced when, quickly and confidently he leaned over and kissed her. This was not like her previous encounters with Cambridge undergraduates. Expertly he opened her mouth with a teasing, firm tongue – only for a split second could she worry about not having cleaned her teeth – it soon didn't seem to matter. She was unaware of how the first barrier between them, a sheet and a scratchy woollen blanket, was removed, but she could soon feel the entire length of his body lying against hers, pressing insistently.

Desire was not something with which she was wholly familiar. The tremors that ran through her, coalescing with an indescribable hunger in some previously un-awakened area deep within her pelvis, were a new and marvellous phenomenon. His hands searched beneath her underslip, growing more impatient, more relentless. Addie's mind became alerted to the presence of an odd sensation. Hot and urgently moving flesh was being forced between her legs. She wanted time to think about this, to know what was happening. Marcel did not seem willing to wait. The more she resisted, the harder he pressed her down on the bed, the harder he tried to achieve his objective, and the harder the fleshy intruder became. Addie's heart began to pound. What had been an exciting experience was beginning to turn into something very disagreeable. She was just drawing breath to shout 'No', though already she feared Marcel might take no heed of her protest, when all was suddenly resolved. She could feel a crawling sensation on the soft skin of her inner thigh as Marcel's engorged penis diminished. He leapt away from her as if from a bed of burning hot embers, clutching his partially removed clothes around him. A tapping at the door saved them from having to say anything to each other. The hostel proprietress, in what was becoming an annoying occurrence, did not wait for a reply before walking in. Her outrage was plain to see at finding them both in the room. Of course, the presence of several crucifixes and paintings of tortured saints should have alerted them to the fact that, in remote villages such as this, carnal sins were still to be deplored and that not everyone was supporting the secularisation of the state. They were ejected forthwith; Addie barely had time to dress.

Most of the remaining journey was spent in an uncomfortable silence. Addie was unsure exactly what had happened. She had wanted him to stop, or at least, take things more slowly, but his sudden loss of interest in her now made her feel guilty and somehow despicable. The sensation of being slightly soiled was not just a result of her lack of opportunity to wash that morning. She wished she could ask him about it but that seemed impossible. Marcel now seemed distant and aloof. He didn't even want to talk to her any more. Despondently, she drove slowly past yet another straggling group of refugees, their donkeys piled high with a strange assortment of possessions – anything from old mattresses to chickens in basketwork cages. The numbers of refugees had been increasing as they grew closer to Murcia. Most people, she noticed sadly, didn't seem to have even a donkey and were limited to what they could carry. They parted to let the ambulance pass, gazing at it with weary, empty eyes.

Marcel left her in the centre of the town of Murcia, announcing that he would be able to find the hospital more easily from there. As he strode off, easily visible for some while amongst the smaller Spanish people in the crowd, Addie breathed a sigh of relief. She decided to put the whole thing out of her mind for the moment and concentrate on the priority of delivering the ambulance safely. Later on, she would try to work out what had happened between them.

III

Rose, drenched to the skin, had just made matters considerably worse by slipping on a wet stone into a large, muddy puddle. Her legs and skirt were now covered in a thick layer of wet clay. Annoyed at her own clumsiness, she crossed the remaining area of muddy forecourt with greater caution. Rain was falling in cold torrents through the pitch black skies, beating loudly on the metal roof of the ambulance which had brought her up the rough track to Villamalea. Rose didn't know that until a few years before, the village had been called San Juan de Villamalea, but that with the coming of the Republic, Saint John had been parted from his flock and consigned to history.

Rose had arrived a few days earlier in the nearby town of Albacete. 'A dismal hole,' she thought. Much to her surprise and disgust, it always seemed to be raining, not at all like the Spain she had seen in the newsreels at the cinema. She had joined a small group of nurses who were staying in a shabby hotel, waiting to be posted to the medical units at the front. The International Brigades were using Albacete as a base. Volunteers of dozens of different nationalities streamed in and out of the unprepossessing town, receiving initial training, waiting for orders, wishing they were somewhere else. Rose was sharing a room with two other girls, a tall, blonde Australian and a wiry little New Zealander with tortoise-shell rimmed glasses. Ada and Madge were good company though Rose was disturbed when talk turned to their experiences of the war. They had already been nursing near the Madrid front. Rose listened to their stories of working round the clock in the operating theatres and sleeping on blood-soaked stretchers with disquiet. She wasn't sure that she would be able to do it. Ada and Madge said that the worst thing wasn't being under fire but fear of the Moors. They had been brought over from Morocco by Franco, as part of the Army of Africa. Everyone knew that the Moors were merciless, raping and torturing and leaving mutilated corpses behind them wherever they went. Ada and Madge managed to remain cheerful despite all this, but even their usual good spirits were dampened after a few days of aimless hanging about. Rose was the first to receive the call from Fritz Beyer, a Medical Officer in the XV International Brigade, the man who would be responsible for deciding her immediate future. She had been told he was a surgeon, a Viennese, and that he was lucky to have escaped from a German labour camp.

The interview was carried out in fits and starts. The phone rang constantly and there was no point in closing the door as, every few minutes, someone would enter with an urgent problem. Rose tried to reply to the questions he was asking her about her experience with fever cases. Yes, she had trained in a fever hospital. Yes, she had worked with scarlet fever. She knew the basic procedures for bringing an epidemic under control, though she had never had to put them into practice.

'The Garibaldis have an epidemic of scarlet fever and their doctor has gone down with it too. I'm appointing you their temporary medical officer till I can find a replacement.'

He looked up just long enough to give her a cursory, dismissive smile.

Rose wondered what Garibaldis were, apart from nice curranty biscuits.

'You must leave at once,' he was saying, 'and don't let it spread'.

'Probably too young and not tough enough,' he said to his adjutant, shaking his head as she left the room, 'but hopefully better than nothing for the moment.'

Rose packed her things quickly. Ada explained to her that the Garibaldis were the Italian battalion of the International Brigades. The battalion was named after a national patriot, Garibaldi, who had conquered Sicily and Naples with a thousand volunteers sometime in the previous century.

Now, banging as loudly as she could on the heavy wooden doors of the improvised hospital in Villamalea, she was bedraggled, cold and more than a little frightened at the thought of all the responsibility that had been laid squarely on her shoulders. A tiny window opened in the darkness of the door, and a face peered out through the grille. She could understand well enough that the guard was saying something in a guttural Spanish that meant, 'Go away, go away.'

'Médico, médico,' she replied, not knowing the word for nurse. Saying things twice was a habit easy to acquire, she noted wryly. The bolt slid back with a hollow metallic clang that made Rose feel she was about to enter a prison. She remembered the sound from the one occasion she had gone to visit her father, 'banged up' for a short while for one of his many misdemeanours. She shuddered, either with cold or at the memory, she wasn't sure which.

'What are we coming to in this war,' muttered the guard under his breath, 'sending little girls to take charge of this mess.' He opened the door to the ward and turned on the light.

Rows of iron beds filled with grunting, cursing men lined each side of the room. They tossed and turned with their heads on rolled up coats instead of pillows. Un-emptied pots of urine overflowed onto the floor. The acrid stench made Rose gag. Those who had been able to eat anything had left the remains of their meal, crusts of bread and half-empty tumblers of wine, by the sides of the beds. The closed windows made the atmosphere stifling; so many bodies so close together, sweating with fever, no sign of bed pans. As Rose walked down the central aisle, she noticed one man lying deathly still. She approached him and touched his chill forehead with the back of her hand, then felt his feeble pulse. 'Almost moribund,' she said quietly, lifting the rough blanket and seeing the lice crawling away from his body. By the time she reached the end of the lines, stopping on the way to briefly examine certain patients, her worst fears were confirmed. Some of them did not have the typical rashes of scarlet fever, they had typhoid. They should be in isolation.

It was a long night for Rose. She battled to make herself understood, finding an unused room in a different part of the house and insisting that the three typhoid patients should be moved there. Firstly though, she cleaned them up as best she could, stripping off their lice-infested underwear and sending it off to be burned. As promised, Beyer sent up an interpreter the next morning. The officers were gathered together and Rose found herself issuing orders for the cancellation of all leave and instructions for a huge programme of disinfection and fumigation that would affect the entire battalion. She inspected the barracks; two-storey barns with ancient straw palliasses as bedding. Eating and drinking utensils were dirty. Cooks must be told about the importance of washing their hands – typhoid was carried from hand to mouth. Pointing to indicate objects for burning, others for disinfecting, cesspools for covering, Rose began to enjoy the feeling of watching people rush to carry out her orders. Her confidence growing, she was able to telephone Beyer and put in a request for medical supplies, new palliasses and a visit from the de-lousing van. The word soon spread that an English nurse had come to help and, as she passed through the wards later on, the men who were well enough called out to her for attention, trying to speak her language, 'Ingleesh, Ingleesh Rosa!' 'English Rose!' The nickname soon spread.

Her work seemed never ending. She examined hundreds

of men as they passed through the process of disinfection and relocation in an abandoned church, which had been designated as their new quarters while the barns were fumigated. During the first few days, several new scarlet fever cases appeared. Then inoculations against typhoid had to be given. The men submitted, on the whole, rather meekly to the injections, but the officers were another matter. They seemed to believe it could not possibly affect them. After a few days not one had not turned up at her clinic. Rose decided to take drastic measures and called them to an emergency meeting. When they saw the tray prepared with the vaccines and realised her intentions, they were all set to flee. Only her threats to tell the men of the rank and file that their officers were too frightened of the needle made them submit.

Just when she thought she could keep up the pace of work no longer, a new crisis arose. One of the officers rushed in to the ward where she was working, carrying a baby in his arms. It was screaming in intense agony, a shrill cry that seemed to cut into Rose somewhere on a deep and primitive level – heart, stomach, or mind – it was difficult to identify where the cry penetrated most. The little feet and legs were horribly burned. 'What am I to do? What can I do? I haven't the right things.' Rose was nearer panic than she had ever been, the baby's screams reverberating in her head. Paediatrics had never been her speciality.

She felt the gaze of the soldier and looked up. He was watching her expectantly, anticipating some instructions. 'A lovely boy, this one,' she had thought as she had given him his inoculation, 'so young to be an officer.' She pointed at the cold water tap in the corner of the room. They held the baby's legs in the flow of water for a long time. The screaming abated a little eventually. Rafael had heard the cries as he was walking through the village. In his broken English he tried to explain to Rose what had happened. Grandmothers were often left in charge of the infants whilst their daughters went to work in the fields. To keep themselves warm in the windowless interiors of the stone houses, they would keep a brazier of hot ashes under the table. This was not the first or the last time that a baby would slip from the dozing grandmother's knee to land in the glowing ashes beneath. He had taken the baby from the outstretched arms of the hysterical old woman and had run as fast as he could to the hospital.

'I have many little brothers and sisters at home,' he told her, his wide eyes with their dark lashes watching her as she gently applied cream to the burns.

Rose nodded, 'Me too,' she replied, smiling a little to see how tenderly he laid the baby in the small wooden box she had prepared for it. 'He probably had more patience with his younger brothers and sisters than I had with mine,' she thought, with a twinge of regret.

Rafael came to see her the next morning to ask how the baby was. She had kept it by her side all night, trying to give it fluids from a spoon, then putting it on a drip, but she knew the poor thing was dying. She tried everything she could think of that might help at all, but the next day, when Rafael called again, she had to tell him that the baby had died in the night. Crossly, she wiped the tears from her eyes. Sentimentality wouldn't do. Rafael, standing at her side, tentatively touched her now wet fingers in an attempt to comfort her. A warm and pleasant feeling began to radiate from her hand as she turned her head and saw his sad expression, the softening in his eyes, the finely-drawn mouth with lips slightly parted. 'Oh, no!' she warned herself sharply, reigning in the emotions that seemed all set to carry her away. She snatched her hand back in haste to wipe her fingers on a towel.

She had asked Rafael to tell the family that their baby was dead, worrying a little that they might think it was her fault. She nearly cried again when later on that day, she came out of the hospital to find a delegation of family members waiting for her, bearing presents of eggs and vegetables. Rafael attempted to translate the speech of gratitude made by the baby's father. They were sorry that they had no money to pay her. She told them no payment was necessary and gave them the box with its pathetic contents wrapped in a piece of linen sheeting. A rare silence encircled the family as they walked away, their rope-soled feet hardly disturbing the dust.

'La vida es dura,' said Rafael, who was already familiar with the Spanish version of a universal truth. He translated for Rose, 'Life is hard.'

Rose wasn't so philosophical. She turned on her heel and stomped angrily away, muttering, 'Well, it wouldn't have been so hard for that poor baby if the stupid old woman had looked after it properly.'

After the baby's death, the conversations that Rose had with Rafael often followed a similar pattern; his idealistic approach countered by her practicality. He would tell her about his hopes and dreams for a new Italy, with equality for all. Rose would ask him, 'What's the point of having equal shares of nothing? There wouldn't be enough to make everyone happy, even if you took all the money from the rich and gave it to the poor. And anyway some of them would just drink themselves straight into the gutter.' At first he was dismayed by her low opinion of the poor. As he gradually learned more about her background, he began to understand. Though he couldn't catch the meaning of all the words she was using, he could sense the atmosphere of deprivation in which she spent her early years, and the degradation she had felt. His own upbringing in a large noisy extended family had been very different. They were poor but the village was full of his relations and he could always get something to eat somewhere. His store of childhood memories was stacked with good times. It wasn't till he moved to the city to find work as a young man and experienced the harshness of urban poverty that he became involved in the unions and politics.

Rose's memories of her youth hung in her mind like

London smogs. She talked about her father, nicknamed 'Bulldog' Baker because of his barrel chest and strength. He didn't hit his children much - except when he'd had a drink, which became all too often. The family were always doing 'moonlight flits' from one slum to another, because they couldn't pay the rent. Rose's older brothers and sisters had gone out to work as soon as they could earn anything. She was the one kept at home to look after the younger ones. The fear she had felt when crouching with her mother under the kitchen table was still vivid in her mind. 'Quick hide, sh! sh! It's the Truant Officer', or the Landlord, or the Never Never man calling for a payment that was never likely to be made. Queuing outside the pawnshop was a nightmare for Rose. Her friends would jeer as they passed by, pointing at her bundle of clothes – her father's suit, or a sister's dress, pawned on Monday morning for a few pence, sometimes redeemed on Friday when it was a payday.

Evening walks with Rafael became an almost daily event. Rose couldn't help looking forward to the hour or so they could spend together. Then came an evening when he didn't arrive. Her first reaction was to think that he had tired of their conversations. It must be laborious work for him, speaking in English and trying to understand her. She said to herself that she didn't care if she never saw him again. Immediately she realised that it had been a mistake to put this thought into words. In wartime, never seeing someone again had a particular resonance, the echo of death. With the quarantine restrictions now lifted, he could be anywhere, perhaps sent into danger at the front on some idiotic mission. He could be lying wounded; he could be dead. Three anxious hours later, after darkness had fallen, he was carried in on a stretcher.

Rafael had been to the American training base at Tarazona, collecting an important package by motorbike. On the return journey, he rounded a corner to find that some fifth columnist had prepared a welcome for him. He caught the glint of the wire stretched across the road just a fraction of a second before his throat would have been sliced through like a Dutch cheese. Without thinking he had thrown the bike sideways, hitting the ground and skidding along the dirt track, his body passing a bare inch below the wire. A rocky outcrop at the roadside impacted with sickening force against flesh and metal, altering their previous trajectory dramatically. Bike and rider finally came to rest in the centre of the track. Rafael lay still, pinned by the bike, blood from his leg slowly colouring a small area of soil a bright red, dripping in time with the beat of his heart. He tried to focus his energies on escaping from beneath the bike, but every time he moved he almost passed out. Whoever set the wire could be approaching to finish him off. A feeling of utter helplessness came creeping into his mind with the mist of unconsciousness.

The screech of brakes brought him to full alert. An ambulance, having taken the bend rapidly, was slithering to a halt in clouds of dust. The driver had jammed his foot on the brakes. His passenger too was involuntarily braking, pushing with all his might on a non-existent pedal. They could see the tangled mass before them, but did not notice the wire still taut across their path. It had sufficient strength to deflect the still rapidly moving vehicle into the high bank at the roadside, before snapping. The wire snaked through the air, whipping through the overhanging branches, cutting twigs and leaves as it fell. The two men staggered from the ambulance, shocked but unhurt. They lifted the bike and hurriedly applied a tourniquet to Rafael's leg before carrying him to the side of the road on a stretcher. A considerable delay followed before they were able to get the ambulance moving again. As dusk fell, the engine spluttered and started up. The nearest hospital was in Villamalea.

Rose could see the wound was deep. Her stomach churned. She realised that she was not able to deal with this particular patient with the detachment necessary for good nursing. It was not the same at all when you knew the patient, when you cared about them, she admitted to herself at last resignedly. Her voice shook as she telephoned Albacete to ask for a doctor to be sent over immediately. None were available. It would be dangerous to leave him with the tourniquet for much longer, or to transport him all the way to a rearguard hospital. She had to do it herself. Deep suturing was not something she had done before, though she had assisted at many such operations. She explained as briefly as she could to Rafael what the choices were. He smiled weakly at her, 'You can do it well,' he said. She tried to switch off the part of her mind that recognised Rafael as she gave him a hefty injection of morphine. The entire procedure took some time. After she had put the last of the sutures into his skin, her knees began to tremble. Tremors spread to her thighs and then from her hands to her shoulders. Sitting down quickly before her legs gave way, she burst into tears.

As much as she intended to maintain her distance while Rafael recovered in the ward over the following week, it just didn't seem to work out that way. Rose felt herself subject to a sort of gravitational pull, a constant desire to move towards him, wherever she happened to be in the building. He would talk about what life would be like after the war, his dream clear to see in his shining eyes. When he slept, she often paused at the foot of his bed to look at him for a moment, a moment that often stretched on for minutes. She would wrench herself away, repeating to herself, 'I am *not* going to get involved with a penniless Italian revolutionary.'

A doctor eventually arrived from Albacete, giving his surprised approval to Rose's handiwork. The wound was healing well. The only problem had occurred shortly after the operation, when Rafael was still too weak to get out of bed. Normally, she washed her patients thoroughly, and was uninterested or mildly amused at the antics of the male genitalia she encountered. When it was Rafael's turn and she approached him with her bowl and sponge, his face flushed red to the roots of the hair on his forehead. She placed the bowl of water on the small table beside him and began to wipe his hot face. He caught her wrist in his hand and gave her a long silent look. Most of other patients in the ward were watching and waiting with delighted anticipation. Rose hesitated. As often and as varied as Rafael's imaginings of their first sexual encounter had been, this public scenario was not amongst them. At last, fumbling with embarrassment, Rose dropped the sponge back into the bowl, saying she had just remembered something she had to do. Laughter from the other patients made her ears burn scarlet as she hurried away. She sent an orderly to finish the task.

As soon as he was well enough to travel, Rafael was sent to convalesce on the coast. Rose filled her days with work in the hospital. She tended soldiers who came to her with small pieces of shrapnel or splinters of bone working their way out from old wounds. She dealt strictly with malingerers, knowing the signs from seeing her brothers try all sorts of tricks to avoid going to work. She began to run a clinic for the villagers too. At first they were unsure of her – she was so different, a strange foreign girl, living alone amongst men. She stitched their cuts and gave out aspirin, slipping a can of condensed milk to the families with young children whenever she could. Soon, they began to invite her to their homes for a meal. With food in short supply, she knew she was being honoured when a chicken was produced for dinner.

The ringing of the phone one day broke this routine. Beyer, more friendly towards her now she had demonstrated her capabilities, had called to tell her of a new assignment.

'How are you, English Rose?' he asked. Her new name had reached Albacete and beyond. 'You must go to Madrid,' he told her, 'they are broadcasting to England and they want nurses to go to make appeals.'

'Me, to Madrid?' She asked in surprise. 'Oh, yes, I'll go.'

IV

Her farewells said, Constance took her 'salvo conducto', the vital document giving her safe conduct to the front, and showed it, as she had been instructed, to the man in charge of the transport depot. He pointed her in the direction of a lorry, just about to set off for the front lines. Fortunately for her, it would actually be stopping at her destination to drop off supplies. Two men were making the final check on the ropes holding down the canvas cover. One of them looked up and grinned cheerfully at the sight of the attractive young woman, presumably looking for a lift with them.

'Where are you wanting to go to, love?' he asked in a friendly voice.

Max was, by this time, bearing more than just traces of grease on his person. It was difficult to tell where the suntan began and the ingrained oil stopped. Demands were high for his skills in repairing vehicles and his fame was spreading for his ability to cobble together a workable engine from the parts of others. When Constance gave him the name of the village where the hospital had been set up, Poleñino, he called his companion over to join them.

'Here, Sam,' he said with a nod of his head in Constance's direction, 'she's going to the same place as you, you lucky blighter.'

Sam held out his hand and shook hers. He was saying 'How d'you do?' politely, but seemed to have forgotten to smile. He suddenly realised that he was staring. Embarrassed, he smiled quickly and took his hand away.

'He's going to be a stretcher bearer,' Max informed her, adding with some envy, 'He's got brains though, he's been to university – you can't keep the working-classes down.'

They all sat on the bench seat in the front of the lorry, stopping now and again to share out oranges from the large bagful that Max had brought with him. It was difficult to carry on any sort of conversation as the lorry jolted noisily along the uneven roads, but when they parked in the shade for lunch, they talked for a while. Constance soon felt at ease with them. Max assured her that the water wasn't fit to drink, 'Better have some of this wine,' he insisted, pouring them each a tin mug full. Sam, relaxing a little with wine and warmth, told Constance about his struggle to get a degree in chemistry. He also spoke of his decision to come to Spain with a good friend, John Gardener, now dead, killed on the road to Huesca. Sam had been wounded too in the same battle and had been sent home to England to recover. He had returned as soon as he could. Constance liked the serious young man. His honest face was far from handsome but the agreeable arrangement of deep set eyes, large nose, and square jaw line, inspired a certain trust. When they arrived at Poleñino, Max dropped them both off at what was now the hospital, an assortment of former farm buildings on the outskirts of the village, converted to provide wards and two operating theatres. She breathed a sigh of satisfaction as she walked through the open arched doors into the courtyard. She was ready to begin work.

At first, they were inundated with wounded, but the Aragon front was falling quiet, and soon only the occasional violent skirmishes brought in casualties. Constance found she did not get on with all the staff at the hospital as well as she would have liked. She had never been renowned for an ability to suffer fools gladly and, despite their splendid qualifications, she certainly considered several of her new colleagues as such. She was annoyed in particular by the behaviour of two English nurses who were seemingly more concerned about the exact position of their starched white hats than the welfare of their patients. They relished the authority they held over the Spanish girls who were helping in the hospital, the 'chicas'. Where Constance saw an ideal opportunity to train more nurses who would doubtless be sorely needed in the near future, others saw the chance to get someone else to do all the dirty work. When she raised the subject at one of the staff meetings, she was pleased to find that she had at least some support. A shy Welsh girl she had hardly spoken to, plucked up the courage to agree with her, and a South African nurse gave an impassioned speech about the need for equality. Little changed, however. The general atmosphere remained elitist, the 'chicas' were still treated by some like skivvies, and the divisions between those who were 'for' and 'against' their training grew ever greater.

Another factor exacerbated the situation. The political differences that were emerging between the staff in their discussions became more firmly entrenched as a result of the debate on the position of foreign medical workers within the newly formed Republican 'Popular Army'. There were those on the staff who were all for becoming part of the army, to be sent where the government decided they were needed most. Others were determined to maintain independence as a 'British Unit', only fully answerable to the Medical Aid Office in London. Constance thought that they would be of more use under the control of those who knew the situation best on the ground, not people who were miles away in an office in another country.

Beneath these tensions the work went on, but with several other irritating distractions. Dominating the nearby village was a zealous anarchist who would appear from time to time, wreathed in the pungent fumes of black tobacco, to observe their activities. With a large-brimmed black hat, crossed bandoliers, and a loaded pistol adorning his imposing midriff, he was a figure to be treated with a degree of circumspection. Due to his resemblance to a famous Mexican revolutionary, ample moustache and violent tendencies included, he was known by all as 'Pancho Villa'. The anarchist Village Committee, over which he presided, had abolished money and set up a bartering system. He was therefore less than happy to have what he considered to be a bourgeois hospital operating within his collectivised zone. Constance had first crossed swords with him in the peaceful setting of a secluded pool fed by a spring of clear water in the hills above the village. As the weather grew warmer, a few of the nurses had gone there to bathe. Those, like Constance, who had no bathing suits, had borrowed from others who had. These costumes bore no resemblance to the styles considered acceptable on the French Riviera. Their built up tops and almost knee length legs made them the epitome of respectability. Nevertheless, Pancho Villa forbade the nurses to use the pool, claiming that they frightened the mules. However radical his revolutionary views in some matters, they did not extend far in regards to women. To avoid further trouble, the nurses sacrificed the pleasures of swimming.

Nevertheless, he continued to make life difficult at the hospital, delaying deliveries of food and fuel, sometimes 'liberating' them altogether. One day, he co-opted a delivery of petrol destined for the hospital. Either through carelessness or machismo, his failure to stub out his cigarette before emptying the small tanker was to prove disastrous. His burns were treated tenderly by the hospital staff and his gratitude notably improved their relationship.

A further annoyance for Constance came in the form of a small group of Englishmen who were inclined to visit on Sundays to check out the female 'local talent'. They were members of the POUM militia who were holding the line to the left of the hospital. Constance now knew something about the POUM, a Trotskyist dissident group, small but very vocal. They were, she was told, a thorn in the side of other groups; it seemed that the communists hated them almost as much as they hated the fascists. The visits of these young men were welcomed by some of the nurses as a pleasant diversion, but Constance did not appreciate being looked over as if she were a prize heifer. She brushed off their flattery, even that of the most interesting amongst them, a tall, dark-haired man with a small moustache and wry smile. He said he was a writer and seemed intelligent, but Constance placed him and his friends beyond the pale when, one day at the beginning of May, the entire POUM unit disappeared, leaving a gaping hole in the front. The communists and anarchists spread out but could only give sparse coverage till reinforcements arrived. They later heard about the terrible fighting that had broken out in Barcelona, the POUM on the losing side. The Trotskyists and anarchists had wanted a social revolution now, others wanted to win the war against fascism first. 'As if we haven't got enough troubles,' thought Constance angrily, 'without fighting amongst ourselves!'

In contrast with the dim view Constant took of those in the POUM who had 'deserted' the front, her regard for Max and Sam increased steadily. They both called to see her whenever they could, and helped if there was heavy work to be done. The result of one such occasion made Constance laugh with delight. There was always so much washing; sheets, bandages, blankets. Constance tried to help the Spanish girls, not wanting them to think she was 'too good' for this arduous task. Max solved the problem. He arrived with a surprise – an enormous makeshift washing machine he had assembled on the back of a beaten up old lorry. It looked like a joke, with its assorted giant fan belts and pulleys, an old boiler to heat water and a tall tin chimney on the top. The 'chicas' chattered excitedly – they'd never seen anything like it; neither, for that matter, had the rest of the staff.

With Sam, Constance could have more serious conversations. They would discuss almost anything - the state of the world, Constance's daily conflicts with the other nurses, Sam's worries about his parents' health and the behaviour of his younger brother, always in trouble of one sort or another. What they never mentioned was Sam's longing for Constance, a dull pain that he knew he would have to learn to live with, probably for the rest of his life. He had seen Constance dismiss admirers without a care. He was certain that she valued their friendship. He preferred to hold on to the possibility that perhaps, one day in the future, however remote, this would become something more, rather than risk losing everything by telling her outright how he felt. For Constance, Sam was an anchor of good sense and reasoned argument. More than anything, she was glad to have found a friend she could trust.

The workload was decreasing. Accidents, general ailments and the occasional wound from a sniper's bullet were all they had to deal with on a daily basis. Constance found relief from the mounting tensions between the nurses by making herself useful in the villages, helping with difficult births. Then, one day in July, Max turned up, obviously keen to tell her something. Constance saw him less frequently these days as work in the maintenance depot kept him busy. Heavy work and rough roads meant that vehicles were breaking down more and more often and new parts were becoming harder to obtain. He had been asked to make a delivery to Madrid and had wanted to see her before going away. Constance sighed with envy at his news. Max came up with the solution. He had overheard someone talking about the appeals that were being broadcast on the wireless from Madrid. They could be heard all over the world, and some of them were very effective, particularly those made by the nurses.

'You could do it, Connie,' Max said encouragingly, 'You'd go down a treat with your posh voice an' all. I'd take you there and back – no trouble.'

Permission was granted for Constance to take leave in Madrid. 'They'll breathe a sigh of relief when I'm gone,' she said to Sam later on that day. Much as he loved her, it was difficult to argue with this statement. Most of the other nurses would find life easier without Constance's cutting remarks, however justified they were. On the other hand, the 'chicas' adored her, and the doctors valued her calmness and efficiency. The patients found her brusque if they were making a fuss about nothing, but full of genuine concern when they were really suffering. They would certainly miss her, but Sam would miss her far more.

V

Murcia's cathedral cheered Addie up greatly. After her meeting with Geraldine she had become much more conscious of the crushingly oppressive role of the Church in Spain. Nevertheless, the style of the building, with its curled and convoluted facade, was enough to make anyone smile, or at least provoke amused disdain by its resemblance to a Baroque iced cake. Now driving with confidence through the maze of narrow streets, Addie extricated the ambulance at last and found her way to 'Pablo Iglesias', a block of flats on the outskirts of the city where she had been told that the refugees were housed.

There were thousands of them. Old men, women, children, babies, the noise was deafening; hysterical screaming, shouting, groaning, crying. The nine storey building was an unfinished shell. There were no doors or windows, very few partition walls and the huge corridor-like rooms were only furnished with straw. The reek from piles of refuse assailed her from all sides. Filthy, bony children crawled in the semi-darkness. In his most graphic portrayals of squalor, Dickens would have been hard pressed to describe it. Wild-eyed and desperate, the refugees surged round Addie as she entered, trying to tell her their tragic stories, pleading for help. Stunned, she stood immobile, uncomprehending, at a loss for words or actions. Rescue arrived in a strange form, entering at the far side of the cavernous ground floor. A floral print dress in crisp cotton stood out amongst the dusty, ragged attire of the refugees, and was moving towards her. The crowd parted to let the incongruous female apparition pass. She had the brittle look of a stereotypical English spinster; flat bosom barely noticeable beneath the frilled collar of her dress, torso firmly encased in Spirella corsets and her gingery permed hair held strictly under control with strategically placed Kirby grips. She stopped to exchange a few words with several women, and to stroke the heads of some of the smaller children. At this point, the stereotype crumbled. The remarkable thing, Addie noticed immediately, was that when she conversed in Spanish, which she seemed to be able to do with perfect fluency, the aura of reserve that surrounded her dropped away. She became animated, open, demonstrative. She grasped Addie's elbow and escorted her out through the gaping hole of the doorway.

'It's a bit overwhelming at first dear, isn't it?' she said kindly, when the noise level had abated. 'I'm Phyllis, and you must be...?

'Addie Maclaurin, I think you're expecting me – from the National Joint Committee.'

Several small boys were already investigating the ambulance that Addie had left parked a few yards down the road. They ran to hide on the arrival of two such alien looking women.

After leaving the ambulance safely under lock and key, Addie had accompanied Phyllis to the flat where she was lodging with Spanish friends. There, she was given a brief, no-nonsense summary of the state of affairs in Murcia.

'Murcia is looked down on by the rest of Spain,' Phyllis told her, 'it's considered backward and uncultured. It was already bursting at the seams with soldiers and wounded. Now, it's been overwhelmed by this influx of refugees from Malaga. Tens of thousands of these Malagans fled the city before it fell to Franco. As they made their escape, the poor things were shelled by warships and machined-gunned from the air. Some of their children are missing or dead, and few have money to buy food. Pablo Iglesias is just one of the refuges here but the others are as bad. They carry out corpses from all of them every day.' She paused for a moment to gather up a notebook and pencil. 'We must get started straight away, there's plenty to be done.'

Addie was relieved to discover that the 'we' included several others, and didn't consist solely of Phyllis and herself. That afternoon, a small group of volunteers, some experienced in refugee work, others not, planned what should be done. 'A stage army,' Addie thought, looking around her at the collection of women, seemingly pitifully few for such a tremendous task. Phyllis, on leave from her post as a Deputy Headmistress in a private girl's boarding school, was however, an old hand at relief work, and without doubt, was accustomed to getting things done. Addie learned that she had been helping the Quakers with refugees since the outbreak of the First World War; Belgians, Serbians, Austrians, Russians, a never ending stream of sorrows.

Over the next week, Addie had little time to think of Marcel. Phyllis set a furious pace. Late at night, Addie could do no more than drop thankfully onto the narrow bed at the flat and sleep. It seemed as if Phyllis was never still, arranging for lorry loads of milk, cocoa and biscuits to be sent from the American Quakers in Valencia, and playing on the pride of local officials to out-do each other in the matter of providing practical assistance. Persuading local women to help was a more difficult challenge. Few women in Murcia could be called progressive by any stretch of the imagination. In Barcelona, women had taken up arms; they were driving the trams, working in the munitions factories. The women of Murcia had put away their mantillas for the moment and were waiting behind barred windows, praying for Franco to bring stability and security. Verminous, disease ridden refugees would go away if ignored for long enough. Only a handful of Murcian women came forward to help them. Nevertheless, gradually some sort of order was established and the Malagans learned to queue for their cocoa. However, it soon became clear that some of the children were too ill to even get to the canteen and the hospitals in Murcia were full. Phyllis's next amazing feat was to persuade the civil authorities in the city to allocate one of the newly built villas for use as a children's hospital. She begged and borrowed equipment, she besieged friends in England with pleas to send out nurses, she was promised the attendance of a doctor from the city hospital for a couple of hours each day.

Addie was soon helping to cope with the arrival of children and babies, often accompanied by their fiercely protective mothers. Her Spanish improved, but when a child died, she could think of no words to say to the distraught mothers in any language. She had dreamed of driving the ambulance to the front, but the ancient vehicle was only fit for use on reasonable roads, not for the rough dirt tracks in the mountains. As the days went by however, she yearned more and more to be at the centre of things, to be in Madrid in particular. Everyone knew that in Madrid, people were holding out against Franco's army with a spirit of resistance to fascism that shone like a beacon throughout the world. But it would take more than just wishful thinking to get there. She resigned herself to the much needed tasks at the villa.

Her daily routine was disturbed sooner than she expected by the arrival of Marcel in place of the usual Spanish doctor. His visits continued for several days. She felt an unpleasant sinking, sick sensation in her stomach when she saw him chatting easily to the young nurse who had recently arrived from England. Obviously flattered by his attentions, the girl followed him happily on his ward rounds. Addie could not suppress a degree of unwarranted resentment. Towards Addie, Marcel remained distant, ignoring her presence almost to the point of rudeness. 'He must be working terribly hard,' Addie told herself. 'He probably doesn't want to be distracted by any emotional entanglements.'

But the silence between them was more than she could bear. She debated with herself what would be the best course to take. They must be sensible and clear the air. It was too silly to continue behaving in a childish manner, avoiding each other in corridors and not speaking. There were real children to be considered, sick children. Just before he was due to leave after one of his morning visits, he went into the small dispensary in what had been a storeroom near the kitchen. Addie grasped the opportunity to speak to him alone. She opened the dispensary door to see him pocketing a handful of vials. Startled, he turned to face her. The flash of hatred in his eyes passed so quickly that Addie thought she must have imagined it.

'Ah, good,' he said, rather too quickly, 'the very person I wanted to see. We haven't had much time to see each other recently. I've missed our talks. I hope we can see each other more when we have any free time – perhaps tomorrow?'

Addie did not reply but stared in curiosity at the half empty box of morphia on the bench.

'I was just borrowing some of these,' Marcel explained with a careless smile, 'we're running out at the city hospital and Phyllis said I could take a few and replace them later.'

Addie knew his explanation was a reasonable one, but somehow still felt uneasy. Drugs were indeed in short supply. The wounded men that Marcel would be treating were far more likely to need morphia than the children in the villa who were mainly suffering from diseases and malnutrition. Better to put them to good use now and replenish the stocks later. Anyway, if Phyllis had agreed..... though perhaps she would mention it to Phyllis when they had a minute to spare.

It was easy afterwards to think what a fool she had been. She had wanted to believe him, still a little infatuated with the character she had invented to match the handsome face, the lithe and graceful body. On reflection, she had also believed him because he was a doctor, and doctors, of course, know best. 'What an idiot I was,' she said to herself over and over again. Phyllis had asked her for 'a quiet word' the next day. Morphia had been disappearing from the dispensary recently. The number of vials in the box had been counted the previous morning, and Addie had been seen leaving the dispensary, after which there was a great deal less. These vague allegations had been corroborated by Dr Boulestin, who said he had suspected her of stealing and selling the morphia. He also claimed he had found her un-cooperative and inefficient. Phyllis had faith in herself as a good judge of character. She had immediately warmed to Addie's genuine good-natured enthusiasm. She had seen her toiling for days, doing more than her share of unpleasant jobs, accepting responsibilities, never complaining. She regretted the fact that, for now, there was little she could do, other than de-fuse the situation by Addie's removal until the outcome of further investigations. On seeing Addie's face change from outrage at the charges made against her, to a dawning comprehension of what had happened, Phyllis was convinced that the accusations were false.

Addie was familiar with the popular English expression 'the penny's dropped' and also with the reality of the loud click that followed the insertion of a coin into the door mechanism which permitted entry to a Ladies' Public Lavatory. The metaphor in this case could not have been more appropriate. Various small incidents came together to fall into place with an almost tangible thud; Marcel's mood changes, his sudden restlessness and need for privacy. She was not aware that the peculiar look in his eyes during their evening walk on the beach had been caused by a restriction of the pupils, a common occurrence in addicts when suffering withdrawal from morphia. She did realise however, that his abrupt loss of desire could be a side effect of the drug. She felt as if the penny had opened the door onto a particularly unsavoury, un-flushed toilet. She assured Phyllis of her innocence, but felt that, as she had no tangible evidence to offer against Marcel, she could say nothing of her suspicions. Phyllis had already resolved to find out more about the altogether too unpredictable Doctor Boulestin.

Luckily for Addie, Phyllis's offer of a substitute position was to be the fulfilment of her wildest dreams.

'Can you type, dear?' Phyllis asked her the following morning. Addie's fear of finding herself allocated to some dreary office in Murcian bureaucracy was dispelled by the news that Phyllis had contacted one of her old journalist friends. She was to go to work in Madrid, typing reports for press correspondents. Jubilantly, she wrote home to her family, 'I'll be there at the heart of it all'.

CHAPTER 3

Golden Threads

I

'This won't do,' Addie repeated to herself firmly, 'it won't do at all.' She closed her eyes and reached out to touch the tiled wall for support. 'There is no point in standing here, trembling like a jelly.' Nevertheless, her knees still knocked. She tried not to think about the unpleasant pulsating sensations beneath her skin, where barely hidden arteries carried surging blood with abnormal speed. Flesh was so vulnerable; shards of steel could pierce it with ease, unleashing red fountains that would gush merrily for a few moments before slowing and congealing. This was the first time she had really felt afraid.

Madrid was being bombarded again. In the street outside the entrance to the Metro station in the Gran Vía, Addie had seen countless pedestrians continuing on their way, barely glancing in the direction of the artillery fire and the ear-shattering explosions. Freshly arrived in the city, Addie had not as yet, clothed herself in the fatalistic armour that allowed people to carry on in the face of death. She felt as naked as in her dreams of walking undressed through crowds. It seemed impossible to leave the Metro and cross the street to the Telefónica building where she was due to report to the Press Office.

The station platform and the tunnel leading to it had been crowded, not with commuters, but with families recently bombed out of their homes. They sat in straggling groups along the walls, surrounded by dishevelled heaps of salvaged possessions, waiting to be allocated new lodgings. Some looked dazed and dispirited, others continued to laugh and argue loudly – no walls now to keep their family secrets - households with no house to hold them. Standing in the shadows near the open doorway to the street, Addie attempted to rationalise her fear. She had evaded academia, but her intellect was always the weapon she chose to use when she had problems. She now attempted to identify exactly what the differences were between the horrid sensations she was suffering at that moment and the delightful trembling and throbbing she had experienced when touched by Marcel. The emotions were so distinct, but the physical manifestations were strikingly similar. Even the overwhelming need to let go that had washed over her for a few seconds as they lay closely together had its counterpart – though now apparently more intimately linked to her bladder than to any other organ.

Insistent tuggings at her sleeve broke into Addie's musings on bodily functions. Rheumy, blue-grey clouded eyes peered from a face that reminded Addie of a particularly disappointing drawing class in which she had ruined a portrait by over use of cross-hatched shading. The shawl-draped old woman was pointing with a crone's finger to the other side of the wide street, and with increasing impatience, was pulling her towards the open mouth of the exit. Rather than fearing the hazards of war, she was obviously just afraid of walking blindly under the first vehicle that passed. Addie, dreading the thought of abandoning the shelter of the Metro station, wondered unkindly what the difference was between a 'crone' and a 'hag'. 'Probably the derivation,' she concluded. But she knew that the analytical bunker in which she was hiding had been breached. Taking a deep breath, Addie ventured forth, her still shaking hand clinging to the surprisingly steady arm of her companion. Together they crossed the road.

As she had drawn nearer to the tall, white, Telefónica building, Addie averted her eyes, not wishing to see its pitted facade where the history of the last few months was heavily imprinted in the limited language of warfare. The elderly woman relinquished her hold once they had reached the opposite pavement. Ignored by the sentry, Addie pushed through the revolving doors to arrive in the reception area, her breathing constricted to erratic, shallow gulps and her palms perspiring. The anxiety did not abate during her search for the press office, when the almost agoraphobic fear she had experienced in the street outside swung instantly to the opposite extreme. Dimly lit, twisting corridors, lined with resolutely closed doors, made her feel as if she were inside the mind of a bigot, claustrophobic in its lack of light and air. With relief, she eventually found the correspondents in a room on the fourth floor, where, fortunately for her frayed nerves, the constant crashing of returning typewriter carriages was a distraction from the sound of exploding shells and gunfire. Unaware of the number of upper-floor rooms within the building that had received direct hits, Addie was able to believe in the illusion of safety within four walls.

Over the next few weeks, Addie somehow became inured to the danger of the bombardment. Like most inhabitants of Madrid, she could soon ignore all but the closest explosions. She loved the excitement of the Press Office, though tensions were rife and frayed tempers abounded. The correspondents had an ongoing fight with the censors to send out their dispatches unscathed. Only those that bore the official censorship stamp for foreign press releases, a blue oval of approval from the 'Oficina de Información y Prensa', were allowed to escape to the wide world. Addie typed away at a furious rate for Ted Allen, a Canadian journalist. She wrote a letter home to tell her family that she was now mingling with the 'great swells' of the newspaper world, like Sefton Delmar and Frank Pitcairn. 'And nobody,' she told them, 'could fail to be impressed by Robert Capa and Gerda Taro.' Addie was sure that Gerda, beautiful and talented, would soon be as famous for her war photography as Capa.

The routine of Addie's days changed abruptly when the commentator for the English language broadcasts was taken ill. Although Addie was still a newcomer, especially in comparison with those who had been in Madrid since the attack on the city had begun in earnest in November, she had already made many friends in the building, and not just amongst the foreigners. Her attempts to speak the language made her popular amongst the Spanish too – her mistakes amused them and brought a little light relief. 'Is it all right if I give birth?' she had asked on one memorable occasion, having meant to enquire if she could switch on the light. When her name was suggested as an emergency replacement for the commentator, the idea was quickly given approval by the Controller of Broadcasting. Addie, he had been assured, was an enthusiastic supporter of the Republic; she had learned fast and knew the ropes from her work with the journalists. Believing himself to be a progressive man, the Controller was even prepared to accept that a woman's perspective might benefit the foreign propaganda broadcasts - for a short time. And, more importantly, she could start that night. 'The Voice of Spain' was, for a while, to be hers.

Late that night, Addie made her first broadcast. At first, the microphone, though inert and unresponsive, seemed to take on the characteristics of an instrument of torture. It loomed before her, threatening to seize the power of movement from her tongue and vocal chords, and paralyse her thoughts with its remorseless presence. Addie felt the darkness in the room closing around her, only held at bay by a pool of light from an overhead bulb, its crinkled carbon paper shade a gesture to blackout regulations. With difficulty, she managed to read out the first few dry sentences from the typed sheet she held in her hand.

Then a radical shift took place in her mind. The microphone became the ear of a vast amorphous creature whose invisible tentacles reached into hundreds of thousands of wirelesses, and to the listeners; her parents in their drawing room in Cambridge, to all those who wanted to know what was happening in Madrid, to the people who hadn't heard about the terrible struggle to defeat Franco and fascism. She had a few minutes to touch them.

Her voice was clear but quiet, with none of the usual rhetorical flourishes. She told her listeners how afraid she had been when she had first arrived in Madrid, but that she had seen how people could carry on their daily lives despite the bombs. There would be no surrender. She asked them to imagine what it would be like if the sandbagged statues were in Piccadilly Circus instead of the Puerta del Sol, if the new London University buildings had been ruined rather than the modern buildings of Madrid's University City. Could they imagine the devastation they would feel if their homes had windows shattered by shrapnel, or had been reduced entirely to rubble? Leaving them with one final thought, she asked if they would reflect upon it, and act on their conclusions. 'If the war is won here in Madrid,' she said earnestly, 'there will be less chance of another world war.'

Addie left the room, her emotions a mixture of elation at having made a broadcast at all, and disappointment, fearing that she had not spoken powerfully enough. She knew she couldn't give speeches like 'La Pasionaria', the Spanish MP who could reduce an audience to tears with her inspiring oratory. 'Better to live on your feet than die on your knees', she had told the suffering Spanish workers. Now her most famous cry of all, 'No Pasarán', 'They shall not pass', was emblazoned on banners and posters throughout the city. 'Well,' thought Addie with resignation, 'I may not be another Pasionaria, but at least I did the best I could.'

Within a few days, she was more cheerful. The response to her broadcast was good. People abroad were asking to hear more from the new commentator; they liked her reasoned approach and were grateful for a change from the usual bombastic rhetoric. Addie busily wrote ideas for her next transmission, typing them with two carbon copies for the censors on the thin, almost transparent, office paper.

She soon found that she enjoyed broadcasting, feeling she was doing something, even if in just a small way, to counteract the psychotic fantasies flooding the airwaves in the propaganda speeches of Franco's generals, especially in the diatribes of Quiepo de Llano. A week or so later, just as she was leaving the studio, the censor, a cadaverous and gloomy-looking man called Arturo, called her over. Addie was now on friendly terms with him, though it was not altogether agreeable to have him sitting there during all the transmissions, ready to break off the broadcast if a commentator appeared to be deviating in any way from the approved copy of the text he had before him. Arturo told her that a British nurse was supposed to be arriving to make an appeal for the medical services. She was late, he added in his customary taciturn manner. Perhaps, he asked, in a tone that conveyed he had little hope of receiving a positive answer, Addie could stay for a while to explain things quickly to her, when, or rather, if, she turned up. Addie willingly agreed, anticipating a welcome change from the conversations that prevailed in the press office; politics, battles and military strategy. The nurse might be glad to be greeted by a friendly face, especially someone who spoke her own language. Just then, a flustered girl entered the office like a small whirlwind, smoothing her fair hair away from her pink cheeks and trying to catch her breath. 'I'm so sorry,' she blurted out, 'we broke down. I had to get a lift on a lorry. Am I too late?'

Rose hated to be late. It put her at a disadvantage. She liked to arrive, cool and collected, and to have plenty of time to go to the toilet. She had made a special effort to look nice for her trip to Madrid, but now she was certain that it had all been in vain. She felt untidy and hot after the tortuously slow and uncomfortable journey. She attempted to brush the creases from her skirt and then reached anxiously to her hair again to verify that all the curls were in their proper places.

Addie reassured her with a smile, 'No, you're not too late, it'll be fine. Let me take your bag and then we'll try to run through a few things together before you start.'

Rose liked Addie immediately. She hadn't met any Americans, but knew from the countless Hollywood movies she had watched at the cinema that Addie's accent was from somewhere in the United States. Rose was normally very cautious when she first met people, always conscious of the likelihood of mispronouncing a silly little word, or revealing her lack of education. A few of the English nurses she had met in Spain had been very snobbish and cutting, 'scenting the gutter', as Rose put it. But she could relax a little with this American girl. A foreigner, she believed, would be much less likely to notice her occasional slips, when the origins she tried so hard to conceal shone out like beacons in her vowels.

After her own recent experience as a new recruit to radio broadcasting, Addie felt sympathy for anyone about to speak on the air for the first time. Besides, Rose had a certain childish quality about her that could stir the protective instinct in people, or, as Addie would find out, could also prove to be exasperating. Rose passed a copy of her appeal to the censor and waited, nerves on edge, till she was given the signal to begin. Addie was surprised at the determined and impassioned nature of Rose's speech. Her nervousness made her hesitate sometimes, then speak with a rush of breath, but this added, rather than detracted, from the emotional power of her words. When Rose spoke about her work with the Garibaldis, Addie was surprised, 'She must be much tougher than she looks.' The talk came to a close with a moving plea.

'If there are any nurses listening to me tonight, please could you think about how much trained nurses are needed here in Spain? I've worked in hospitals with hundreds of wounded soldiers and only one or two properly trained nurses. Could any of you come to give us a hand? These courageous people are fighting for their right to democracy. They need our help.'

Addie felt rather ashamed after hearing Rose talk about the work nurses were doing. Not only was her own contribution to the war effort insignificant in comparison with that of Rose, but to make matters worse, she had to admit to herself that her initial opinion of her had been somewhat derisory. She had judged Rose too quickly, believing that someone with such vain little mannerisms was unlikely to be anything other than shallow. This was clearly not the case.

'I do envy you,' Addie said warmly when the broadcast was over, 'having the skills to save lives, and to know that you are really doing something useful.'

'Sometimes it seems nowhere near enough,' said Rose feeling a stab of regret at the memory of the baby who had died from burns.

Addie offered to walk with Rose to one of the small hotels nearby where she would be staying for a few days. Rose was to wait in Madrid for a consignment of surgical equipment expected later in the week and take it back with her when she returned to Albacete. 'I can show you round a bit if you like over the next few days,' offered Addie, 'as long as there isn't a rush on.'

The next day they lunched together in one of the workers' canteens. Both were now used to the copious quantities of beans that formed the basis for most of the meals. For Rose however, the monotony of the diet in Villamalea had sometimes been relieved by a meal from a grateful villager, even a bit of rabbit on rare occasions. Since coming to Spain, they had both learned to eat almost anything available. Addie would even have welcomed the sprouts she used to reject so forcefully in the nursery. Rose's former plump curves were now less rounded than before, something she was not altogether displeased about. They chatted while they ate, exchanging little bits of their lives, mainly the nice parts, chosen for display like photographs in an album of the best memories. But soon they moved on to the important business of examining their present lives, probing the people they knew, and dissecting relationships with incisions as keen as scalpel blades.

Rose didn't say very much about Rafael, but even so, her face betrayed her. When she mentioned him, an uncomfortable lump in her throat suddenly made speaking difficult. Before she realised what was happening, her eyes prickled annoyingly and watered a little. She certainly didn't want Addie to think that she was crying like a love-smitten adolescent over an Italian romance, so she quickly thought about emptying bedpans to obliterate the image of Rafael's face, radiant with his hopes for the future. But Addie was observant when it came to human emotions. She saw the impatience with which Rose suppressed her tears. 'She still hasn't admitted to herself that she loves him,' thought Addie with a flash of insight. She knew that before long, Rose would be forced to return to the subject of Rafael, that it would lure her back with the irresistibility of a half eaten bar of chocolate.

Addie managed to make the story of her journey to Murcia with Marcel into a humorous episode that caused Rose's eyes to water again, but with laughter. In recounting the tale of her rejection, Addie too began to find it funny rather than painful. She decided to confide in Rose and tell her the sad sequel, the missing morphia, the accusations against her, and her own suspicions. Rose, familiar with the symptoms of morphia addiction, both theoretically and from experience with patients in great pain, confirmed Addie's conclusions. Marcel's impaired night vision, sudden mood swings and impotence were typical side effects that came with prolonged use of the drug. Addie still had the nagging worry that she had put the welfare of patients at risk by keeping quiet about the matter. But, as Rose pointed out, given the limited availability of morphia, Marcel's thefts would probably be discovered sooner, rather than later.

They left the building, still talking cheerfully. Rose felt

more at ease with the unpretentious Addie than with anyone she had ever met before. Nevertheless, she knew that under normal circumstances they would have been most unlikely to form anything remotely resembling a friendship. The war had brought them together, but after a few days they might never see each other again. She felt a twinge of regret at the thought.

Addie thought Rose intriguing. A veneer of superficiality hid a complex mix of strength and weakness. Rose could deal efficiently with diseases and death, but had squirmed with badly concealed revulsion when Addie had offered to share a little of her lipstick before they sallied forth to face whatever the enemy might decide to hurl at the city that afternoon. It would have dismayed Rose to learn that her new friend had already guessed a great deal about her past. Addie had quickly realised that Rose had grown up in a world bearing no resemblance to her own comfortable, cushioned, childhood. Just the action of picking up her knife had given her away, although she had changed her grip on the handle almost instantly. Since her recent wholehearted adoption of socialist tenets relating to equality, Addie had often wondered if, in practice, class differences would be easy to forget. She intended to try her hardest to prove that such old-fashioned concepts could be discarded once and for all.

As they walked down the Gran Vía approaching the Calle de Alcalá, Addie answered the question put to her by a puzzled Rose, 'Why is almost everybody walking on the same side of the road?'

'According to Arturo, the censor you met, everyone calls this 'Shell Alley' because it leads in a direct line to the front and the Fascists fire straight down it so often. There's a widely held superstition that on this side there is less chance of being hit.'

Rose couldn't help noticing that this belief was to some extent countered by the numerous shell holes and ruined buildings on both sides of the street. Not far away, they could hear desultory fighting taking place in University City, where machine guns chattered harsh conversations full of hate and rifle shots cracked dry and deathly jokes.

'Aviación, aviación!' The warning was taken up and passed along till it echoed through even the narrowest streets. Whistles started to shriek. Addie drew Rose into the shelter of an immense stone doorway as several aircraft approached. For a moment, the entire population of Madrid shared one thought. 'Would the planes be "ours" or "theirs"?' Whilst boys competed to be the first to identify German, Italian or Russian wing shapes, engine noises, or markings, others held their breath waiting for the bombs to fall - or not. There was a brittle tension in the air when time seemed to take on curious qualities of elongation - a washing line on which events hung suspended. Air-raids had been slightly less frequent of late. When the attack on Madrid had begun, the bombardments and the massive poster campaign urging civilians to 'Evacuate Madrid', had persuaded some that it would be better to leave. Thousands of school children had been taken to safety by their teachers. Pregnant women and nursing mothers had been moved to country refuges, but other families had stayed. They didn't want to abandon their city and their homes, or be parted from their children. Danger and food shortages had not deterred them. Eventually, the government dropped the idea of a forced evacuation. The city endured.

Time returned with the exploding bombs. The ground shook beneath Addie and Rose, sending tremors through their shoes. Powdery mortar from crevices between the stones of the porch fell gently onto their hair and shoulders. From her position in the centre of the roundabout on the Calle de Alcalá, the goddess Cybele could peer with her stony eyes from between the sandbags to watch another tragedy unfurl. The walls that were falling in waves of suddenly disassociated stones would inevitably land on the women who had been waiting below with their food rationing cards.

Most had no time to run. Mothers crumpled, folding themselves around their infants in a pitiable mockery of security. Addie listened with horror to the interminable cacophony of the impact, 'a composition for demented gods,' she thought, glaring with a newfound loathing at the statue of the indifferent Cybele.

Before the clouds of dust had settled, while planes still circled like vultures overhead, Rose shot out of the doorway and ran towards the ruins. She pulled at the loose stones, heaving splintered wood aside, ignoring the broken glass. She had seen the woman at the end of the queue hurl her small child with all her strength to the outermost perimeter of the falling masonry. Landing like a doll tossed aside by an angry little girl, the child had soon disappeared under a relatively thin layer of rubble. Quickly Rose found a small soft hand protruding from the mass of brutal stone. Addie came to help her, but even between them, they couldn't lift the iron rail that imprisoned the unconscious child.

The eerie silence that now surrounded them was broken by the noise of a lorry, squealing to a halt, and the sound of running footsteps. Rose, covered in dirt and bleeding from several cuts, was kneeling to excavate the area where she thought the child's head would be. She looked up into the steady brown-eyed gaze of Constance. A fraction of a second later, they were both scrabbling with bare hands to clear the debris. Max was strong enough to lift the rail. As he held it aloft, Addie crept underneath to remove the remaining stones. Gently they lifted a limp figure from the small depression in the heaped wreckage. Addie was struck by the very modest amount of rubble that is displaced by a boy of about two years old. His leg was almost severed above the knee. In the short time it had taken them to dig him out, the litre or so of blood he needed to keep him alive had drained out onto the hard pavement beneath him. Rose clutched the limp child to her, supporting the dangling leg, now only attached by the vestiges of sinews and skin. She could feel the leg still wiggling, wriggling, in her grasp. But she knew it was too late. It wasn't life, just the last spasms of severed nerves. Constance asked her if they should take the boy to the hospital in the lorry, but with a slow shake of her head Rose put the body down in the shelter of a doorway.

More people were now climbing the wreckage, searching, shouting. The next few hours were spent in the desperate hunt for survivors, but none were found. Constance, ever practical, had brought a First Aid kit with her in the lorry. Its meagre contents were soon exhausted by those who had received minor injuries. Before long, a small crowd had congregated round the two nurses, showing their wounds and asking for help. A hysterical mother appeared, searching for her daughter who had been in the queue. When she realised that there was no hope of finding her alive, Addie tried to comfort her. Eventually, leaving the Madrileños to the task of clearing the ruins from the road, Constance, Addie and Rose squeezed into the lorry beside Max to go in search of a respite from the sound of guns.

They entered the cool, shadowy vestibule of the Hotel Gran Vía. Subconsciously, all four chose to sit as far inside as they could, in a dimly lit corner behind the telephone boxes. Belated introductions broke the silence. Addie and Max were delighted to meet again, Constance and Rose less so, though both had begun to revise their former opinions of each other a little. Constance observed Rose closely, seeing signs of incipient delayed shock in her pale face and trembling hands.

'We all need a stiff drink,' announced Max, hurrying off to the bar.

'Are you all right?' Constance asked Rose quietly.

'I'll be fine in a minute,' she replied, 'it's always when it's children....' she added, stopping in mid-sentence when she realised that she could not control her tremulous voice.

Without Max, they would probably have sunk into an ever deepening gloom, but he would not allow anyone to wallow in grief except in the rarest of circumstances, and then not for long. He returned with the drinks and an International Brigader on leave that he had met at the bar. Before long, he had captured them all with his animated action replay of a small incident during the Battle of Cable Street.

'It was like this, you see,' he began. 'Mosley and his Blackshirts wanted to march through the East End, showing off like, but they hadn't reckoned on thousands and thousands of us blocking the way. The coppers tried to clear a path for them, charging us with their horses, but we was too many for them. Me and a group of mates who'd been what you might call, 'resisting arrest' tried to duck into a side street out of sight for a bit, but the coppers saw us, and soon they was chasing us, hell for leather, waving their bloody batons and saying they was going to give us what for. But they made a mistake when they chased us into a dead end down by some shops and the lock ups. Just before they'd got us collared, another lot of our lads blocked off the end of the street. It were a stand off with the coppers in the middle. Then, would you believe it, all the windows of the rooms above the shops opened and the women, them that was too old to come to stop the Blackshirts in the streets, or with little kids and that, well, they all started to pelt the coppers with bottles – mainly brown sauce and vinegar – you wouldn't believe the smell when them bottles broke on the cobbles. Phew, and the language – those women swore like troopers. Well, the coppers was taking a hammering so they dived into one of the open lockups and then we had them. We slammed the door shut. The coppers hollered and shouted inside and the lads danced about and whooped outside, and the women up above clapped and cheered. Cock-a-hoop we were. But then, we began to wonder, 'What the 'eck are we going to do with them?' We couldn't decide. A few was for setting fire to the lock-up, but most thought we should just keep them there till things had calmed down a bit, like. Then someone had the bright idea of rubbing their noses in it a bit – so we made them surrender their helmets! They had to pass them outside and when we had our pile of trophies, we let them go. Were their faces red! And laugh – we laughed till we cried.'

Max was pleased to see that his story had the desired effect. The gloom receded. Soon Addie and Constance had made the effort to be polite and were chatting to the Brigader. Only Rose still seemed a little quiet. She became more interested in the conversation when the Brigader mentioned fighting alongside the Garibaldis at Guadalajara and began to praise their bravery. They had come face to face with the Italians sent by Mussolini to fight for Franco, and had won a resounding victory. Several drinks later, the Brigader's admiration began to be directed towards the three ladies at the table, whose beauty he extolled in an increasingly persistent manner. Deciding it was time to make a graceful exit, Constance suggested they should say goodnight. Max insisted that he would escort all three back to their lodgings.

On the way out, Addie was able to take a good, careful look at the intriguing-looking people occupying one of the centre tables. The centre of attention within the large group seemed to focus almost entirely on a well-built figure, square-faced and moustached, exuberantly holding forth on the subject of bullfighting. When still sober, the Brigader had identified this 'larger than life' figure as the famous writer and reporter, Ernest Hemingway. At his side was an elegant, tall, blonde woman. She had an air of confidence and intelligence, even though she was actually saying very little. Several women in the group were gazing at Hemingway admiringly. Addie thought him too florid to be attractive. She had read some of his books with interest but without much enjoyment, and couldn't help being curious to see what the author was like in person. Fortunately, all those round the table were too engrossed in their own circle to notice her impolite stares.

Constance was tired and pleased to accept Rose's offer

of the spare bed in her room. Although she would normally have preferred to be alone, her conscience had kept nagging her, reminding her of their earlier uncomfortable meeting in London and insisting that she try to make amends. Professionally too, she couldn't deny that having shown signs of shock earlier on, it would be better for Rose to have company. She had acted very bravely, thought Constance, despite being afraid. An hour later, admiration was overcome by irritation when Rose continued to keep her awake, talking of trivialities non-stop as she used all the water in the jug on the washstand to meticulously clean first herself, then her clothes, and finally her shoes, before getting into bed.

They awoke early in the morning, their sleep pierced by breaking glass. This was not just the melodious chiming of a single broken pane falling, but a chorus of discordant crashes that immediately set teeth on edge. Women were sweeping their balconies, clearing the remnants of their shattered windowpanes after the previous day's attack, and showering the street below with glassy splinters. While Rose busied herself getting ready to go out, Constance prepared the appeal she would be broadcasting that night. She had recently been shown an 'auto-chir', a type of small lorry completely kitted out as an operating theatre. It meant that the wounded could be treated much closer to the front than ever before, tremendously improving the chances of survival in certain cases. An appeal for funds for something as useful as that would be really worthwhile, thought Constance. As the auto-chirs were a modern innovation, their use showed that the Republic was trying to do the best it could for the wounded. 'As soon as I get back to the hospital' Constance vowed, 'I will get a posting somehow to the front – perhaps in one of these if I'm lucky.'

When they met Addie later in the day, she was bursting to tell them her news. After weeks of trying, she had at last managed to obtain permission to visit the front in University City, a privilege normally only granted to visiting dignitaries.

Her resourcefulness and persistence had paid off. She had explained to the military official in charge of issuing passes that the visit was necessary for the propaganda purposes of their radio broadcasts. And, she had added with a flash of inspiration, the presence of two attractive young nurses would act as a morale booster for the soldiers, now becoming bored with the stalemate that had become a test of stamina rather than bravery. Addie had been within earshot of the fighting for weeks, now she was going to see the front for herself.

II

The mutilated trees in many of the parks and gardens gave a good indication of how desperately cold the previous winter had been. An assortment of leafy shoots now sprouted from the stumps, vainly endeavouring to replace branches that had been lopped off at night by people searching for firewood. As they drew near University City, the guide suddenly left the street and turned onto a path that passed through one of the gardens. Rose, Constance and Addie followed him, surprised to find that this former quiet haven was now the entrance to the trenches.

The guide had warned them to duck when they came to the more exposed sections, but even so, the angry rattle of bullets against the rocks in the wall made them jump. For a little while, the impressive buildings that had been the pride of the Republic's educational reform plan maintained the illusion of perfection. The yellow walls shone in the evening sun like a mirage on the horizon. But the Medical Faculty turned out to be not much more than an empty shell. Once inside, Constance looked sadly at the gaping hole in the roof. At her feet, the torn pages of scientific journals lay trapped amongst the fallen debris. Instinctively, the three moved closer together as they entered another trench, a darker, deeper gash in the earth which muffled the frequent thuds from above. In some places, they had to feel their way along the dirt walls. Just as Rose was wishing fervently that she hadn't come, a glimmer of light indicated that they had almost arrived.

The trenches that marked the front lines in Madrid bore no resemblance to the grim images from the First World War showing sodden ditches surrounded by desolate, never-ending seas of mud. Lining these Spanish trenches were dugouts that had been transformed with loving care into substitutes for domestic bliss. Homesick soldiers had planted flowers outside their earthen caves and hung name plaques over the doors; Casa Florida, Villa Pasionaria, Hotel Rusia. The popularity of each general could be judged by whether or not his name featured as a residential address. The men were keen to talk, to show them the carvings they were working on to decorate their dugouts, and to serenade them on battered guitars in their harsh flamenco voices. One group was the proud possessor of a gramophone. Addie listened with as much appreciation as she could muster to the strident rendition of a fandango, the record worn and scratched by repeated playing. What impressed them most was the improvised library, packed tight with everything from text books to thrillers. Rose could sympathise with the craving of the illiterate soldiers to learn to read; she remembered the hunger for education she had felt as a girl, never able to keep up with the others because she had to miss so many classes. In the end, she had taught herself to read, longing to explore the secrets that lay hidden in penny novels, newspapers, and even the text books that lined the walls of the headmistress's office. She wasn't surprised to learn that many of the soldiers attended the reading classes that were held there every day. A portrait of Goethe was suspended precariously over the door of the library. 'Who ever would have thought that Faust would have a fan club in the middle of a war zone?' thought Constance with delight.

They were escorted to a look-out position where a

machine gun had been mounted facing away from the city. Entrenched opposite them, a mere two hundred yards or so away, were the Moors. Franco had deployed part of the Army of Africa to attack Madrid, and when the offensive stalled due to the unexpectedly tenacious defence of the city, he had been content to leave them there, waiting, while he waged a war of attrition on the rest of the country.

'Would you like to fire a shot at them?' the soldiers asked excitedly.

Constance said 'No thank you,' as politely as she could. Somehow, it was absurdly difficult for her to contemplate inflicting a wound on someone, even the enemy. Rose had no such reservations. She happily complied, her face alive with pleasure at the attention she was receiving. The soldiers competed for the chance to show her how to take aim and fire, laughingly asking her to come and serve in the trenches with them when she managed to shoot straight at the target they had selected for her.

Then it was Addie's turn. She was asked if she too would 'fire a shot for freedom'. When put in that way, it was difficult to refuse. The men were all waiting eagerly for her reply, wordlessly encouraging her to show support with a gesture that, although futile in practical terms, was charged with symbolic meaning. Addie, feeling cowardly and underhand, aimed wide. If by some miracle, an enemy had popped up at just that moment to be killed, she knew she would have been haunted by the memory for the rest of her life. Fortunately, her shot did no more than kick up a spurt of dust. The soldiers guffawed good-naturedly at her ineptitude, but were content with her puny efforts. Usually, the guests who came to the trenches were less welcome. They were inclined to make impromptu political speeches, or harangue them unnecessarily to keep up the effort to defend Madrid. Women visitors were more often than not the same age as the soldiers' own mothers, certainly offering nothing much to gladden the eyes. 'But,' they said to each other cheerfully, 'good-looking girls like these, who have come all the way to Spain from other countries just to help us, well, no one would complain about that.'

The following evening, Addie gave what all agreed was her best broadcast to date. The visit to the front had left them all in high spirits and Addie gave voice to their feelings. In Cambridge, her mother and father listened entranced, almost holding their breath as they followed her description of the front lines. They leaned closer to the wireless to catch her final words as the signal weakened.

'Although the dream of a new University City has been destroyed for the moment by the war, there is a Trench University in its place where culture and education are still very much alive.'

The atmosphere in Madrid seemed charged with energy when they went out to celebrate her success that night. Wine, a little rough but acceptable under the circumstances, bestowed its welcome warming glow. Even Constance, who normally would stop after one glass, loosened her grip sufficiently to have two. They were repeatedly approached by a remarkable variety of men, all hoping to make their acquaintance, offering to buy them drinks, and to take them to fascinating places where they would have the time of their lives. They took it in turns to reject these advances, vying with each other to come up with the most ludicrous, but nevertheless convincing, excuse. The hilarity engendered by this game had the curious effect of creating a cocoon around the three of them. They were surrounded by a million tragedies, great and small. That knowledge made them all value the moment more when they drank a toast to their new friendship.

The correspondents in the Press Office who had been crying out for an interesting human story after the long days of the stalemate, were granted their desire in an unexpectedly disturbing manner. Gerda Taro was crushed to death at the front by a tank. Not, sad to say, even an enemy tank, but a run-away Republican one. The correspondents wrote of the tragic loss of a gifted and beautiful young photographer, but for a short while, all were uncomfortably aware of their own mortality. They were forced to see that the cloak of invincibility they had contrived for themselves was as much a sham as the Emperor's new clothes. Addie raged at the pointless stupidity of Gerda's death, crying with anger rather than sadness at the thought of such a senseless waste.

'At least,' she later told Constance and Rose, 'her work will be given some recognition at the Writers' Congress. I saw the programme and there's going to be a eulogy.'

There had been great excitement in Madrid for the last few weeks at the prospect of the forthcoming 'International Congress of Writers for the Defence of Culture'. Despite the war, authors and intellectuals from all over the world were going to attend to show their support for the Republic. Constance had feared that she would have to return to the hospital with Max and miss it all, but he had been given work to do in Madrid for a few more days. If nothing else, this would allow her to attend the opening and listen to the first speakers. She and Addie began to plan who was definitely in the 'not to be missed' category, such as Malraux, Heinrich Mann and Alexis Tolstoi. They were both keen to hear the British poet, Stephen Spender, and Addie had been told that Pablo Neruda was wonderful. Eventually, they stopped talking for long enough to notice Rose's dejected face.

'Who would you most like to see?' asked Addie, attempting to draw her into the conversation.

'I don't think I'll go,' replied Rose, smiling as brightly as she could.

Constance and Addie exchanged a brief look of understanding, unfortunately intercepted by Rose. Her lips tightened but a tremble escaped, followed by a tirade of angry recrimination.

'It's all right for you, you know who these people are. You know their books, you understand what they're saying, even when they speak French. I won't understand any of it - even when it's English they might as well be speaking in Chinese. And you'll laugh together at the jokes at the right moment, and say, 'Oh, isn't that just like so and so,' and I'll just look like a fool!'

Constance and Addie tried hard to comfort her. They told her that she would soon get to know who the people were and promised they'd explain things if she didn't understand.

'You'll enjoy it if you give it a try,' said Addie, 'just screw your courage to the sticking-place.'

'Exactly,' agreed Constance, triumphantly.

As Rose burst into tears, Constance and Addie wished desperately that they could retract their last words. Of course, Rose did not share their familiarity with Lady Macbeth's advice.

'I don't know where your bleedin' sticking-place is and I don't care. Screw you!'

Rose flounced from the room, her features contorted into a grimace of distress. The sheer vehemence of her parting words, rather than the coarseness of her vocabulary, stunned Addie and Constance for a few moments. As the sound of the slammed door faded, they leapt to their feet and hurried after her, managing to catch up with her before she reached the street. Appeasement took quite some time.

III

The Congress took place in the heat of late July. Audience and contributors grew steadily hotter as the temperature rose along with the fervour of the occasion. Most of the intellectuals cast off layers of clothing like old, discarded ideas, but those who were in the International Brigade felt duty demanded that they stay in uniform. Ardent renditions of the 'Internationale', salutations and ceremony, outweighed the serious intellectual content for much of the time, but Addie, an avid watcher of individuals, found plenty to entertain her.

Constance had at last persuaded Rose to come with them, pointing out that it would be a pity to miss the chance to see such a famous collection of people who might never be gathered together again. Rose was thrilled when Addie pointed out Geraldine Rees Jones. Someone she had heard of at last! Betty had lent her a novel – she remembered the name of the author, but not the title. She now regretted that she hadn't actually read it.

'Who's the tall girl beside her?' Rose asked Addie.

'That's Vivien Erroll. She's a poet I think.'

Addie didn't comment on the relationship between the two women. She wasn't really sure about her own attitudes towards them, and had no idea what Constance and Rose would say. She had heard lesbians described as freaks of nature, as perverts or inverts. 'It seems sad though,' she thought to herself, 'that people should be persecuted for loving each other, even if they are of the same sex.'

As the day drew to a close, they left the Congress happy and elated, following along behind quite a large crowd that headed into the Hotel Gran Vía for refreshment. As they were about to sit down, Geraldine waved to Addie from the next table to call them over. They couldn't believe their luck when, after brief introductions had been made, enough room was made for them to sit down, almost rubbing shoulders with the writers from the Congress. At first, Vivien seemed engrossed in an altercation with Stephen Spender about the ideals, or lack of them, in the Communist Party, but Geraldine, not much interested in the subject of party politics, drew them into a discussion more to her liking. She was thinking about her new novel, a satire on the problems that currently beset rural Spain, but set in the eighteenth century. Tentatively exploring the theme of the Spanish peasant and culture, she began to rhapsodise about the welcome they had been given as they had passed through the countryside. Even in the poorest agricultural areas they had been greeted with shouts of 'Viva los intelectuales.' How strange, she was saying, to be labelled as an 'intellectual' and to feel none of the usual disparagement that was evident in England and elsewhere. Here, one could feel proud to be an intellectual rather than embarrassed. During the Congress, one of the speeches had been made by an ordinary Spanish soldier. Everyone had been moved by his noble words about fetching peace and culture at the point of a bayonet to bring a happier life to his children. He had seemed the embodiment of the proud Spanish peasant. 'I'm going to write about him,' said Geraldine ardently.

Opposite them sat Hemingway, this time without his blonde companion. Addie now knew that the woman she had seen with him before must have been Martha Gellhorn, the American writer and correspondent. There was plenty of gossip in the Press Office about them and their frequent tempestuous arguments. Someone had also related the story of how Hemingway's extra-marital liaison with Martha had first been confirmed. They had been staying in Madrid's Hotel Florida when a shell hit the hot water tank. Water gushed through the ceilings, and guests rushed from their bedrooms. They were not the only couple having an affair who were seen leaving a bedroom together, but theirs was the one that caused most comment.

At Hemingway's side on this occasion, a tall American Brigader sprawled rather untidily in a chair that seemed too small for his long limbs. Addie noticed his large brown eyes resting appreciatively first on Constance, then on Rose. His languid appraisal came to an abrupt end when he encountered Addie's amused glance. He quickly returned to the general discussion, now centred on the films being made about the war, 'To Die in Madrid' and 'The Spanish Earth'. Geraldine and Vivien were taking their leave, saying they had a dinner to attend. Their departure left empty chairs between

Hemingway's party and Rose, who was sitting nearest to them. The three stayed in their seats, uncertain what to do next – to leave, smiling politely, or to move up and join the others. Their indecision was ended when Hemingway, beaming expansively, beckoned them to come closer. He asked if they would be going to see 'The Spanish Earth', the film he had helped to make. He had been working with a group of contemporary historians, following closely behind the tanks and infantry to film the action. Unperturbed when Constance replied that there was little opportunity for nurses to go to the cinema with so much work to be done, he proceeded to regale them with stories of the dangers he had encountered during the making of the film.

Rose listened, enthralled by real-life movie adventures. She had no trouble laughing at the right moments during these stories, Constance thought, sighing inwardly. She had heard that the film would raise a great deal of money for the Republic, and Hemingway must be given due credit for his efforts. Nevertheless, Constance detected a subtle undercurrent of menace in his personality that she found abhorrent. Flirting with him would certainly not be a good idea. Rose's dimpled smiles and fluttering lashes were asking for trouble. Rose was so practical in many ways, Constance concluded, but she didn't seem to have much common sense about some things.

Leaning forward over the table, the tall young American Brigader now entered the conversation.

'And what are you lovely young ladies doing in Madrid?' he asked in an easy drawl, offering cigarettes as he spoke. His question was directed mainly at Constance and Rose. Addie, who was sitting furthest away was able to adopt the role of observer for the moment. His smile was broad and charming, perhaps too much so. Was it a genuine overture of friendship, or a predatory crocodile's smirk? She looked at his eyes, searching for clues, but in the subdued light of the hotel interior it wasn't even possible to distinguish the borderline between his pupils and the dark brown irises. Addie could come to no firm conclusion, but feared that as a friend of Hemingway's, he was, more likely than not, a man who could be categorised as 'macho'. She had recently come to understand the full implications of this Spanish word. It seemed to describe a certain type of arrogant man very well indeed.

'I'm Byron, by the way,' he was saying, extending his large knuckled hand across the table to each of them in turn. 'Byron Fox'. He shifted uncomfortably in his seat to reach over to shake Addie's hand, before turning back to the others. His grip was firm, but surprisingly gentle. He told them that he was a machine-gunner in the Abraham Lincoln Battalion, but that when the war was over, he would be able to concentrate on becoming a writer.

Soon, the evening was passing in a very pleasant manner. Addie struck up a conversation with some of the others at the table, and managed to talk in Spanish to a young woman from Madrid, Carmen. 'With so many Carmens, how does anyone know which one they're talking about?' she wondered. This striking beauty, with enviable long black tresses, gradually lost interest in their conversation. Her barely suppressed anger was growing ever greater as she watched Hemingway and Byron. A competition was developing between the two men, with Rose and Constance as the trophies. With Rose, they both flirted outrageously, whilst with Constance, they tried the sincere and serious approach. Incensed that she was being ignored, Carmen looked as if she was about to grab Rose and Constance by their fair hair and drag them from the bar, a sight which doubtless would amuse the men greatly, thought Addie. Which man, she mused, was provoking the girl's jealousy? Perhaps both?

Byron, although outwardly relaxed, was inwardly seething. Hemingway had enough on his plate, not only with Martha, but now that she was away for a while, with Carmen too. 'Those of us who have just come on leave should be granted some privileges,' he thought, put out by Hemingway's attempt to capture the attentions of both British girls. But, unable to resist a challenge, he turned on the charm again and returned to the fray. In reality, he was well aware that it was unlikely that either of them stood much of a chance with the two nurses. Almost certainly they were 'nice girls'. Even the giggling Rose was unlikely to want to indulge in a brief fling. What was irritating him above all, however, was the way in which he was unable to stop his attention wandering away from the battle in hand. Why was he trying so hard to tune in to what was being said by the ordinary looking girl at the other end of the table? At first, she had been talking about Cambridge University, and muttering, 'typical blue-stocking' under his breath, he had been able to disregard her for a while. With the well-developed peripheral vision of a soldier at the front, he had seen her looking at him, in what he interpreted as amused disdain. She was, he decided, too thin, not very pretty, and definitely not his type. But now she was talking about something that he found particularly interesting, the need for artists and intellectuals in wartime. He heard her mention the death of the poet and playwright, Federíco García Lorca, and caught references to Picasso's painting of the devastation of Guernica. Just for a moment, he desperately wished he could stop the pointless rivalry at the table; leave the hotel and Madrid, and especially the war, and be far away, talking quietly with someone like her. 'Hell,' he shook off the mood, ''I'm on leave, that stuff can wait.'

Later on, Constance and Rose squashed beside Addie on the small bed in her room to review the evening.

'Ernest Hemingway,' said Constance, straight faced, 'is possibly not a gentleman!'

They all burst out laughing at this blatant understatement.

'But what about that Byron?' asked Rose, 'he seemed

nice.'

'Well, you certainly thought so,' Constance teased, 'you were giving him the eye all evening, apart from when you were flirting with Hemingway, that is.'

Rose hit her with the pillow. 'Oh, Hemingway's much too old, not my type at all. It's just fun to make men like you, don't you think?' Constance shook her head doubtfully.

Rose turned to Addie instead, 'What did *you* think of Byron then?'

'Well,' Addie deliberated carefully before replying, 'I would say he definitely prefers blondes.'

'Natural or bottle?' asked Constance with a mischievous smile.

'I don't suppose he cares for a moment,' answered Addie, 'he probably wouldn't notice the difference until morning anyway.'

Laughing like schoolgirls, eventually they parted company.

The next day they found out that the interlude that had turned out to be a happy time for all three was drawing to a close. Max arrived to tell Constance they would be setting off late that night. Rose's delivery of medical supplies arrived, and she was instructed to leave Madrid very early on the following day with two doctors who were travelling to Albacete. Addie knew that she would miss them. It was strange, she reflected, how quickly friendships could arise in unusual circumstances. But although they were parting, she was sure that a bond had formed between them, perhaps a long-lasting one. A picture flashed into her mind of a tapestry hanging in the Fitzwilliam Museum in Cambridge. Its intricate pattern had fascinated her, the golden threads glimpsed amongst the colours, sometimes hidden for a while but always emerging again to brighten the entire design. Addie suddenly saw friendships as the golden threads weaving in and out of life, occasionally running all the way through to the end.

They managed to meet for one farewell drink together, choosing the place they were beginning to feel was like a second home, the Hotel Gran Vía. It was almost deserted at that time in the evening. They sat with their drinks, all determinedly keeping up light hearted conversation, despite the worries they all felt to some degree as to what the future might bring. Just as they were promising to meet again in England, if not before, Byron loped through the entrance hall, looking like a lone wolf hungrily scouting for dinner. He was restless. After the debacle of the loss of Brunete, he'd been eagerly anticipating his leave in Madrid, but now he was actually here, an empty feeling was lurking in his entrails, and this time he knew it wasn't just for food or a woman. Catching sight of the nurses he'd met the night before, he smiled, thinking that perhaps good company and lively conversation might hold the hollowness off for a while, like a camp fire to keep away wild animals. He drew nearer to their table, hoping the warmth of their companionship would bring some respite from the tiresome emptiness.

When Byron asked if he could join them, Addie wasn't pleased. The little farewell gathering of those she now thought of as friends would be disturbed by the presence of this intruder. Rose and Constance had no such objections and willingly made room for him, telling him that it was their last drink together before leaving Madrid. They introduced him to Max as 'a poet in the making'. This, to his credit, he obviously found embarrassing, explaining that he hoped to be a writer but that as yet he had nothing published. He didn't seem so brash this time, Addie noticed. He was friendly towards Rose, but the flirtatious banter of the night before was gone. He listened carefully when Constance spoke about the contrast in atmosphere between Valencia and Madrid, adding some observations of his own about attitudes amongst people in the rearguard. His most scathing comments were reserved for those whose only complaint about the war was that they needed extra security measures to safeguard the proceeds they'd made from profiteering. Max seemed to enjoy talking to him, and they exchanged a few wisecracks about the vagaries of machinery. But, even when the opportunity arose, Byron still said nothing directly to Addie. She could feel him watching her though, more and more often, with what seemed to be curiosity. Disconcerted by the tension that was hovering between them, she hadn't been able to think of anything to say to him either. 'What *is* he thinking when he looks at me like that?' she thought with irritation. 'It's as if I were some sort of rare species being examined under a microscope.'

Byron was, in truth, curious, wondering what would have happened if this strangely attractive girl hadn't been leaving with her friends tomorrow. He would have liked to get to know her better, but he didn't want the complications of a serious relationship in Spain. Who needed that extra worry in wartime? Besides, he had a girlfriend in the States who wrote to him faithfully every week. Sometimes a pile of her letters arrived all at once, sating what little need he felt to be reminded of home. But, as his eyes rested on the unexceptional features of this... 'Addie,' as he suddenly remembered she was called, a certain sadness was undeniable. Regret was a funny thing, he decided. Why was he looking at this particular girl and feeling miserable about a relationship they had never had, just because her eyes held some sort of lightness that he found intriguing? When at last conversation turned to Rose's return to Albacete and the imminent departures of Constance and Max, he suddenly addressed her for the first time.

'You're not leaving then?'

'No,' she replied, taken aback by the abruptness of his question. 'I'll be broadcasting for a while longer, and I've also been given the job of working on an English and Spanish phrasebook for the Brigades – translations of useful expressions, 'pass the ammo' and things like that I suppose.'

He had risen to his feet and was staring down at her. The

silence lengthened till the others noticed it too. Addie stared back at him, forced to look up awkwardly to meet his eyes, reluctant to lower hers. As it was, she was aware of an infuriating blush spreading from her cheeks to her forehead. She certainly didn't want to make herself look even more like a heroine in a Victorian novel by casting her eyes down demurely. But then she saw a gentle look on his face that she hadn't noticed before, softening the harsh lines round his mouth and eyes that had formed during the months spent at the front. They both smiled at the same time.

'I could help,' he said.

'Help?' asked Addie, who had quite forgotten what they had been talking about.

'I could help you with the phrasebook. I know what needs to be in the book, essential things at the front, like "This rifle has a rusty firing mechanism." Do you know how to translate that?'

'I'll have to look that one up.' Addie smiled again, having to admit to herself that the prospect of seeing him again was actually far from displeasing.

The others, Max included, had been watching with interest to see how the long silence between Addie and Byron would be resolved. There was no doubt in their minds that they had witnessed the beginnings of what could be a memorable romance.

CHAPTER 4

Eager Hearts

I

Addie's task of compiling a phrasebook for the Brigades had been the bright idea of a formidable American journalist, Anna Louise Strong. Anna Louise had passed through the press offices like a tornado, demanding a pass for the front on short notice and getting her own way in most things. Addie had been caught in her wake as a fellow compatriot and useful 'aide de camp'. 'What we need,' Anna Louise had drawled, fixing Addie with a look of inescapable authority, 'is a vocabulary for our men - you get down to making us a vocabulary, Spanish into English, English into Spanish.' As Addie would soon no longer be needed for broadcasting, and her typing had speeded up sufficiently to allow her more time for other work, she felt unable to refuse.

Being with Anna Louise was certainly stimulating. She had friends in high places, and through her, Addie was brought into contact with people she would otherwise not have met. One of these was the famous 'man of the moment', General Miaja, who was acting as Governor of Madrid. Addie had seen his portrait on enormous posters, his round, bottle-bottom glasses perched on his long nose, their steel rims and glinting lenses giving him an unyielding air of determination. His bronzed features were superimposed over a woman's face in profile, recognised by everyone as 'La República', serious and statuesque. Before the war, she had been young and carefree, known as 'La Niña Bonita', 'The Pretty Little Girl'. Such was the level of illiteracy in Spain that, like many of the posters, this one had few words, relying more on symbolism to convey the message. 'General Miaja' and 'Defender', written in firm, square capital letters, was considered enough. Addie was glad to have seen Miaja in the flesh, and afterwards was full of admiration for the artist's skill in changing the image of a short, paunchy, unprepossessing man into the heroic figurehead of the city.

But the most memorable encounter Addie had with a public figure was not through Anna Louise. Ever since her arrival in Madrid, Addie had wanted to meet the other champion of Madrid's resistance, La Pasionaria, but the opportunity had never arisen. Reviled by the Right and idolised by the Left, La Pasionaria was a rare phenomenon in Spanish politics, a woman MP who had risen from the masses. She had been born into the black misery of a poor mining town in Asturias. As a young married woman, her articles on workers' rights under the pseudonym, 'La Pasionaria', had led to her transformation from Dolores Ibárruri into the 'Passion Flower'. Now the country was at war, her potency as an icon arose not only from the fact that she was female, like the image of the Republic she represented, but also because she was a mother, and a mother who had known the bitter anguish of loss more than once. When Spanish people spoke of her, Addie always listened closely, trying to understand why this woman, certainly neither young nor glamorous, had captured so many hearts. There were some who admired her as a role model for women, a symbol of egalitarianism, but these were few and far between. Women, it seemed to Addie, felt that she shared their pain. The church had offered them a 'Mother Mary' whose son had died on the cross, now the Communist Party gave them 'La Pasionaria' whose children had been crucified by poverty. For men, she was a mother figure in a different way, reminding them perhaps of their own mothers, or of an idealised mother they had never had. La Pasionaria cared about them enough to visit them at the front, however dangerous it was, and in the hospitals. But like their own mothers when they were little boys, she also expected them to be brave, to act like men. It was as if, Addie concluded, she even expected them to sacrifice their lives to make her proud of them.

Byron had met her once, briefly, when she had visited the International Brigades at the front near Madrid. He had thought her speech was 'inspirational'. When Addie heard that she was to have the chance to meet La Pasionaria too, she could hardly wait to tell him about it. A cross-party delegation of British women had arrived that day in Madrid, on what was called a 'fact-finding mission.' Leading this group was the Duchess of Atholl, the Scottish Conservative MP. It was thanks to her that Addie had managed to get to Spain in the first place and she was keen to show her gratitude by helping the group during their visit. Although the Duchess was an old friend of her mother's, Addie hadn't met her before. She was surprised to find that the scourge of the Tory Party on Spanish issues was an unobtrusive, rather tired-looking lady, seemingly older than her years. In pro-Franco propaganda, she was often referred to as the 'Red Duchess' or worse, because of her outspoken views against the government policy of non-intervention in Spain. Nevertheless, undaunted, she continued to raise questions in the House at every available opportunity, ignoring the boos and catcalls from her own party. Addie was greatly impressed by her sincerity. One of the journalists had mockingly referred to the delegation as the 'monstrous regiment of women', and indeed there were some who were formidable in their commitment to public service. Eleanor Rathbone, the epitome of female philanthropic traditions, was an independent MP of long standing, elected by the university vote. Dame Rachel Crowdy had come as a representative of the League of Nations. The group was fortunately enlivened considerably by the presence of Ellen Wilkinson. With her red hair and tiny frame bursting with energy, she had been appropriately described as 'The Fiery Particle'. She too, as a Labour MP, had problems with her own party, repeatedly calling on them to help the Republicans, or at least to support their right to buy arms.

Byron was watching Addie whilst she talked about the planned meeting. She was as vibrant as a hummingbird, thoughts hovering, darting suddenly forward to probe ideas. The night before they had talked for hours before parting, and he'd spent the long day looking forward to meeting her again. He'd wandered round the city, collecting cameos of Madrid at war. For a while after the daily bombardment had finished, he watched as people picked up shell splinters, still faintly warm, to be hoarded as keepsakes. On 'Shell Alley' the cleaning squad had arrived and were washing dark trickles of blood from the pavement. A curtain flapped in and out of a window frame, but now there was no house behind the facade.

For long stretches of time however, he didn't notice what was going on around him; he was trying to think. Being a soldier at the front tended to focus the attention on survival. When there was a break in the fighting it was better to concentrate on practicalities rather than grieve over the friends who hadn't made it, or start to get jittery about whether or not the next bullet could be heading your way. Now he was on leave and had time to put things in perspective a bit, he was realising that he had been a pretty straightforward sort of guy before leaving the States, one who perhaps hadn't been aware quite how many shades of grey there were in the world. Spain was teaching him greys. He was beginning to lose faith in politicians and generals, their motives were so often shrouded in murky mists of deceit. Worse, perhaps, were the things that he'd seen at the front. He had seen men he had believed to be good men, doing things that he knew were not so good. It would take a while to get a handle on it all.

Now, there was Addie. He'd thought he knew a lot about women, and in some respects, that was true. He understood how to charm them, to make them laugh, to enjoy sex with him. But he had never thought much about how the world looked through their eyes. Certainly women should have the right to vote – equality was after all, one of the things he was fighting for, but feminists..? Well, he'd gone along with the general view of those around him; they were ball-breakers, the butt of contemptuous gags at times, not given serious consideration. But Addie had given him a new slant on such things, and after talking to her until sunrise cracked the shadows, he felt he was floundering in uncharted waters. Her eyes must see the same things as his, but in her mind everything seemed to have passed through a kaleidoscope. She saw shifting fragments of colour, he saw geometric patterns. An oversimplification, he knew, and one that she would doubtless like to dissect. They disagreed about lots of things, and argued their points ferociously, never wanting to give up. If one of them admitted defeat, they both laughed with relief. Sometimes a temporary truce was declared. This was happening more frequently. It was difficult to keep hold of the thread of the argument, Byron found, when you were imagining your opponent naked and eager in your arms.

The story of the Duchess of Atholl's encounter with La Pasionaria was related to Byron the following lunchtime in the Bar Chicote, another well-known haunt of journalists and Brigaders. Delighted to have witnessed such an historic event, Addie was reflecting on the reactions of the women to each other. Byron, with his new found curiosity about the workings of female minds, was more interested than he had expected to be in the subject.

'The Duchess didn't want to go to meet her at first,' Addie told him, 'she said to Ellen that anyone with a name like Pasionaria must be a rather over-emotional person. But eventually, we all persuaded her to come, and afterwards she was really pleased she had gone.'

'If the Duchess is one of these stiff upper lip British types,' asked Byron, 'what did she like about Dolores?'

'She said afterwards that she had been astounded when La Pasionaria had swept into the room like a queen, that you would never have known she was a miner's daughter, married to a miner. But I don't think it was just that. When they were introduced, they looked rather droll together; this quaint glinty-eyed Duchess, tiny and frail, and a solid Spanish working-class woman, radiating a sort of intense vigour – chalk and cheese you would have thought. But then, you could see that there was a spark of recognition between them. They each knew that the other was fighting tooth and nail for Spain in their own way - La Pasionaria at the barricades and the Duchess in the House of Commons. They're saying now that the Duchess may lose her seat in Parliament over her stand on Spain.'

'Those true blue Tories in Britain sure won't want a Red in their ranks,' said Byron shaking his head, 'even aristocrats, as much as they love them, can go too far.'

Addie had to agree.

'Choices are like pebbles thrown into a pond,' Addie was thinking a few hours later, 'the ripples may carry further than you expect.' The nickel silver bed head was decorated with ornately swirling flowers. Opulent but appropriate, thought Addie, feeling rather like a newly opened bloom herself. She laughed at the mental image and stretched her arms out wide across the huge mattress. It was wonderful to be able to spread out luxuriously, an action quite impossible in the confines of the narrow bed in her lodging house. Byron was standing, naked, looking out through the dustily draped window, giving Addie time for an objective overview of his long, lean body, rather than the detailed close-ups she had been enjoying a short time before. Light and shade accentuated the hard muscle masses lying beneath his skin, except where the dark jungle of pubic hair absorbed the light. Sharing physical pleasure had been as satisfying as sharing ideas, she concluded happily. He turned and crossed the room at a charge, landed heavily on the bed beside her, demanding to know if she had been laughing at him again.

'Not this time, no,' replied Addie, 'and anyway, I wasn't really laughing at you before, it was just your friend here who was so funny.' She gingerly prodded his now quiescent penis with her finger. 'It grew so amazingly quickly, like Jack's magic beanstalk. Does that happen often?'

'Yep,' said Byron as the beanstalk stirred again, 'it's more rampant than weeds.'

'Good,' said Addie drawing back the sheet so he could slide in again.

After leaving the bar, they had wandered through unfamiliar, rather grand residential streets in Madrid, radiating benign good will to all they met, partly as a result of the wine they had just drunk. Many of the houses in this rather affluent area were boarded up, their owners in areas under Franco's control. Although some of the houses had been requisitioned, others were still unoccupied. The hot streets began to empty as siesta took hold of the city. Byron could think of nothing he would like more than to spend the siesta with Addie, but his hotel was full of rowdy Brigaders on leave, hardly the place to invite her. He wanted something special. If he had believed in God, he would have thought that the board hanging loosely in front of the broken doorway had been sent as the answer to a prayer. The house, impressive once, had obviously been left abandoned for much longer than the year of civil war. Looters had wrecked the ground floor – little was left.

'Hey!' Byron exclaimed, 'come and look at this'.

He moved the loose board to one side and climbed in through the gap. The entrance hall was spacious and grandiose. Dominating the room, the staircase rose in sweeping splendour, dividing before reaching the top and curving round to the two upstairs landings. The newel posts and banisters were heavily carved dark wood. Shafts of light entering through the door revealed that the carpet, now dirty and torn in places, had been a rich, dark red. Dominating the entire scene was an enormous stained-glass window, situated at the point where the stairs divided. It was a glorious example of modernism, a swirling web of flowers, creamy white lilies and purple irises, with leaded roundels of pistacchio green, lilac and violet appearing like jewels in the intricate pattern of the border.

'This,' said Byron, gazing up the stairs, 'seems like a perfect setting for a romantic and passionate interlude – as long as there's a bed up there.' He turned to look at Addie. She too was staring at the staircase, knowing that this would be a moment she would surely remember all her life. When his eyes met hers, he saw that she was smiling. Honesty, he was certain, was the best option with Addie.

'I would like to sweep you into my arms, carry you to bed, and make love to you,' he said, reaching out to touch her neck just beneath where the brown curls fell.

'It's a long way up,' Addie answered, 'do you think you can make it?'

'You are addressing a man who walked into Spain across the Pyrenees,' he said as he lifted her from her feet and cradled her easily against his chest. She put her arms over his shoulders, feeling like a heroine in an epic historical novel, and laughed in delight as he ran up the steps. Byron gave her a rather breathless kiss when they arrived on the landing. Even with the heavy breathing, Addie liked it more than any others she had experienced. Perhaps it wasn't so much a matter of technique as trust.

They found the bed almost immediately, a dull glimmer from the silver bedstead just discernable in the darkness of the shuttered room. Byron opened the slatted shutter enough to reveal the brocade bedcover, covered in a pall of undisturbed grey dust. They carefully folded it with the dust inside and moved it to the dilapidated ottoman at the foot of the bed. The sheets and pillows gave off a vaguely musty smell but were otherwise clean. They began undressing each other slowly. Byron made softly appreciative comments on seeing Addie's neatly rounded firm breasts for the first time. Addie was less complimentary. As she helped rid him of trousers and underpants, a startled gasp escaped her lips.

'I know it's good,' Byron exclaimed, looking down at his erection with not a little pride, 'but it's not that remarkable.'

Addie put her hand over her mouth smothering nervous laughter. 'Sorry,' she mumbled through her fingers, 'I had an idea of the size but it's the glorious Technicolor that's so amazing. It looks as if it's about to explode.'

'Well, in a manner of speaking, it will.' Byron sighed, resigning himself to waiting rather longer than he had anticipated before arriving at the moment of detonation. He could see that Addie's eyes were full of unanswered question. He would try to answer them all as best he could.

Addie's sheltered upbringing had certainly been less than enlightening regarding the momentous event she was about to experience. Her mother had given her a small booklet describing the advent of 'certain times of the month' for girls. Biology classes at an all girls school had never proceeded beyond the reproduction of frogs. She had never lived on a farm, and copulating animals were rarely seen on the streets of Boston or Cambridge. During her visit to Italy, she had studied Renaissance art, much of which was awash with strategically placed drapes and fig leaves. In the absence of such niceties, girls were normally hurried along by embarrassed parents or teachers, and anyway, as Addie now knew, penises were prone to change.

Outside the confines of the school room, Addie was nothing if not a willing student, and to Byron's delight, was certainly a quick learner. He taught her that there was no inch of skin on their bodies that could not give rise to desire, no crevice that could not yield hidden secret pleasures. As his erection reached hitherto unknown proportions, he mentally rooted round for a first-rate distraction. He turned his thoughts in desperation to the process of dismantling and reassembling his rifle, a subject that had the required effect until he got to the stage of inserting the bolt back into the breech. Summoning the very last vestiges of will power, he somehow managed to abide by his promise not to enter her until she was ready. When eventually she cried out for him and he pushed hesitantly inside her moist, softly resistant vagina, their shared orgasm resembled the volcanic eruption of Krakatoa.

Byron had also promised that he would take measures to avoid an unwanted pregnancy. With no knowledge of birth control, Addie was not really prepared for him to take his leave quite as abruptly as he did. All became clearer when a stream of hot viscous liquid landed like a translucent lava flow in her navel. Addie examined it curiously while Byron searched for some sort of cloth. She realised with belated understanding why the strange smell was vaguely reminiscent of her brother's bedroom. Byron returned with a lace-edged handkerchief he had found at the bottom of a drawer. After he had tenderly wiped her clean, they debated with much amusement as to which of them should keep the hanky as a souvenir, then decided they should cut it in half so that years later, when they were unrecognisably old and decrepit, they would know each other by matching the halves together.

But the handkerchief was soon forgotten. The next time they made love, the pace was slower and the union deeper. They lingered ecstatically for as long as they could on the summit. As the hot afternoon passed, they achieved a variety of expression that would have made them worthy models for the stone reliefs adorning an Indian temple. In between, they had languorous conversations about trivialities and dozed a little. When Byron slept, Addie listened to him snoring lightly. She didn't mind, it was a comforting sound. She put her head close to his and watched his lips moving rhythmically as the air passed in and out. As the day cooled, they curled like cats together in the gathering dusk.

The pattern was followed for the next two days; mornings apart whilst Addie worked, afternoons together for 'research' as Addie euphemistically named their passionate physical explorations, and evenings spent talking intently about everything, except whether or not they had a future together. Byron decided that there was such a strong likelihood that he wouldn't survive the war that there was no point worrying about whether they would make a success of a long term relationship. Although they were both American, their backgrounds could hardly have been more different. His father, a Hungarian immigrant, had managed to find work sometimes in New York, but with five children it was never easy to keep the family afloat. Most of Byron's education had been gleaned from books. There were library loans and cheap drugstore novels at first, then when he was fifteen or so, he began to read left-wing paperbacks and newspapers that circulated amongst the men in the factory where he worked. His mother he regarded with a deep affection. She had done her best to bring up her children decently and put food on the table for them, though she often cursed men long and hard for making her task so difficult. Byron hadn't told her that he was going to join the International Brigades. She would have tried to stop her only son from doing anything so foolish. Wanting to avoid an argument and to spare her the worry, Byron had said he was going to support the Republic by working in a factory in Barcelona. All this was a world away from the comfortable realisation of the American dream in which Addie had spent her early years.

When Byron didn't arrive at their arranged meeting place the following day, Addie felt a surge of nausea slowly rise from her stomach as the minutes went by. The thought that he might have tired of her was distinctly disagreeable. Although in her mind she had set out clear guidelines regarding the need to accept their relationship on a day to day basis, it appeared that this decision had been overridden by a stronger biological directive.

'Why,' she thought angrily, 'does the fact that I have allowed him to make love to me leave me with the feeling that I can't live without him. I managed perfectly well before.'

In the end, unable to resist finding out for sure, she went to the hotel where he was staying. Rucksacks and bags filled the reception hall. Men crowded round the desk, arguing with the clerk. Addie waited for some time, but losing patience and determined not to be ignored any longer, she pushed through to the front and in reasonably fluent Spanish, asked to see 'el americano, Capitán Fox.'

'He was one of the first to go, Señorita, they've all been recalled to their battalions.'

Addie felt her heart sink with a palpable thud. She'd known his leave was nearly over, but even the loss of a couple of days left her with a pervasive ache that seemed to originate around the region of her uterus. She had reached the door when a chorus of shouts from the assembled Brigaders called her back. The clerk had remembered a letter Captain Fox had left for a girl. 'Is it for you, darling?' one of the Brigaders asked, with a distinctly suggestive grin.

Not even noticing his expression, Addie snatched the letter with her name on it, saying hurriedly, 'Yes, thank you.' She repeated her thanks several times to all and sundry, and clutching the letter tightly, rushed out to read it.

She was going to return to her room before opening the letter, but just couldn't wait that long. With her back pressed against the wall just round the corner from the hotel, she opened it with exasperatingly shaky hands. It was little more than a scribbled apology and farewell, apart from one memorable sentence.

'Helping you with your "research" has been one of the most rewarding and enjoyable experiences of my life.'

Addie didn't want to cry in the street but the tears rolled out anyway. Her body seemed to be over-ruling her brain most of the time these days. He ended the letter saying that he would try to keep in contact with her, and telling her that she could send letters to him through the Battalion. That was it, just the initial 'B' scrawled in worn-down pencil, scraping the thin paper with the final flourish.

Attempting to follow her mother's customary advice to 'stop moping about and do something useful,' over the next few days Addie concentrated hard on finishing the phrasebook for the Brigades. She worked well into the evenings but the nights on her narrow bed still seemed long. She tried to write to Byron but the tone of the letter was never quite right. Several sheets of useless efforts were ripped out of the typewriter, making her feel guilty because paper was so scarce. The Brigades, she had heard, were fighting in the town of Belchite. Unofficial reports were suggesting that casualties were high. It was difficult not to think about what that could mean for Byron.

Distraction for Addie arrived in two letters, one from Phyllis in Murcia, and the other from the Medical Aid Committee in London. Phyllis had tracked down some of Marcel's past employment records and discovered that he had been removed from his post in France somewhat ignominiously. He had been given the chance to leave without a fuss after the disappearance of quite a considerable quantity of morphia. There had never been an official investigation, but Phyllis had reliable unofficial sources. Any suspicions that had been laid at Addie's door had been erased. The other letter was a welcome surprise, possibly also something for which Addie had reason to be thankful to Phyllis. The Medical Aid Committee asked if she would accept the job of travelling between the medical units to help the English speaking staff with their assorted problems, a sort of welfare officer. But this would only be part of her work. They also suggested that these visits would allow her to collect material to write articles and appeals for propaganda magazines. Her experience in the press office and broadcasting might thus be put to good use in raising more funds. They already had confidence in her driving skills, and had been assured of her capacity for hard work by those in charge of the hospital in Murcia. The letter finished by saying that should she accept, she would be based in Barcelona, and that a car and a camera would be provided for her.

Addie took a deep breath. Like a pilgrim arriving at a shrine, she had felt drawn to Madrid, the symbolic heart of the struggle. In a few short weeks, there had been so many new experiences that the days had seemed to expand to months. But since Byron had gone she felt as if she lived each day wearing spectacles with lenses of monochrome grey. The River Manzanares still curved like a shining arc through the city, the spirit of the people still endured, but all was tinged with a sadness that had lodged as heavily inside her as yesterday's cold rice pudding. When she had walked past the doorway of the abandoned house, the board had been nailed securely back in place. She hadn't wanted to go in anyway. A change, she decided as she looked at the letter, would do her good. The job would suit her perfectly. She would be relatively independent, meeting people, travelling, doing worthwhile work, what better? Her spirits lifted a little as she repeated John Milton's words under her breath, 'To-morrow to fresh woods and pastures new'.

II

A welcome party awaited Rose when she arrived back at the hospital. The villagers had turned out to greet her, giving her small gifts with their kisses. The single brown egg placed in her hand almost moved her to tears. They had so little to give. Someone had put up a sign over the door saying in English, 'Welcome to our English Rose.' A contingent of Garibaldis were lined up in the courtyard, but many familiar faces were missing. Along with the rest of the International Brigades, they had been fighting at Brunete, near Madrid. After a desperate hand to hand battle through the streets, they had managed to recapture the town but then with the arrival of Franco's heavy artillery, they had lost it again. Casualties had been very high. There was only time to return for a brief respite before the next campaign began.

The Garibaldis saluted Rose smartly before breaking ranks and giving her a voluble reception, cheering and whistling. She looked impatiently for Rafael, but he wasn't amongst them. Her relief when she found out that he was alive was quickly replaced by annoyance that he hadn't come to welcome her.

'Oh, damn,' she thought with irritation, 'why should I care?'

She had left Madrid, truly determined to put Rafael out of her mind, and now, she was thinking about him again. Rafael hadn't wanted to be part of the welcoming group. The others would have made fun of him, he knew, encouraging him to kiss her so that they could make lewd comments. They meant no harm, he was sure, but he had often wished he looked older, tougher perhaps, and that his boyish face didn't betray his feelings so clearly. But his friends had to admit, when it came to women, Rafael with his youthful charm and poetic good looks, was the one who had the most success. What they found even more galling was that most of the time, he didn't even take advantage of the fact.

In the late evening Rafael escaped from his duties to stroll, as casually as he could, to the outskirts of the village, hoping that Rose would be walking somewhere along the route they had taken together. But there was no sign of her. He searched the hospital for her but she wasn't there either.

Just as he was wondering where to look next, he saw her coming out of one of the houses in the village. He recognised the house, he had been there himself, bearing the news of their baby's death. As small as she was, even Rose had to bend her head to pass through the dilapidated doorway. She didn't lift her head again, just rushed towards him without looking where she was going. He stood in her path, and she almost bumped into him before noticing his presence. As she raised her head, he could see that she was crying.

'Rosa,' he said, catching hold of her shoulders, 'what is the matter?'

' Miscarriage,' she said though gritted teeth. She pulled away from him and began to walk back to the hospital. They hadn't seen each other since Rafael had gone to convalesce after his accident. He had thought they were growing so close before then. Now he was not so sure. She was so unlike the Italian girls he knew. It was easy to understand what they were saying in the messages conveyed by their dark eyes and swaying hips. With Rose he was unsure; he had believed she wanted him, but now she seemed so distant. Perhaps Madrid had changed her. Rafael walked with her back to the hospital. When the office door was firmly closed and they were alone, he gathered her into his arms in an attempt to comfort her. She leaned against him. Had she missed him after all? A sudden surge of renewed hope gave him courage and he tried, rather clumsily, to kiss her. For a few brief seconds he thought that she was going to turn away and that he had made an irrevocable mistake. But, before he had time to release her and make an abject apology, she returned his kiss with a fervour that amazed him, her softness gone, replaced by a hungry need.

Rose was in turmoil. Long suppressed memories raked her with their long claws, gouging fresh wounds above old scars. Although she had seen the results of a few miscarriages during her nursing training, the sight of the foetus in the bucket had been a shock. She could see it had been a late abortion, and rather than a strange hybrid animal shape, the bucket contained the mangled remains of a tiny person. She had at first presumed that the foetus belonged to the mother of the baby who had died of burns, but then had discovered that it did not. It belonged to one of her daughters, the daughter who could not be more than twelve or thirteen. When she saw the girl lying on the wooden cot, Rose almost fainted at the sudden vivid memory of invasive instruments, fear and pain. God only knew what they had used on this child; Rose had never seen clearly what they had done to her when it had been her own childish body that was being probed and pierced. She had covered the episode with a blanket of oblivion that had lasted for years. Perhaps it was the poverty in the dismal room that had brought the memories to the surface, the inevitable presence of filth in the absence of hope.

Rose's abortion had been the unfortunate result of her mother's generosity. A woman that Rose had known as 'Auntie', who in reality was no relation at all, was convicted of dealing in stolen goods. Her prison sentence was substantial, a deterrent to others. With no one to turn to, she begged Annie to take in her son, rather than leave him to the doubtful mercies of the church orphanage. Billy had arrived to share their cramped accommodation; a two up, two down condemned terrace house in Hackney, when he was thirteen, two years older than Rose. She had liked him more than her brothers, he talked to her and didn't push her around. He was strong and protected her from the street bullies. She began to follow him like a puppy, doting on him with childish devotion. If she did what he asked, strange things sometimes, he gave her some sweets from the endless supply he kept in his pockets, taken from the corner shops for miles around. It was their secret. When her parents were drinking at the pub, and older brothers and sisters were out, Billy was left with Rose and the younger ones. While the little ones slept at one side of the old sagging bed, he would crawl in quietly at her side. As time went on, Rose found she didn't like the new games he wanted to play at all. Sometimes they hurt. She'd heard her mother moan when her father lay on her in bed, like Billy was doing with her. Perhaps it hurt her too. But Rose couldn't tell anyone. Her mother had said that she mustn't let boys touch her, that it was dirty to let them, so she knew she had been doing something wrong and the punishment would be dreadful. Billy told her she mustn't tell either or he'd go away, and despite everything, she didn't want him to leave. She was trapped. When she was just fourteen and pregnant, the truth was discovered. Billy never even said goodbye.

Rose didn't want to tell Rafael about the girl she had just seen. Better he should think it had been the mother who had needed help. Rose remembered the importance of secrecy surrounding the gruesome matter of abortion. It had been drummed into her by her mother. It was something between women. Men, like her father, were to be kept out. This, she had realised later, let them nicely off the hook. They didn't know about the agony that resulted from their actions. But, of course, if the news of a girl's abortion leaked out, like dark blood through a bandage, the stain on her character could never be wiped out. Rose's mother told her to forget about it, that she would soon get over it, and indeed Rose did stop thinking about it consciously. But she became obsessed with cleanliness, a fixation that was tidily rationalised when she became a nurse. Rose would certainly never tell anyone what had happened to her. The lost child would be a secret companion, carried with her to the grave.

Unknowingly, Rafael had weakened the barriers that Rose had put up to keep such grim realities at bay. She liked to think of him as a romantic figure, as handsome and dashing as a celluloid star, but actually here with her in the flesh, a real-life hero. However, that was not all that attracted her so much to him. He also possessed another quality she found desirable – although he was only slightly younger than she was, he looked like a boy. Billy, with his snub nose and smooth cheeks, had made a lasting impression on her in more ways than one. The days when she had been his willing victim still exerted their subliminal power. She felt strongly drawn to this almost androgynous boyish type of beauty that had been imprinted on her mind when the first haunting sexual fingerprints were left on her body.

But Rose was now no longer so defenceless. After the abortion, she had begun to learn her strengths, and revenge is sweet. Her eye-catching figure and honey-blonde prettiness drew men like bees. Within a short time, she found she could play on their admiration as skilfully as a concert pianist. But things were not allowed to progress much beyond flirting. Rose wanted to be worshipped like an unattainable goddess, not to be mauled like a sixpenny tart. Sex as far as Rose was concerned, was something that never actually occurred, just like a movie romance in which everything ended with the kiss. Sometimes it was difficult to persuade men of this fact so, if men were not two-dimensional screen idols but fleshy reality, it was better that they were dependent on her, like patients, or that they were young enough to be her eager acolytes.

Although Rose was by now telling herself firmly to extricate herself from Rafael's embrace, her body was reluctant to obey. Even Errol Flynn had not aroused such passion in Rose, though she was an ardent fan. For quite some time, they remained locked in a Hollywood clinch of steamy intensity. At last Rose pulled away, exhilarated to see the adoring look in Rafael's eyes. Another conquest. This time however, she felt overcome by an unusual tenderness rather than triumph.

Rafael never did things by halves. His feelings for Rose burned as fiercely as his hopes for revolution. Nevertheless, he realised that although on the surface she seemed as perfect as a china doll, her childhood had somehow left her damaged inside. He was still young enough to believe that he would be able to repair the harm that had been done. It would just take him a little time.

During the days that followed, Rafael could tell that Rose was falling more deeply in love. Sadly, it was the idea of love that had captivated her, far more than Rafael himself. She was living in a dream world, retreating from the realities of war and from her past traumas as far and as fast as she could. Their evening encounters grew increasingly torrid, but there would always come a point at which she would stop his advances. With mouths soft and wet, they simulated other pleasures; it was tantalising, never satisfying. Even Rose was becoming frustrated, but held on like a limpet to the make-believe virginity she had created in her imagination. Rafael had dreams that left him exhausted. The situation could not possibly continue for much longer. It was ironic that matters should be brought to a climax by the sexual aspirations of the single remaining donkey in the village, long suffering and hardly more than a bag of bones.

Rose was with Rafael in the village square. It was market day, formerly a bustling affair, now reduced to a few items of sad looking vegetables spread out on the shawls of a handful of local women. Barefoot, several children played near the slow trickle of water issuing from the fountain. Piled high with his burden of twigs, the donkey was being taken to drink from the nearby trough. There was quite a stir when a sorry assortment of beasts was brought into the square, also to be allowed a welcome drink. Lame horses, mules and donkeys with the scars of old beatings on their backs, they looked more like moth-eaten hides draped on coat hangers than flesh and blood. They filed into the square with heads low and hooves dragging. Meat for Madrid, the drover said. Then the village donkey caught the stimulating scent of a jenny, or perhaps it was only a memory on the air. His muzzle wrinkled upwards, snorting and sniffing, exposing long yellow teeth in a death-like rictus. A tragic comedy began as he careered around between the other animals, scattering them all over the square in his search for fulfilment. Rafael joined in the rowdy laughter of the troops and villagers, until he realised that Rose was not laughing. She was shouting, crying out in near hysteria, 'Stop, stop, watch out for the children.'

When the donkey was recaptured and all was calm again, it was clear that no child had been trampled, or even slightly injured. Quick and surefooted, they had all managed to get out of the way by climbing up onto the plinth of the fountain. But Rose was still shaking with emotion. Rafael led her to a stony seat they had discovered during their walks round the village. They would often sit there to talk, dwarfed by the harsh mountains of the nearby sierras.

'Rosa,' he said softly, taking her hand, 'tell me.'

Her words all came rushing out in a flood, but his English was improving quickly and he could understand most of what she said, filling in here and there with wild guesses that seemed to make sense.

'The coal man had a horse to pull his cart,' she began as the tears rolled down her cheeks. 'I always liked that horse, though he was a scrawny old thing. He had long fringes on his hooves and a long mane, but his tail had been bobbed so I felt sorry for him when there were flies. He would put his head down so I could pat him on the nose. I could see his sad eyes inside the blinkers. If I could pinch a piece of carrot from the kitchen I would always give it to him.'

She smiled, but as she gathered her thoughts to continue, her face took on a tense, pained expression, as if she were screwing up courage to open a door knowing there was something horrible on the other side.

'The coal man had left this poor old horse tied up outside the pub while he went in to sort out opening the coal chute. I was sitting right by the horse singing him a song to keep him company. I was supposed to be watching my younger sister, but I wasn't. I was playing in the gutter, rolling marbles, just a little bit. When the coal man came back he shouted at me to get away and made me jump. I was always afraid of him, all black with the coal dirt, and he whipped the horse sometimes.'

Rafael was startled when she cried in distress, 'I forgot them. I left them there. The horse moved and trod on them and slipped and panicked and reared up and the cart went backwards where my sister was. I heard her scream. I saw the hooves coming down on me and the next thing I knew I was in our house on the sofa. The doctor was talking to my mother. He was saying, "She's going to die, I'm afraid, there's nothing more I can do." I prayed and prayed so hard that it was my sister who was dying, not me. And it was. They took me in to see her the next morning, all laid out, looking like a beautiful white angel, except you could see there were places she looked squashed. All the neighbours came in to see her and cry a bit. They looked at me as if I was a monster, they knew it was my fault. I knew too. I'd left the marbles behind, I hadn't watched her, I'd prayed for her to die.'

'But you were so young Rosa, just a little girl, it was an accident.' Rafael wanted to take the pain away, but Rose seemed to have withdrawn behind a grey veil of guilt. He understood now why she was always so distraught when disaster struck children. She always took the burden of responsibility to save them on her own shoulders, and if she failed to do so, her remorse was overwhelming. He could only think of one way to help her. She needed someone who could make her forget such terrible things, someone to care specially for her, to make up for the love she had lacked as a child.

'I love you, Rosa,' he said earnestly, 'marry me.'

At that moment, everything conspired against Rose to prevent her from making a sensible refusal. Rafael, suffused with radiant sincerity, was offering to fulfil the romantic dreams she had cherished for years. The impact of raw childhood memories, resurfacing after so many years of quiescence, had rendered the normally dominant, practical side of her nature, temporarily inactive.

'I will be going to the front soon. I want you to be my wife before I go.' He could have chosen no finer finishing touch. Rose could no longer resist the building pressure to say 'yes'. The thought of their imminent parting, a scene entitled 'young woman waves goodbye bravely as her husband sets off to war,' tipped the scales in Rafael's favour.

'The Battalion Commander can marry us now,' Rafael told her excitedly, 'then, after the war, I promise we can marry again in England, with your family there.'

Rose wasn't so sure about a wedding with her family in attendance, she didn't want to think about the world outside Spain at the moment, but the rest all sounded perfect. Imagine how surprised Constance and Addie would be when they heard her news.

Reality was now suspended almost completely for Rose. She held the small bunch of wild flowers that Rafael had picked for her while the Battalion Commander conducted an incomprehensible Spanish ceremony for them later that evening. He had agreed to carry it out, though he wasn't quite sure if he had done everything correctly. He knew the Battalion would soon be given orders to leave. Afterwards there was wine and opera and a rousing rendition of the Battalion song, 'La Guardia Roja'. Rafael went with Rose to her narrow bed in the hospital. Like Neapolitan ice-cream, they lay together, his suntanned brown body against her pink and white skin, melting into each other.

Rose didn't really wake from her dream until two days later when the Garibaldis left for Belchite. She contacted Beyer at Albacete to request a transfer, hating the feeling of being left in Villamalea. There were patients to care for but not enough to keep her busy. Sometimes she cried for Rafael, missing the devotion in his eyes and the excitement of their lovemaking. At other times she cried for herself, thinking what a fool she had been to marry a revolutionary instead of a doctor with a practice in Harley Street as she had intended.

III

Constance slumped against the wall. Sleep didn't come to her like a drift of blossom on the breeze, it slammed into her brain, shutting off consciousness with the speed of a plummeting guillotine blade. She had been in the theatre for a day and a night, swabbing and sterilising, intuitively passing the correct instruments at the right moment, steadying the slippery bones and organs while the surgeons sawed and sutured. At last, her turn had come for a brief respite, but casualties continued to arrive in a relentless tide. The front was now less than a mile away from Quinto, the dusty town where the Lincoln-Washington medical unit had set up the hospital. When two American doctors had arrived in the quiet backwater of Poleñino, scouting for recruits, Constance had seized the chance to leave. A new front was opening up between Huesca and Teruel and they were short of nurses. Constance didn't wait to ask for permission, agreeing willingly to be abducted. Her only regret was not having time to say goodbye to Sam. He had been so pleased to see her again when she had come back from Madrid, insisting that she read the transcript of her broadcast to him, and showering her efforts with what seemed to Constance to be unnecessarily effusive praise. She hadn't seen him since then, but knew that he would probably soon be posted to the new front too. Perhaps they would meet there.

A nightmare of grotesque proportions had greeted their arrival in Quinto. The long shadow of Franco's army had barely receded. The dead still lay in the streets, piled up as high as five feet in places. An unrelenting sun had bloated the bodies into bizarre Humpty Dumpty figures. Swollen soldiers and civilians, hugely inflated horses and mules, all were tangled together to form an immense abstract composition that shifted its outline occasionally when clouds of fat bluebottles rose in the air and landed again in yet another flyblown paradise. The smell of putrefaction wormed its way into every corner of Constance's mind and she knew that she would never be able to rid herself of the memory.

The women who had helped to prepare the buildings for the hospital had cried for their dead husbands and sons as they scrubbed the floors with sand and water. There was not enough soap to waste it underfoot. The boys who had survived the slaughter in the village also came to help, carrying water from the well; moving equipment, then as the wounded began to arrive, carrying them from the ambulances and trucks into the triage area. Constance was always glad when it wasn't her turn for duty there. It was a dreadful strain on the nerves – deciding those who should go straight into the operating theatre and those whose chances of survival were so negligible that they should be left to die.

Propped up by the wall, she slept without stirring, head hanging down on her chest, legs sticking out in front of her like a rag doll. Her slender limbs were pitted with small ulcers, the result of infected insect bites that would not heal. Angry red swellings marked the smooth skin of her face. With her hair drawn ruthlessly into a tightly coiled bun at the base of her neck, she appeared to have aged years since the recent days in Madrid.

'Triage! Triage!' The call woke her and she struggled to her feet. More casualties were arriving. She must go back inside. For twelve days there was no respite.

She returned to Poleñino, weak and exhausted, to find herself in disgrace. If she had been able to muster the energy, she would have been outraged at the injustice of having to stand in front of the other staff and be admonished, still dirty and dishevelled, with traces of patients' blood smeared on her clothes. Even as tired as she was, she was not going to agree that she had been wrong to leave without waiting for permission.

'There was no one at the hospital to ask just then,' she protested tersely. 'I left a message. I thought I should go where I was needed most.'

Constance, her emotions anaesthetized from the sights she had witnessed, seemed uninterested in her accusers, led by an officious newly arrived Political Commissar, now responsible for morale and certain aspects of discipline within the unit. Much to his annoyance, Constance gave the impression that he was not worthy of her attention. She said, 'goodnight,' tersely, and then left the room.

The Spanish Medical Aid Committee in London had been deliberating whether to recall Constance from Spain, despite the fact that she was undoubtedly a good nurse. Reports they had about her conflicted greatly, some praising her dedication to the work and her efforts to train Spanish girls, others criticising her dismissive attitude towards superiors and certain colleagues. More to the point, they were not sure that she could ever be relied on to do as she was told. Fortunately for all concerned, a solution materialised within a few days. The nurses who were still on speaking terms with Constance rushed to tell her the news that a visitor had arrived. The Chief Medical Officer of the XI and XV International Brigades was, at that very moment, finding out if any nurses were willing to leave Poleñino and join the Brigades. Constance immediately liked Dr Walter, even though it was sometimes difficult to understand what he said, his Russian accent heavily overlaid with a Scottish burr, a result of having been trained in medicine in Edinburgh. He looked askance at the marks of bites and sores all over her face and arms, and the black rings beneath her eyes, then asked kindly, 'And where have you been?'

When she heard the sympathy in his voice, Constance felt a tear escape from her eye and trickle down her cheek. Blinking furiously, she told him about the work at Quinto as calmly as she could.

'And would you be prepared to work like that again?' he asked, the serious look in his eyes revealing that he believed there were hard times to come.

'Yes,' she answered firmly.

Dr Walter took note of the strength and determination he could see in her eyes and fervently hoped that it would be enough to get her through the coming months.

'If you join the Brigades, you will be under the military discipline of the Republican Army; no longer a volunteer for Spanish Medical Aid.'

'That,' said Constance dryly, 'will be a pleasure.'

'Well,' Dr Walter added with a smile, 'the good news is that you will be paid 10 pesetas a day, just like the soldiers.'

'Splendid,' thought Constance, 'I'll be able to afford new underwear at last.'

The Brigade hospital had been set up not far away on the south side of the River Ebro that flowed, wide and green, between the mountains and down to the lush plain of the Delta. When they crossed the bridge, Constance could see it snaking away into the distance, and fell instantly in love with its languorous beauty. She soon began to recover her strength and spirits in her new environment. All seemed well-organised, even the improvisations were efficient. Apart from the normal routine of the hospital, preparations were also being made to send more mobile units to the front the following week. Constance was relieved that no one had the time, or the inclination, for petty squabbling. The nurses were far more politically motivated than those at Poleñino. For the first time, Constance met a black American nurse. Selena was in the Communist Party and had been involved in a nurses' union back home. As they worked together, she quietly told Constance what it was like to be a Negro in the States. Constance was horrified. She knew a little about anti-Semitism, but hadn't thought much beyond that. America, she had naively presumed to be civilised and modern, a place where people believed in the credo 'All men are created equal.' She was angry at her own ignorance. It was at least, good news to hear that the American Battalion in Spain had a black officer, Oliver Law, commanding white troops – an impossibility elsewhere. 'The Brigades are setting an example to the world,' thought Constance with a sudden flush of pleasure. It was strange how she was feeling an increasing pride in the Brigades, and how satisfying it was to be part of a group that had such a sense of purpose.

Over the next few days, Constance spent as much time as she could with a Spanish girl who showed particular talent in nursing. Aurora had been studying English in Madrid when the war broke out and had been one of the first to volunteer to work in the medical units. She was tiny but strong, and her small hands deftly carried out tasks of cleaning wounds and bandaging. The patients were so captivated by her smile that they hardly noticed when she gave them injections. Best of all, Constance could see that she had the instincts for nursing, for knowing when something wasn't quite right with a patient, even without knowing exactly what it was. In a mixture of Spanish and English, they managed their shifts together remarkably efficiently.

When Sam arrived to join the unit, Constance was delighted. But she gradually detected that something had changed about him. He was more cynical than he had been before. His acidic comments slipped into their conversations, leaving a bitter aftertaste, especially if the subject related to the Communist Party. He could see that Constance was burning with a bright new hope when she talked about what the Party was doing, and what it would be able to achieve in the future. Sam was reluctant to be the one to tarnish her golden illusions. Eventually, he knew he would have to tell her about the less savoury activities of the communists, particularly in Barcelona, during what was now coming to be known as the 'May Events' earlier that year. Even more alarming were the stories he had begun to hear about what happened after the street fighting had finished. A formidably efficient repression had been carried out to grind the anarchists into the ground and the Trotskyist POUM into oblivion. There were rumours of brutal torturing and murder, and the leader of the POUM was dead. It was still unclear exactly what had happened, but it seemed beyond doubt that the Soviet Secret Police and certain communists had played some part in the matter. Sam was filled with a dreadful despair, fearing that the Left would never be able to overcome their differences and concentrate on fighting fascism. But, that discussion could wait a while longer, he decided, enjoying seeing Constance in such high spirits.

When she was asked to organise a team to accompany two surgeons and an auto-chir to the front, Constance was jubilant. 'There'll be you and an orderly,' she told Sam, 'and another nurse, probably Selena, and Aurora to help us, and an extra driver for the supply lorry who can do most of the cooking too.' She threw herself into the preparations with enthusiasm. The team and their patients would be under canvas. Constance knew all about camping. Her years as a Girl Guide and Akela of a Wolf Cub pack were to be put to good use at last. She fussed about, organising and improvising the usual type of camping equipment and finding things that would be needed for post-operative care till the wounded could be moved on. Constance thoroughly approved of the neatness and practicality of the auto-chir. Inside there were fitted shelves and cupboards to store the hundreds of items needed for operations; instruments, gowns, gloves, anaesthetic, ampoules of glucosade and saline, the list seemed never ending. They left for the front as the dawn was breaking, heading for the mountains near Belchite.

The fighting in the town was intense, house to house slaughter. The surgeons were rarely short of work. Yards of intestines passed through their hands as they searched for perforations to be repaired or sections to be removed. Shrapnel and bullets were gouged out from countless pounds of flesh. Sometimes Constance would bear away the grisly relics of amputations. But their success rate was good. Quick attention reduced the number of deaths considerably, and now that the blood transfusion service was up and running, they were saving some who would never have survived before. New techniques had recently been developed for the preservation of blood. Before, they had relied on direct arm to arm transfusions. Constance had been a donor on a few occasions, watching in wonder as the colour returned to an ashen faced patient when the blood left her veins and flowed into his. But there were never enough people available nearby to meet the continual demand. Now the blood could be collected in the cities from willing volunteers and brought to the hospital units at the front in specially adapted lorries.

The town of Belchite finally fell to the Republicans at the beginning of September. The wounded passing through triage considered themselves lucky. Not only had they survived, but they were in the hands of surgeons and nurses who knew what they were doing. Others hadn't been so fortunate. Rumours soon began to fly round the ranks about the 'poor sods' who had been discovered in the fascist hospital when Belchite was taken, left behind when their army retreated. Eighty wounded men were found, two to a mattress on a floor slippery with urine and vomit. Tourniquets, applied days before, had choked the life from living limbs. Dressings, rigid with dried blood and pus, hid nothing but rotting flesh and gas gangrene. Some had gone mad, some were dying, and some were dead. The orderlies who had evacuated the survivors to a hospital on the coast returned to their units, nauseated and shaken. Constance heard the stories with disgust. How could the nuns who had been responsible for these patients have allowed them to get into such a state? Even if they had no professional nursing ethics, where was their sense of Christian duty towards these men? How could they abandon their patients? Full of righteous indignation, she was sure that she would never behave in that way.

After a while, the soldiers' faces had blurred together in uniformity for Constance. They all reflected pain and exhaustion, they were all unshaven and dirty. What she saw were the details of their wounds, what she heard, whether spoken or silent, were their needs. She lost all track of time, till one day, when she approached the last few wounded waiting on stretchers in triage with the detached skills of an automaton, a familiar American voice triggered a response in her memory.

'Not much like the Hotel Gran Vía, is it, Constance?'

She looked more closely at the drawn face on the stretcher at her feet. Byron managed to smile. Constance moved to examine the wound in his side which had leaked a considerable quantity of blood onto the stretcher beneath him.

'It's not serious,' he assured her, 'just a flesh wound. If you see to these others, you can fix me up afterwards. What I need more than anything is the chance to talk to a pretty girl.'

He was not expecting the antiseptic. 'Sonofabitch!' he cursed in surprise as Constance cleaned the wound thoroughly. She dismissed his apologies lightly, accustomed to hearing much worse. With a clean dressing, she decided he was fit to be moved to a rear-guard hospital on the next ambulance. They had a few minutes to exchange news. Constance asked if he had heard from Addie.

'No,' he replied, 'I was hoping that you would know something.'

He looked so dejected that Constance, even despite her tiredness, laughed a little.

'I take it you two became good friends in Madrid after I left.'

Byron's smile returned and broke into an uncontainable grin. 'She's something special, that one,' he said, with a longing that Constance sensed was not only carnal in nature.

'If I see her, I'll tell her you're OK,' she offered, adding 'Do you want me to give her a message?'

'Yeah. Tell her to put her research on hold till I can get back to help her again. I've thought of some new possibilities we should follow up.'

Constance was puzzled but decided it wouldn't be much

good asking Byron for an explanation. Better to wait till she met up with Addie again to find out what had really gone on between them.

IV

Barcelona had changed. The exhilarating atmosphere Addie had felt on her first visit was gone. After the 'May Events', the revolutionary period had drawn to a stifled close, and society had reverted to its former divisions, the bourgeoisie and the rest, the disparities somewhat muted perhaps, but nevertheless, unmistakeable. The first thing Addie noticed was the transformation that had taken place in the posters. Where there had been a rash of acronyms and initials now there were impressive hoardings lauding the heroic Popular Army. After a while, she noticed a marked difference in the way the posters portrayed women too. She remembered those from her earlier visit, already fraying a little round the edges, showing women with guns, the 'milicianas', leading men into battle in defence of the Republic. Wearing workmen's overalls, albeit tightly cinched at the waist, they had been portrayed in the vanguard of the action. Such posters were now in tatters, replaced by others using more traditional representations of women. Now they were more often shown as the victims of bombing, helplessly clutching their children. A few of the new posters encouraged women to work in heavy industry. Addie knew that large sections of the economy were dependent for the first time on women in the workforce, and that their labour was essential in the dangerous work of manufacturing armaments. Sadly, she noticed a considerable number of posters about venereal disease in which skeletal females enticed innocent soldiers to a terrible fate. 'Something not quite right there,' Addie muttered. Byron had told her such diseases were rife in the army and they had talked about the failed attempts to close the brothels. The posters all appeared to uphold the belief that women alone were guilty of disseminating the disease. Addie could see that this said a great deal about the real attitudes within the government towards equality between the sexes.

She found her way to the flat maintained by the Medical Aid Committee at 167 Balmes, the street that led from the Diagonal to Mount Tibidabo. She had been told by the Committee that the 'responsable' for the flat, someone called Mary Davis, would let her in and give her a set of keys so that she could use a room there when she was between tours of the medical units. Addie stood on the pavement outside the entrance, ringing the bell for the flat on the fourth floor. No one replied. Addie was beginning to think the bell must be broken. Just as she was about to give up, the street door opened and a small woman, middle aged and round, peered out at her. This must be the 'portera', decided Addie. It seemed to her that on reaching maturity, Spanish women were doomed to be dressed in black and to wear their hair scraped relentlessly into the tightest of buns.

When Addie asked for Mary Davis, the portera was at first confused. It took a few seconds before she broke into a smile and nodded, saying, '¡Ay! sí, María, arriba.'

Despite Addie's protests, the portera, Asunción, insisted on climbing to the fourth floor with her, asking questions all the way, only stopping to draw breath on the landings. She banged loudly on the door of the flat and announced Addie's presence. Addie understood enough of the voluble reply, shouted angrily from somewhere inside, to know that her arrival was not welcome. Asunción shrugged her shoulders and rolled her eyes expressively, the ill-tempered response had come as no surprise to her. Eventually the door was flung open by an unsmiling, hard-eyed young woman, who immediately turned on her heel and walked away, saying, 'I suppose you'd better come in.'

Addie thanked Asunción, and followed her unwilling host into the flat.

María, as Mary insisted everyone should call her, was the most difficult person to get along with that Addie had ever encountered. From the nurses who were living in the flat, she learned a little about her, but nothing that explained why she was so disagreeable. Addie at first thought the nurses were just gossiping unkindly. They had clearly decided she was 'a suspicious character', and enjoyed reviewing her dubious activities. María was a British subject but had been born in Poland. It was rumoured that she had titled relatives living in England somewhere. Because of her impressive language skills, she had been given the job of liaising between the Committee in London and the Spanish authorities overseeing the medical units. She was known to speak Russian and German as well as Spanish, French and English. She had come over to Spain with the first unit to be sent from England, arriving within a month of the start of the war. Everyone knew that after only a short while, this group had been split by an insidious, deep-seated factionalism. María, it was said, had been the instigator of much of the trouble. After a few days, Addie could see how that could be true. María wormed away at people's worries and grumbles like a maggot in an apple, gradually turning things rotten from the inside.

Addie found out even more about María from Max when she went to the vehicle depot to collect the car she had been assigned. Arriving in the workshop, she heard familiar curses coming from beneath a nearby truck. Max was so pleased to see her that, overcome by newly acquired Spanish habits, he greeted her with a kiss on both cheeks, then apologised for leaving oily smudges on her face. Addie didn't mind in the least. He showed her the car, a dilapidated Citroen with a variety of dints and holes in the mudguards and running boards. 'She's a good runner, don't you worry,' he said reassuringly. They went to a nearby bar to catch up on news. Max knew that Constance was near the front at Belchite, and that there were terrible casualties. Sometimes he drove the ambulances taking them to the rearguard hospitals. He hadn't heard anything about Rose though.

Addie told him about the work she would be doing, but when she said she would be based at the flat, he shook his head and uttered a breathy whistle through pursed lips.

'You've met María then? She's a rare bird. When she was in Valencia earlier on this year, the word was that she was a fascist agent, or at least, a British government agent, which is pretty much the same thing in this war.'

These accusations, Addie discovered, were based on rumours about her hiding deserters in the flat and helping to smuggle Franco supporters across the lines.

'There's been nothing proved of course,' he added, 'but I know for a fact that she messes things up on purpose. That's sabotage in my book.'

He proceeded to enumerate a string of instances in which María had delayed, misdirected or disregarded important messages. Unfortunately, all the ordering of supplies from the Medical Aid Committee passed through her hands. Her actions therefore affected not only the medical units, but the maintenance work on the ambulances in the transport depot too. María, however, had friends in high places. Complaints about her inefficiency were ignored, and those who had dared to make them were sure to have a very long wait before receiving any of the goods they requested from then on. Addie wondered if all these stories were true. She had tried hard to befriend María, sad to see that she had no friends, but any conversation she had with her always left behind a feeling of uneasiness. María's remarks about the people she knew in the medical units were full of insinuations and gossip. Addie couldn't decide if she really might be a fascist supporter, finding a thousand small opportunities for sabotage, or if she was just an exceedingly objectionable character.

Whatever the truth of the matter, Addie was glad that she would be spending much of her time travelling round to visit the medical units. Being in close contact with María would surely prove to be disheartening over even a short period of time. The poor nurses who shared the flat were certainly finding it so – María's petty rules and restrictions were always causing problems. She wouldn't even let them use the kitchen until she had finished eating. Addie hated such conflicts, pathetic at any time, but especially pitiable when there was a war to be won. She decided that the minute she had the camera, she would begin her first tour of the hospitals. It would be good to see Constance and Rose again.

V

The rains came early that year. It didn't really seem appropriate to call it 'rain', Constance thought, as she ran from the bell tent to the auto-chir. The word suggested that water was falling in drops. The size of drops might vary, the density and speed too, but it was not the word to describe the emptying of a giant's bathtub all at once onto your head. A few patients, bunched together in the limited dry areas that remained in the tents, were being evacuated as quickly as possible. Fortunately, the deluge had stopped the fighting for a while and there were no incoming wounded. Constance, soaked to the skin, was helping with the packing, trudging back and forth with arms full of wet bedding whilst the men carried the heavier items. They were to return to base till the rains abated.

The drive was interminable. They lurched and slithered over the muddy road, unable to avoid the pot-holes that lay in their path. Constance had no idea how the driver could see where they were going at all. The rain beat against the windscreen, rendering the wipers almost useless. The incessant drumming of water on the metal roof drilled ever deeper into her brain. She sat, squashed tightly on the bench seat in the front of the lorry between the driver and the two doctors. Sam was driving the auto-chir following behind them with the rest of the team. Constance was growing tetchy. Her legs were cramped to one side of the gear stick, and the tuneless droning of the driver, singing the same song over and over again was getting on her nerves even more than the sound of the rain.

'I think we've had quite enough of 'Ay Manuela' for the moment,' she said testily.

He lapsed into silence and Constance drifted into a stupor.

The rain lessened just enough for Sam to see the lorry on the curve ahead of him slide slowly from the road and plunge down the precipitous bank below. He accelerated dangerously till the auto-chir reached the same spot then slammed on the brakes, his heart pounding. Leaping from the cab, he followed the fresh tyre tracks to the crumbling edge where they seemingly led into mid-air. Through the rain he could just make out the shape of the lorry below, frozen in mid-descent by a bizarre miracle. He arrived at the scene some seconds before the others, his fears for Constance making him ignore the dangers of the treacherous slope. He wrenched open the lorry door but she was not inside. Through the shattered windscreen he could see that only a stunted old olive tree stood between the lorry and a deadly vertical drop to the valley below. With dawning horror, he realised that hole in the windscreen would have been made by the soft form of Constance's body, travelling at high velocity. He held on to a slim hope that she had not fallen far. He found her lying, face down in the mud, at the other side of the cab. The exposed and twisted roots of the tree that clung to the stony slope so desperately had caught at her clothes as she rolled past. As he turned Constance over, an anguished cry escaped Sam's throat. Beneath the mud, her face was an unrecognizable mess. Nose and jaw were grotesquely misaligned, smashed by the brutal impact of the metal emblem that adorned the bonnet of the lorry. There was so much blood it was impossible to see if her eyes were damaged or not. Sam held his breath till he had managed to find a pulse and re-assure himself that she was still alive. Intermittent sobs, painfully tearless, shook him to the core as he clumsily disentangled her clothes from the roots with one hand, holding her tightly with the other to prevent her from sliding over the edge of the cliff.

Sam could hear groans coming from inside the cab as he staggered up the steep slope, Constance in his arms. He knew that the others would be coping with the rest of the injured. He glimpsed Aurora covering the face of the dead driver who had already been lifted out. Sam cursed him for his carelessness. At that moment, if the man hadn't been dead, Sam would have throttled him for losing control of the vehicle. Possibly the idiot had fallen asleep – he deserved to die, thought Sam bitterly.

Constance was a light burden for Sam, too light. 'You've been working too hard, not getting enough to eat,' he mumbled to her, though he knew she couldn't hear. As the rain washed some of the blood and mud from her face, he could see that her neat white front teeth now protruded at a strange angle through her top lip. But the globes of her eyeballs beneath the closed lids seemed intact. Sam had seen every possible horror on the battlefield, from brains pulsating within skulls cracked like eggs to the gaping void left by a direct hit to the genital area. For him, this was a thousand times worse. This was Constance. He placed her gently on the small area of floor space in the back of the auto-chir, then quickly proceeded to tear out some of the larger pieces of equipment, throwing it to the side of the road. By the time the others arrived, he had made the still inert Constance more comfortable, and had cleared enough room for the two doctors. The discarded equipment and the body of the driver could be collected later. He doubted that the tree would support the weight of the lorry for long enough to salvage the contents. Now all he could think of was the need to get Constance to hospital as quickly as possible.

Constance was wishing fervently that people would stop coming in to her room, bursting into tears and rushing out again. She had seen her face reflected in the steel kidney bowl, and knew it was bad, but things seemed to be nearly in the right place again at least. The blue-black swollen bruises were still a shocking sight, but at least her features no longer made her look like the distorted portraits of a woman painted by Picasso. The worst thing was that she was unable to move her jaw, so talking was nearly impossible. A few words could be forced out between clenched teeth, but mainly she had to resort to writing things down. As quite a few of the Spanish girls who were making a rather poor job of looking after her couldn't read, this was not much use. Eating was a problem too. Sweetened condensed milk was all she could manage.

Sam had stayed with her in the hospital in Valls until she had regained consciousness, but then had to leave, promising to return as soon as he could. The days were now passing slowly for Constance. Word had spread through the hospital about the beautiful English nurse whose face was now a monstrous mask. The Spanish, unlike the British, Constance had noticed, made no pretence of hiding their reactions to physical injury. There was no polite attempt to disregard disfigurements, no aversion of eyes, no carrying on as if nothing had happened. They would stare and grimace, or, as Constance now knew from the last few days, shed copious tears of sympathy for another's plight.

A week later, by which time Constance was totally sick of the sugary taste of condensed milk and of enforced inactivity, the mayor arrived with a group of local dignitaries to present her with flowers and to thank her for 'giving her all' to the Republic. Still unable to speak intelligibly, Constance tried to protest in her broken Spanish, furiously declaring that she had not 'given her all', that her face was nothing like her all, there was still lots of her left. The delegation left in confusion, unsure why their expression of gratitude had caused such garbled hostility.

Sam eventually came to the rescue. He had moved heaven and earth to find the best treatment for Constance. Somehow, he found out about an American plastic surgeon working near the French border. Luckily for Constance, the lack of awareness about this new field of treatment meant that he had room to take her case. After several operations on her face, Constance knew full well that but for Sam's efforts and this surgeon's skill, she would have born conspicuous scars forever. As it was, her previously perfectly straight nose was never quite the same again.

The lapping of the waves on the beach at Benicasim was a soothing balm for raw nerves. Constance sat looking out to sea, her fingers idly working their way through the warm sand. She slowly let the grains trickle from her cupped hands, feeling them run between her fingers and fall back to the beach. The scene was surreal. In sun-bleached pyjamas, figures wandered slowly along the narrow strand, stopping to rest, to watch the sea, to wonder by what miracle they had survived. None looked towards the mountains that rose from the plain a little way inland where battles continued to rage. Why would they wish to be reminded of the nearness of death? Although Constance's face was still marked by fading bruises, the haggardness she had acquired at the front had gone. She looked healthier than she had ever done, her skin lightly tanned and the blemishes from ulcers healed.

The verandas of the villas were crowded with men playing board games or cards, reading or talking. There were far too many of them, thought Constance, too many wounded, too many who needed to convalesce. Far too many of them, she knew, would return to the front and never walk by the sea again. She pushed such sad thoughts aside, and rose to her feet as the sun sank lower over the water. It would soon be time for the concert.

Quite a crowd gathered every day in the villa used mainly by the convalescent German Brigaders from the Thaelmann Battalion. There were many nationalities at Benicasim, ranging from Cubans to Finns, and even one Chinese. Most of them tried to spend the time till they recovered as constructively as possible, but it was the

Germans who were the leading lights in the organisation of a more formal educational programme. Spanish language classes were of course very popular, but others were well attended too, everything from Marxist theory to chess. Constance had become a great favourite with this group of serious-minded Germans. Felix, Otto and Ernst, resolutely committed to communism after their experiences in the unions in Germany, decided they would take on the task of bringing Constance into the political fold. She carefully studied the books they gave her to read and struggled to understand when Felix attempted to clarify the basic economic practicalities that would bring social change. Sometimes the theory was so complex that she couldn't understand it at all, but some of the ideas were so beautifully simple that they seemed to make perfect sense. Tonight though, instead of giving classes, they were going to sing.

The choir had been recruited by Ernst, and they had worked hard during the last week to prepare a concert for all the patients. Their voices were strong and true, and although Constance did not understand the words, she was moved by the power of the music. Arrayed in bandages, leaning on crutches, some in wheelchairs, they nevertheless were impressive. 'Perhaps it's something in their eyes,' thought Constance as her gaze flitted across the faces that had now grown familiar to her, 'so full of zeal and glory.' For a moment she imagined they could be the direct descendants of German gods, like Wotan and Thor. She raised her head to see those at the far end of the back row and her world changed.

He was blonde; of course, many of the Germans were - and his eyes were blue; but no more so than a dozen others. He must have just arrived. Constance had no idea why her legs felt suddenly weak and her heart raced when she looked at him. It was certainly not something that had ever happened to her before. He was singing with a sad intensity that seemed to come from the depths of his soul, all his attention on the conductor. Karl was still weak from the surgery to remove a bullet from his arm. The doctors had told him that he should make a good recovery. He had wanted to join in the concert, not only because he loved singing, but also to celebrate his good fortune in having emerged alive from the confused nightmare of battle. He knew the songs well and, full of the pleasure of being alive, he was singing with all his heart. But as the bold notes of the song of the Thaelmann Column rose to a crescendo, he was struck by a tight fist of emotion that hit him in the stomach with the force of a prize fighter. Grief. After he had been hit, he had crawled between scattered bodies to safety. Once or twice the dead had shielded him from further outbreaks of machine gun fire. In hospital, he had concentrated all his will on the need to be well enough to return to the fight again. He looked to the future, not permitting himself to think of the past. The song had released all the feelings of loss he had not wished to face. Now, he was singing in memory of the friends he would never see again.

Constance had watched, mesmerised, as the traces of this emotional turbulence transformed the expression on his face. When the pain had surfaced in his eyes, she felt as if a steel-tipped arrow had pierced her own heart. A resonance between the music and his emotions seemed to rise into the air and flood over Constance like a tidal wave. As the last notes died away, she left her seat and hurried away, fearful of the feelings that she did not understand. She couldn't face everyone with her thoughts in confusion and her emotions blazing with the brightness of Blackpool illuminations. What *had* happened? It didn't seem possible that she should now feel herself as defenceless as any of the girls she had scorned for having fallen victim to something as silly as love at first sight.

By the following morning, she had managed to impose a veneer of calm, enough, she hoped, to fool everyone, including the new arrival. She was bound to be introduced to him at some point in the day, a moment she both longed for and dreaded. As it turned out, no introductions were needed. As she sat on the beach, a prescient prickling of her skin let her know that the shadow cast upon her must belong to him. She had not heard his approach through the soft sand. Before she turned to face him, he spoke.

'Why did you leave so quickly last night?'

Constance had not prepared an answer to this question, though she had rehearsed a thousand other possible conversations with him in her mind. He sat beside her. His nearness made her feel so dizzy that she was sure if she had not been already sitting down, her legs would have given way. He seemed to sense some of her discomfort, because rather than waiting for an answer, he continued, 'I'm so sorry, I am being very rude. My name is Karl.'

'Constance,' she croaked in return, unaware that he had already found out her name.

'Did you enjoy the singing?'

'Oh, yes,' Constance replied, 'it was wonderful. The German songs are so beautiful. I hadn't heard some of them before.'

She was extremely pleased with herself for having managed to complete at least a couple of sensible sentences and decided to risk looking directly at him. He looked older in the strong sunlight, she thought, a man who has been fighting for a long time. But there was no sign of the weariness of spirit that she was beginning to see more and more often in the men who came under her care.

'I will teach them to you,' he said, his English grammatically precise, but with no hints of the conversational informalities that are learned outside text books. As the concert had finished, the quick movement as she had risen to leave caught his attention, and he had watched as she made her hasty departure. The pale bruises on her face didn't hide the strong lines of her strikingly fine features. A wistful desire to bring laughter to her solemn eyes had washed over him unexpectedly. Later in the evening he had found out all he could about her from Felix and the others.

Constance smiled a little at his offer of tuition, though not much. She had lost the habit of smiling during the weeks when it had hurt her to move her mouth. Laughing had become a forgotten art since the accident.

'What did you do before the war?' she asked abruptly. Suddenly, it seemed important to learn all about him and his life in the increasingly distant world that had existed before the war began. This in itself was unusual. There were so many meetings and partings, different faces coming and going. People had become less inclined to talk about such things. What mattered was the present; defeating Franco, and what was to come, building a better world. But Constance wanted to know everything about this man, she wanted him to share his past with her, almost as much as she wanted to be part of his future.

'I was a teacher,' he said, 'in the University of Dresden. But it was long ago. Would you like to walk as we talk?' He stood up and extended his good hand to pull her to her feet. Neither of them doubted that there would be a great deal to say to each other.

Passionate love, when combined with a passionate commitment to an ideal, can create a potent cocktail. Constance never really could separate the two in her mind ever again. The ardour of one became inextricably tangled with the fervour of the other. The intensity of the days that followed made Constance glad to be alive, not just a comfortable, contented gladness, but a joyful, elated gladness that reached her soul. Karl was a dedicated communist, not the sort who debated the finer points of ideology in the drawing rooms across Europe, but one who wanted to demonstrate by example how communism should work. To find someone like Constance, who would toil alongside him to this end, was rather like a Protestant missionary having the good fortune to meet a vicar's daughter, willing to become his wife and follow him up the Amazon. In truth, Constance would have been surprised to discover how much she would have had in common with many a missionary's wife. In her childhood she had been drawn to religion. For a while, the blessings offered by the Church of simple answers and a sense of belonging had been sufficient to captivate her totally. But as she discovered the writings of atheist authors like George Bernard Shaw, the doubts she had already forming in her mind were confirmed. Despite having rejected a belief in a loving God, the capacity for faith had remained. Communism and Karl had filled the void, offering her a clear path and comradeship, and a considerably more tangible form of love. Irresistible!

The sea sparkled in the late autumn sunshine. In the early mornings it had an exhilarating chill that set the body tingling. Karl and Constance would be amongst the first bathers, Constance swimming strongly, Karl standing waist high in the gently rolling waves watching her, with his wounded arm held aloft, following instructions to keep his dressing dry. When the bandages were removed and he was told that salt water and swimming would be beneficial, they ran to the beach laughing with the excitement of children let out of school. Their bodies touched in the water with the jolt of electric eels, lithe and slippery.

By now much recovered, Constance offered to undertake light nursing duties in the clinic. They planned something special for her last free day – an excursion together. The village was hewn from the soft, oxblood-red rocks of the mountain, a short way inland from Benicasim. Houses clustered together, piling upwards to form an irregular pyramid that had changed little since medieval times. Karl was delighted by the fortifications, the castle, the immense walls, and the narrow zigzagging streets that dated from Arab days, long before the Re-conquest. One of the ambulance drivers at the hospital had told them about the place, and the mineral waters that gushed from a spring into several pools nearby, ideal for swimming. He had offered to drop them there on his way to Valencia and collect them on his return. They had longed for just such a chance to spend a day alone together. Privacy was virtually impossible in Benicasim. The walking wounded were everywhere, exercising to regain strength. Those who were confined to the verandas often killed the boredom of the long hours when there were no classes by watching everyone else.

The day was still cool when they left the village to walk to the spring that lay hidden in the hills. The path meandered between pale green olive trees and small dark, evergreen oaks. Their bare legs brushed against the leaves of rosemary and thyme by the side of the path, releasing a fragrance that lingered on their skin. They rounded a corner and the pools lay before them, deep and tranquil, only disturbed by the cascades of water falling from above, flowing over the rocks to form an eddy between the banks at the far end.

'Well,' thought Constance pragmatically, 'if ever there was a time and place to lose one's virginity, this is it.'

She didn't want to alter the mood of the day, however, by announcing her decision to Karl. It would be better, she decided, to allow things to take their natural course. In truth, she was rather nervous about the whole thing. It was of course, a healthy, normal biological function, but Constance, desperately anxious to please Karl, had no training or expertise to rely on in this instance. She had no fear of men's bodies; the problem was rather that she knew them so well - unfortunately, inside as well as out. Ruptured organs, severed muscles, fragmented bones, if she closed her eyes she could see them all vividly, freshly imprinted on her mind. Could the act of love that inflamed the passions of other men and women turn out for her to be no more than a brief encounter of fleshy tissues?

As the sun warmed the water they swam together in the pool. Karl was growing stronger, he could nearly keep up with her. Nobody disturbed them, the pool was theirs, the world was theirs. Wrapped in each others arms, they sank beneath the surface, to emerge spluttering and laughing a few moments later. Lying side by side on towels spread on the warm sandy earth by the side of the pool, Karl captured her hand in his and examined it, stroking the palm with his forefinger. Despite her enforced rest from nursing, there were still traces of roughness from the constant scrubbing needed when working in the theatre. Constance turned over his hands, and tenderly touched the calluses there, sad for a moment to think that a man like Karl, who so obviously loved to teach, should have to wield a gun instead of a pen.

When Constance looked into his eyes, she was overjoyed. Frequently, it was no more than the gleam of lust she saw lurking in the sly glances of men. She could identify it with ease and abhorred its power of devastation. She had heard many women in childbirth scream curses on the men whose lusts had led to their pain. But although desire burned in Karl's steady gaze, there was love there too. With confident hands, each slowly explored new terrains, smooth curves, exciting textures. Constance discovered a beauty she had never noticed before in the sweep of a thigh, in the ripple of muscles. The sensations that enveloped her left no room for the doubts that had troubled her earlier – she was lost in the moment.

Karl knew that this was no transient affair. His home and his country were lost to him for the present, but here in Spain he had found a woman who could fill the emptiness in his heart. Carefully, remembering her injuries, his lips caressed hers. When she responded to his tentative overtures with unmistakeable enthusiasm he ventured further. It was disconcerting at first for him to find that Constance, usually so self assured and knowledgeable in matters physical, obviously had no previous personal experience of lovemaking. But slowly, with infinite concern for each other's happiness, they moved together.

As they lay with their limbs peacefully and contentedly

interwoven, Constance felt as if her senses had all been finely tuned. Birdsong that she normally didn't notice was filling the air with melodies. The greens of the leaves above her had a multitude of shades that shifted as they moved. Karl's hair, still slightly damp, had the merest touch of wet dog about it, a smell she remembered from her earliest childhood when the spaniels had come in from the rain. The nearness of death, she knew, was largely responsible for this increased awareness of life, and for the rapid development of her relationship with Karl. There was no point in wasting time when time might be so short. Karl's thoughts drifted too, raising questions with painful answers. 'How many soldiers rest wearily on this warm earth when the guns fall silent for a while? All of us... How many are lucky enough to lie on that same hard ground in the arms of the woman they love? Very few... How many will be held forever in the intimate embrace of the Spanish soil, till their bones are chilled by winter? Too many...'

They had brought a picnic. The bread was rather stale, but the small tin of processed meat was a special treat. They toasted each other's health in the robust local wine, and drank to victory. Karl told her about his life in Dresden, how he had been sent to a labour camp for protesting against Hitler's programme of repression and murder. With another two prisoners, he had escaped. His friends had been captured but he had been luckier and had fled across the border. Fighting in Spain was the best way to begin the long struggle to win back his homeland. They made plans for their future, what they would do and where they would live when the war in Spain was over. The idea of not sharing the future together was inconceivable.

As they talked, Constance idly touched the newly healed skin of his arm, appraising the progress of scar tissue. But her fingers gradually lost their professional approach and sent quite different messages to the sensory nerves all over her body, especially those that had been newly awakened. When

Karl suggested that they went for another swim, at first she felt disappointed. But he held her close to him in the water beside the rocks and as the water lapped against her breasts, her disappointment was soon replaced by delight.

They swam again in the late afternoon sunlight, diving deep into the pool where the water was cool, then warming themselves on the bank, sleek and content like well-fed otters. As they gathered up their belongings, Karl showed her the photographs that he kept in his wallet, his father and mother, and one of himself taken just before he left for Spain. He gave it to her. She had nothing to give him. He said it didn't matter, he would never forget her face as she looked at that moment, even if he lived to be a hundred. Constance knew that she would love him for ever.

CHAPTER 5

Winds of Change

I

Rose sat between Constance and Addie in the auditorium, wishing she could escape the echoes of a thousand female voices. Her hands moved unceasingly, fluttering in her lap, the fingers picking round the nails like enamoured budgerigars nibbling each other's beaks. Constance had been shocked to see the transformation in Rose a mere three months after they had met in Madrid. Although she knew that her own face had acquired several visible scars since then, Rose's eyes, heavily ringed by purple-grey circles, showed signs of deeper damage within.

Nightmares were tormenting Rose till she feared to sleep. After leaving the hospital at Villamalea, she had been sent to work with a mobile unit near Zaragoza. Within days, a flood of casualties arrived, the human wreckage from a disastrous attempt to recapture the nearby town of Fuentes de Ebro. Rose's friends from the first days in Spain, Ada and Madge, went with a small team from the unit to set up a casualty collecting post just behind the front lines. Meanwhile, Rose worked for hours on end in triage, having to choose over and over again - theatre, transfer to the rearguard, no further treatment. Then the startling high notes of a woman's cries pierced through all the usual noises of pain. Rose looked up and saw that Ada and Madge were amongst the newly arrived batch of wounded, together with the Catalan doctor they had all been working with for several weeks.

Never had the choices to be made in triage been so agonising. Fortunately, Madge only had superficial wounds and was transferred to a base hospital immediately. Rose chose to send Ada straight into the theatre, believing that there was a good chance she would survive. Meanwhile the Catalan doctor had slipped into unconsciousness, despite all Rose could do. He was bleeding internally and needed surgery, but both operating tables were in use. He was such a nice man, stocky and kind, always polite to the nurses. Rose had been full of admiration for his neat, quick incisions, his gentle handling of tissue, and the precision of his suturing. Helplessly, she watched him die.

Afterwards, she couldn't stop going over the episode in her mind, hearing his last light exhalation, then returning again to the moment when he had been carried into the tent with Ada. She had only checked his injuries very superficially, relying more on his quiet reassurances that he would be fine, although she could see a ghastly pallor creeping into the mucous membranes of his gums and round the rims of his eyelids. Ada, however, had been almost incoherent, whimpering with pain. A tourniquet was controlling the bleeding from a deep wound on her thigh. She could lose her leg if surgery was delayed. For a moment, Rose was undecided. Suddenly, she felt an overwhelming affinity with Ada; a nurse, just like she was, but with an overall soaked in her own blood instead of other people's. Scrawled on the sticking plaster in the middle of her forehead was the quantity of morphia she had been given at a first aid post. It had been a large dose, yet still she was in pain. Rose told the orderlies to take her through to theatre. Now, her tired mind kept asking the same question. Had she made the right decision? Would the doctor have lived if she had sent him in first? Would Ada have died or lost her leg if she had not been sent in straight away? Such decisions were a normal part of the work in triage, but when the faces of friends emerged from the mass of the wounded, the choices were torture.

In the harsh light of day, Rose was aware that she could never know for certain whether she had made the right choice. The re-awakened memory of her sister's death had left her raw with remorse. Now the new guilt piled heavily on top of the old, landing like an immense black crow on a heap of carrion, cawing at her unceasingly from its grisly perch. At night she dreamed of standing in triage, surrounded by the dying, in agonies of indecision. Who to choose? Who to leave? She wanted to escape from the groans of pain and run away, but where could she go? The distant explosions would grow closer, but still she couldn't move. She would awake sweating and rigid with fear at the very moment when a blast ripped her apart, her own screams still ringing in her ears.

The shrill clamour in the hall reached a crescendo and Rose felt her skull would split. A sudden silence fell on the voluble crowd as La Pasionaria entered. As delegates to the National Conference for Women, they had all been eagerly waiting for this speech. Addie watched Rose anxiously, casting sidelong glances at her as surreptitiously as she could. She had thought that bringing Rose back to Barcelona would help her to pull herself together and that the conference would be a distraction. Now she was not so sure. Rose seemed unable to cope with anything at the moment and Addie was beginning to regret that she had not arranged for her to go back to England straight away. Though apparently pleased to see her friends again, Rose's attention was inclined to drift elsewhere in mid-sentence. She barely noticed their amazed reactions to the news of her marriage to Rafael, despite the relish with which she had anticipated the moment a few weeks earlier. But, Addie decided, her usual optimism predominating, perhaps it was better to wait a while before sending Rose home. She had so often shown that she was tougher than she looked. Maybe she just needed to rest for a few days.

La Pasionaria spoke clearly and slowly. Constance found she could understand nearly all that she said, perhaps because her recent conversion to communism had given her a whole new vocabulary, one that she shared with the sturdy woman speaking so eloquently on the stage. The Spanish phrases relating to the fight for peace, liberty and justice were very familiar to her after hours of intense conversations with Karl and friends of different nationalities. Who could fail to be stirred by La Pasionaria's cry, 'Better to die on your feet than live on your knees'? Another familiar slogan was greeted with cheers from the audience, 'Better to be the widow of a dead hero than the wife of a live coward.' A fleeting uneasiness crossed Constance's mind. The possibility of over-zealous women, eager for vicarious glory, goading their meek and mild husbands into playing the role of intrepid heroes, did seem in rather poor taste. But, the thought was soon lost as she was caught up again in the flow of the rich oratory.

Constance had been asked to represent the British medical staff at the conference before returning to full-time duty. Karl had already rejoined the Thaelmann Battalion. She had received one letter from him - a beautifully written avowal of his love for her, followed by several pages clarifying the benefits of socialism. When she moved, she could just feel the thin paper, folded four times, tucked safely into her brassière. The talk Constance had given on medical advances in front-line hospitals had been well received by the other delegates. Now she listened to La Pasionaria with a hungry intensity. It was not Karl speaking, but the words could have been his.

Addie could see the fervour in Constance's eyes. She too thought La Pasionaria was a remarkable person, and that her ability to lift the morale of soldiers and civilians was vital to the war effort. Nevertheless, she could not wholeheartedly share Constance's enthusiasm for the Communist Party. They hadn't had time to talk properly yet, but they could both sense great changes in each other since they last parted. As they were all staying together at the flat, there would be plenty of opportunity for talking later on. At the moment, apart from María, the flat was empty, though a new contingent of nurses was expected to arrive at any moment. Addie had been spending as little time as possible there. The atmosphere of the place was contaminated somehow by María's malevolent personality. Rather than offering a shoulder to cry on when nurses were homesick or ill, she often brought them to the brink of hysteria, telling them they were useless and ought to go home. Addie also had heard a string of complaints about her from the staff she had been visiting in the units. It was said that she didn't bother to send on the letters that arrived for them in Barcelona and that she sent them parcels of medical supplies so badly wrapped that the contents arrived broken. She was also accused of having a certain select group of favourites within the medical units to whom she would divert supplies that had been designated for others. Reluctantly, Addie was coming to the conclusion that she would have to write a letter of complaint to the Committee as the situation seemed to be getting progressively worse.

Barcelona too, was in marked decline. The streets, like the people, were slowly taking on a weary, hard, grimness. Empty shop windows led to nothing but bare shelves inside. Another winter loomed ahead with the cold prospect of hunger replacing the hope of a swift victory. Since May, Italian aircraft based on Majorca had been bombing the city. Each time they appeared, yet more neat lines of buildings would be interrupted by surprising new voids, and rubble-lined hollows would make even more roads impassable. To escape the bombardments, entire neighbourhoods were banding together to burrow under the city with pickaxes and shovels, excavating complex refuges that ran like rabbit warrens below the streets. The delegates at the conference might be speaking bravely about the way forward for women after the war, but Addie sensed that in the secret corners of their minds the fear of defeat lurked, as terrifying as the Jabberwock that had waited hungrily for her in the shadows of the nursery. Franco had already demonstrated the sort of treatment 'Red' women should expect under his regime. In the areas that had fallen under his control the humiliation of ritual head shavings and castor oil drenches had signalled the return of repression for many women deemed to have been tainted by association with the Left.

Gathering together at the conference had been a wonderful way to raise spirits, Addie reflected, as they rose from their seats to applaud enthusiastically. It was as if their individual hopes reverberated round the room with the applause, merging together and returning to each person, amplified a thousandfold. The delegates spilled out onto the street, an animated and colourful tide, clutching the flowers they had each been given as they left the hall. A few blooms tied together with a thin ribbon triggered a range of thoughts and emotions in those who held them. Rose looked at their cultivated splendour with a melancholy sadness, thinking of the wild flowers she had carried when she married Rafael. Constance, although revelling in their heady scent, couldn't help thinking that the money and effort it had taken to grow the flowers would have been better used in food production. For Addie, their significance was poignant. Even in these troubled days, the importance of beautiful things, of the arts and culture, should not be forgotten. The delegates drifted away, bearing their bright reminders of renewed optimism, not thinking for the moment, of how short-lived cut blooms could be.

María and Constance clashed before they even set eyes on each other. Rose was obviously exhausted when they arrived back at the flat, and Constance wanted to make her some hot chocolate. The door to the kitchen at the end of the long unlit corridor was closed and when she tried the handle, it turned round uselessly. Hearing someone moving at the other side, she called out.

'Hello! I can't seem to get in. Can you open the door for me from that side?'

'You'll have to wait till I've finished eating,' came the

discourteous response, slightly muffled by a mouthful of food.

Constance rightly presumed that the voice must belong to the infamous María, subject of much gossip and speculation in the medical units at the front. Their paths had not crossed until now, but Addie had already mentioned some of the problems she was causing. Constance looked briefly into the adjacent room that overlooked the narrow well in the centre of the block of flats, thinking carefully for a few moments before returning to the kitchen door. In cut glass tones, sharp as a knife, she addressed María again.

'I think you may wish to reconsider and come out now after all, in view of the fact that there appears to be an increasingly strong smell of smoke coming through the bedroom window here. Does the kitchen have a fire escape?'

Fires were becoming a frequent occurrence as fuel shortages forced people to use more dangerous combustibles for cooking and heating. María had seen a block of flats ablaze only the week before, the flames spreading rapidly out of control from what had begun as nothing more than a small accident in a kitchen. Fully aware of the fact that there was little likelihood of a fire escape or any other safety measures in such old flats, Constance listened with a smug satisfaction to the hurried rattling noises coming from the other side of the door as the inside handle with the spindle were hastily replaced.

'Thank you,' she said condescendingly when the door opened to reveal María's alarmed face. María was poised to dash for the stairs, but instead was forced to stand back as Constance swept past her into the kitchen saying breezily, 'The smell appears to have gone now.'

María, mute with anger, could think of no appropriate retort to make for the moment but, giving Constance a look that would have cowed a less confident adversary, she silently vowed to exact revenge at a later date.

When Constance returned to Rose's room with a tray

bearing three cups of cocoa and described the difficulties she had encountered, Addie laughed gleefully.

'One in the eye for María at last. She's always taking the handle off so no one else can go in the kitchen when she's using it. Sometimes she doesn't put it back on properly when she leaves and it falls off. It had rolled into the corner right over by the cupboard the other day. Next time Max is here, I'm going to ask him if he can fix it so it won't come off at all.'

As they sat closely squashed together on the bed just as they had done in Madrid, Rose gradually relaxed, her nerves temporarily calmed by a warm feeling of security. She didn't say very much until Constance produced her photograph of Karl.

'He's very handsome,' she said to Constance, 'but not as beautiful as Rafael. I wish I had a photograph of him to show you.' They debated the finer points of masculine good looks for a while, Rafael's wide eyes with long dark eyelashes versus the classic lines of Karl's features and his soft golden-blonde hair.

Addie was still wondering if her affair with Byron had any long term prospects at all. When Constance told her about having seen him in Belchite, her immediate thought was that he might have been seriously wounded. Constance, seeing her shocked expression, had hurriedly reassured her that his wound had been slight and passed on the message she had been given.

'What is this research he's talking about then?' she asked with curiosity.

Addie, despite being a modern American girl in many ways, felt a warm flush rising to her cheeks and knew her face must be as red as the carnations amongst the flowers from the conference.

'Aha!' cried Constance, 'this blushing indicates an underlying heart condition. We must learn more about the causes. Rose, will you help me with the diagnosis?'

The process of finding out a little more about Addie and Byron's interlude in Madrid revived for a while the buoyant mood of their days together three months earlier. 'Well,' said Addie at last, 'Byron may not be so handsome as Karl or Rafael but it would be difficult to find a better bottom, especially in action.'

'How on earth do you know?' asked Constance in disbelief, 'I wouldn't have thought you were in any position to see.'

'Wardrobe mirrors,' answered Addie, 'are useful for more than just checking the seams of your stockings.' Even Rose managed a watery smile. But it was not easy to keep to light-hearted subjects for long. All three now had more personal reasons for worrying about what was happening at the front in addition to their concerns for the fate of the Republic. There was always a high price to pay for love in wartime.

II

The next morning, with the first real taste of chill autumn breezes, the new nurses arrived from England. María, who hated getting up early, was still in bed so Addie let them into the flat, chattering and cheerful as they surveyed their new surroundings. Excitedly, they plied her with questions about the medical units. Addie was taken aback by their youthful freshness and enthusiasm, wondering in amazement if she had appeared so 'green' to others when she had first arrived. It seemed so long ago. She still believed in the aims of the Republic, but perhaps influenced by talks with Byron, she had doubts about some of the leaders and their methods. A cold shard of cynicism had touched her, as icy as the fingers of the Snow Queen. And what about her friends? She suddenly could see clearly how much they had changed too. Beneath her usual cool veneer, Constance was consumed with love for Karl, passionate about her newfound beliefs, her emotions aflame as if with a virulent fever. Could her energies burn so brightly for long? Poor Rose was a wreck. Even though Addie knew nothing about the memories that were haunting Rose so tirelessly, it was plain to see that she was retreating from reality.

'We've all been changed by the men who've entered our lives, and almost as much by their absence as their presence,' Addie concluded sadly. A few brief days of happiness would now be followed by months spent anxiously waiting to know if they were alive or not. Even when a message from them got through, it was old news, and anything could have happened since then. Addie suddenly knew there was no possibility of ever again being as they had been before, or as blithely carefree as these new arrivals seemed to be. She looked properly for the first time in months at her shabby clothes, comparing them with the neat, clean attire of the newcomers. Almost everyone who had been working in Spain for a while wore rope-soled sandals and odd mismatched remnants. Even Rose had been unable to maintain former standards. The ravages of war made a distinct impression on sartorial elegance. 'Without even noticing,' mused Addie, 'we've moved from wearing the styles on the pages of Vogue or Woman's Realm to modelling jumble sale rejects.'

One of the new nurses, Harriet, drew Addie's attention immediately, and not only because the sight of her well-cut, warm woollen coat and comfortable hand-made leather shoes filled her with envy. Harriet was the daughter of a prominent Liberal MP who, much to her father's embarrassment, had recently caused quite a stir by getting herself arrested for throwing red ink all over the steps of Number 10 Downing Street. 'The blood of Spanish people, spilled because of British government support for non-intervention,' she had shouted as she was being escorted away by two burly policemen. Her decision to volunteer to go to Spain was given wide coverage by the press. Over breakfast, she showed them a newspaper article that had appeared a few days previously, with photographs showing her in an evening gown and in nurse's uniform. The article said that they would be following her 'adventures' in Spain, and already they had taken pictures of her at the docks when the group set off from England. She was also the subject of much local interest in her home town of Manchester. A committee had been formed there to collect money and medical equipment. This would be sent directly to Harriet in Spain so she could set up a 'Manchester Ward' in the hospital where she was working. Although her manner was a little flashy, she was good-natured and charming. Addie liked her, and was sure that with her many high-profile friends and supporters in Manchester, she would doubtless attract substantial sums in donations.

The other two girls seemed good sorts, both recently qualified. Janet was a big-boned Scottish redhead with hundreds of freckles that were already burgeoning into a previously unattained prominence in the Mediterranean sunshine. Her two brothers were in the Brigades. Elsie was a Lancashire girl with an accent so broad it was an effort to understand what she was saying. She also had the habit of speaking in a series of never-ending clauses with no pauses for punctuation. Nothing short of interruption would stop her when she was in full flow. Harriet had already mastered a technique for doing this without seeming too rude. With Janet, Harriet had begun to form a humorous double act, based on quick-witted banter. It was clear to Addie that if Harriet were as skilful at nursing as she was at getting on with people, she would be a great asset. They all sat round the table for a while, hungrily eating the breakfast prepared by Asunción who, in addition to her duties as caretaker, now did much of the cleaning and food preparation in the Medical Aid flat. These responsibilities had originally been María's but she had managed to offload them by telling the

Committee that she had too many other things to do.

During breakfast, Elsie began talking about her work in the cotton mills before she began to train as a nurse. She had tried to start a union because the working conditions were so bad, but the other girls just laughed and called her 'Bolshie'. Then she showed them her hand. Part of a finger was missing. It had been lost in the machinery of the mill along with countless other severed fingers of the women who worked there, all desperately rushing to fill quotas. Rose was the only one at the table who turned her head away, not wanting to see the disfigurement. She was accustomed to war-time amputations, but hated to look at Elsie's hand, so irrevocably branded by poverty. She loathed Elsie's voice too, wincing inwardly at her grammar and the distinctive Lancashire vowels. Elsie continued to talk about the mills. How the girl went on! Why wouldn't she just shut up. Rose gave her a look of undisguised scorn. Elsie unfortunately caught sight of Rose at just that moment, whereupon her monologue faltered to be followed by an uncomfortable silence.

Rose inwardly cursed herself for being so careless as to give her true feelings away in front of everyone. Some people were content to be 'common', she thought crossly, and she couldn't help it if she disliked them, but it would be better to keep her views to herself. Suddenly, her mind flashed back to her first meeting with Constance, when she had thought her so snobbish. She was struck by the realisation that in truth, she was more of a snob herself. Certainly, Constance often treated others with condescension, but this had little to do with their social class. It was just that she never suffered fools gladly, whatever their upbringing had been. Rose experienced a brief twinge of envy for Elsie, who was obviously not ashamed of her family and was proud to be working-class. For a few seconds, Rose wished she could feel the same way, and was almost embarrassed by the disdain she had felt for Elsie, but the moment passed quickly. She'd pulled herself out of the gutter, and she wasn't about to befriend those who were happy to have their roots firmly planted there. It didn't occur to her that the past would always be with her, it had made her what she was, that it was impossible to leave it behind.

María eventually appeared, in a particularly foul mood. Even Harriet was unable to make much headway with her. She crashed and banged around the kitchen, sulking because she had been asked to write a report on the distribution of medical supplies to the various units. Her belligerent presence soon led the others to make hasty exits. The new nurses set off to look round Barcelona before leaving for Albacete that evening. Addie was going to take Constance and Rose to visit the Quakers at the canteen. María called out to her from her room just as they were leaving.

'I'll need to use your car today. Where are the keys?'

Sighing, Addie went to the room María had co-opted as an office to give her the keys. It was no use expecting María to ask for anything politely, or to thank you for it either. As she came in with the keys, María was scooping together piles of papers spread out on her large desk to put them in a folder. Amongst them were quite a number of unopened letters. Addie's attention was suddenly drawn to one of the envelopes because the writing was in her mother's familiar hand, clearly addressed to Miss A. E. Maclaurin.

'I think this letter is for me,' she said in surprise, snatching it from the pile. When she saw the date on the postmark, she could feel hot anger boiling up inside her. The letter had been posted over a month earlier. It had probably been sitting in María's office for ages. Beneath it was another, also addressed to her but in handwriting she did not recognise.

'These seem to have been here some time,' she said through clenched teeth, 'are there any more?'

'Oh, are they for you?' María replied carelessly, 'I'd forgotten your surname. You can have a look through if you want.'

Addie furiously sorted through the letters, some addressed to nurses she knew in the units. Another was for Constance.

'I'll take this too, to give to Constance now. What about these others? Do you want me to help deliver some of them?'

'If you like, or I'll give them to the drivers at the depot sometime.'

Addie could feel that she was rapidly losing patience. 'María,' she exclaimed angrily, 'some of them may be urgent, and the nurses are always longing for news from home. You shouldn't just leave the letters sitting here.'

'You deal with them then,' María retorted, 'I have more important things to do.'

Picking up all the letters she could find, Addie left the room, more determined than ever to complain to the Committee about María's incompetence as soon as she could find a free moment.

The letter from her mother had a few lines of family news, but much more about the Basque Children's Colony that had been set up in a village just outside Cambridge. Twenty-nine orphaned refugees from the northern regions of Spain were now housed in a former vicarage. Virginia, Addie's mother, chaired the committee responsible for their care. Fund raising was nearly a full-time job, as there was no support from the British government. The children were helping by performing their national songs and dances all over the country, and had even been invited to give concerts by the hotel manager in a Swiss ski resort. A press cutting was enclosed with a photograph, showing the children in traditional dress, with the headline, 'They Embraced Our Cameraman'. Apparently, the warm-natured Spanish children were making quite an impression whereever they went. The other letter for Addie was from Professor Burchill. The rather pompous style in which he wrote did not entirely mask his feelings. He obviously still held on to the hope that they would see more of each other when she returned. The thought that she had, even for a second, contemplated a physical relationship with the Professor now seemed incredible to Addie. Byron had certainly set a standard that would be difficult to surpass. She resolved to write to the long-suffering professor as tactfully as possible to avoid prolonging his misery any longer.

Constance's letter was from her mother, parts of which she read out to Rose and Addie. Jessica had been gathering news from Lady Cunningham about Diana's experiences in Spain, nursing Franco's troops.

> Diana is in Jérez at the moment having a holiday from nursing. She is staying there on her way back from Gibraltar where she had picked up a car her father sent out for her, a rather nice one I understand, with green leather seats. Nancy tells me that Diana has been seeing a lot of Freddy. I believe she has high hopes for a good match there before long. They have been going about with a group of Freddy's pilot friends from the Luftwaffe - swimming, dancing, and riding at an Arab stud. I fear Diana may be becoming a rather fast young woman without a strong hand there to guide her, but should she marry into the Spanish aristocracy it would certainly be a feather in Nancy's cap.

'German pilots!' exclaimed Constance angrily, 'How can Diana be friends with them after what they did to Guernica? They blasted it to bits. How on earth can my mother worry about Diana's reputation and not be the slightest bit concerned about the fact that she's helping the Fascists?' She angrily returned to reading the letter.

Apparently Diana will be returning to a hospital near the front again soon, in the Teruel area I believe. Nancy was horrified to learn that the nurses are even expected to look after the Moors. Can you imagine it? I would have thought that they would have been cared for separately by their own kind. I'm so glad that there aren't any Moors on your side, dear.

Constance grinned sardonically at the thought of what her mother would say if she knew that her daughter too occasionally nursed Moors when they had been captured. When they were brought in they were often terrified, believing that they were going to suffer the same treatment as they meted out to their own prisoners. But rather than torture, they received a reasonable level of care as a matter of principle, though usually without quite the degree of concern given to other casualties. That was the general rule with enemy wounded, standard medical treatment with no frills. Constance folded the letter impatiently and put it away, annoyed with her Mother's blinkered attitudes and lack of understanding about the seriousness of the situation. She had quite forgotten that only a year earlier she had known nothing about Spain either, and that politics had been no more than the distant droning of nameless men, and that she had never even heard of Moors. She decided to embarrass her mother by sending her one of the rampantly 'red' propaganda postcards that were currently popular in the Brigades. 'Let's see if she takes that to tea at Lady Cunningham's,' she thought with a touch of malicious satisfaction.

Feigning deep regret, Addie reminded her friends of their agenda for the day. 'I apologise ladies, I'm afraid I have no new car, or even an old one, to take you to a glittering array of social events. Instead we will be walking to the Quakers' canteen to serve cocoa till we drop, and then returning for a meal of garbanzos and bacalao - the chickpea and dried cod dinner of your dreams.'

III

As they rounded the corner, tired from the hours they had spent on their feet in the canteen and wearied by the endless stream of suffering they had seen, they were confronted by a scene that would remain forever imprinted on their minds. Dusk was falling and the unlit streets were uniformly sinking into shadow, except for one large rectangle of flickering luminous orange that stood out against the matt dark walls of the building, high above the street. A silhouetted figure moved from side to side, outlined like a shadow puppet performing in the candlelight. Mesmerised for a moment, they watched open mouthed until Addie murmured, almost under her breath, 'Oh God, the flat's on fire!' Together they ran down the road, realising as they drew nearer that the person now balancing so precariously on the windowsill was Harriet. Neighbours were starting to drag mattresses out on to the pavement, but they were getting in each other's way and blocking the doorways. Smoke began to billow out of the window, and fanned by the gusts of a cold night wind, fingers of flame caught hold of the frame. For a moment, Harriet stood on the window ledge, as silent as the screaming woman in Picasso's painting of Guernica. Then she leapt outwards, her dress a blazing comet's trail as she fell.

Constance pushed her way through the neighbours to where Harriet lay, but could see instantly that the sickening impact had been fatal. Her face was unmarked save for a few smudges of smoke, but the strange angle formed between her head and shoulders left no room for doubt. Constance covered her with the singed blanket that had been used to smother her flaming clothes. From inside the flat came the noise of splintering wood and shouting. Addie was already running up the stairs, and her friends followed close behind her. The door to the flat was open, and the corridor leading to the kitchen was full of smoke. Several men had managed to break down the kitchen door and were carrying the unconscious Elsie to safety. She was still alive, but mingling with the smoke fumes was another, more nauseating smell that both Rose and Constance recognised instantly, even before they were close enough to see the burned flesh. Listening to Elsie's rattling breaths, Constance looked at the splintered and charred remnants of the door hanging on its hinges, and remembered with horror how only the day before she had stood outside the same door, luring María to open it by pretending that there was a fire. For a fleeting moment she felt as if her careless words had tempted the Fates too far.

More and more people were rallying round, forming a chain to pass buckets of water to the kitchen. Fear that the fire would spread to their own flats spurred them on to make prodigious efforts and the flames were soon being doused continually. The black-grimed face of the neighbour who had carried Elsie out, father of a huge brood of children, stopped for a moment to ask how she was. He already had a theory worked out for the cause of the fire.

'Looks to me like an explosion, probably the can of fuel for the stove blew up. This poor little girl must have been knocked out or something so she couldn't open the door.'

Another neighbour who had witnessed the events in the street was puzzled.

'I wonder why the other one tried to get out of the window? She must have thought there was a way down outside, or perhaps she tried the door and it was jammed. The explosion could have blasted it shut with tremendous force.'

'That must be it,' said their neighbour, 'we couldn't open the door from outside either.'

Addie bit back what she had been about to say. In their haste to break into the kitchen, the men hadn't had time to examine the door carefully. When they had broken in, they hadn't noticed that the handle on the other side had probably been missing. A painful lump rose in her throat at the realisation that the newly arrived nurses hadn't been told about María's peculiar habits - they wouldn't have known where to look for the handle. They had been trapped, Elsie probably injured in the blast, Harriet unable to break down the door. Suddenly, she gasped as another dreadful thought came to her. There were three new nurses. 'What about Janet? She must still be in there.'

'There wasn't anyone else,' said Elsie's rescuer. Nevertheless, a hint of uncertainty crept into his voice at the thought that they could have left one of these young foreign girls inside. He pushed his way as fast as he could through the line of neighbours to the kitchen, shouting to others to help him search the room again, though all knew there would be no chance of finding anyone alive. He came out, shaking his head. The dripping, blackened remains of the kitchen held no further horrors, only the sweating shapes of those who were beating out the last flames amongst the wreckage with soaking wet rugs. Turning to Rose and Constance, Addie said with relief, 'Janet must have gone out somewhere on her own. She'll probably be back soon. I'll stay here till she gets back, you go with Elsie to the hospital and we'll join you there later.'

But within an hour, Constance and Rose were back from the hospital. Mercifully, in view of her extensive burns, Elsie had died without regaining consciousness. Asunción embraced them both warmly as she let them in, and took them to her own remarkably uncomfortable living room. There, sitting on straight-backed hard chairs at the table, surrounded by a typical selection of bizarre Spanish bric-a-brac, Addie was talking to a trembling Janet. She had not known how Janet might react to the news of what had happened, and had steeled herself to face the worst. But Janet was grimly holding her emotions in check, her lips compressed into a thin resolute line, though her face was drawn and her freckles had paled almost to invisibility. She stared down at the small cup on the table before her. Asunción had filled it with syrupy coffee substitute and had kindly added a sizeable shot of brandy. At the news that Elsie too had died, silent tears ran down Janet's cheeks, but she didn't say a word. She downed the coffee in a single gulp. 'This girl's got her fair share of grit,' thought Addie, watching her closely. It was a habit she was acquiring as part of her job, always observing the nurses carefully, alert for signs of impending problems. She was good at her work; the nurses confided in her, knowing that she didn't gossip, and when it came to sorting out practical problems, they could rely on her completely. She would be keeping an especially close watch on Janet after such a traumatic introduction to Spain.

Indeed, Addie too felt very shaken by the tragic deaths of the two girls. 'But I'm getting hardened to such things,' she realised with astonishment, 'and so is Constance.' This wasn't the first time that people she had known had been killed, and it certainly wouldn't be the last. War stalked through their lives, a skeletal figure animated by a daily ration of deaths, growing strong on the diet of destruction which it consumed with an insatiable greed. Both Addie and Constance took its presence for granted, and even recognised that it sometimes came accompanied by a surprising companion - the joy of being alive. However sad they felt about the tragic events of the day, they knew they would be able to carry on. At first glance, it appeared that Rose too had born the evening's events well. She had been calm and efficient when dealing with Elsie, and had said the same sort of sympathetic platitudes to Janet as everyone else. But Addie now had time to notice that Rose was functioning like a clockwork doll, her eyes always vacant, as if the deaths of Harriet and Elsie had not actually touched her in the slightest.

Asunción had decided to take them all under her motherly wing. The flat upstairs reeked of smoke, so she made up beds for them in the rooms left empty by her sons. They were away fighting battles in parts of Spain she had never seen, nor wanted to see. Barcelona was where she had been born, as had her parents and grandparents. There couldn't possibly be anywhere better. She liked these foreign girls, though she couldn't understand how their mothers could have allowed their unmarried daughters to travel alone to a foreign country. If she had daughters, they would be kept safely at home, despite all the modern talk being bandied about these days. In her opinion, females who stood on the street corners shouting about joining associations of 'Free Women' just weren't respectable at all. Taking Janet off to one of the bedrooms, Asunción left the others sitting round her table. They were exhausted but not in the right frame of mind for sleep.

'I wonder when María will turn up?' said Addie in a desultory fashion.

'And the gentlemen from the press,' added Constance, with a grimace. 'It won't just be the newspapers here that will be writing reports. I don't suppose it will be of that much interest to people in Spain when there are so many dying all the time, but the British press will be on to it as soon as they realise that Harriet was one of those who died. It sounded as if her father was someone quite important.'

Rose unexpectedly entered the conversation, her former distracted air dispelled at the mention of the press. She had dreamed of having her photograph in the newspapers as a heroine home from the wars, but this story sounded like trouble. 'It will cause a terrible scandal when they find out about her being trapped in the kitchen. I don't want to have anything to do with it.' The nervous movements of her hands were back with a vengeance.

'Oh God, you're right, it will be headline news,' said Addie, her heart sinking.

'The Tory papers will have a field day,' added Constance, 'Imagine what they'll say about the Committee, sending girls out to die in such a senseless way, through the idiocy of their own staff rather than under enemy fire. I think we should all just keep quiet about the stupid door handle business. Things will be bad enough without that.'

'But María mustn't get away with it,' protested Addie crossly. 'She should be punished, or at least be given the sack for what she did. I know I'm partly to blame. I should have reported her ages ago, but I can't stand by and say nothing, even if I get into trouble myself.'

'You're being selfish,' Constance said stonily. 'You feel guilty, and you want to make a futile gesture to make up for it. What's done is done. They're dead and we can't bring them back. You can find another way to get rid of María. If you make a fuss about this and tell the press the truth, it will do nothing but bring bad publicity for the cause. Any donations to the Spanish Medical Aid Committee are bound to drop dramatically, and then where will we be? We'll have even fewer medical supplies for our wounded than we have now, and goodness knows, we have little enough of them as it is. How many legs will we have to amputate without anaesthetic just because you needed to clear your own conscience?'

Addie bridled angrily, knowing that there was an element of truth in the accusation, and that she did indeed feel guilty about her own shortcomings. But the more she had thought about it, the more she wondered if the rumours about María being some sort of enemy agent were true, however far-fetched they seemed. There was no doubt she was a troublemaker, but the question was, 'why?' Addie snapped back at Constance, her anxiety making her unusually abrupt.

'If we do nothing, and María remains in her present post, do you want to take the responsibility if she does something even more damaging? She has plenty of opportunity to sabotage our work, not just in small ways as she has already been doing, but to do something much worse.'

They had both disregarded Rose during this exchange,

but at this point she leaned forward and grasped Addie's arm with a fierce intensity. 'Please don't say anything about it, Addie,' she begged, 'the journalists would ask us all so many questions, and ...' Her hands flew to her mouth and she paused, as if by smothering the words she could stop the thought, but it came tumbling out. '...and the police too! We could all be taken to prison.' Everyone knew that in Spain people were sometimes kept locked up for weeks, just for questioning. Childhood memories of visiting her father in Wormwood Scrubs were bringing her to the point of hysteria. She had no doubt that Spanish prisons would be much worse than even the Scrubs.

Addie was torn. Leaving María in her post would be like having a loose cannon at your back. You'd never know when she might cause a catastrophe. And anyway, making compromises about the truth was singularly abhorrent to her. Her outspoken nature had combined with an upbringing based on George Washington's 'I cannot tell a lie' to make it difficult for her to dissimulate in any way. She knew that it was unlikely there would be much of an investigation into the circumstances surrounding the fire unless she spoke out. 'Accidental death' would be the verdict. Everybody had far too many other pressing problems these days. It would be written up as a terrible tragedy by the British press, then the journalists would quickly move on to something else. No one else was likely to say anything - the few other people who knew about María's habit of removing the handle were not in Barcelona, they were in the units scattered along the various fronts. But how unjust it would be if María was not held responsible for what she had done. Two girls had died because of her.

Addie had almost made up her mind to tell the truth when she looked up to see the faces of her friends. Constance, regarding her with a baleful glare, was wondering how Addie could even be contemplating damaging the cause in any way. For her it was a matter of the greater good, not individuals. Addie looked at her with concern. It was worrying, she thought, how Constance seemed to have fallen for a man and an ideology so completely that her critical faculties had atrophied to the point of non-existence. Nevertheless, Constance was right about the likely loss of donations. Addie knew from her experience with the Aid Spain Committee in Cambridge that they would lose supporters if the story were made public. The respectable middle-class matrons who did so much fund-raising for Spain would turn to one of the other charities desperately needing their help if they thought things were being mismanaged. Meanwhile, Rose was looking at her with the vulnerability of a child wanting protection from the dark. Addie found her exasperating, but despite the fact she knew Rose was sometimes weak and selfish, she still couldn't ignore the pleading in her eyes. There was real pain there, as surely as there would be more pain if the already intermittent flow of medical supplies were to diminish. Reluctantly, she capitulated.

'Very well,' she sighed, 'I'll say nothing unless someone asks me a direct question about it.' Relief spread across Rose's face, and Constance gave her a barely noticeable nod of approval, but Addie frowned, knowing that silence would rankle till she had somehow solved the problem of what to do about María.

A new and uncomfortable tension overlaid their parting. They had never really disagreed before and were not sure if their friendship was strong enough to survive the quarrel. When the time came to say goodbye, Addie was acutely aware of how much their paths had diverged, and couldn't help resenting the rather self-righteous air of frosty disapproval that Constance radiated in her direction. Towards Rose, Constance was a little more friendly, saying that she hoped she would feel better after spending time convalescing in the mountains. But even there, a hint of impatience was creeping into her voice. Constance didn't wholeheartedly share Addie's view that a week away from the bombardments would do Rose good. A good sleep followed by hard work was the best remedy in Constance's opinion, rather than sitting around dwelling on things too much.

When Addie had asked Rose if she wanted to go back to England, she had been surprised by her firm 'No'. However much Rose longed to escape from the war, she didn't just want to crawl back home with her tail between her legs. She knew she must somehow get in touch with Rafael too. He had talked about them both going to Italy when the Fascists were defeated, and somewhat belatedly, she had begun to realise what their future together could be like; living in a little village where she couldn't understand the language, surrounded by bambini, and waiting for a husband to come home from some political meeting or other. Such a life was not what she had wanted at all. Her mind was a torment of confusion about what exactly she did want. Perhaps, she hoped, after a week's rest, she would be able to look at things more calmly.

Driving back from taking Rose to the mountains, Addie had time to think over the events of the previous few days. Although not normally one to hold a grudge, she still resented having been forced to stay silent. María had not arrived till late morning on the day after the fire, breezily sailing in after having spent the night on the coast with friends. Her tendency to take impromptu bourgeois vacations at the seaside was another of the many criticisms levelled against her. This time Addie was irritated too by the fact that she had not mentioned that she would be taking the car overnight. Addie could well have needed to use it herself. Once María had verified that all her own possessions were still safe, she showed no concern about the fire and very little about the deaths of Harriet and Elsie. Addie cornered her in the ruins of the kitchen on her return. Idle curiosity had drawn her to the room, but as she had listened to Addie's account of the tragedy, she had merely shrugged her shoulders.

'I didn't know them anyway,' she said carelessly.

'But you were the one mainly responsible for their deaths,' Addie retorted, her voice rising accusingly. 'They were trapped because you had taken the handle off the door.'

'Prove it!' replied María, her hard eyes glinting and the triumph in her voice clear as she regarded the smashed and burnt remains of the door. It was unlikely that any incriminating evidence could be found there after the destruction wrought by neighbours and the fire.

Swallowing her fury, Addie vowed she would watch María carefully until she found a way to remove her and send her somewhere where she wouldn't be able to cause so much damage. Through gritted teeth, Addie asked, 'As the person in charge of the flat, are you at least going to write to the girls' parents?'

'Well, I wasn't here and you were, so you'd better do it. I've got to find another flat till this one can be sorted out.' With that final imperious remark, María marched out of the room, leaving Addie to wonder what ways María would choose to make life difficult for her in the future.

IV

The absurd idea of gigantic rabbits hopping in and out of the round cave mouths almost brought a smile to Constance's chapped lips. She shivered and pulled the old cape closer round her shoulders, trying to gather the folds tightly in her hands without exposing blue fingers to the cold. The high plain of Teruel was covered in deep snow. As far as the eye could see the white hills rolled, their monotony only broken by the outcrops of low dark pines that merged together to form irregular black patches in the distance. The air entered her lungs like icicles, clear and sharp, a world away from Benicasim and the soft humid air of the coast. She longed for vivid colours. Here in the village of Cuevas Labradas the women wore black, the scrawny goats were black, even the bark of the stunted almond trees was black. Before the snow had fallen, relief from the barrenness of the landscape had been provided by a striking palette of reds and oranges in the bare earth, echoed by the tiles on the steeply pitched roofs. But now the rich hues had gone, blanketed in unforgiving whiteness. The only remaining traces of colour to lighten her spirits were in the vast skies of palest blue and in the frosted greens of the olive leaves.

The town of Teruel was just a few miles away. It had fallen to Franco, but the Republicans had launched a new attack to recapture it, hoping to draw the fighting away from Madrid. Constance and several other nurses had travelled to Cuevas Labradas with the medical unit led by Dr Walter to set up a hospital in an old woollen factory on the outskirts of the village. The journey had been a nightmare. Even inside the lorry the temperature was freezing. Their hands and feet ached with cold but there was no room to move to restore circulation. As they climbed up to the plateau, the roads grew more treacherous so at first, the sight of Teruel in the dawn light was a relief. But something about the town, clustered tightly around its Moorish towers and surrounded by a deep gorge, made Constance feel uneasy. Men were dying by the hundreds in the bleak landscape that spread out before her. Was it worse to die amidst such icy barrenness rather than in the warmth of the sun and with a final glimpse of blue skies? Constance didn't know, but was certain that many more men would die because the cold would kill them even if their wounds did not.

She looked up at the caves, set in the cliff above the river bed where the tiniest trickle of water still ran between thickly iced edges. The caves were usually inhabited by a few local families, but now they were filled to capacity because of the shelter they gave from the bombs. Constance had come to the caves looking for young women willing to help with the laundry in the hospital. Uncertain of what courtesy demanded of a visitor, she gingerly pulled aside the thick material hanging inside the first cave mouth just a fraction and nervously called 'Hola' into the shadowy interior. As her eyes grew accustomed to the gloom, she could see an old woman whose guarded features were illuminated by the flickering light of a single lamp. Several children peeped at Constance from behind their grandmother, hiding in her skirts at the sight of the tall, blonde foreigner. The woman invited Constance to enter with a brusque beckoning of her hand.

Once inside, it was a surprise to find that the sandy walls of the cave were dry, and that the fire that sent its smoky plumes through the cave roof gave enough heat to make everything seem almost cosy. Constance, looking at the wary expression on the old woman's face, hesitantly asked if any of her daughters would be prepared to work in the hospital. The wages were not high but would help them a little in these hard times.

'Yes, they will come,' replied the old woman with fierce pride, leaving no room for doubt that her daughters would be turning up for work even though they had not been asked personally. She took Constance to the other side of the table, nearer the fire, where a variety of drawings were propped up on a battered shelf leaning against the wall.

'My grandchildren did these pictures with coloured pencils at school. Before the Republic there were no pencils in the village and no school. Now they are learning to read and write. This is why my daughters will come to help you and,' she added with a toothless grin, pinching Constance's cheek with affection, 'I will come too when I can. I'm not too old to work you know.'

Constance flinched a little at the pain of the old woman's sudden vice-like tweaking of her cheek, already red and sore from the cold. 'I'll never get used to these ferocious displays of affection,' she thought, casting a pitying glance at the children who seemed to tolerate such demonstrations with resignation.

With assurances that several women would arrive at the hospital for work the following morning, Constance ventured out into the cold again to walk back to the hospital. The village houses were ramshackle affairs, with crumbling walls and broken shutters. The only building with any glass in the windows was the church. Despite the shortage of firewood, the villagers had not cut down the remains of a huge elm tree standing in front of the church door. With its knobbly roots and gnarled trunk, it was an object of veneration in the village. She had been told by the locals that 'el olmo' was a thousand years old, a rare specimen. By the time she got back to the hospital her feet were completely numb. Like most people, including the soldiers, she only wore roped-soled 'alpargatas'. She had been horrified to see that some of the women and children in the village didn't even have those. Anyone with boots that didn't leak was considered to be lucky indeed.

One of the constant problems in the draughty old mill they had taken over, was keeping warm. The cavernous hall was open to the high roof, apart from a section separated by a flimsy partition wall where the nurses snatched some sleep if the beds were not being used for wounded men. The operating theatre was in the only other room, formerly the foreman's office. Sometimes it was so cold that the surgeons' hands became too stiff to work and they had to resort to burning alcohol in a bowl to give a few moments of warmth. The nurses' quarters were in the storerooms next to the mill. Old sacks they had hung in the windows to keep out the freezing winds made the place dark and depressing. Their only light came from a small wick burning in olive oil. Despite their efforts to clean the place up, at night a wide variety of suspicious rustling noises came from the roof and the holes in the thick stone walls. Constance preferred to sleep in the ward after her shift on duty. Most of the time she worked with the Spanish girl, Aurora.

Ever since the early days when Constance had shown

her the basics of nursing, Aurora had remained fiercely loyal to Constance, despite anything others had said. Constance was a good teacher and Aurora a willing pupil. The relationship was entirely satisfactory. Constance would ask politely, 'Would you wash the instruments please, Aurora?' and Aurora would always feel a thrill of exaltation at being asked to do something instead of ordered to do it. All her life she had obeyed the orders of her father, her brothers, the priest, her mother, the nuns at school, an endless list of authoritarians who ruled her life with their strictures and demands. However hard the work in the hospital, it was worth it to escape a life where she had felt the weight of tradition bearing down on her with unrelenting pressure. The educational reforms introduced by the Republic had helped her a little, but the war had made her free.

When Constance returned to the ward, she could see no sign of the nurse who was supposed to be on the ward, a normally conscientious, hardworking Welsh girl. A few moments later, she emerged from the empty operating theatre with an obviously captivated Spanish medical orderly in tow. Their smiles disappeared when Constance reprimanded them both for dereliction of duty, not quite as fluently in Spanish as in English, but nevertheless making her message clear. Constance found Aurora behind the partition wall. She had been hoping to snatch some sleep now she was off duty, but her 'lodgers', as Constance always called them, were particularly lively. Despite the cold, lice continued to multiply at an astonishing rate, and everyone was infested with the hungry parasites. Even enduring the paralysing chill of washing oneself brought no relief; they were there in all the clothing waiting for another meal. It was impossible to heat enough water to boil their clothes regularly. Keeping bandages and bedding washed was a full time job in itself. Aurora, with growing desperation for sleep, had resorted to a radical solution to stop the itching. When Constance entered the partitioned area, she was nearly bowled over by the heady smell of ether.

'Aurora!' she exclaimed, 'Whatever are you doing?'

'The lice itch me so much, Constance, I am putting them to sleep for a while,' she replied, her eyes slightly unfocussed.

Aurora was dabbing herself with a small gauze swab soaked in the anaesthetic. The fumes were strong enough to send Aurora to sleep as well as the lice.

'But Aurora, don't you know that ether is highly inflammable? You could go up in flames if someone came near you with a cigarette.'

'I didn't think, I'm sorry, Constance,' said Aurora as she flopped back on to the bed and closed her eyes. Constance took the bottle from her just before she dropped it, and replaced the lid. She opened the curtain hanging across the partition doorway and flapped it about as much as she could to get the air to circulate. With a sigh, she marched back through the rows of beds to take the still damp swab outside, saying clearly in her best Spanish, 'No smoking for a while gentlemen,' adding in English, 'Better to be safe than sorry.' The men protested but did as they were told. Aurora slept on.

A small group of women from the caves arrived the next morning, and attacked the washing and cleaning energetically. They had gathered round Constance to be given their instructions and she had felt herself to be huge and pallid in their midst, rather like an albino pigeon she had seen in Hyde Park, surrounded by excitedly chattering brown sparrows. One of the pleasures most keenly anticipated by all, was smoking. Constance was no exception. Cigarettes were prized like gold dust, even the last few remains of the butts were carefully saved. When Constance lit up a cigarette after the work was done, the local women regarded her with fascination, watching her closely as she inhaled and then blew out the smoke.

'I'm sorry,' Constance said to them as she looked at their rapt faces, 'Does my smoking bother you?'

The old woman she had met in the caves answered her, curiosity and admiration combined in her voice.

'We were always told by the priests that it was wicked for women to smoke. That was just one of the many things women were not supposed to do, whereas they could do what they liked, even seduce the prettiest girls in the vestry. But we've learned a lot since then about the world outside the village and we're not so shocked to see a woman smoking. Do you always hold your cigarette in the same way? Do women always breathe in the smoke like you do?'

Constance soon found herself answering a barrage of questions regarding life for women in England. They wanted to know about everything, from clothes shops and the availability of ready-made dresses, to the frequency with which Englishmen demanded their conjugal rights, a subject upon which Constance was unable to expound in any detail. When she told them that if they learned to read, they could find the answers to many of their questions in books, they excitedly asked if she would teach them. This was something that greatly appealed to Constance. Soon, most of the nurses were helping to teach the women too, spending spare moments in what became known as the 'Reading Corner' in the ward. They amassed an eclectic collection, newspaper cuttings, political pamphlets, and cheap Spanish novellas. A class on signing names ended in triumphant beams all round after each legible achievement. Constance didn't know much about the educational theories of Pestalozzi or Makarenko that she had heard Karl discuss with Felix, but the women were making good progress. Constance was sure that Karl would approve wholeheartedly.

V

As the battle for Teruel intensified, more and more vehicles could be heard passing the village, their engines grinding as they churned through the snow. Ambulances arrived with increasing frequency, but it wasn't just the numbers of patients that grew worse, it was also the injuries they suffered and the brutality of the surgery they required. In Teruel, the ground was rocky and frozen. The men were unable to dig deep trenches so instead of the usual head and chest wounds, they were also being wounded more often in the abdomen and the groin. Constance was always on the alert when the groin cases came back from theatre, hoping to be able to break the news to them gently as soon as they regained consciousness. Spanish men were the most difficult in that respect. As soon as they started to come out of the anaesthetic they would fumble around with their bandages and guess something was wrong. They would feel the tubes they had in their bladders, and what was left of their urethras, and there would be a ghastly shout, 'Madre mía! I'm not a man any more.' The staff had to rush to sedate them and watch to make sure that they didn't commit suicide. Nurses also had to share the agonizing waiting of the men with frostbite. After persuading the drivers to part with some petrol for the primus stove, the nurses would place the patient's affected limb in a bath of tepid water. Eventually, sometimes hours, sometimes days later, a line of demarcation formed. The part that could not be saved turned black and died; a tap on the skin would produce a hollow sound, making one think of the hollow shells of Egyptian mummies. But it had to be done if possible, otherwise the surgeons had to rely on guesswork for their incisions, and who would want to amputate a foot when it was only necessary to sacrifice the toes, or sever the limb above the knee instead of at the ankle? Half-starved rats ventured into the precincts of the hospital to gorge themselves on the amputated limbs awaiting burial. Aurora, catching a glimpse of suspicious movements under a blanket, discovered a particularly strapping specimen gnawing at the stump of an amputee, as he lay fresh from theatre and still under the anaesthetic.

Just when Constance was feeling that nothing would ever relieve the monotony of the chilling cold and the unceasing stream of men suffering from frostbite and worse, Max arrived in a supply lorry. He was working in the transport park in the next village of Perales del Alfambra and, hearing about the English nurses in the hospital, had decided to investigate. From the depths of the lorry's interior, he produced all the essential requirements for a brew-up. The nurses' quarters seemed less daunting with the added presence of Max and the tea. He joked with Aurora, making the normally serious girl laugh more than ever before. Because all the men in her family were so dominating and stern, she found Max's easy humour intriguing. Constance noticed that Max watched Aurora closely as she left the room, and teased him a little about falling for every pair of dark Spanish eyes he met. This he denied vehemently.

They sat together for a while, exchanging news as they cradled the tin mugs of hot tea in their hands. Max told her that Sam was near Teruel too. Constance could vividly imagine what his work as a stretcher bearer must be like, battling through the deep snow. She told Max a little about Karl, hoping that his travels might take him to the Thaelmann Battalion. She scribbled a note for him just in case. There wasn't time to say much more. As Max was leaving, he grasped her hands between his own warm, roughened palms. He knew Constance well enough to realise that the few words she had spoken about Karl were not the whole story. His acute ear for anomalies and strains enabled him to identify the underlying problems of both engines and people. That look of tense anxiety on her face was certainly not for her own safety.

'Don't you worry, luv,' he said, looking steadily into her eyes. 'I'll find your bloke and let him know you're alright.'

Christmas day passed almost unnoticed. The only gift Constance gave was a curious one. An Australian Brigader arrived with an open fracture of the thigh bone. She was preparing him for theatre, cutting through the leg of his trousers to expose the open wound for surgery. When the scissors reached his underpants, he groaned loudly.

'Do you need another shot of morphia?' Constance asked.

'No, no, but please nurse, don't cut my underpants, I shall never be able to get another pair so good and it's so cold in the bloody trenches.'

Constance appraised his grey and tattered underwear with fresh eyes, noting their winceyette warmth rather than their lack of cleanliness. She could see that once upon a time, they had been top quality. Carefully, she rolled up the leg of the underpants as far as she could and secured it neatly with a length of bandage tied in a small bow, hoping that the surgeon would find the exposed area of flesh large enough for his work. Bizarrely, it reminded her of tying up presents, bringing to mind images of other Christmases spent at home. Determined not to become maudlin at the thought of roaring fires, roast turkey and plum pudding, she smiled at her patient, wishing him 'Happy Christmas' as he was carried through to theatre. He gave her a grateful wave. The day did not pass altogether uncelebrated in the end. Max arrived, well scrubbed, with firewood and a couple of chickens. He had paid an exorbitant price for them in bartered goods, but all the staff savoured the taste of their small ration. Constance had never seen Max looking so clean. She wondered if the presence of Aurora had anything to do with it.

For the next few days, the news was good from the front. Most of Teruel was in Republican hands. Could the tide be turning? Everyone in the hospital was fervently hoping that it was so. Medical reinforcements arrived; two nurses and a recently qualified young doctor, originally from South Africa - Reginald Aston. He was working on improving techniques for collecting and storing blood for transfusions in ampoules. Visiting ambulance and lorry drivers tolerated his rather ghoulish habit of waylaying them to replenish supplies because he took their blood painlessly and with such good humour. 'Transfusion Aston' soon featured in a series of anecdotes that were transported with the supplies round the different battalions. He had the appearance of an aesthete; tall but with fine boned hands and small feet, making it easy to characterise him as Count Dracula. One of the two nurses who arrived with him was Janet, the Scottish girl. Neither she nor Constance mentioned the tragic deaths at the flat in Barcelona. It already seemed so long ago, there had been so many deaths since then. Janet was a hard-worker, and soon earned approval from Constance. Florence, despite bearing a name so irrevocably associated with selfless nursing, did not. She was unmistakeably a girl who belonged in the category 'flighty', Constance concluded, after watching her for a few days. She had a habit of flirting with all and sundry that was likely to cause trouble before long. Her manner was open to misinterpretation, especially in the light of cultural differences. The patients' response didn't worry Constance too much, it gave them something to think about other than the war, but the ambulance drivers were a different matter. Men of certain nationalities would have no respect at all for a girl who sent out the wrong signals. Flo, as everyone soon called her, was already being talked about. It wasn't so much that Constance cared on a personal level what Florence got up to, but she minded terribly if nurses were being brought into disrepute. As senior nurse, Constance decided she must find an opportunity to give Florence a quiet word of warning.

The New Year of 1938 began with hopes for victory still hanging in the balance. But the endless biting cold continued to eat away at strength and spirits. By the last days of the month, the rumours of Franco's preparations for a new offensive to retake Teruel were growing. The wind howled. The wounded tried to hold their own howls behind clenched teeth. Constance felt she would never be warm again. She wore several layers of old shirts and two pairs of men's trousers, rolled and gathered at her waist with a canvas belt that was so long it wrapped round her twice. And still she was cold. She shouted in annoyance at the bulky figure, enveloped in a long overcoat, who entered the ward and let in a blast of freezing air. He didn't reply, just removed the blanket that had been wrapped round his shoulders, and the cap that had been pulled down low on his face. When Constance saw the pale gleam of blonde hair, and realised that the face below belonged to Karl, she felt she would faint with joy and relief. She certainly didn't dare try to take a step towards him, fearing her legs would give way. Fortunately, Karl was a man of action. He swept through the ward and gathered her into his arms, holding her as closely as their numerous layers of clothing would allow. Constance, though disconcerted by the cheers of the bedridden men, was not going to let that stop her from returning his embrace. She clung to the rough fabric of his coat and pressed her warm cheek against his ice-cold face. His skin felt as chilled as that of a corpse, but he was alive.

One of the other nurses volunteered to finish her shift for her, so the couple could spend longer together. The nurses' quarters offered little privacy, but in a village like Cuevas Labradas in winter, there was no alternative shelter. For Karl the surroundings were not important anyway. He knew Max was right to call him a lucky man when he had passed on the note from Constance. It had been no easy task to find him, and he was grateful to Max for all the trouble he had taken to track him down. He told Constance how happy he had felt when Max had told him she was nearby.

'I came as soon as I could get leave, but I have had to walk much of the way. I can't stay long.'

He didn't tell her that this was because they were certain another attack was imminent. He only had a few hours to be with her. Constance tried to rub back the circulation into his fingers, automatically checking for signs of frostbite. She noticed his boots were better than most, so his toes were probably alright. There was no talk of whether they still felt the same about each other or not. There just wasn't any doubt. Faces close together, they looked at each other intently. Constance saw new sufferings written in the lines on Karl's gaunt face, adding to those he had borne before Benicasim. She wanted to smooth them all away. Karl saw only his beautiful Constance, the woman he loved and desired above all others. His hunger for her rose from a chronic ache to an exquisite torture.

Making love was not something that Constance would have been likely to choose to do under the circumstances. She was acutely aware of her body, primarily of the variety of impediments to her feeling in any way attractive. She could feel the lice perambulating over her skin, reaching even the most intimate warm places. Her chilblains itched incessantly. Her hair had not been washed for weeks and her armpits smelled. It wasn't that she minded Karl being similarly afflicted, it was just that she didn't want to be like that for him. Added to all that, there was the suspect scratchy straw mattress, and the fact that someone could walk in at any moment. But she couldn't push him away, couldn't say anything hurtful. He was kissing her with a desperate need – it could be the last time, he knew. She knew too. How could she possibly send him back to the front, 'spurned' was the word that sprang to her mind, when she loved him more than anything in the world?

Horribly aware that she was just one of millions of women who had faced the same decision, she chose pretending rather than protesting. A pathway was eventually cleared through the layers of lousy clothing. Constance wondered if these rank bodily smells and uncomfortable sensations would remain with her as clearly as all the pleasurable ones she remembered from the first time they made love by the pool. She couldn't help hoping that they would not. This time, there was no smooth blending of bodies. She tried hard to recapture those feelings but knew she was failing. These desperate, dry, abrasive thrustings defeated all her powers of imagination. She opened her eyes to see Karl looking intently at her face. He stopped moving within her, waiting, watching. A longing grew then within Constance, not so much of physical desire, but passionate nonetheless. How she wished the war was over, that they were making love in a safe world where they were always together, that she could have his child. When they moved again, they were in harmony, but when he cried out with pleasure, she was crying out for the future that they might never share.

Surprisingly, no one came in for the next hour and they were able to spend the precious time talking together, huddled closely. 'Like Babes in the Wood,' Constance thought. Having just experienced her first ever yearnings for maternity, memories of nursery stories were strangely vivid. She was used to witnessing the strength of the biological instinct to survive, but was amazed by the power of the urge to reproduce. 'Quite out of the question.' She buried the sharp pain of it as quickly as she could.

During his walk to the hospital, Karl had been thinking over what he wanted to say to Constance, although he knew however carefully he chose his words, their meaning would be grim and hard. He must say these things quickly, while there was still time.

'I may die, Constance, and you may not. It will be more likely to be this way because I am at the front and death is close to us all the time there. If I am killed, you must go on. You must go on working for the cause and, I ask you this from my heart so I can think of you without worries when I am fighting, you must try to find happiness in your life again, all the happiness that we should have shared. You must live your life to the full because you will be living it for both of us.'

It was no good denying what he said, Constance knew it was all true. A trail of unmarked graves had been left near the hospitals where she had worked; on the battlefields thousands of corpses were buried a few inches below the stony soil, and thousands more lay stiffly frozen in the snowdrifts of Teruel.

'I promise,' Constance replied, hoping that he would believe that she could be strong enough to keep the promise. She very much doubted it herself. She might manage to keep on working, but achieving happiness would be another matter entirely. She wished she could think of something noble and valiant to say to him in return, but nothing came to mind at all. It was easier to stick to practicalities. 'I shall send you some gloves as soon as I can,' she said, remembering that he hadn't been wearing any. 'You mustn't forget to wear them. Though I will love you anyway,' she said with a fragile smile, stifling the words 'whatever happens,' before they were born.

Neither Karl nor Constance realised that Aurora was responsible for their hour alone. She had rushed round warning the other nurses to stay away from their quarters for a while, and had been standing guard at the end of the street despite the freezing temperatures, just in case an unexpected visitor turned up. When they emerged, she pressed her small frame against a doorway, and from there she watched them walk towards an ambulance, engine revving ready to leave. Karl was going to get a lift, at least part of the way back to his unit. He climbed in beside the driver. The tears that came to Aurora's eyes immediately chilled on her cheeks as she saw Constance, as rigid as the statues of the Madonna, standing in the street till the ambulance had driven out of the village, across the frozen stream and out of sight. 'She doesn't even weep,' thought Aurora in amazement, 'how strange it must be to be English.' Wailing inside, Constance walked back to the ward.

CHAPTER 6

Gathering Clouds

I

Rose lay full length in the bath, the water almost unbearably hot but ineffably pleasurable. Teruel was far away, though when she closed her eyes she could still see images of what seemed to be distant black birds of prey in an ice blue sky – Franco's planes. The bombs they dropped sometimes landed in deep snow, raising only faint white flurries. It was like watching a silent movie. She opened her eyes again quickly, not wanting to think of Rafael in a freezing trench whilst she luxuriated in blissful warmth.

The huge roll-topped bath tub with its cast iron claw feet was bigger than any she had ever seen before. But then, life at the moment was full of things that were totally new to her. There were more books in the house than in a public library, and more comings and goings than at Paddington Station. A constant stream of people passed through 'Fen Gate', the rambling house that belonged to Addie's parents. The door was always open for visitors; students and colleagues to see Hugh, members of the Basque Children's Committee and other charity groups to see Virginia and now, in the Christmas holidays, friends dropping in all the time to see Addie's brother and sisters. Everything was free and easy. Rose could never work out exactly when the meals were supposed to be as everyone arrived and left at different times. This haphazard arrangement was rendered even more unpredictable by the unexpected guests who were always invited to pull up a chair and share whatever food appeared from the kitchen. The seemingly endless talking frequently escalated into passionate debates though, much to Rose's amazement, the arguments always remained terribly polite.

Rose was convalescing from pneumonia. The unforgiving environment of Teruel took a hard toll. By the time Rose had begun to feel ill, many of the nurses in her unit had already succumbed to a virulent form of influenza. Knowing they were desperately short staffed, she had tried to keep going by taking massive doses of aspirin. For a while, this made the blinding headaches bearable and dulled the bouts of coughing, but eventually the fever had won. One night she was found outside the huts where the nurses were sleeping. She was barefoot and delirious, wandering around in the snow. The doctor in charge of the unit had summoned Addie to arrange for Rose to be sent back to England. This time there was no question of her staying in Spain. She was going to need plenty of good food and complete rest, and even then Addie feared that she might not be fit to return to duty. Although Rose's resilience was amazing and she had seemed to recover quickly from her last collapse, her life was an ongoing drama as full of highs and lows as a roller-coaster ride. You never knew quite what would happen next. Addie was fairly sure that with good care, Rose would regain her health physically, but this time, after weeks of unrelenting pressure, she could have lost her nerve permanently as far as nursing at the front was concerned. It was impossible to judge. But where could she be sent to convalesce? Clearly, sending her home to the backstreets of Hackney would be far from ideal. After much thought, Addie came up with what seemed a much better idea. She arranged for Rose to go to stay in Cambridge with her own parents. 'Mother will sort her out if anyone can,' Addie had concluded after considering all the alternatives, 'and anyway, she loves having lame ducks under her wing.'

The sound of laughter echoed up through the spacious stairwell and along the corridor to the bathroom where Rose was trying to sum up the will power to get out of the now tepid water. It still seemed odd to hear English voices all around her again, like being in a foreign country. Everything was strange – even her own body, thin after her illness. 'I look like a scraggy old hen,' was Rose's verdict when she finally rose from the bath and wiped the steamy mirror to examine herself full-length. Even though the lice were apparently all gone, she checked to reassure herself that there were no nits lurking anywhere, waiting to hatch and plague her again. Much to her relief, not a single sticky egg clung to the fine-toothed comb.

Wrapped in a comfortable towelling bath robe, she returned to the bedroom that had been hers for the last two weeks. The heavy furniture exuded an air of permanence and stability. Fortunately, the rather ponderous effect they created was softened by the intricate flowing designs on the drapes. As she drifted off to sleep each night, Rose loved to let her eyes follow the patterns made by the leaves and flowers, each section interwoven at strategic points with brightly-coloured small birds. She appreciated their beauty even though she was unaware of their value; the heavy cloth had come from the famous workshops of William Morris, a leading figure in the Arts and Crafts movement. When she woke in the mornings, Rose could see the spires of churches and colleges through the leaded panes of her window. After the harsh brightness of Spain, they always seemed mysteriously insubstantial in the weak, wintry English light. Sometimes they appeared as mere grey silhouettes piercing the sky, barely visible through the dawn mists. 'If only,' she would think with longing, 'I had grown up in a place like this.'

Rose was truly grateful to Hugh and Virginia for their kindness to her, and deeply regretted her inability to be a more cheerful guest. She tried to enter into the festive spirit of the season, but stark images of war came to her mind continually and never before had all the trappings of Christmas struck her as quite so irrelevant. 'What exactly is the point of Christmas trees anyway?' she wondered idly as huge efforts were made to erect a gigantic evergreen in the hallway. She felt disgusted at herself for eating such copious quantities of food, enough to have fed a whole family in Villamalea. When she went with her hosts to a carol service in King's College Chapel, the gulf between Britain and Spain seemed to widen even further. Sitting on the slippery wooden pew, she had at first been stunned by the sheer scale of the architecture. The stained-glass windows soared upwards to unbelievable heights, and for a while, she was mesmerised by the complex structure of the fan vaulting. Soon the chancel was reverberating with the piercing sweetness of choir boys' voices and the sonorous tones of the organ. Rose looked at the congregation around her; the women in their elegant hats and furs, the men in bespoke suits with their faces shaved so closely that they shone. She wished fervently that she belonged to the same social class and could share their enviable self assurance. The scent of wealth permeated the air. With every breath she took she inhaled a heady mix of expensive perfumes, wax polish and altar candles.

But envy was quickly overcome by another emotion, so strong that it left her gasping for breath. She wanted to shake these complacent people till their teeth rattled. How could they sit here, mouthing platitudes about 'Peace on earth and goodwill to all men', without lifting a finger to help people in Spain who were dying in their thousands; defending democracy, fighting fascism - whatever you called it, these complacent fools in their cloistered halls ought to realise it was their fight too. She tried to suppress the rising fury, tried to maintain an outward calm, but politeness finally failed during the pompous delivery of the Latin Litany. What was this man doing in his ridiculous garb, chanting his incomprehensible rites? Telling his flock that they would be better off in the next world than they had been in this one? Like many of the priests in Spain, what he really wanted, Rose knew with a sickening certainty, was to ensure his own powerful position in the world around him, not in the next. She squeezed past the others in the pew and rushed down the aisle towards the door, her footsteps echoing to the roof. Virginia followed her, believing she might have been taken ill again. Once outside, Rose sat miserably on a bench overlooking the exquisitely tailored lawns, not knowing quite how to explain her behaviour without seeming to be rude and ungrateful. It would be better, she concluded, just to say that she had needed some fresh air.

Virginia, however, was not to be fooled so easily. She had some idea of what Rose was going through. Indeed, she was often infuriated herself by the smugness of the society in which she lived. The women of her generation had grown up restricted by innumerable spoken and unspoken rules. It had taken all the intelligence and feminine wiles she possessed just to persuade her family to allow her to study at university. After her marriage, she had eventually found an outlet for her energies in the traditions of philanthropy that sustained so many women of her class. Men had their boardrooms, women had their committee culture. Thousands of them formed networks right across the country raising money for charity, campaigning for good causes, serving soup, and now with the escalating problems in Europe, caring for refugees. Looking at the dejected figure of Rose, hunched miserably on the bench, Virginia decided action was needed. 'Come along with me, Rose,' she said in her brisk, friendly tones, 'I want to introduce you to some friends.'

Rose reluctantly followed her, though the thought of having to make the effort to converse with yet more well-intentioned Cambridge intellectuals was the last thing she wanted to do. They walked through the busy streets, past rows of substantial town houses, their yellow bricks toned down to a variety of greys from the smoke produced by winter fires and the engines on the railway nearby. Gaunt trees lined the straight road leading to the train station, heavily pruned into knobbly fists ready to punch the sky. They turned into the entrance of the last house on the corner, slightly more dilapidated than most. Climbing the steps to the door with the sure tread of familiarity, Virginia opened the door without knocking.

'Hello, anybody home?' she called out loudly as she took off her hat and gloves, placing them on the stand near the door.

A loud clattering of footsteps began above and grew rapidly louder as running feet descended the stairs. An excited chattering foretold the arrival of a large group of children, who were soon milling round the visitors in the entrance hall. They were of mixed ages, the girls all with ribbons tied in huge bows in their dark hair, the boys with bare and vulnerable knees appearing in the space between their voluminous short trousers and heavy grey woollen socks.

A mixture of English, Spanish, and what Rose presumed must be Basque, assailed her ears. 'Who is this lady?' and 'Has she brought presents?' seemed to be the two most frequently recurring questions.

'It is not good manners to ask for gifts,' Virginia said firmly, 'and I have brought this lady to meet you because she is missing Spain at the moment, just as you are. She has been working there as a nurse.'

Rose was then besieged by children. Order was restored to some extent by the presence of the teacher, but their exuberance and curiosity didn't remain subdued for long. As they settled themselves onto a well-worn sofa in the sparsely furnished living room, Virginia told Rose that the children in the Cambridge colony were nearly all orphans, their fathers had fought and died in Socialist militias during the first months of the war, and their immediate families had been killed in the bombardments of Bilbao. They had arrived with the other Basque refugee children in the spring of 1937. Groups were now scattered all over Britain in homes run by special committees, wealthy individuals, political parties, church councils, all completely un-aided by the British government. Rose looked at the children, watching her expectantly, eager for news. At first glance, they had seemed just like any other group of small boys and girls excited at the prospect of Christmas, but now their tense faces and solemn eyes revealed that they had seen in reality what other children only imagined in their worst nightmares. Rose knew she couldn't tell them the whole truth of what was happening in Spain. They were the children of political activists, and well versed in the causes of the war and the horrors that came with it, but nevertheless, they were still children. She forced herself to think of the good things to tell them – how the people of Madrid continued to resist Franco, that soldiers from all over the world were still joining the International Brigades to fight in Spain, that Teruel was about to be retaken by the Republicans, and finally, trying to convince herself as much as them, she told them that the war would soon be won.

Even after the art class, when Rose had seen with sadness the violent scenes of war most of them painted, Virginia was sure that the visit had been the right medicine for someone she considered to be suffering from too much introspection. Rose walked with a more positive step as they left the house, knowing that at least a few children had escaped from the destruction and suffering. It was a small comfort to know that some of the people in England were trying to help, even if the government was not. The children had asked her to write to them when she went back to Spain. She hadn't been able to bring herself to tell them that she might choose not to go back at all.

When the Spanish Medical Aid Committee asked her to speak at a series of public meetings, she felt her throat turn dry in nervous apprehension. She had spoken on the radio in Madrid, but how much more difficult would it be to stand on a platform and face an audience? Nevertheless, she knew she would have to do it, and even if her efforts only raised a little money, it would be better than nothing. The first time, her knees trembled as she rose to speak, and her hands holding her notes shook so much that she couldn't read them. But she soon learned that it was better just to tell people about the things she knew well, describing her work and the patients, and what she had actually seen herself in Spain. Before long, she rather enjoyed sharing a platform at big meetings with famous speakers from different political parties, like the English 'Pasionaria', Isabel Brown, the fiery Ellen Wilkinson, and even with Conservative MPs, such as the aristocratic Duchess of Atholl and Robert Boothby, memorable for being the first man she had seen wearing suede shoes. Sometimes the collections taken were splendid - it was said that Isabel Brown could make people part with the last pennies for their bus fare home. Rose's greatest success was with the members of the Cooperative Guild who were inspired by her speech to collect enough money for a complete new set of surgical instruments for her to deliver to a Spanish hospital at the front.

With each day that passed, Rose grew more frightened at the thought of returning to Spain. She sometimes thought she must be mad even to consider it for a moment, when in England shop windows burst with riches and food, and people didn't look upwards in fear when a plane flew overhead. But as time went on, she grew increasingly uneasy as the ties binding her to Spain tightened. Christmas passed in a dreamlike haze of comfort, punctuated by the insistent barbs of her conscience reminding her that she must soon make a decision. Eventually, she calmed these annoying demands by vowing to decide after she had faced one particular challenge she had been dreading since her return to England. With the arrival of the New Year, a visit to her family in Hackney could not be postponed any longer.

Tears streamed down Annie's face when she opened the door to find her daughter standing outside. Rose had been there for quite some time, trying to summon the strength to knock. She had stared down at the shallow depression on the top step where the stone had been worn away by the scrubbing brushes of countless unknown women. She could see no trace of the white scouring that was traditionally used to smarten doorsteps, this one wasn't even clean. To cross it and enter the house would be, Rose felt, like taking a step into the abyss.

For a fleeting moment, Annie thought Rose could have returned home to live with them again, and would be able to help look after her father, but the expression on Rose's face as she went down the stairs leading to the confines of the basement kitchen told her that she had been wrong. Rose had been steeling herself for what she would find on her arrival. She had seen terrible deprivation in Spain and had believed herself to be quite prepared for whatever she encountered at home. Though of course, this place wasn't really 'home' in any real sense of the word. Her parents had moved several times since she had been away. But in this house too she smelled the all too well-remembered odours, and listened to the usual sad catalogue of calamities. Things had not been going well it seemed. Bulldog Baker, now a shadow of his former self, was unemployable after falling down the basement steps on his way back from the pub and damaging his back. Maybe, thought Rose as she listened to her mother and tried not to look at the peeling walls and the cracked sink in the corner, it wasn't so much the poverty and the lack of anything beautiful that was such a shock; it was the hopelessness that oozed from every nook and cranny. An aura of despondency surrounded Annie too, and she seemed smaller than Rose remembered, as if she were disappearing, her identity seeping into the unvarying grey patina of her surroundings. Rose thought of the Spanish women of her mother's age she had known in the villages, ruling their homes and families with vociferous pride, black skirts swaying as they went to fetch water from the fountain, sitting in the evening sunshine outside their doors, usually surrounded by swarming relations. Annie wiped her eyes. She could no longer even imagine that there were green horizons outside the kitchen window. She only saw the wall a mere three feet away, and leading up to the pavement above, the broken steps that had been Bulldog's downfall.

'Mosley's right, we should look after our own people first. What's Spain got to do with us? We should be getting rid of all these refugees and Jews that are taking our jobs away.' Rose's oldest brother thumped his fist on the kitchen table to emphasise his point, not a wise thing to do in view of the instability of the rickety legs.

'You are a fool,' Rose replied angrily, 'not to see that what's happening in Spain will soon be happening here too, unless we fight now. Will you only understand when bombs are falling on London?'

He raised his hand sharply, as if he were going reach over the table around which the family were sitting and hit her. She used to be scared of her brother's bullying, especially when his thick-set neck turned flaming red in anger and the veins protruded and throbbed on his forehead. But she wasn't frightened now. She had a whole new perspective on fear after living in the midst of a war for so long. She stood up, facing him with her shoulders squared and her hands bunched into tight fists. Whatever it was that her brother saw in her eyes made him waver. His hand fell back to the table and he slumped a little in his chair. He was unsure of exactly what she would do, but instinctively sensed that she was capable of retaliating in a manner that would not be to his liking. 'Bloody Reds' he muttered under his breath. Rose looked round at her family and despaired of them all. This brother was nothing but a fascist, the others thought only about which horse would win the two-thirty and going to the pub. Her sisters regarded her with sullen distrust, except for the youngest who talked of nothing but the boys she met at the cinema. Her father grumbled discontentedly, sometimes gripping the greasy upholstery on the arms of his chair when a spasm of pain shot through his spine.

An uneasy truce reigned for the rest of the meal, the

likelihood of any conversation having been eliminated by the realisation that they had no common ground whatsoever. Annie took refuge for a while in telling Rose the latest news about the ex-king and the former Mrs Simpson. Rose feigned interest for her mother's sake but felt herself even more distant from her own family than Addie's. She toyed with the mutton stew on her plate, trying in vain to swallow the gristly bits she had always hated.

After the meal, there was only a little time to spare before she had to catch the train back to Cambridge. Her mother stiffened when she heard that Rose wouldn't even be staying for the night. 'You could easily share with your sisters,' she was saying, but Rose couldn't bear the claustrophobic atmosphere any longer.

'I can't stay, they're expecting me back in Cambridge to speak at a meeting,' she lied, trying to avoid seeing the hurt she was causing her mother. Out of the blue, her next words tumbled out, 'and I must start getting things ready to go back to Spain again.' Immediately she had spoken, she realised that this wasn't a lie, that she would go back as soon as she could.

Her mother's sharp intake of breath made her wish she had prepared her words more carefully before speaking, though it would have come to the same thing in the end.

'I have to go back,' Rose said as gently as she could, 'there are still things I have to do there.' As the image of Rafael came unbidden into her mind, she remembered that one of those things must be to give him an honest explanation of her feelings towards him. She hadn't mentioned him at all to her family. 'Perhaps,' she wondered, rather ashamed of having forgotten him entirely for a while, 'I was just worried what their reaction would have been if I'd told them about him.' Deep down in her heart however, a hard kernel of truth was putting forth a penetrating shoot. Rafael never really seemed to fit anywhere in the dreams she had for the future, when the war was over.

Her mother was attempting to wash up their plates in cold water, opaque and faintly greenish with fat and old kitchen soap. Rose had never felt so alone. She certainly didn't belong here with her family, she didn't even belong in England at the moment, where hardly anybody seemed to care about the war. In Spain she didn't really fit in either. She wasn't brave and committed to communism like Constance, she wasn't as clever as Addie, who seemed to understand all the complexities of what was actually happening there, but she did know it was important to try to help. She put her hand on her mother's shoulder, asking her to listen for a moment.

'Please try to understand. Often I'm scared in Spain, and sometimes I make mistakes, but I can still be useful. Every hour I spend here, wounded people are dying there because there aren't enough nurses. I can't just leave them.'

Annie knew there was nothing more to say.

II

Once again, Teruel was falling to Franco. In the blackness of the cold February night, Constance could barely make out the stone arches that enclosed the main square, until the next flash of light came from the exploding mortars. Constance never had liked mortars. Apart from everything else, they were so dreadfully noisy. There was that particularly horrible 'crump' when they were fired, triggering a sick sensation in the pit of her stomach, followed by a tense period of waiting as they whistled through the air, and finally the ear-splitting bang of their impact that nearly always made her jump even though she knew it was coming. And now they were landing much too close for comfort. She was alone, crouching in a rickety ambulance which offered little protection from the ricocheting machine gun fire whipping round the square, let alone the mortars. The rest of the staff and patients had already been evacuated from the hospital in Cuevas Labradas and were travelling in convoy to set up again in a safer place. Everyone was exhausted. All the medical staff were worn out, and the mechanics and drivers exhausted with the extra work of keeping the vehicles running in temperatures constantly far below zero. Without anti-freeze the radiators had to be drained every night and refilled each morning. Usually they had to light primus stoves or bonfires under the engines to thaw the oil so that the tired batteries didn't fail completely.

Constance had been the last to leave the hospital at Cuevas Labradas. Max had waited for her while she packed the remaining precious supplies into the back of the old ambulance he was driving. He had grumbled about the time it was taking her to wrap up the glass syringes, saying that it didn't seem worth them both getting killed just so some poor sod could have a needle in his backside, but then had helped her as much as he could. Now he had disappeared, leaving her alone, and rather annoyed, in this most unpleasant spot in the middle of a battle. The truth was that Max had not wanted her to know just how close Teruel was to falling. He had been ordered to deliver a last message to the few Republican soldiers who remained in the town, telling them that the evacuation of the transport depot and the hospitals on the north side was complete. When he at last returned to the ambulance, he got in without a word and drove as fast as he could, pushing the old engine to its limits. The urgency of the situation became clear to Constance as they reached the outskirts of the town. Teruel, its squat buildings anchored firmly to a rocky prominence, was surrounded by a ring of destruction. As they crossed the ravine by the one remaining bridge, they could see tanks burning below them. The flames illuminated numerous small, unmoving black figures that lay sprawled on the flickering pink snow. Mortar fire rained down on the town. There was no longer any sign of resistance. Max drove on, sliding on the ice, lurching over pot holes, and the glass syringes, shaking free of their wrappings, rattled alarmingly in their boxes.

The retreat was a desperate affair, though the Republican Army repeatedly turned to make a stand and halt the rapid advance for as long as they could. If he were still alive, Constance knew Karl would be there with the rest of the Germans. She lost track of the number of times they stopped to set up the hospital in some deserted building to take and treat new wounded, then evacuated again hurriedly before they were caught by Franco's advancing troops. There were not enough vehicles to transport them all at once and a system of leapfrogging had to be worked out to keep them all ahead of the enemy. It was terrible to be waiting in the last group, hearing the sound of trucks drawing nearer and not knowing to which side they belonged. Each time they raced away from the approaching front, skidding through villages on the unmade roads, they would lean out of the windows and bang on the cab doors, shouting 'ambulancia' to clear the streets. Sometimes they would discover later that the villages had already been occupied by Franco's soldiers.

'Nowhere to take cover for miles,' Constance whispered to Aurora as they sat in the back of a truck during yet another interminable stage on the retreat. The narrow road was bordered by ditches on each side but had nothing to offer shelter from an aerial attack, no sign of rocks, trees or bushes to give even partial cover. There were far too many stretches of the road that left them exposed like this to passing aviators, looking for a spot of target practice. Aurora had been talking to the young mother beside her, who held her small child tightly in her arms. 'Must be about a year or so old, still a baby really,' Constance decided, though it was difficult to be sure of ages when children were so often small and undernourished. The child looked at her expectantly, listening intently for any repetition of the strange sounds that Constance had made when speaking in English. 'What's your name then?' Constance asked her with a smile, to be rewarded by a dribbly grin. They had picked up the refugees just as they left the last village, cramming as many as they could in amongst the equipment on the truck. This woman appeared to be on her own apart from the child, not travelling in a large family group like most of the refugees. Her few possessions were wrapped up in a shawl. Constance looked at her pityingly, thinking, 'She's got nothing, nothing at all, poor woman. Well,' she hastily added with a touch of jealousy, 'nothing but her child.' She tried hard to imagine how it would feel to hold a baby of her own; warm, soft, vulnerable, to know that this tiny person depended upon you for everything, and loved you without reservations.

Suddenly, above the noise of the engines and the rumbling of the tyres on the rough road, they could hear the drone of a distant plane. The driver heard it too, and slammed on the brakes just as the first shots hit the far end of the convoy. The canvas tarpaulin under which they sheltered gave no protection at all, and there was always the possibility that the fuel tank could explode. They leapt from the truck, scrambling down to the road and then into the deep ditches at each side – there was nowhere else to go. The mother and child slithered down the bank beside Constance and Aurora. The earth around them rose in a series of small spurts as the bullets hit the soil. Overhead, the small plane circled, returning for several runs before losing interest in the now unmoving targets. In silence, people began climbing out of the ditches.

While the drivers looked over their vehicles to see if they were still roadworthy, the injured were checked by the doctors and nurses. The dead had to be left behind as there was no time to bury them and some of the lorries had been put out of action. Everyone still alive piled into those that remained serviceable. The mother who had been with Constance and Aurora seemed unhurt, and was helped on board the truck again, still clutching her child. It was quite some time before Aurora began to worry. At first she had thought the baby had perhaps dropped off to sleep, but the strange rag-doll manner in which the baby's head lolled against its mother's breast made her nudge Constance and nod in their direction. The mother was staring fixedly at the road as it receded into the distance behind the truck. Constance gently moved the shawl enveloping the baby's head, to be met by blank staring eyes, all curiosity gone. Together with Aurora, she tried to release the mother's iron grasp to take the baby away, but it was as if the blood seeping from the baby's body had turned to insoluble glue. Aurora tried to talk to her, to ask where she had been intending to go, to find out if she had family somewhere nearby, but there was no reply. Some of the other women in the truck were going to remain in the next town where they had relatives. They said they would take the woman and her child with them. She would let go eventually.

As Constance watched her walk away with her precious burden, she felt a devastating sense of loss. 'Could there be anything worse than knowing that you were unable to protect your children, that you had brought them into the world to suffer and die?' Constance thought not. Her sympathy for this solitary mother was compounded by something more personal. For weeks she had carried a small secret hope that she could be pregnant. It was easy to believe it could be so, because poor diet and exhaustion meant that neither she nor the other nurses had normal menstrual cycles, a fact they all considered a blessing under the circumstances. Now, reluctantly, she realised that this desire to be carrying Karl's child was no more than a need to have a kind of insurance for herself in case he was killed, to leave her with at least some small part of him. But, she thought sadly, it had been a shamefully selfish wish. How could she have contemplated for a moment wanting to bring a baby into this terrible world? The war might go on for months, years even. Afterwards, it might be too late for her ever to have a baby of her own. The bitterness of this realisation was as persistent as the taste of ashes.

It was not until several weeks later, as they unpacked their equipment yet again, that Constance realised with surprise that she was feeling an emotion other than fear and sadness. There was activity all around her; everyone on the team was working together to set up the hospital, knowing what they should be doing and getting on with it without slacking or griping. She began to feel a warm glow of pride in the unit; doctors, drivers, orderlies, nurses – all of them. Janet was proving to be an excellent nurse, especially good at caring for post-operative patients when careful observation was needed. Aurora was growing more confident in her own abilities every day. Even Flo was pulling her weight properly. In the nightmare of the retreat, the Chief Medical Officer, Dr Walter, had managed to keep order throughout the various units. They hadn't panicked, they were still organised. The disagreements and tensions between the staff had been set aside, at least for the moment. 'Just as well,' Constance muttered to herself, 'because working in this place will really test our mettle.'

The black entrance to the railway tunnel loomed before her, and even though she knew that the other end was blocked, it was hard to dismiss the horrid fear that at any moment, a train could come rushing down the track to obliterate them all. The tunnel had a damp, sooty smell, and tarry drips fell intermittently from the centre of the curved roof. But the uninviting site had one saving grace. It offered sanctuary from the increasingly heavy bombardment. The ambulances and trucks had drawn up onto the platform of the station just in front of the tunnel. Equipment and patients were unloaded and carried the short distance down the tracks. A small group of drivers led by the ever-resourceful Max searched a few of the large empty houses nearby. Some of their finds were 'organised' for hospital use, including the contents of a store cupboard which contained the most beautiful white linen sheets, some of them bearing embroidered crests. With these it was possible to rig up a structure reminiscent of a sheik's pavilion within the tunnel, to be used as a soot-free operating theatre. There were enough sheets left to provide a canopy for the post-op cases too.

For the first time in her life, Constance endured the horror of nursing men with gas gangrene. Half a dozen of them had been picked up from a hospital they had passed on the retreat. Their wounds hadn't been debrided properly and they had been sewn up too tightly, allowing the dreaded gas gangrene to take hold. They were slowly dying, slowly, so slowly. 'It shouldn't have started,' Constance thought in cold fury, 'they shouldn't be in this state. We know how to stop it happening now.' But there was no treatment, only morphia. When there was time to rest for a moment, Constance would sit for a while at the mouth of the tunnel in the sunshine, trying to clear the stifling air of the tunnel from her lungs. She no longer thought of what might happen next, or even of her whereabouts. If ambulances arrived, she would go back inside, not only to see to the new arrivals, but also because planes sometimes followed hot on the trail of the ambulances, firing at any sign of movement.

'I need help here,' called Florence urgently, 'Constance, come quickly.' Plunging further into the depths of the tunnel, Constance followed the sound of the urgent voice through the gloom. Florence was crouched beside a young woman who was sweating profusely in the close atmosphere, each laboured breath causing her tremendous effort and pain. Constance hadn't seen this woman before. Doctor Aston had found Constance slumped over fast asleep, midway through changing a patient's dressing. He had given her strict instructions to go and find somewhere to rest for a while.

'She was brought in with a group of injured villagers a couple of hours ago,' Florence said trying to check the woman's pulse. They didn't make it to shelter in time when the last lot of shelling started. She's been in theatre for ages, a pretty straight forward fracture of the humerus,' said

Florence, pointing at the arm now in a wire splint, 'but it was the compound fracture of the femur that took the time. And now, as if that weren't enough, she's gone into labour. There's not much hope that the baby will have survived. She was very shocked when she arrived.'

All the nurses knew that shock could be a killer sometimes, even when there had been little haemorrhage. It would certainly have affected the baby. Constance's old skills in midwifery rushed to the fore as she examined the woman. She was certainly going to give birth quite soon, though she was probably less than eight months pregnant. Constance left Florence in charge of the woman whilst she carried out the round of treatments for the other patients, returning to check on her progress every now and again.

'Un hijo, un hijo,' Florence shouted in delight to the mother when the baby eventually arrived; a son, tiny but alert, taking a first breath immediately and soon nuzzling hopefully at his mother's breast. They all smiled. Constance didn't really know why, things couldn't have been much worse. 'Death all around, but an infant still fights for life,' she thought as Florence reassured the mother that her child was fine.

'She wants to call him after me,' said Florence happily a short while later, 'so we've decided he can be named Florentino. It's as near as we can get. What do you think, Constance?'

Constance nodded, but didn't smile this time, knowing that she couldn't delay telling Florence the orders she had just been given.

'We have to evacuate straight away, Florence, we're under attack from both ends of the tunnel. Franco's troops are clearing the rubble at the far end, and this end is being bombed so much that it might give way. We have to get out. And Florence,' she said as gently as she could, 'we can't take civilians.'

'We can't leave them,' cried Florence in horror, 'and

what about Florentino.'

'We have to,' said Constance, 'there isn't room, and anyway, they may not want to leave their village. And even if the roof falls in at this end, they will be found when the troops arrive from the other end.'

Florence, angered to the point of tears, suddenly rushed off towards the tunnel mouth, shouting back, 'I just need a few minutes.'

'Wherever is she going when there is so much to do?' Constance wondered, anxious because time was so short. The enemy would probably be coming up through the tunnel slowly, checking for time bombs and booby traps, but they might appear at any moment.

Florence returned with her small bag of possessions, and fished out a silver crucifix from somewhere in the depths. She fastened it onto the mother's torn dress with a safety pin, telling her that she must insist that she was a Catholic when the soldiers found her.

'I was once,' said the mother, gratefully touching the familiar form of the crucifix.

'You are again,' said Florence. She kissed the baby and settled him close to the mother, within the circle of her uninjured arm.

As they left, Constance remembered how critical she had been of the nuns that had abandoned their patients at Belchite.

'I believed we would never do that, never leave people behind, helpless. What a fool I was to be so conceited and naive.'

Before she opened her eyes, Constance tried to remember where she was, but everything was far too confused. She knew they had been travelling for a long time, probably for two whole days and through at least one whole night with the enemy close behind them. They had arrived somewhere in darkness and had all staggered from the vehicles to collapse in one large room, she had no idea where. She half opened her eyes to see the ragged shapes that were her companions all around her. The room was hot and airless. Constance watched the dust moving languidly in the narrow beams of light that came shooting in through the slits in the shutters. She tottered over to the window and flung the shutters wide, and there was the sea, bright and glinting and to Constance, unthinkably shocking. 'How have we been driven back so far? We started such a long way inland.' She knew enough about their situation to realize that if Franco had forced them to retreat to the coast, what remained of Republican Spain must now be cut in two, Valencia on one side and Barcelona on the other. What chance was there for victory now?

III

Rose looked up to see small flashes of red moving in the distance. In the brilliant sunshine she had to half close her eyes to work out what they were. Eventually, she could make out a few men straggling along the track leading down from the nearby hills. They wore the red scarves of the Garibaldis. Her heart pounding, she asked the driver to stop for a few minutes and rushed to meet them at the crossroads. The thought that Rafael could be with them filled her with a mixture of hope and anxiety. What would she say to him? She certainly couldn't tell him the truth in a few brief moments as their paths crossed. She couldn't say that now, in Spain, she loved him as much as ever, but that during the weeks she had just spent in England she had never been able to imagine him as part of her life after the war was over. 'Why do things have to end up being so complicated?' she asked herself in vexation. She always felt torn like this, as if her mind was being pulled apart by conflicting emotions when all she really wanted was peace and stability.

The Garibaldis halted briefly at the crossroads, but Rafael was not amongst them. Nobody knew where he was either – so many soldiers had become separated from their units during the retreat. One man tilted his head sideways, gesturing vaguely towards the mountains where the noise of gunfire could still be heard in the distance. She heard a shout, 'English Rose,' and saw a face she remembered from Villamalea. Knowing Rafael would try to rejoin his unit if he could, she hurriedly scribbled a pencilled note for him and gave it to the man. 'Dearest Rafael,' she wrote, 'I am well. Do not worry about me. Be careful. All my love, Rose.' It seemed totally inadequate.

'Please give this to Rafael when you see him again,' she begged as the men prepared to set off, already tired and hungry and with a long march ahead of them to Tarragona where the rest of their unit were waiting.

Perversely, when everyone else was retreating to the north, Rose was heading in the opposite direction to rejoin her old unit, still working in the south. The doctor in charge had asked for her and she was going to do her best to get there, even though everyone warned her that Franco's troops were about to succeed in driving a wedge through Republican Spain. She was determined to overcome her fears and prove, once and for all, that she was as good as any of them. Finding anyone to take her was not easy, but eventually she heard of a driver who was travelling south to pick up some British nurses and bring them back to Barcelona. He agreed to take her, admiring her courage although thinking she must be mad.

When at last she found her unit again, she had been given a warm welcome, and the instruments she had brought back from England sent the surgeons into raptures of delight. The gleaming scalpels, forceps and clamps were the only new surgical equipment they possessed. The barn they were using as a first evacuation station was a poor affair, badly equipped with only two bare operating tables. Outside, they could hear the last remnants of the Republican army in the south fighting and retreating, fighting and retreating towards Valencia and the coast.

After several days with barely a break, a lull had allowed Rose to take a short walk away from the barn and the sight of mangled flesh. As she walked wearily back along the track, several more ambulances overtook her and began to disgorge their wounded in the triage area. Camouflaged amongst the pine trees slightly off to one side of the barn, this was no more than a large tent where the men could be laid out on stretchers till they could be classified. It was perhaps only an illusion that it was safer for the ambulances to unload under the trees, rather than in the cleared area round the barn, but the trees offered shade at least. It was not Rose's turn to work in triage, but no doctor or nurse seemed to be on duty there. 'Wherever is everybody?' Rose asked, unaware that in the barn they were already beginning to prepare patients for evacuation.

'Over here nurse, this one's bad.' Rose had no alternative but to answer the call and cover till someone arrived. They were now using a system of coloured tags to speed up the sorting process; red for extreme urgency, yellow for secondary importance, and blue for not so urgent. Rose examined the wounded as quickly as she could, tying the tags to the wrists of the patients she had seen. Few drugs remained, she only gave morphia to the worst cases. She issued orders perfunctorily to the orderlies, 'This man's haemorrhaging badly - he needs a new dressing.' 'Give each of these men 10ccs of anti-tetanic serum and 10ccs of anti-gas serum.' 'This man's in shock - help me set up a drip.' She called for stretcher bearers to carry an urgent case up to the barn, and to ask for help in triage.

The bombardment now sounded horribly close. Everything suddenly seemed completely familiar to Rose. She was awake, but living in her nightmare. As the explosions grew nearer, some of the half-conscious men grew restless. Rose tried to calm them, talking to them in a firm clear voice, or touching them gently as she passed on to the next person needing attention. An enormous wave of relief swept over her. She wasn't going to panic, she didn't want to run away, she knew the job she had to do and she was just going to get on and do it. She turned to the next man...........

It was difficult to open her eyes. When she had managed to partially raise one eyelid, Rose could see moving shapes and what looked like the inside of a barn, though not the one where they had been working. This one was lower and had patches of blue sky showing through the roof in several places where tiles were missing. Wounded men lay all around her. She moved her hand gingerly and discovered that beneath the coarse blanket, tight bandages swathed her chest and stomach. She wanted to ask someone what had happened but the all Spanish she knew seemed to have disappeared. For a while, she drifted in and out of consciousness, feeling nothing except the sharp pain of an injection, badly administered. A little later, she had enough strength to raise her hand to her face to try to rub away the dried blood encrusted on her eyelids. Licking her dry lips, she noticed the salty taste of yet more blood. The sounds around her seemed muffled; 'Perforated eardrums?' she wondered. Lifting the blanket a little, she could see the garish redness of the bandage that encircled her ribs. 'Chest wound, poor prognosis,' she diagnosed as she slipped back into a welcoming blackness.

When she woke again, she could see stars through the holes in the roof. They were not enough to distract her from the pain she now felt hammering her into near insensibility. A doctor who spoke some English came to give her an injection of morphine and to tell her that she was to be evacuated to the coast soon.

'What happened?' she managed to ask him.

'A direct hit.' he replied, 'Don't try to talk now.'

'But, the others?' she whispered urgently.

'They were not so lucky.'

She pointed to the now hardened blood on her chest. The doctor knew that as a nurse, she would want a more detailed explanation of her injuries than he would normally give to his patients.

'You were coughing up blood, the force of the blast caused contusion of your lungs, but there are no open chest wounds. You have multiple lacerations and abdominal injuries.'

He was relieved that the morphine took effect quickly and that Rose drifted off again before asking him to say anything about the considerable quantities of shrapnel lodged in her abdominal cavity.

Days and nights followed in a sequence of events that for Rose seemed as disjointed as a flicker book with some of the pages missing. She was in a hospital bed in Benicasim with the sound of Spanish voices all around her for an indefinite number of days. Then she was on a stretcher again, being carried into a station, her hospital notes pinned to her blanket. She had a clear memory of a long train, with the carriages converted to take the stretchers. At village stations, locals would bring oranges for the wounded. At one of the larger stations more stretcher cases were waiting. Sirens sounded - an air-raid alarm. Rose was again amongst the lucky ones; she was quickly taken from the train to a refuge. Those still outside were unfortunate, the enemy planes bombed the station to rubble, and the hospital train was nothing but a twisted mass of wood and metal.

In all the chaos of the journey that followed in jolting lorries, her notes were lost with the diagnosis of her injuries. She spent days in growing frustration in the military hospital in Valencia. She overheard doctors speaking of a laparotomy. 'No, no!' she screamed as loudly as she could, 'Not here. England.' She didn't want them opening her up for abdominal surgery under these conditions – she'd rather wait, even with the pain.

'Rose, Rose,' a woman's voice came into her dream, speaking English in a way that Rose knew she had heard somewhere before. She opened her eyes to see Madge, her tortoiseshell glasses perched lopsidedly on her nose, now held together with wire.

'You're still here!' Rose exclaimed in surprise, at first because she had believed she was only dreaming, and then because she had presumed that Madge had returned to New Zealand months ago after being wounded with Ada.

'Ada went home, but I stayed,' Madge replied, 'and a good thing I did too, seeing as you need to be rescued. I'm putting you on board a British ship tomorrow.'

When, after a scarcely remembered journey, Rose was eventually carried ashore on a stretcher at Dover, tears trickled slowly from the corners of her eyes. She wasn't crying from pain, or even with happiness at having reached the safety of British shores. She was crying with a tremendous sense of relief, knowing that she wouldn't have to face the agonising decision of whether to stay or return to Spain again. Her injuries were serious enough to put her out of the fight for good. Rose sighed peacefully, unaware that someone was watching her closely. The Medical Aid Committee had sent a young doctor to meet her at the boat and take her to a London hospital. The sight of Rose's ashen face, almost transcendental in its serenity, triggered all the protective instincts he possessed. She looked so ethereal he feared she might be dying. He spoke a few words to her gently. Rose's blue eyes fluttered open and her tears stopped.

IV

The battered Citroen crawled along the narrow road between tall plane trees, their bark mottled with silvery greys and browns, a medley of constantly shifting tones orchestrated by the shadows falling from translucent green leaves above. Addie was reminded for a moment of the stately trees in Cambridge, but that was where the similarities ended. Here, there were no examples of soaring gothic architecture. Instead, the wide valley was surrounded by mountains, each vista with its own distinctive character. In one direction, majestic ranges receded into the distance till they looked like cardboard cut-outs in various shades of blue. In another, it seemed as if an enormous flat-topped craggy tooth had erupted from the valley floor, scrubby bushes clinging to the lower slopes like gingival flesh. Far behind her, stretching for miles, a sheer wall of deeply striated rock rose up like a ruched Odeon curtain. But much closer, immediately before her, lay the small village of Marsá, nestling companionably against the foot of a much less daunting hummock. Its almost perfectly oval form was dramatically interrupted by a large step-like segment missing from one side of the summit. The curious shape and the terraced slopes, partially covered by late spring foliage, conjured up an unlikely image in Addie's mind. As a child, full of eager anticipation, she had often watched Cook invert the heavy glass moulds to turn out something delicious and wobbly for tea. She had liked the rabbit shape, but had hated to watch its jellified body being brutally dismembered, so her favourite had always been the oval mould, its rising ramparts ascending to a splendidly tremulous citadel.

'Look!' Addie said out loud, pointing ahead, 'A lime blancmange castle with the first spoonful scooped from the top.' Her passengers laughed at the improbability of the image she had conjured up.

The car was packed with nurses, squashed in as tightly as undergraduates heading for a party. And surprisingly, the mood was indeed remarkably light hearted. A short while before, the same nurses had been running for their lives in the retreat, almost cut off by the enemy's advance to the coast. They had eventually managed to reach the safety of

Catalonia, the largest region still in the hands of the Republic. Amongst the nurses was Madge, who had told Addie the sad tale of Rose's departure for England. After making sure that there was someone to look after Rose on board the British ship, Madge had managed to find a boat to take her to Barcelona. But now, after all the tragedies of the retreat, they all felt a new heady feeling in the air. Morale was lifting, they weren't giving up. The Brigades were regrouping all around this area, and better hospital facilities were being set up. The nurses would have plenty to do.

The road meandered through fields punctuated by gnarled low-growing vines and hazelnut bushes, then crossed a brick railway bridge into the village. Addie turned into the narrow streets between the houses, hoping her brakes would hold out as they descended a series of miniature San Franciscan-like undulations to reach the main square. She had been told that someone there would be able to give her detailed directions to the place where the nurses were to stay. The village, apart from a few larger houses, had a dilapidated appearance and looked just like many others Addie had seen recently, except for one immediately noticeable difference. Marsá was seething with activity. There were people everywhere; marching soldiers dogged by groups of children, men carrying boxes of supplies, and women cooking huge quantities of something that smelt very appetizing over a large fire in the open air. By the fountain there was a large rectangular water cistern where some of the younger women were scrubbing vigorously at piles of washing. The smallest children played nearby, watched by beady-eyed grandmothers.

Addie and her passengers were all glad to get out and stretch their legs. The car had been growing rapidly hotter and more uncomfortable as the strength of the sunshine intensified towards midday. The imposing facade of the Town Hall overlooked the square, directly opposite a two-storey building which boldly proclaimed in red above the door that it was the Brigade Stores. Addie sat in the shade on the stone slabs of a low wall that ran along one side of the square, glad to rest quietly after the long drive. The others went to search for a bar that might offer something resembling coffee. Addie could see a great deal of bustling about taking place further down the hill on a flat and dusty open space that was possibly the village football pitch. Truckloads of soldiers were arriving, and then, catching Addie's interest, a couple of ambulances. With a rush of pleasure, Addie saw a familiar figure alighting from one of them. It was Constance. Addie called her name excitedly and waved frantically to attract her attention before remembering that their last parting had been somewhat strained.

Whatever their differences had been, they were, at least for the moment, forgotten. Constance returned Addie's embrace with a warmth that was far from characteristically British, leaving Addie reassured that they were indeed friends once more. They even kissed each other's cheeks in the nervous way of those who are not quite sure which side comes first, however long they have spent in Spain. Constance had been through so much in the past few months that it seemed years since the fire in Barcelona. She remembered having been very annoyed with Addie then, but the overwhelming feeling of finding her, still alive and well, was one of pure joy. Without any shadow of doubt, she now knew that life really was too short to hold grudges over such disagreements. They were both on the same side after all. Addie too wanted to put the episode behind her though unfortunately, the problem of what to do about María still remained. It was proving impossible to find any clearly defined grounds to ask for her removal. María was being more careful since the fire. She continued to annoy almost everyone with her inefficiency and surly manners, but Addie couldn't bring herself to write a report to the Committee which would be no more than a list of María's snide remarks and petty lies and subterfuges. But, Addie thought as she looked at Constance, still proud but perhaps a little less self-assured than she had been before, it would be stupid to let the problem of María poison their old friendship.

'What are you doing here?' asked Constance as they walked along arm in arm.

'I'm bringing reinforcements,' Addie replied, 'several more nurses to help set up new hospitals. I've got to take a couple of them to a railway station near here – there's going to be an operating theatre on a train parked inside one of the tunnels next to it. Several units will be working in large farm houses in this area, and one is even going to be in a cave, I believe.'

'Oh, Dr Walter told me that I'll be going there soon,' said Constance, 'it's somewhere higher up in the mountains. At the moment we're all in a huge old house on the way to the next village. We've got quite a few pneumonia cases to nurse. During the retreat, the men had to swim the Ebro to get back to our side because the bridges had been bombed. It was still very cold at night then, and some of them were wet and hungry for days before they got back to safety – no wonder they came down with pneumonia. Most of them are recovering now though.'

'Rose hasn't been quite so lucky,' said Addie with a sigh. She told Constance what had happened to Rose, the bombing of her unit near the front-line and her evacuation home to England. From what Madge had said, they both knew that her wounds were serious. If she had recurring fevers, there was probably shrapnel in her abdomen, and the likelihood of extensive long-term damage.

'And what's going on here in the village?' asked Addie brightly, trying to lighten their spirits again, 'They seem to be putting all the flags out for something. Is it always so lively?'

'Not quite,' replied Constance, laughing, 'but there's a fiesta this afternoon. You will be able to stay, won't you?'

Addie thought a fiesta sounded like a wonderfully good reason to stop, just for a short while at least.

As the heat lessened, the celebrations began. The military commanders were keen to foster good relations between the locals and the Brigades, so with that aim, a programme of sporting and cultural activities had been planned, and most importantly as far as the villagers were concerned, the Brigades were providing the food for everyone. There was a huge turnout, including as many of the medical staff as could possibly be spared. Some of these foreign visitors caught the attention of the village children. Selena, the black American nurse, tolerated their persistent curiosity with remarkable good nature. They had never seen skin so black or curls so tight. She showed them the palms of her hands where the skin was lighter, and after she allowed them to touch her wiry hair they skipped off gleefully. Addie was surprised that Janet's red hair and freckles didn't cause a similar commotion, till she realised that some of the locals were redheads too. Invasions from Europe rather than Africa had given the locals a very different ancestry from those in the south of Spain.

The football matches between the foreigners and the locals caused great excitement. As some of the Brigaders had boots, the bare-footed villagers were at first thought to be at a distinct disadvantage, but, they were playing on their home ground and repeatedly emerged victorious. In the midst of all the cheering, Max arrived escorting Aurora, both beaming at everyone in undisguised happiness. Max introduced Aurora to Addie as his fiancée, saying that they were hoping to be married soon.

'We're planning a great party so make sure you'll be here for that. Hey, you can be a witness too.'

As they talked of the wedding, an unscheduled competition was beginning at one end of the football pitch that turned out to be the most hotly contested match of all. Even Constance, despite her initial disgust, was drawn into the spirit of the event. A group of Americans from the Lincoln Battalion accepted a challenge from several local men to a spitting match. Not just force, but accuracy too was to be put to the test, so a large target was set up leaning against one of the trucks. The locals presented a fairly uniform team image, similar in height, build and attire. They were shorter than the Americans, their wiry frames garbed in almost identical baggy trousers supported by a broad band of black material wrapped round their waists. The main difference that Addie could see was in the number of teeth they had missing, the gaps increasing proportionately with their age. The older ones also sported traditional Catalan elongated caps which flopped gently over one side of their heads. Addie considered the headwear definitely gnome-like rather than dashing. In contrast, the Americans were a varied bunch both in stature and in dress, each having adapted the basic notion of a uniform to meet their own individual sartorial style. The team was composed of several second-generation Italians from New York, a few recent arrivals still red-faced and fresh, and a tough looking bunch led by a lanky cowboy known to everyone as 'Tex'.

The locals were renowned for their spitting and fully expected to win. As a team, they were undoubtedly the stronger. Tension mounted as the match progressed, and the contestants were positioned ever further from the target. Weaker contenders rapidly fell by the wayside but Tex was a star, and seemingly unbeatable. Constance was amazed that it was possible to produce such quantities of saliva. Everyone, Constance included, was soon in hysterics as the churning of mouths became more animated in the effort to accumulate a good 'gob'. A momentary silence fell as each person took aim, then the arrival of a viscous 'buong' on the target would be greeted by deafening cheers or boos. Much to the delight of the Lincolns, Tex continued to out spit all his rivals till at last, dry-mouthed and slack-jawed, the village team conceded defeat. Fortunately, wine was still plentiful and there was no problem in the rapid replacement of lost fluids.

But when the contest was over, Addie grew thoughtful.

All the worries she kept as firmly repressed as possible about the safety of Byron had come surging to the surface of her mind on seeing the Lincolns. She sought out Max again in the crowd, knowing that he always seemed to have more information than anyone about what was going on.

'Major Fox he is now, love,' Max told her when she asked if he had news of Byron, 'didn't you know? You get rapid promotion in the Lincolns if you make it through. He was captain of a machine gun company at Belchite, now he's been promoted again. They all thought he was killed in the retreat from Aragon but, blow me, he showed up again after four days wandering about trying to get back to the battalion through the fascist lines. He swam the Ebro – rather 'im than me – it's a big river and a helluva lot faster than the Thames. I think he's the ninth commander the Lincolns have had since the start.'

This was not a fact that Addie found at all re-assuring.

'Sorry, love,' added Max quickly, seeing her worried face, 'I didn't mean to upset you, and the good news is, he's here somewhere – with the top brass I expect, and he's sure to be along later.'

The evening air was suddenly rent by the sound of strident reedy music - Catalan pipes, strangely eerie, playing along with an odd assortment of brass instruments. Addie had heard them before, but the music had never seemed so moving, reverberating through the village streets as the sun was setting. Just at that moment, several large black cars drew up on the road at the far side of the football pitch and an assortment of local dignitaries rushed over to greet the new arrivals. Unfolding as he climbed out from the interior of one of them, Byron was immediately identifiable, even though the light was fading.

'There he is,' Max called out cheerfully to Addie, 'he's with all that lot from the command post.'

If Addie had not already known that Byron was now the commander of a battalion, she would certainly not have been able to deduce the fact at first glance. Most of the men he was with were wearing smart military uniforms. Addie could see that some of them, possibly the Russians, sported surprising quantities of gold braid and what to her seemed ostentatiously large hats. Byron, however, wore a zip-up corduroy jacket, fitted below the waist, and an open-necked shirt. Nevertheless, there was some almost indefinable change in him since their days in Madrid. Addie tried to think calmly, not an easy task with a racing heart, and work out what it could be. 'Ah, the aura of authority,' she decided as she watched him casually talking to someone who looked like a general. But she was not the only one who appeared to be aware of this particular quality, and others, that he possessed. The bevy of girls emerging from the cars gravitated towards him, attempting to entice him from the general's side. They reluctantly dispersed to find alternative prey on the arrival of a sophisticated looking woman, mature but still beautiful, who in a skilful and proprietary manoeuvre, captured Byron's arm and clung to it with well-practised assurance. Not wishing to be forced to vie for Byron's attentions whilst he was obviously otherwise engaged, Addie shrank back further through the crowd till she found a spot beside the steps leading up from the fountain where she could listen to the music and watch the festivities un-observed.

A sadness settled over her, like damp leaves falling to earth. Byron was dancing passably well with his elegant companion, despite the slightly alien quality of the music. She had to admit to herself that seeing Byron with another woman was painful. It created a sort of dissonance in her heart, echoed in the peculiar harmonies and rhythms being played by the band. A sudden flood of homesickness added to her miseries as she remembered the limpid melodies in Purcell's 'Faerie Queen'. The present lull between battles had given her more time to think of home. She leaned her head back against the wall and closed her eyes. The day had been long, and the drive tiring. She wasn't sure how much time had passed, she must have drifted off for a few moments, but she gradually became aware that the tune had changed. The musicians were now attempting their own distinctive rendition of 'The Quartermaster Stores'. Before she was fully awake, she experienced that uncanny feeling of knowing that someone was watching her. She jumped visibly when she opened her eyes and saw Byron's face close to her own.

Suddenly seeing her on the steps had stopped Byron in his tracks as he was slipping away for a few moments alone. The fact that she seemed to be asleep took him instantly back to the times when he had watched her resting contentedly in his arms. There had been several other girls since then, and the sex had been mostly passable to good, but it had never brought that same intense feeling of being alive he had always found with Addie. Since the retreat, there had been no one. When, without warning, she opened her eyes and looked straight into his, the same spark flew between them again.

'I didn't want to wake you,' he said as he sat down beside her on the step, 'you looked so peaceful.' Addie was close enough now to see that there were more changes in him than she had realised. Outwardly confident, even brash, there had always been times when he had seemed more thoughtful. Now, despite his relaxed smile, there was a brooding darkness in his eyes that gave him a slightly haunted air. Addie noticed it immediately, although it would have been barely discernable to anyone who hadn't known him earlier in the war.

'How are you?' she asked, falling back on polite convention as she was quite unable to find any other words amongst the turmoil in her head.

'I am a deserter on the run,' he joked, attempting to break through the barrier of the months they had spent apart. 'I am escaping my assigned duty of escort to a lady diplomat from a far-away country about which I know very little indeed. She is as formidable as an entire battery of field guns and I shall need reinforcements to escape unscathed.' He looked at her hopefully till they both burst out laughing.

'Are we to be comrades-in-arms?' asked Addie with a quizzical smile, quite unable to resist the chance for verbal innuendo or indeed, Byron himself. Apart from the scribbled note he had left for her when his unit had been recalled to the front, they hadn't written to each other, though both had started letters that they couldn't finish. The thought had occurred to both of them that perhaps their days in Madrid were best left in the past. They might never see each other again, and if they did, things would probably be different.

Now, under an improbably large and luminous rising moon, that didn't seem so certain. If, decided Addie, for some reason Byron was choosing her company over that of the prestigious group from the command post, it was no good pretending that she wasn't pleased. As he took her hand to walk down the steps to join the dancing, her spirits soared. She knew that on the sand-covered dance floor they made an ill matched pair. Unlike the leggy diplomat, she was much too short to be an ideal dancing partner for him. However, they whirled round together in a most satisfactory manner, Addie's feet often barely touching the floor. When they stopped to draw breath, Byron's officially designated date came to claim him, claws unsheathed. He quickly attempted to mollify her by introducing Addie as the love of his life, lost at the front for months, and now miraculously found again by amazing good fortune at this remote village fiesta. Although she had at first glared at Addie with blatant ferocity, Byron told his story convincingly enough for her to soften and forgive him a little in the end, perhaps because there was sufficient truth in his explanation to make it believable. Addie found little difficulty in playing the adoring girlfriend.

When they had collected their portion of supper, served from something reminiscent of a cannibal's cauldron, they sat down at the long trestle tables with Constance, Max and

Aurora. The food was the best most people there had tasted for months – still the inevitable beans, but with the occasional meatball as an added luxury.

'Are you down in Chabola Valley?' Max asked Byron, 'the lads are turning it into a regular holiday camp.' The troops had been ordered to build rough shelters for themselves all along the narrow valley that ran between Marsá and the next village. Most of them had adopted the Spanish word, 'chabola', to describe their improvised sleeping quarters, usually dugouts covered by branches and any other materials they could 'organise'.

'What's coming sure won't be a picnic though,' Byron replied, then stopped abruptly, obviously not wanting to say any more. 'The British Battalion are down at the far end near the Canadians, aren't they?'

'Lucky for them,' Max said with a grin, 'right next to the village where there's a good supply of vino. All this training is thirsty work.'

A wary glance passed between them, an acknowledgement that it was better not to discuss details of the training. Everyone had been given strict orders about the need for secrecy. The men were spending hours in the dry river beds, rehearsing for what all of them knew must be the crossing of the River Ebro.

The music was slower and the night growing cooler when Addie and Byron danced again. Her head rested against his chest and she felt his arm gently pulling her closer. It was all so pleasant, she found herself wishing that time would stop, or better, that she could capture these moments and keep them in a sort of album of experiences, to be taken out and re-lived whenever she wanted, rather than just admired like photographs.

'Excuse me, sir,' she heard a voice say in slightly deferential tones, 'the cars are leaving now to go back to Falset. Everyone is going for drinks at the hotel I believe. Will you be joining them?'

Addie saw Byron hesitate before he answered. She guessed that he wanted to ask her to come with him to the hotel, but there were still certain social conventions to be observed, even in wartime. She waited to see what he would say.

'Where are you staying tonight?' he asked her cautiously, 'Some of us have rooms at the 'Fonda' in the town just down the road as we're supposed to be entertaining the visitors. I'm sure I could get you a room there too, if you like.'

Addie was surprised at how relieved she felt to be able to hide behind this subterfuge. It was one thing to enjoy uninhibited passion when she was alone with Byron, quite another to go into a hotel with a group of senior officers and brazenly go up to share a room. 'Will we ever succeed in changing these outdated attitudes?' she asked herself in annoyance. 'And I'm as much to blame as anyone. We're all supposed to be fighting for equality and yet it's still impossible for me to ignore the rigmarole of what a 'nice' girl should do or not do.' She grudgingly came to the conclusion that this was not the right time to make a stand on the issue of women's sexual freedom. After the war, she would think about it again. She smiled and answered graciously, 'That would be most kind.'

They followed the young officer, obviously a new recruit who was somewhat in awe of a battle-tested veteran. Addie found Constance and checked that Madge and the other nurses she had brought would be able to stay at the hospital nearby. 'Stacks of room,' replied Constance, adding with a slight smile, 'you two enjoy yourselves.' She was pleased to see Addie looking so happy, though there was something that worried her about Byron. She had often nursed men with eyes that had a veiled look about them. Usually, they were trying to hide something from themselves as much as from others. That night, she had glimpsed the same intangible quality in Byron's eyes too.

The Fonda was still noisy even though it was very late. The bar was full to bursting and people spilled out into the gardens behind. Songs were sung in various languages, rising and falling in volume, sometimes all at once. Byron spoke to the landlord and money changed hands. An unoccupied room had miraculously been found for Addie. They joined those from the command post at one of the marble-topped tables. She sipped her drink slowly and tried to work out why she felt so ill at ease. It wasn't just because she was in a bar that was clearly a predominantly male preserve. This was a rural market town, not a cosmopolitan city like Madrid, and old traditions were strong. Though there were a few other women to be seen in the bar, they were mostly foreign ones. She knew that she was being carefully looked over by several of the men there, and that she was still being closely scrutinised by the formidable lady delegate who had apparently not given up all hope of regaining her former position. Addie felt sure they all knew that she longed to be in bed with Byron. It was as if they could see into her imagination; their soon to be realised intimacy lying bare and exposed, sex on a slab. The scenario reminded Addie of all the seedy encounters she had ever imagined taking place in hotels.

Byron could sense that Addie was uncomfortable and knew that he must do something quickly if he wasn't to lose her. She was retreating further from him every minute. It wasn't so much that he wanted a night of passion, though of course, he wouldn't deny that the idea was certainly agreeable. In reality, he just wanted to be with her again, to re-create the private world they had shared. Without the adrenalin surge of battle, the painful truths about the war and what it did to people came frequently to the forefront of his mind, and though he knew he had to stick with the bloody business till the end, this mental fatigue was far harder to overcome than physical exhaustion. Addie though, had a way of making him feel that things balanced out better. With her, he was sure he could be himself again for a while instead of this 'Commander' character who had taken over his life. Right now, he had to come up with a strategic plan of attack or Addie might well change her mind and leave after all. It was pointless trying to talk properly in the bar and the crowd showed no sign of diminishing. He leaned closer to her and said so that only she could hear, 'I've got to stay and have one more drink with the General. Would you prefer to go up to your room? If there's anything you want, I'm in number four, at the other end of the hall from you.' Addie nodded in agreement, relieved that she would be able to escape the noise and have time to think things through before deciding what to do. Byron had clearly placed the outcome of the evening in her hands.

The diamond shaped pattern of the black and white tiles on the floor in the hotel had a distinctly Alice in Wonderland quality about them, thought Addie. Perhaps the last glass of wine was making her a little light-headed. She quite expected to find a small bottle on the side table in the hall with a label saying, 'Drink Me'. Certainly, she felt as if she was in a dream as she collected her key and climbed up the stairs to the first floor. There was a surreal quality about the building. A few isolated lamps cast pools of feeble light amidst the shadows, and the noises from the bar became strangely muffled as the double doors swung together. The first floor retained vestiges of its former glory as a spacious, smart 'salon', with numbered doors leading off to each bedroom. Addie couldn't help noticing that several vast chessboards of the black and white tiles would have to be crossed to cover the distance between her room and Byron's.

In the relative quiet of her room, Addie wrapped herself in the counterpane and sat hugging her knees on the bed. The dismal decor was enough to depress a saint, she thought gloomily, wishing she was with Constance and the others instead of alone in a hotel room. Then, drifting through the open window came an impromptu rendering of 'El Quinto Regimiento', one of the best known songs amongst the troops. The verse was for one voice alone, and whoever the soloist was in the garden below, he was singing the poignant melody from his heart. Addie was surprised to find that fat tears were rolling down her cheeks. For months she had been driving miles along dangerous rough roads, sleeping fitfully wherever she could lay her head, and taking on her shoulders all the problems that the nurses shared with her, trying to boost their morale. During all that time, she hadn't cried once.

'What an idiot I am,' she muttered angrily as the final chorus reached its resolute conclusion, 'I can't believe I'm letting myself be bothered by a few lewd men in a bar and a lascivious old witch. I'm not going to spend the night by myself in this dingy room just because of them.'

Her normally rebellious nature now rapidly reasserted itself, and she could see quite clearly that she and Byron should be together again, even if the circumstances were far from ideal. Her mind made up, she went to wash her face in the sink. Grateful to the previous occupant who had left behind a rare luxury – a sliver of perfumed soap – she washed herself slowly and thoroughly to remove the cares of the day along with the dust of the journey. Half an hour later she walked with determination across the hall and opened the door of Byron's room.

At first she thought that the room was empty. The light was not switched on, and in the wedge of light that had entered through the door, she could see that the bed was undisturbed. Then she realised that there was another door, opening onto a terrace. A shadowy figure was standing there, looking out over the garden, apparently listening to the ongoing concert being performed by the men drinking at the tables outside. Byron was not really hearing the music, he was gazing at the mountain ranges that were just discernable against the starry sky. He hadn't heard her enter the room, or lock the door behind her either, but as she stood by the terrace door, shivering slightly from the chilliness of the night air, or perhaps from anticipation, he sensed her presence and turned to face her.

When he saw Addie watching him, Byron at first felt a moment of triumph, but this was soon overwhelmed by something he would have described simply as happiness. For a short time it seemed as if this, in itself, was more than anyone had a right to expect, but when he took her in his arms and kissed her, he knew there was much more they both wanted. However hard they tried, it was impossible to temper desire with technique. Byron only had time for a brief moment in which to be glad that Addie's reluctance for any further delay seemed as strong as his own. He entered her with a shout that was loud enough to have brought the men below to attention, had they not fortunately still been singing too loudly to hear. He felt that the power of his thrusting could drive out demons. Then, in a split second, the demons turned to plague him. His mind was filled with their foul darkness. He faltered, unmanned by the suddenness of their ambush. He could feel Addie tensing, knowing there was something wrong, then freezing to immobility. She was afraid of what would happen next, remembering with a horrid vividness the last time she had been aware of such a dramatic turn in the tide of passion. Would Byron turn from her as Marcel had done before? The hurt rejection she had felt then would be nothing in comparison to the pain she would feel this time. Even though she knew logically that Marcel's problem was of his own making, she couldn't help thinking that she must be doing something to cause such a distressing loss of desire.

But Byron didn't turn away. Instead of his own unwelcome visions, he began to think of Addie, of not wanting to bring sadness into her bright eyes, of how much he loved the way she questioned what she saw in the world around her. Then he thought of her warm breasts, aware that one was, at this very moment, beneath his hand. He could detect the faint smell of soap coming from her body. She must have washed before coming to his room. The thought of her spreading the smooth lather on her skin and enjoying the sensual pleasure of its touch, made him recover with an amazing rapidity. Within seconds, he watched her body arch and shudder, and felt her rise to meet him in a lightning union that seemed to contain enough of a charge to blow all the fuses back home in Brooklyn.

Addie, curled on her side, could feel him all along the length of her back, his knees tucked up behind hers because the bed was too short, his chest against her shoulders. Despite the intermittent tickling sensation on her bottom whenever he moved, she was happy to stay where she was, looking at the night sky through the open terrace doors and listening to him breathing in her ear. He'd gone to sleep almost immediately after they made love; so deeply it was almost as if he had fallen into a coma. She drifted a little, but woke again when the pace of his breathing began to change, becoming faster, more staccato. He grew restless, and the arm that lay across her twitched repeatedly. When he twisted away from her, she could see his face contorting in the pale dawn light. At first she thought it would be best not to wake him, that the nightmare would pass, but instead it grew worse. He was struggling to say something but despite his efforts, no words would come. Addie woke him as gently as she could. For a few moments he lay rigid, sweating and disorientated, trying to accept the reality of what he could see around him. She knew it would be stupid to say 'Is anything the matter?' when obviously something was seriously amiss. Instead, she asked 'Is there anything I can do?'

'No,' he replied with a slow shake of his head, but he held on to her hand like a lifeline.

They sat up, side by side, leaning against the wooden headboard of the rickety bed, so they could see the sun rising. The mountains were soon perfectly defined in the clarity of the morning light, their brutal ridges suddenly looming far too close at hand.

CHAPTER 7

Lost Dreams

I

Marsá and the mountains became Addie's world in the weeks that followed as she travelled between Barcelona and the village, taking nurses and supplies to the medical units. Each time she made the journey there, she could hardly bear the anticipation as the car twisted and crawled slowly upwards, away from the coast. Finally the moment would arrive when she rounded the last corner and could look down and see the wide valley opening out below her, Falset and Marsá looking as tiny as model villages fitting neatly within a random geometry of meticulously cultivated plots. She always wished she could launch herself from the summit and fly there in a straight line but instead, she had to descend cautiously, hugging the verge on blind bends in case any trucks were laboriously climbing up the steep gradient in the opposite direction. On her arrival, she would sometimes find that there were staff problems to be resolved, giving her an excuse to stay near Marsá for a few nights. Constance and the other nurses had been working hard to convert two of the houses on the largest rural estates into respectable hospitals. The arched terraces and towers made the buildings rather imposing, but they were not what could be called comfortable. At least with their thick walls and stone floors, they were cool inside. Addie fervently hoped they would not still be in use by the time winter arrived when the draughty halls would be impossible to heat. Their Catalan names sounded strange when she first heard them. She tried to copy the local pronunciation of 'Mas de l'Arany', and 'Mas Magrinyà', but it was not easy, and very frustrating after she had made so much effort to learn Spanish. Some of the villagers hardly spoke any Spanish at all and when they talked to her in Catalan she could only understand a few words.

As soon as she arrived, she would send a message to Byron hoping that he would be able to escape from the battalion for a while. When he could get away for a few hours, they would walk together, deep in conversation, often barely noticing their surroundings, unless one of them saw something that they wanted to share with the other. Addie was the first to see the bee-eaters. She stopped in her tracks, clutching Byron's arm. Swooping as they hunted, the birds filled the air, the sun glinting on their shimmering gold and turquoise feathers and shining through translucent wings. Addie thought them unbelievably beautiful, more like creatures from fables than flesh and blood. A soft burbling sound came from their long sharp beaks as they perched on the vines. She watched enchanted as they disappeared into their nesting holes in the bank at the side of the road. The hot sandy soil of the bank was perforated with their tunnels and appeared to have as many residents as a tenement block.

Sometimes, Addie and Byron would climb the oddly shaped mound next to the village. The locals had told them that it was called the 'Miloquera', after a type of bird now long extinct. 'All eaten probably,' said Byron wryly. The views as they climbed became ever more dramatic, but they preferred to stop before reaching the top, where a lookout had been posted to watch for signs of enemy movements. There were other places to pause for a while and look at the world spread out at their feet, or to sink for a brief time into happy seclusion. The tumbled walls of Iberian ruins and a variety of large spiky bushes offered shade and privacy, though Addie soon came to regard the inhospitable shrubbery with less favour after a few prickly encounters that were too close for comfort.

As the weeks passed by, the official programme designed 'to maintain the morale of the troops and the goodwill of the local population' gave them even more chances to meet. There were concerts in village halls, theatrical performances in barns, propaganda talks and parades on the football pitches. Afterwards, Addie and Byron could occasionally spend the night together at the Fonda, even though Byron swore that the bed had been designed to cripple him. The springs sagged alarmingly and his feet crashed into the wooden bed end with monotonous frequency. But, of course, it was worth it.

In Madrid they had talked mainly of writers and politics, ideas and dreams. But now, in this interlude that they both well knew was the calm before the storm, Addie learned more about Byron and his life before the war. He had already told her with seeming indifference, that times had often been hard for his family. Now however, she began to understand that his childhood had probably had more effect on him than he cared to admit. He had learned a lot about survival as he grew up, everything from fighting in street gangs to making unscrupulous deals to defraud exploitative employers. Any signs of weakness were kept well hidden, only fools allowed themselves to be vulnerable to others. It was becoming clear to Addie that the streets of Brooklyn had given him a core of toughness he could still draw on at will. Sometimes it was covered with a thin veneer of easy charm or the type of literary intellectualism that she found fascinating. Nevertheless, she now knew why he had become the commander of a battalion so quickly. He was capable of doing whatever needed to be done; perhaps, she thought with concern, even at whatever the cost might be. Could it be that this toughness ran right through him like the lettering in a stick of seaside rock? Very occasionally, she thought she caught a glimpse of something softer, though it was as fleeting as the glint of sunshine on the bee-eaters' wings.

Addie was vaguely aware that the undercurrent of danger she sensed in Byron was partly what attracted her to him. This, she found extremely disconcerting.

Subconsciously, she had always believed that her ideal man would be rather like her father; kind and reasonable, always a gentleman, someone who would make her feel safe and secure. Byron was very different. She suspected that it wouldn't be at all wise to put herself at the mercy of a man who at times had more than a hint of the savage about him. Unfortunately, it seemed that she was not entirely in control of her feelings. Whenever she saw him, her whole body seemed on the point of dissolving into hot, viscous treacle. She thanked her lucky stars for the strong independent streak that was the only thing standing between her and total liquefaction. Their relationship, so intimate on one level, was charged with latent tension as they circled each other as closely as they dared, both secretly afraid to risk too much.

By the time of Nehru's arrival, everyone had grown accustomed to the visits of important dignitaries who were still prepared to show their support of the Republic. A string of them had been already. They watched displays of training exercises put on by the troops and had their photographs taken with the generals, smiling and confident of victory.

'Jawaharlal Nehru,' said Constance to Addie, as they waited with the crowd on the football pitch for the Indian politician to arrive. 'What a mouthful, no wonder everyone just calls him "Nehru". Can you see him yet?'

'No,' replied Addie, 'but they're always late. I don't think the men are ready for the display yet either. I can see Max over there though, let's go and join him.'

Max was sitting on the wall by the fountain, looking unusually downcast.

'Oh dear,' Constance said to Addie with a grimace as they approached him, 'I do hope Aurora hasn't given him the brush off, he'll be miserable if she has.'

'Bad news, Max?' asked Addie as they drew near.

'Rotten,' replied Max tersely. 'The word is, and it's more or less official, that Sam was with that lot who took a hammering at Calaceite. They were marching along the road in heavy rain, poor visibility, they say, and round the bend came these tanks. The commander and the commissar were killed before they realised that they were Italian tanks, not ours. The lads put up a bit of a fight but only a few got away.'

'Is Sam dead?' Constance asked with a lump in her throat.

Addie knew Constance had a soft spot for Sam. She had often spoken of him.

'Well,' Max said, rubbing his hand through his hair several times with unaccustomed agitation, 'they say that he was taken prisoner – plenty were.'

'But that means he could be alright then,' said Addie earnestly, 'they're starting to keep prisoners alive now to make exchanges, aren't they?'

Max nodded in agreement, making an effort to be more optimistic about Sam's chances. 'They'll probably be back home before us,' he assured them. He certainly wasn't going to mention what he had heard about the sort of conditions prisoners had to endure. If you weren't taken out and shot, you were lucky to survive starvation, dirt, disease and torture. Max knew that Sam wasn't only out of luck in getting himself captured either. When their paths had last crossed in Teruel, Max had told him about Constance being mad keen on a German bloke, and how grateful she had been when Max had found him. Sam's downcast expression soon made Max regret he'd opened his big mouth. 'Cheer up, mate, women are always changing their minds.' Even as he said the words, he knew that neither of them believed this old chestnut applied to Constance.

'Sam's got his head screwed on, he'll be alright,' Max smiled as confidently as he could.

'We've just got to wait for news then,' said Constance, sighing in resignation, 'we mustn't give up hope yet.'

Before they had time to recover from this upsetting

information, something else happened that dampened their spirits even further.

'It never rains but it pours,' Constance muttered gloomily as María emerged from a car that had just screeched to a halt by the town hall. Hoping that she hadn't seen them, Constance and Addie merged into the crowd as quickly as they could.

The VIPs arrived just as the last soldiers shuffled into line. A buzz of interest greeted Nehru, in his white hat and distinctive clothing. Addie could see Byron and the Lincolns over at the far side of the football pitch. They had arranged to meet after the afternoon's events were over. She could see him, head high, eyes searching the crowd. When he caught sight of her, he gave a very relaxed version of a salute in her direction. The display began with the sun beating down on the columns of men as they marched back and forth. Part of the training was to get new recruits fit for fighting in the heat. Even though she was in the shade, Addie could feel her head beginning to ache from the glare of the sun on the sand. The machine gun companies usually put on the final display. There was an ongoing competition between them to see which company could dismantle and re-assemble a machine gun in the fastest time. The rest of the assembled men closed ranks to watch them, urging them on, aware that their own lives often depended on the speed with which a machine gun could be set up in a new position. Constance and Aurora were cheering loudly in Addie's ear as the contest reached its climax. She was finding it more interesting to watch Nehru and the Indian woman at his side that she believed to be Indira Gandhi. Their faces both had fixed expressions, polite, but impassive. Addie resolved to find out more about the motives for their visit from Byron later on.

She didn't see the accident, only heard the sharp shot and the gasps of dismay. Her eyes followed the direction of the stunned gazes of the audience, to see an agitated circle of men forming around two soldiers lying on the ground.

'What happened?' she asked Constance and Max in dismay.

Constance was about to run over to the injured men, but others had been nearer than she was and were swiftly dealing with the emergency.

'Must have been a bullet still up the spout,' Max replied in disbelief. 'They should've checked that the chamber was empty, because they always pull the trigger last of all. And every idiot knows not to point a gun at your mates, even if you're sure it's unloaded, let alone fire it.' That one carelessly fired bullet could have so pointlessly injured two men seemed cruel indeed. The display was brought quickly to an end with a short speech of thanks to Nehru and his party, and most of the soldiers were marched back to Chabola Valley as fast as possible.

The crowd dispersed more slowly, rumours were already spreading of the death of one of the wounded men, and the imminent demise of the other. Constance and Addie sat despondently by the fountain with Max and Aurora, stunned into silence at the grim turn of events. María's breezy greeting was less than welcome.

'Well, what a display of efficiency that turned out to be!' Her voice, heavy with sarcasm, grated on their ears.

'Hello, María,' Addie said reluctantly, 'I see you haven't lost your knack for making tactless remarks.'

Their eyes met, fully aware of the enmity that lay behind their insincere smiles. María eventually looked away and tossed her head to cast off the weight of Addie's contemptuous glare. She turned to Constance, saying, 'Oh, I've got a note for you from some German chap. I forgot to bring it with me, but it wasn't urgent - he says he's fine.' The implications of this nonchalant statement took a few moments to register with Constance. That María should have read Karl's letter was bad enough, but then to have left it in Barcelona, discarded as unimportant, was sufficient to make her want to rip María's heart out. On top of everything, she knew that she would never see the letter if she let any of her feelings show.

'I'd be grateful if you would let me have it as soon as you can,' Constance cast her eyes downwards so María couldn't see the resentment burning there. Aurora caught a glimpse of the fires that raged within them and, once again, was amazed at Constance's steely self-control. She would quite willingly have torn María's heart out herself, knowing how much Constance must be suffering. Gratified to detect the traces of suppressed pain and anger emanating from her audience, María basked in the warm glow of revenge accomplished. Just then, a car stopped beside them and Byron got out of the back. He hurried over to Addie and, smiling briefly at the others, took her arm to draw her aside.

'Are you OK?' he asked in concern, knowing that it was likely that the accident had upset her. Deaths by 'friendly fire' were always hard to take, even for the men, who had probably all witnessed quite a few.

'I'll be alright,' Addie replied, 'Do you know what's happened to the men who were shot?'

'Both dead,' he replied, 'that's why I've got to go now – formalities to go through, you understand. I'll try to get back as soon as I can. Can you wait?'

Addie so wanted to be with him that she felt like saying she would wait all night if necessary. But instead, she just briefly and lightly stroked his hand, saying, 'I expect I'll be here for a while.'

María's sharp eyes didn't miss the gesture of affection, or the intensity of the looks that passed between them. It was obvious that something was going on, and it didn't take María long to work out how she could turn this to her own advantage. Ever since the fire in the flat, María had been aware that Addie was watching her. This had presented her with all sorts of irritating and inconvenient problems. When Addie returned to her friends, María was ready to wreak her revenge in full.

'Funny,' she said, a slight smile playing across her lips, 'I hadn't put you down as the type to fraternise with a man who shoots deserters.'

There was little hope, María was thinking as she dropped the acid remark into the already overwrought atmosphere, that the gossip circulating in Barcelona about Byron had not yet reached Addie. But the shock on Addie's face told her that she had been the first to tell her the news. She watched with pleasure as the body blow she had given her enemy took effect.

'What do you mean?' Addie at last managed to ask, trying to keep her voice steady. She was too stunned to care that her distress was delighting María.

'Oh, I thought everyone knew by now. He shot at least one, probably more, on the retreat, I think. He didn't order a proper execution. It was a quick bullet in the dead of night, so I've heard. Perhaps he likes to do it himself. You never know with a man like that.'

Constance spoke out in dismissive tones, 'I don't believe it – it's just gossip. What proof have you got, María?'

'Well,' María replied, the final victory almost in her grasp, 'it doesn't matter to me what you believe, but it would be easy to find out for sure.' She drew closer to Addie and fired her poisonous parting shot, 'Why don't you just ask him?'

Addie felt the words hit home. She stood silently as María triumphantly walked away, though inside she felt as if she were sinking to her knees in defeat. She knew that all María had said could easily be true. It could explain the uneasiness she had felt about Byron, about the changes she had sensed in him ever since they had met again in Marsá. What was worst of all was that she knew María's poison was already coursing through her veins. However hard she tried to avoid it, sooner or later she would have to ask Byron the question. If he admitted it, she doubted she would ever be able to forget what he had done. If he denied it, whether guilty or truly not guilty, they would still both know that she had believed him capable of murder. The venomous question would contaminate their relationship whatever he replied. She could think of no antidote, the damage was done.

As she sat outside the church on the benches where they had arranged to meet, Addie tried once again to put the whole thing in perspective. She told herself firmly that terrible things always happen in wars. The priest of this very church had been shot by vengeful extremists from the next town in the first days of the war. Men had been killing each other by the thousand for the last two years. It was stupid of her to let just one more name on the casualty list destroy something she held so dear, even though it was a death that she believed never should have been allowed to happen. Above the church door, a statue of John the Baptist stood in its niche, obviously symbolic of something, though Addie wasn't quite sure what. His image had suffered less than the priest when the time had come for the settling of old scores, just the lower part of one arm was missing. Had his hand been raised in benediction over the village or had he been pointing to the heavens to warn sinners of the wrath of God? Wasn't it enough to know in your heart that something was wrong without having the threat of divine retribution hanging over you? But what a comfort it must be to believe that your sins could be absolved. Without blind faith to call on, where did one find forgiveness? Addie's head throbbed and she pressed her fingers hard against her temples trying to ease the pressure.

She could see Byron looked tired as he walked towards her. His loping stride was less energetic than usual and his shoulders hunched, hands thrust deep into the pockets of his jacket. It had grown chilly sitting in the shade of the church now evening was approaching and Addie stood up to meet him. Together they set off along the now familiar path to the Miloquera. They were both at a loss for words. Byron was reflecting with bitterness on the debacle of the afternoon's display, angry at the loss of two good soldiers for the sake of a public spectacle that had prevented the men from concentrating as well as they should. He assumed that Addie was quiet for the same reason. Indeed, she was sad too at the thought of such futile deaths, and also because of the news about Sam being captured. But the waves of sickness that washed over her were because she dreaded the moment when she would have to ask him the question, knowing that the words, once spoken, couldn't be recalled. They stopped when they had climbed the pink rocks of the path to the point where the tiled roofs of the houses and the church tower were below them, warm in the soft evening light. The ever-present backdrop of the distant mountains framed the scene with a peaceful stillness but Addie, for once, was oblivious to their beauty. She could wait no longer.

'Is it true that you shot a deserter?'

For weeks Byron had expected that Addie would hear the rumours sooner or later. Such things were difficult to keep secret for long. He looked deep into her eyes and hated what he saw there – a reflection of his own disgust at what he had done. He didn't want to talk about the soldier he'd shot, quickly and neatly, before there'd been time for him to feel fear for more than a split second. The man had already deserted on several occasions, but had managed to worm his way out of trouble with excuses when he was caught. Finally, when they had been ordered to make a stand during the retreat, he'd pushed his luck too far by feigning injury and nearly getting two stretcher bearers killed rescuing him. He had even let them carry him out under fire, whilst comrades around him were really bleeding to death. Afterwards, he had claimed he was concussed but there wasn't a mark on him. He was a coward and a liability; everyone knew he was a danger to them all. Even so, when Byron had received instructions from HQ to get rid of him, he had been loath to do it, or to order anyone else to do so. But they were having to move fast then, fighting and retreating, no time for niceties like trials and firing squads. He had to think of the men in his battalion first, not just this one miserable liar. How many others would desert if they knew that this man had been sent back to the rear? He'd done his best to make it easy, waking the poor sap to tell him he was needed for night sentry duty outside the camp. Half-asleep, the soldier had followed as trustingly as a lamb to the slaughter. In the end, it had been more like shooting a loyal, sick dog than butchering a lamb, only much worse. As planned, he'd fallen tidily into the trench that Byron had ordered to be dug that afternoon. The sound of the last breath leaving his lungs as he hit the bottom, and the smell of the damp earth that was shovelled on top of him afterwards, were recurring elements in Byron's nightmares.

Byron failed completely when it came to putting any of this into words. He didn't want to talk about the doubts that he now felt about whether he had done the right thing or not. At the time, it had seemed unavoidable, and in a way, better for the man's wife and family, who would be told simply that he had been lost in action, not executed for cowardice in the face of the enemy. But now he wondered if he should have tried harder to find another option. He wasn't sure any more that he could convincingly justify his actions to anyone, especially Addie, and right at that moment, after such a goddamn awful day, he wasn't prepared to even try.

'Someone had to do it,' was all he said, turning away so he couldn't see Addie's face any more.

He didn't want to watch any longer as her features hardened into an expression he had never seen on her face before when she was looking at him. He was suddenly filled with a cold resentment. She was far too ready to think the worst of him. She didn't seem to be trying at all to understand the terrible responsibilities that came with leadership. The men in the battalion trusted him, but she didn't. He wanted to retreat and redeploy his forces but she continued to pursue him further, crying in anguish, 'How could you kill one of your own men, just because they were too afraid to fight for a while? Maybe he had a good reason.'

Addie knew a great deal about the deserters who had been executed in the First World War. Her mother campaigned on a committee trying to get pensions for their widows. She had shown Addie some of the last letters written from the condemned men to their wives. The latest research on shell-shock would have exonerated nearly all of them. Surely the International Brigades were more enlightened than the British Army had been? Could Byron be so callous?

'It's nothing more than cold-blooded murder to shoot someone who's defenceless.'

Addie felt like a murderer herself as she saw him flinch. Why wouldn't he defend himself? She waited desperately for him to retaliate, to convince her that she was wrong.

If Byron had realised that this was the only chance he was going to get to mount a counter offensive, he would have used every strategy he knew and would have fought till he dropped. Instead, he made the biggest tactical error of his life.

'I guess that makes me a murderer then,' he said quietly.

For a moment, as Addie stared at him in silence, he seemed like a stranger, his customary half smile replaced by an expression as hard and immutable as the statue above the church door. She tried desperately to suppress the insistent thought that now welled up in her mind, but with a dreadful and pernicious persistence it formed itself into unspoken, unwanted words. Perhaps Byron was really not the person she had imagined him to be at all.

The church clock chimed the hour. It might as well have been a death knell. Addie stumbled down the path with tears in her eyes, her feet sliding on the stones that now glowed a dull blood red in the setting sun.

II

As they drove ever higher above the Ebro, Constance felt the sweat soaking through the back of her shirt and adhere damply to the seat of the ambulance. The hot breeze from the open window did little to make her more comfortable. 'Ladies never sweat,' Constance recalled her mother saying, but 'perspiration' did not seem an adequate word to describe the rivulets of bodily fluid trickling down her neck. 'Flaming June' however, was a totally appropriate description. Constance looked forward eagerly to their arrival at the cave, now designated for use as a hospital. In her imagination she could see it hovering as tantalisingly as a mirage before her, a cool leafy grotto with a cascading waterfall.

'Poor Addie!' The memory of her friend, sobbing miserably after parting from Byron, made her reflect for a while on the events of the last few days. It annoyed Constance intensely to think how overjoyed María would be if she ever learned the true extent of the damage caused by her spiteful remark. Although Constance could sympathise with Addie's distress, she didn't actually share her point of view. She saw the whole thing as another example of Addie's tendency to overindulge in righteous indignation, just as she had done following the fire in the flat. In Constance's opinion, which she imparted to Addie in no uncertain terms, Byron had only done what he had to do – a very nasty business, but completely necessary when viewed from a practical perspective. One had to think of the greater good in these situations, not just the individual. Karl had taught her the importance of that. And anyway, Byron had been given his orders. What would have happened to him if he hadn't carried them out? Byron was due some credit at least for having done the job himself, rather than delegating the dirty work to someone else. Though she had tried her utmost to persuade Addie to talk to Byron again, she had left for Barcelona the next morning, the pinched tenseness of her face betraying her wretchedness. Addie could only think of one reason why Byron had been so reluctant to discuss the matter – he believed that what he had done was right. In the face of such arrogant conviction, what was the point of arguing?

The ambulance was now passing beneath massive rounded rocks that hung over the narrow road. Their strange formations seemed to ooze from the mountain, like gelatinous darkly golden syrup, petrified in mid-flow. The narrow houses in the village of La Bisbal de Falset seemed to have sunk their foundations into a molten rocky embrace, to become an integral part of the mountainside. Once past the village, the driver suddenly veered from the road. Constance almost shrieked, fearing a repetition of her earlier accident. But to her relief, once over the brink, a path descended abruptly, eventually leading to the cave at the other side of a small valley. It was not at all as she had envisaged. Beneath an immense slab of rock was a large opening, like a gaping toothless mouth, wide but shallow. There was no waterfall, but when Constance stood beneath the arching grey and ochre walls and her eyes grew accustomed to the shadows, she could see a small spring of fresh water trickling quite rapidly into a natural channel at the back of the cave. When she turned to look at the world outside again, she was dazzled by a landscape of brilliant blue and green, set within a ponderous curved frame of stone.

Work had already begun on converting the cave for its new role. The earthen floor had been divided into two distinct levels where the patients would be safe from bombardments. With a practised eye, Constance estimated there would be room for around a hundred and fifty beds. One end of the cave was being separated from the rest by an improvised partition wall, which Constance presumed would be for the operating theatre. In the newly turned earth at her feet, she suddenly caught sight of a small strangely-shaped stone. She picked it up and rubbed away the soil to expose a primitive flint arrow head, its crafted facets still smooth to the touch. Constance shivered slightly. The cave obviously had a long history of human habitation, but she feared that what was to come would be more tragic than anything that had happened there in the past.

Further modifications were made to the cave in the days that followed. Max helped a Canadian engineer to run a power line from a temperamental generator that they had rigged up to provide light in the operating theatre. An enormous curtain now hung in the cave mouth in front of the low metal framed beds, not only in an attempt to keep out the flies, but also to conceal the patients from the searching eyes of passing enemy aircraft. Down in the valley below, amongst the olive trees, Reggie Aston's transfusion lorry was parked next to the triage tent and supplies of preserved blood were being brought in from Barcelona. June passed into an even hotter July, and the tension mounted. No one knew the exact date, but the increased traffic along the road was a sure sign that something would be happening very soon. There was time for one last morale boosting fiesta before the offensive began.

Constance had been given the task of organising the village women to help with the preparations. They were much more wary of her than the women of Marsá had been, perhaps because in Marsá there was a railway station and people were used to strangers and travelling to the nearby cities. La Bisbal de Falset seemed as isolated as a distant island in a mountainous sea of olives and almonds. Preparations for the fiesta in the tiny village were simple. Constance had wanted at least one of the women to take part in the speeches, joining the mayor on the platform and the representatives from the Brigades, but this was not to be. 'Women don't make speeches,' the mayor told her categorically. 'What about La Pasionaria?' Constance retorted. 'She's different,' was the taciturn reply. So the women stuck to tradition, much to Constance's annoyance, content to heighten the festive atmosphere by adorning balconies with their shawls, to cook the communal meal, and to organise games for the children. There was no football pitch for the sports as there had been in Marsá. Instead, races were held on the only flat site available, the road that ran past the village towards the river Ebro. Every now and again, the races would stop to allow convoys of trucks to pass, piled high with assorted equipment for assembling pontoons. By now, everyone knew that a surprise attack was planned across the Ebro, but nobody would betray the secret. The trucks might as well have been invisible for all the comment they received.

Above all that day, Constance enjoyed the picnic. Some of the International Brigaders had contributed scarce luxury items of food to the meal and seeing the expressions of amazement on the faces of the smallest children as they tasted delicacies such as chocolate for the first time was truly memorable. But as the day progressed, it became clear to Constance that a confrontation with Florence could no longer be avoided. A group of Spanish soldiers had invited Flo to drink with them, passing her a leather bottle of rich dark wine. With the bottle held high and her head tipped back, Florence was soon trying to master the art of catching the arching stream of liquid in her open mouth. Her failure to do this successfully was the cause of great hilarity amongst the men. Constance watched uneasily, noticing the disapproving stares from the village women in Florence's direction as the comments from the soldiers grew increasingly ribald. Heedless of the muttered criticisms of the women, Flo wiped the wine from her face with her shirt sleeve, greeting each joke with unrestrained laughter. If she drank much more, Constance was sure things could easily get out of hand. Reluctant as Constance was to interfere, she knew that Flo's behaviour was likely to cause problems for them all in the future.

Trying hard not to appear disapproving, she approached the group with a smile, saying 'Florence, could you spare a moment, please?'

'Bye for now, boys,' said Florence rising to her feet rather unsteadily, 'duty calls.'

'Really, Florence,' Constance began, once they were out of earshot, 'you might think a little more about the reputation of the nurses rather than behave so irresponsibly. It's hard enough sometimes to make the men treat us with respect, and now you are making the women here think we are all shameless hussies. We want them to work with us, not put us beyond the pale.'

Constance had expected Florence to apologise when faced with the obvious logic of this criticism, but she was disappointed. Florence immediately went on the attack. She had a fiery temper and usually didn't much care what people thought about her.

'Oh, it's alright then for you and your friends to have relationships with men, but not for me.'

A ripple of apprehension at the turn the conversation had taken made Constance feel even more uncomfortable than she had before.

'We all know what you get up to when a certain German comes to call, and then there's Addie's fling with the dashing commander. Oh, and let's not forget Miss Aurora butter-wouldn't-melt-in-her-mouth and the cheery cockney mechanic. You're all at it, so don't think you can look down on me with those superior airs of yours.'

The truth in Flo's statement left Constance momentarily at a loss for words. None of them were following normal conventions when it came to relationships with men, even if Florence was more liberated than most. It certainly seemed totally ridiculous to be talking about the need for discretion in such matters when they could all be dead tomorrow. Constance remembered that Addie had mentioned something very similar when telling her about the first night she had spent at the Fonda with Byron. All the intellectual posturing on the subject of open marriages and the prevalent socialist theories of equality for women hadn't made much difference so far, and definitely hadn't reached La Bisbal de Falset, despite the efforts of the Republic to change society.

Constance was prepared to cede the point, but not the battle. Flo, arms folded and face flushed, waited in angry anticipation for Constance's outraged response. To her surprise, Constance merely sighed, 'You're right, Flo, I've no right at all to sound superior, and the people here probably think we are all scarlet women anyway, but it doesn't help us right now to rub their noses in it.'

Florence looked at Constance's tired face and shrugged her shoulders. As usual, her temper had flared quickly but soon subsided. 'Oh, I suppose you've got a point, we haven't got time to be missionaries for the feminists as well as nurses.' Constance didn't expect an apology, and Florence had no intention of giving one, but the tension between them lifted as they walked back up to the cave together. The brief comfort of forgetfulness brought by the wine was fast dissipating as Florence turned to Constance with a sad smile saying, 'I get the feeling the party's nearly over anyway.'

Under the cover of darkness on the night of July 24th the River Ebro was crossed by an army of men who just a few months earlier had swum its green waters in desperate flight. Now, they were in high spirits, well organised for the crossing, and determined to take the enemy by surprise and push on to recapture the territory they had lost. The Republic was at last on the offensive. The progress of the battle was as clearly written in the casualty lists at the cave hospital as it was in the dispatches from the front, if anyone had wanted to look. At first, as the advance moved forward without meeting much resistance, casualties were light. Those unlucky enough to be injured were quickly brought back across the river in boats or on the pontoon bridges, and taken in trucks to the cave. In the makeshift operating theatre, their wounds were checked for rifle and machine gun bullets or painstakingly probed for small shards of shrapnel from hand grenades.

There was a sudden influx of Italian prisoners, conscripts sent by Mussolini to help Franco. They were put in the beds on the lower tier under guard, but showed no inclination to escape. They just wanted to go home.

By the end of the week, the wounds were telling a different tale. Heavy armaments were being brought into play, and the Republicans had nothing to compare with the force of the weapons that Franco could command. The human body was dramatically restructured by even the most fleeting acquaintance with artillery shrapnel, mortars, and bombs. But what made the death toll rise to new heights was the ever increasing length of time it took to bring the wounded back for treatment. Outside Gandesa, the attack had stalled. Day after day the Republicans tried to take the hills surrounding the town, but failed. There was little cover on the scrubby slopes below the enemy strongholds on the summit of each objective, and assaults on Hill 481 and Hill 666 resulted in nothing but losses. The wounded couldn't be retrieved till nightfall, and then they often had to wait agonising hours on the banks of the Ebro because the bridges were bombed almost as fast as they were built. As air attacks increased, makeshift rafts carried the heavy cargo of maimed men back across the silent river. If they were fortunate, only the moon illuminated their passage. The lucky ones made it to the operating tables, but many didn't last that long. Shock, blood loss, dehydration, infection, all reduced chances of survival.

By August, Constance was waging a continual war against scabies. Every new arrival bore the marks of infestation. She scrubbed her arms with Lysol till they were red to keep the parasites under control, but then they found a way through her oversized shirt where the buttons gaped at the waist to feast on her body too. Her shins were a mass of bruises and sores from banging into the bed frames. Constance cursed their higgledy-piggledy arrangement, dictated by the irregularities in the walls and floor. It was difficult to avoid them as she rushed from patient to patient in the gloomy light that penetrated the cave if the curtain was lowered during the day, and impossible at night when the only light came from burning wicks, flickering feebly in their battered tins of oil. She longed for tidy, straight rows of beds and floors that could be scrubbed clean. Each day she hoped for news of Karl, but heard nothing. She worked mainly at night when most of the wounded were brought in, though sometimes she was needed in the daytime too. She slept whenever she could on a straw mattress in a little dry conduit under the road, crawling out of the blazing sunshine into its welcome shade. She felt safer there from the planes that occasionally strafed the valley than in the tents where some of the others slept.

Addie's arrival broke the routine. As her battered car pulled in alongside the trucks and ambulances in the valley below the cave, Constance was walking back from the conduit to begin another shift. At the sight of Addie's face she felt a rush of pleasure, recognising for the first time that this was probably the best friend she had ever had. Though still a little subdued, Addie looked much less strained than the last time they had seen each other. Her characteristic air of optimistic determination was returning and a smile lit up her face when she saw Constance hurrying to meet her. A large woman was struggling to extricate herself from the passenger seat, her smart white blouse, rather tight black skirt and lisle stockings completely out of place in the heat and dust of the countryside. Addie introduced her to Constance as the former Labour MP, Leah Manning, who was in Spain on a propaganda gathering trip. With great enthusiasm, despite the fact that she was obviously suffering from the heat and constantly mopping her brow with a handkerchief, Leah explained to Constance how a renewed effort was being made to gain support for the Republic in Britain. If the Republicans could just hold on a little longer, they would be able to fight alongside the Allies when Britain and France declared war on Germany.

'Then we shall soon see the end of this farcical policy of non-intervention in Spain, and once the Republicans are allowed to buy proper weapons, nothing will stop them from defeating Franco.' Addie and Constance nodded politely, though both of them rather doubted that it would be that easy.

Addie had at last managed to get María to hand over the letter Karl had sent to Constance. Hurriedly scanning the contents, Constance smiled gratefully at Addie, and put the letter carefully in her pocket for closer examination later. Addie had also brought her camera and was keen to start taking photographs of the patients while there was still enough daylight in the cave. She was going to write a long article about the hospitals for a pamphlet that the Committee wanted to use for fund raising. They unloaded the car, and set off up the hill to the cave, Addie and Constance carrying boxes of new syringes and thermometers, more bandages and a few precious sachets of sulphanilamide. Leah found it quite difficult enough to negotiate the stony track in her smart leather-soled shoes without carrying anything extra. She had enough breath however, to tell them some news about Rose. Leah had been to visit her in hospital in England where she was recovering slowly after several tricky abdominal operations to remove pieces of shrapnel.

'I met her before she went to Spain, you know,' said Leah with a slight smile, 'quite a little heroine our English Rose has turned out to be. I always thought she might. When I saw her last she was sitting up in bed wearing a most becoming pink bed jacket and sorting out her press cuttings to stick in a scrap book. She seemed in good spirits and was obviously being well taken care of by a very devoted young doctor. She's out of hospital now, I believe, in a convalescent home on the coast, paid for by the Committee which of course, is as it should be.'

Addie and Constance exchanged questioning looks, wondering if Rose had heard anything about Rafael's whereabouts. It seemed she hadn't mentioned him to Leah at all.

'Now,' Leah turned to Constance, 'I don't want to be given any special treatment whilst I'm here. You just tell me what to do and I'll pitch in and make myself useful till Addie is ready to return to Barcelona.'

Constance tried to think of a job suitable for a visiting politician. Even one as eager to help as Leah might not be grateful to find that she had acquired parasites at the same time as propaganda. But the problem was soon resolved. As they entered the cave, one of the first things they saw was Reggie Aston and his assistant setting up a blood transfusion for an unconscious man.

'Ah! Constance, good. This man will need checking frequently, though I'm afraid there's not much hope at all – liver shot to bits. He may regain consciousness. He's Welsh I think.'

Leah was looking closely at the hollow-cheeked unshaven face, exclaiming at last, 'I know this boy. It's Jack Griffiths, he's from my constituency. He came to a talk I was giving on Spain at the start of the war. I remember him very well, because he was so keen to join the International Brigade. He invited me home to tea with his mother because he wanted to ask me more about how to volunteer.'

'Would you mind sitting here beside him then?' asked Constance, relieved to have found a useful task for her. 'If he wakes up, it'll be good for him to see a familiar face, and you can call me if he needs anything.'

The heavy curtain was drawn aside in places to allow more light to enter and Addie busily took photographs and jotted down what Leah had said about the wounded Brigader so that she could use it in her article. With a practised eye, she began to look around for other likely subjects. Nearly every patient would have a heart-rending tale to tell but the trick was to choose stories that loosened purse strings as well. In a way, it made her feel like a vulture, picking over people's tragedies to bare the bones of their misfortunes, but perhaps in this case, the ends justified the means.

'Who's the boy over there at the far end with Aurora?' she asked Constance.

'That's Manuel. He had a lucky escape. When Corbera was being bombed, he took shelter under the water tower but it received a direct hit. He nearly drowned when it collapsed. A Canadian soldier fished him out just in time. He needs more surgery on his leg, but he should be alright. His friend was killed.'

Addie, recognising a sure-fire winner, took several more photographs as Aurora changed his dressings, whilst answering the boy's questions about Canada as well as she could. 'That Canadian soldier, he was so tall, are all the people in Canada tall too?' Addie told him that mostly they were much taller than Spaniards. Manuel looked disappointed. He had hoped he would be able to find the man again easily just because of his height. 'I shall have to think of another way to find him then. I didn't say thank you.'

'I'm sure you'll find him if you keep trying,' Addie reassured him, 'but it might take quite a while.'

'If I haven't found him by the time the war ends, I can go to Canada to look for him.'

He seemed delighted at the thought, and Addie decided not to mention that Canada was very large and far away.

'I don't suppose you know any Finnish?' Addie looked up to see Constance, gazing sadly in the direction of a man sitting wedged against the back wall of the cave, propped up in his bed by blankets and pillows. His chest was swathed in tight bandages and as Addie approached him, she could hear his breathing, an irregular rasping noise, each one sounding as if it could be the last.

'Isn't it terrible, a beautiful blonde thing like him must have a last message to send to someone and we can't understand anything he says. We think he's a Finn, but no one here speaks Finnish. I've tried other languages but it's no good. I asked one of the chaps to try Yiddish. That often works because there are lots of Jewish Brigaders from all over the place who can talk to each other in Yiddish, but he didn't understand that either. He'll die soon and we don't know anything about him. I don't think he can talk at all now, so it's too late.' Constance patted his arm gently while she checked the position of the needle for the drip. 'It seems,' thought Addie, as she watched Constance expertly locate the collapsed vein, 'that however many men nurses see die, they never become completely blasé about it.' She wondered if the accumulation of deaths they saw built up within them like the waters of a dammed river. If the river was in full spate for too long and there was no way of easing the pressure, would the dam eventually give way?

'I couldn't do your job, Constance. You nurses must be so strong to see all this suffering day after day and still keep going.'

'Humph!' snorted the ever practical Constance, 'just get on with your own job then, and get us some more money for supplies. Remind me to give you a list.'

Addie returned to her note-taking with a smile, Constance still seemed to be holding up well just at the moment anyway.

She was surprised when, in the farthest corner of the cave, she found an injured woman. At first, seeing only her close-cropped hair, she had thought it was another soldier, only realising her mistake when a croaking voice, still identifiably female called out to her as she passed by the bed. All that remained of the woman's black hair were a few ragged and burned tufts. Her lashes and eyebrows had been singed completely away. Addie could make out that she was calling for her daughters, but it was clear that she was delirious.

Aurora hurried over to give her an injection, saying 'Shhh! Teresina, I'm giving you something to make you sleep again.'

'What happened to her?' Addie hardly dared ask, fearing to hear the answer.

'The fascist planes bombed La Bisbal de Falset last week,' answered Aurora in her simple English, a bitter fire in her eyes. 'Teresina's house was hit. Her children were in the bedroom and they are dead. The house was on fire but Teresina was taken out. She has many burns. We have sent a message to ask if her husband can come from the front to see her. She calls out for her daughters all the time and we give her more morphia.'

'Oh, yes,' said Constance as she swept past to set up another drip, 'we're very generous to the local people. We come here and disrupt their lives, we use their caves for our weapons and our wounded, and when the enemy comes here looking for us and the villagers are caught in the crossfire, we always treat them really kindly.' Something about the brittle way in which Constance delivered this statement made Addie begin to wonder if Constance was not quite as far from breaking point as she had believed.

After this, Addie felt she had collected more than enough material for her article, but when she returned to Leah, she discovered that Leah had no intention of leaving. She settled herself down more comfortably beside Jack Griffiths' bed, saying, 'He opened his eyes and knew me straight away. He said he wanted me to take a message to his mother, but then he drifted off again. I'll have to stay to be here if he wakes up again.'

Leah stayed till the dawn was breaking and Jack slipped into death without regaining consciousness.

'What shall I say to his poor mother?' she asked as she stood up, stiff and tired after her vigil. She was a sensible woman, but couldn't help feeling somehow responsible for having played a part in encouraging Jack onto a path that had led to his death.

'You tell her that he said he loved her dearly, that he knew he was fighting for a worthwhile cause, and that we must all keep on fighting so that he didn't die in vain. That's what they all say,' said Constance with a deep sigh.

III

'Guilt,' Addie thought as she drove back along the same road to La Bisbal de Falset, this time alone, 'we're all riddled with it.' Several weeks had passed since she had made the trip there with Leah, but she would always remember the cave particularly vividly. This, she knew, was partly because writing the stories of the patients there had imprinted them clearly on her mind. The photographs too, hurriedly glimpsed before sending them off to the Committee, had crystallised the memories even further. Soon there would be another reason to remember the cave.

'Leah felt guilty because she had encouraged that poor Welsh boy to leave his mother and go off to get killed, and Constance believes we are all guilty of bringing death from the skies down on the villagers. Now I'm probably going to feel guilty for the rest of my life for being the one to shatter all the hopes Constance had for the future.'

She took a deep breath and gripped the juddering steering wheel tightly to swing the car round yet another tight bend on the potholed road. Perhaps it wouldn't make things the slightest bit easier for Constance that she heard the news from a friend, but even if it only made things a fraction less horrid, Addie knew she had to do it. She was sure too that Constance would prefer to know the truth straight away, rather than spend weeks of uncertainty listening to rumours and platitudes.

There was something much more claustrophobic about the interior of the cave this time, thought Addie as she stood by the gap in the heavily curtained entrance, looking through the gloom for Constance. She held her breath as she entered, hoping she would be able to find Constance quickly, before having to take in much of the fetid air. The wounded now stretched from wall to wall, the low beds closely packed, making it difficult to pass between them. Then she saw Constance with Reggie Aston and others grouped around one of the patients who lay unmoving on the bed. A great deal of blood had spread and splattered over everything in the immediate area. When Constance came towards her, Addie could see that her clothes and arms were flecked with red, the distribution of spots varying in density like spatter pictures painted with toothbrushes.

'Do you have a moment free to come outside?' Addie asked her, unwilling to deliver her dreadful tidings in such dismally sad surroundings.

'I think so. We lost him - post-op haemorrhage.' Constance wiped her face on the relatively clean corner of a surgical drape, smudging the minute specks of blood that Addie now noticed had even sprayed onto her cheeks. She turned and moved towards the cave mouth, not wanting Constance to read her expression. Even outside, the sickly smell of death blew on the light breeze. They were downwind of the corpses waiting to be taken for burial. 'It's so hard to make a man and so easy to blast him to pieces,' thought Addie as yet another lean brown body was loaded onto the lorry.

'Oh! good grief,' grumbled Constance, wrinkling her nose, 'it's time they moved that last lot to the cemetery.' They took the path leading away from the road and the cave, climbing a little higher above the valley where the air was clearer. The September sun had lost little of its searing heat, but clumps of pines shaded the rocks here and there. As they walked, Addie nervously picked sprigs of thyme, rolling the leaves beneath her fingers to release their lemon perfume, finding as she breathed the scent in deeply that there was a hint of something vaguely acrid behind the sweetness.

'What's wrong, Addie?' asked Constance softly as they reached a point where the path dwindled to nothing, 'you haven't come all the way up here for a stroll in the countryside. Just say what you've got to say.' As she looked more carefully at the solemn expression on Addie's face, dread gripped her in a petrifying embrace, and she realised that within seconds, the world would change for her. She leaned against a smooth boulder, already anticipating that she would need solid support. Desperately, she tried to absorb everything that she could sense around her before Addie spoke; the colours in the landscape, the sounds of birds and distant human voices, the scent of pine needles and rosemary in the air that brushed warmly against her face. She wanted to savour them all and fix them in her memory. The sudden touch of her friend's fingers on the rough skin of her arm told her time was up.

'Yesterday I went to see Janet on the hospital train in the tunnels near Marsá. They had just operated on a German Brigader called Felix. When he came round from the anaesthetic and heard us speaking English he asked if we knew a nurse called Constance. He said he was Karl's best friend.' Addie hesitated, not knowing how to continue, even though she had practised in the car over and over again what she would say. She could tell from Constance's distant expression that it was almost as if the words had already been spoken. When she began again, it felt as if they were replaying a scene that had been enacted countless times before.

'When I told him I knew you very well, he asked me to tell you what happened to Karl. The Thaelmanns were leading an assault on a hill and some of them couldn't reach cover in time when a plane flew over, bombing their position. He saw the explosion that killed Karl before he was hit himself. I checked his story with some of the others from the battalion to make sure there was no possibility he had been mistaken.'

Addie could see a terrifying blankness settled over Constance's eyes. She wished Constance would scream or cry hysterically, but her silence was seemingly endless.

Addie picked up Constance's passive fingers and squeezed them painfully hard but there was still no reaction.

'Felix said he was quite sure Karl died instantly. He said that Karl was always talking about you. He knew how much you loved each other, that's why he wanted you to know exactly what had happened – that Karl didn't suffer.'

'No,' thought Addie as the words still hung in the air, 'it's Constance who will do the suffering.'

A cold grey numbness began to envelope Constance. She remembered Karl describing a lovely day like this one in Germany before the war; sunshine, birds singing. He had been taken outside the concentration camp with a group of others to form a work party. Some S.S. men had told them to stand facing a wall and shouted, 'Now you'll all be shot!' They had pressed their pistols against the backs of the prisoners' necks – and then roared with laughter, saying 'You know now what will happen if you don't obey orders.' Karl had smiled at the memory, saying that the realisation he was going to live had turned every day afterwards into a bonus. From now on, Constance knew that for her each day would be more like a penalty in a game she could never win. A small part of her mind, an automaton without identity or memory, detached itself from the unbearable pain of being the person called Constance and took control.

'Constance, what can I do?' asked Addie, breaking the silence at last, 'Would you like me to try to arrange a few days' leave for you?'

'No,' Constance replied, shaking her head slowly and mechanically, 'there's lots of work to be done, I'd rather stay here, thank you.' Her voice was a little unsteady and her limbs seemed unwilling to move from the rock that was partially supporting them, but they were forced to obey. As they walked back to the cave, Addie was careful not to look in the direction of the lorry waiting to leave for the cemetery.

Constance had no idea of how many days and nights she spent nursing the never-ending flow of wounded men. Some left in ambulances for the coast, far too many were taken to the cemetery. She fought like a wild cat when the dead were being removed from the hospital beds. The Spanish orderlies always wanted to bury the bodies wrapped in the blankets. 'You can't take that,' Constance would shout at them, 'I need blankets for the living – the dead won't feel the cold.' Sometimes she would actually end up tussling over the bedding with the elderly Catalans who were helping on the burial detail. They thought it the height of disrespect to bury someone without a shroud. Faced with Constance's fury, they would give in, but she had to be on guard constantly or they would slip past with a corpse cloaked in one of her precious few remaining bedcovers when she wasn't looking. Deep in her mind, hidden under a weighty blanket of denial, lurked images of Karl's body, or what remained of it, lying unburied on the hillside. A nurse of her experience knew more than enough about human bodies and the ways they could be blown to bits and how they looked when they decomposed in the open air. Those who died in the cave were at least covered by the warm earth.

A small number of enemy wounded were still arriving, though nothing like as many as there had been at first. Constance treated them with detached efficiency, barely viewing them as individuals. Still existing in a cold greyness despite the sunshine, it was surprising that such a small detail should trigger a distant memory of days before she came to Spain. The distinctive white scar was just below the eye of a young pilot from the Condor Legion.

'This one got what he deserved,' said one of the stretcher bearers as they unceremoniously dumped him onto the bed before rushing off to get another casualty. 'His plane crashed not far from here. I reckon he's had it – not really worth the trouble of carting him here. We should have left him to rot anyway.' As Constance looked closely at his pallid features, it slowly dawned on her where she had seen his face before. She remembered the photograph in its ornate silver frame, and the voice of her childhood friend, Diana, telling her that this was Alfredo; Freddy she had called him, aristocratic object of all her affections. Now he lay before her, his smart uniform in tatters and his life in her hands.

Around her was the tumult that always greeted a huge influx of wounded. There were too many patients and not enough staff. Some would have to wait and perhaps that delay would be fatal. The orderly left with a parting curse of 'Bloody Fascist', over his shoulder. He cared nothing about what treatment the pilot would or would not receive. Constance examined Freddy quickly. As she automatically worked on his wounds to staunch the bleeding, her hands froze. Without a blood transfusion, he stood next to no chance of making it to the operating table. She could call Reggie or she could pass on to the next patient. Her heart hardened, why should she try to help this man who had probably crashed his plane whilst bombing innocent villagers? Her hands began to tremble violently as she suddenly realised that he could have been the one who had killed Karl. She wanted to pull out the swabs and let him bleed to death like a stuck pig. The temptation was almost overwhelming - no one would ever know. She eased the pressure she was applying to stop the flow of blood from the torn vessels, but then as the gauze turned rapidly red, she changed her mind.

'*I'd* know,' she murmured to herself. 'And all that matters to me now is being a nurse, and a good nurse wouldn't do this. I'd be ashamed of myself forever if I did.' Hanging on by a thread to this need for professional integrity, Constance called loudly for someone to get Dr. Aston as quickly as possible. The haemorrhage was under control, but she didn't dare release the pressure again.

She had thought her tortured anxieties about Freddy's life or death were over, but the outcome still hung in the balance. When the Spanish orderlies realised she was calling for a transfusion for a fascist pilot, a passionate debate began amongst them as to whether the blood of the women of Spain should be given to a sworn enemy. Some of them argued that even if the answer was 'yes' in principle, stocks of blood were low, and would be better kept for the wounded on their own side. Constance longed to let the argument continue till Freddy's life had ebbed away, but she knew that by doing nothing, she was merely attempting to take an easy way out. Her conscience would never be clear if she remained silent.

'What do you think of the Fascists who leave our wounded to die, or shoot them without mercy?' she shouted at them in exasperation. The numbness that had anaesthetised her senses since Karl's death was replaced by a raging anger at having to fight so hard to save this man for whom she felt nothing but loathing.

'I'll tell you what you think of them,' she continued, 'you think they are animals. And now you are behaving as badly as they do, or worse, because you know what you are doing is wrong. Are you civilised men or wild beasts?'

Exchanging shifty glances, the orderlies fell quiet. A half-mad foreign nurse was not a problem they wished to confront, and though they were all reluctant to let such a stimulating, passionate discussion end so unsatisfactorily, there was still urgent work to be done. A tacit agreement was made to call a temporary truce on the issue and, to placate the glowering Constance, one of them hurried away to find Reggie Aston.

The inferno of anger burned away the kindly grey fog which had been protecting Constance from the full force of grief. Then, when the rage finally subsided, desolation and bitterness emerged to take its place. She watched with macabre fascination how Freddy fought for life, how the colour came back to his face and the strength to his limbs like Lazarus returning from the dead. How she hated him for being alive instead of Karl. How she resented Diana's continued chance for happiness when her own was gone. Amorphous dreams of revenge drifted through her troubled sleep.

'Connie, Connie, I've brought you a present,' Max called to her as he jumped from the driver's seat in the truck. 'It's not much, just a stray I found wandering along the road.'

Sam climbed slowly and carefully out of the back, thankful that the jolting journey up from the River Ebro was over. His mouth twitched into a questioning smile when he saw Constance.

'Max promised me a cup of tea and the possibility of seeing you, so I couldn't turn him down.'

From the awkward way he had moved, Constance knew there was more to it than this. She managed to smile, pleased and relieved that he was alright, not incarcerated in one of Franco's prisons. 'It's good to see you Sam, but it looks to me as if you need treatment before tea.'

'He never was captured. He got away, but he nearly died of pneumonia after the retreat.' Max, as usual, was forced to fill in the gaps when Sam was at a loss for words with Constance. In truth, Sam was stunned into silence by the changes he could see in her. It wasn't just that she looked tired and gaunt – he had seen her like that before. It was her eyes that scared him, perhaps he was even more scared than when he had picked her up with her face smashed and bloodied after the accident. The expression in her eyes had always been changeable, often solemn or determined, sometimes disdainful, at times fervent, occasionally gentle, but never hard and embittered as it was now. He could tell that she was indeed pleased to see him, but her welcome was no more than a fine veil over a black abyss. Max had told him briefly what had happened to Karl and how worried he was that Constance had 'gone a bit barmy in a quiet sort of way.' Sam could see exactly what he meant.

'He's been fighting up by Gandesa, Connie, and his backside's had a close shave from a fascist bullet, so I'll take him up to the Doc. See you for a brew up and a chat after?'

'Yes, fine,' replied Constance, watching Sam begin to

walk rather painfully up to the cave. She knew they were trying to cheer her up but felt only exhaustion at the effort that would be needed to pretend they had succeeded, even for a few minutes.

Sam returned to the front. He was told that he would be evacuated to a hospital in Valencia for further treatment, but cadged a lift with Max back down to the Ebro as soon as he could. Constance was sorry to see him go. Their chats had not proved as wearing as she had feared. It had been a comfort to sit when she came off duty with the mug of tea, and listen to Sam's voice talking quietly about things that had nothing to do with war, or to wince at Max's excruciating jokes. But when Sam had gone back, and Max disappeared to God knows where, she sank deeper and deeper into despair. The battle was going badly, their losses were appalling, but still sometimes she heard the sound of singing as troops marched past the cave on the road to the front. Haunted by their voices as they went to meet their fate, she went closer to the road and discovered with horror that they were no more than children; some little more than sixteen, the last call up, 'El Quinto del Biberón' - 'Baby-Bottle Conscripts'.

'It isn't worth it,' she whispered as she stood by the roadside, wringing her hands together in an age-old gesture of anguish.

Returning sadly to work, she felt overwhelmed by the numbers of maimed and dying soldiers in the cave. Soon, she knew, many of the boys she had just seen marching past would be carried in to occupy the very same beds, youth ruined. As she carried out the routine duties of nursing, she talked to herself, repeatedly asking the same questions because she couldn't find the answers.

'We can't go on much longer, surely everyone can see now that we are losing the war? What point is there in sending those boys to die?' The sound of singing once again came echoing across the small valley from the road.

Near the entrance to the cave, a local man sat on the end

of one of the low beds. His weathered face was vaguely familiar to Constance, and then she recalled that he regularly brought supplies of fresh fruit for the unit from one of the other villages nearby. Relaxed and jovial, he drew deeply on what remained of a cigarette, guarded carefully within the circle of his hand. Wisps of smoke curled between his stubby fingers to fill the air with the distinctive smell of black tobacco. He was laughing loudly at a joke shared with one of the orderlies. His seeming indifference to the horror and misery that surrounded him brought Constance to breaking point.

'Can't you hear those children singing? Can't you see what's going on around you? How can you be talking and laughing as if nothing was happening?' The man stared at her, patiently waiting for her to finish. 'Well,' she demanded finally, 'is it really worth it, all this?'

Calmly and with great seriousness, he answered her. He told her of life as a peasant in his isolated village, before the days of the Republic. Like nearly everyone in the village, he had been not only poor, but illiterate and totally ignorant of the outside world. When the time came to vote, the landowners voted on behalf of their workers, who were just so many numbered souls. But then he heard there was going to be an election in which they could all vote, so they went over the tracks and voted. The next thing they heard was that the village next to them was measuring out the land, so they went to find out what was happening. They learned that the Popular Front had been elected and was bringing in land reforms. When the reforms reached their village, they didn't know how to measure and they hadn't got anything to measure with, so they had to learn how to do these things. When the local landowner fled, the village elected a council, and he became the mayor and had to learn to read and write. A few months ago, a letter had come for him, the first letter he had ever had, and he could read it. He was called to a meeting in Barcelona. A car picked him up, it was the first time he had ever been in a car. It had leather seats. In Barcelona he was told that there was going to be a great battle, and that roads were going to be built up to his village, and that it would be his job to supply as much food as they could for the army and the hospital and to help with refugees. So he went back to the village and organised all the things they had to do, and did them all well.

'I became a man,' he said simply, 'and that is what we're fighting for.'

Constance looked at him and tears came to her eyes. He had achieved so much, she felt ashamed for being so defeatist. He would fight to the bitter end in the hope for a better future, and so must she.

For a few moments, she stood in the mouth of the cave, noticing the cool hint of autumn in the air on her tearstained face. A flock of birds rose up from the undergrowth to soar high in the cloudless sky. Since she had heard of Karl's death, the monotonous repetition of 'dead, dead, dead' in the depths of her brain throughout her waking moments had nearly driven her mad. She hadn't dared to think of him. Now, for the first time, she remembered Karl as he had been when he was alive. He had loved to sing, just as the birds above her were singing, and like them, he had loved freedom. With a soothing touch as light as a feather, the thought came into Constance's mind that Karl had died like a bird in flight, and that he would have wanted it to be that way.

CHAPTER 8

Worlds Apart

I

France 1939

As the lapping wave receded, small hillocks of sand formed behind the heels of the man who stood at the water's edge. His dirt encrusted toes curled deeper into the beach every time the sea shifted the grains beneath his feet. He remained there for a long time, cleansing his sores in the salt water, tiny flecks of dried blood peeling from his skin and floating away on the tide. Dispirited and weary, he gazed out to the horizon, eyes unseeing, raw wind and icy ocean numbing his flesh, his thoughts elsewhere. He wasn't alone. Some of the men who had been his comrades in arms for the last two years were beside him, waves washing around their ankles. Beyond them, figures straggled all along the shoreline far into the distance. Thousands more were herded together on the sands, the boundaries of their freedom delineated by unassailable barbed wire fencing and armed guards.

The hordes of Republican refugees that had climbed the snow-covered Pyrenees to cross the border into France had found a cold welcome awaiting them. The humiliation of every soldier, forced to disarm and thereby acknowledge his defeat, was followed by the indignity of being corralled like cattle on an open beach. The February gales harried them constantly, so they gathered the flotsam that came in on the Mediterranean tides, using any fragments of wood to shore up the shelters they excavated in the soft sand. Those still with a shred of optimism told themselves that the world would soon recognise their plight. Some were too stunned to think at all, others were driven mad by their thoughts. Meanwhile they died, by the hundreds, of old wounds and diseases.

Addie couldn't believe that the golden sands of Argelès would ever again be crowded with summer visitors, spending carefree holidays relaxing at the lido. 'The shore here's poisoned,' she thought bitterly. 'Even if the wind and the sea can eventually eradicate the germs, the lice, and the pollution from the latrines, surely everyone will remember how shamefully these brave people were treated here? Who could want to come here for a vacation after this?'

Since news of the exodus of soldiers and civilians from Spain into France had reached Britain, the National Joint Committee for Spanish Relief had been fund-raising to charter a ship to take several thousand refugees, men, women and children, to Mexico, where the government was offering them asylum. Addie was amongst the volunteers helping in the mammoth task of distributing aid to the refugees and organising their dispersal. 'But the efforts of all the relief agencies are no more than a drop in the ocean,' Addie thought despondently as the enormity of the task became apparent, 'and it's no use believing the British establishment will lift a finger, and the French certainly don't seem as keen to help Franco's enemies as might have been expected.'

On top of all this, the Committee had told her that Constance was missing. She had become separated from her unit somehow when they left the cave hospital. She hadn't been in Barcelona with the other International Brigaders when a huge farewell parade had been held in their honour. All the foreign troops had been withdrawn from the Popular Army by the Republican Government in the desperate hope that international pressure would force Franco to send home the Italians and Germans fighting on his side. It had been a futile gesture. The desire for appeasement in Britain and France was too strong. One never to be forgotten day at the end of October, the departing Brigaders had marched through the streets of the city, showered with flowers and embraces by the grateful crowd. Addie had seen a group of nurses in the parade as she stood on the Diagonal to cheer their passing, but Constance was not amongst them. For a moment, she thought she had glimpsed Byron at the head of the Lincolns, but he was too far away to be sure. Along with many of those around her, she was moved to tears by La Pasionaria's speech to the Brigaders:

> You are history. You are legend. You are the heroic example of the solidarity and universality of democracy. We shall not forget you, and when the olive tree of peace puts forth its leaves, entwined with the laurels of the Spanish Republic's victory, come back! Come back to us and here you will find a homeland.

Addie had watched the anguished faces of the Brigaders whose countries were under the sway of fascist dictators. Where would they go now? La Pasionaria's words were especially significant for them. She hoped with all her heart that their wait for a homeland wouldn't be too long.

No one had seen Constance during the parade or in the evacuation by train that had taken place afterwards. Addie had got as far as Paris before reading the latest reports in the newspapers of the tragedy taking place at the frontier. Tens of thousands of refugees, the human detritus of war, were streaming into France. She had persuaded the Committee to send her south to help. Since then, she had asked everywhere for news of any English speaking nurses, but her questions were always met with blank stares. Her daily fight with French bureaucracy almost drove her to screaming point. Soon after she had first arrived, one officious camp commandant told her that the aid parcels could only be given to named individuals, and at that point she didn't know the name of a single one of the thousands of men interned. After what seemed like hours of arguing in French, she got him to agree to her request for a list, to be drawn up by one of the internees. She copied the scrawled names on the list as quickly as possible onto the dozens of parcels, after which they were allowed to drive the lorry into the camp. With great restraint, the men waited in an orderly manner until they heard their names called. Addie knew she would never forget the pitiful sight of a man with half a leg missing, dragging himself through the sand in agonising slow motion till he was beside the lorry. His look of disappointment was heartrending when the last name to be read out was not his.

One day during the following week, she found Constance. From the camp adjutant, she learned of two nurses who were working with a Spanish doctor, trying to help the refugees within the camp.

'One is Spanish,' he told her in a confidential manner, 'but I don't know about the other. She says she has no passport. I suspect she is a Russian. She is always very secretive and won't say where she is from, but I have heard her speaking English sometimes as well as Spanish. She is certainly not Spanish,' he added with a frown, 'too fair, and too cold. So many English girls are cold, but you, you are American, are you not? Warmer than the English I think?'

He sidled closer to Addie with an eyebrow raised hopefully, His small moustache was not quite long enough to twirl suggestively as villains did in silent movie melodramas, but Addie was sure that if it had been, he would have twirled away with the best of them. She tried to keep smiling for the sake of maintaining an 'entente cordiale', replying as she edged away, 'Well, I'm half British actually, so perhaps a little on the tepid side.' However, her reticence did not seem to deter him at all, and, possibly in the hope of building a more intimate friendship over subsequent visits, he allowed her entry to the camp to look for the nurse.

'Ah! I was wondering how long it would be before you found me,' was the first thing that Constance said when she saw Addie.

'Did you know I was here looking for you?' Addie asked in surprise.

'Not you personally, but I presumed that someone from the Committee would turn up eventually.'

'Are you alright? We've been so worried about you. Why didn't you tell the commandant who you were?'

Constance didn't reply at first, just gestured at the human wreckage around her. Windbreaks of sticks and tattered old blankets partially shielded the sick men lying prostrate on the sand nearby.

'I thought I could help,' she said with a shrug of her shoulders. 'We don't have proper medicine, but I bring them water and try to make them more comfortable. It isn't much, but I do what I can.' Her eyes lit up with a flare of anger, 'It's disgusting how they've been treated. These men have fought the Fascists for over two years and instead of being welcomed like heroes, they're being treated as pariahs.'

Seeing Constance once again filled with righteous indignation brought a tremendous sense of relief to Addie. When she had broken the news of Karl's death to her, it had seemed that the light had left Constance's eyes so completely it might never return. But, despite the fact that Constance was as thin as a rake, dressed in what could only be described as rags, and obviously tired, it was clear she was not totally dispirited.

'I knew they were sending as many foreigners as they could back to their own countries straight away, but I didn't want to leave,' Constance explained as she gave one of the men a few sips of water. 'The commandant likes to think I am a Russian spy, and I don't like to disillusion him. He gets very excited about it. Men do so love their spy games, don't you think?'

'But why weren't you with the rest of your unit in Barcelona? I looked for you all over,' protested Addie, a little annoyed with Constance for having deliberately kept her identity secret and caused her so much worry.

'Do you remember the woman in the cave whose children had been killed when the village was bombed? When the order came through to withdraw all the foreigners, I helped move her to one of the small caves where her family was living. I stayed to show her relatives how to treat her burns, change her dressings, that sort of thing. I was going to catch up with the others, but it didn't work out quite like that. There were still a few Spanish staff working in the cave, and we were about to set off when another truck load of casualties arrived, so we didn't go. And then it went on and on, you know how it is, how the wounded flood in after a battle, only boys really.'

Addie certainly did know how it was. Constance would have stayed till the bitter end. In fact, it was a miracle that she had been persuaded to leave before Franco's troops had arrived.

'You must go home now, Constance. We've been given strict instructions to repatriate as many people as possible. Food is terribly short as you know. And besides, there's so much you can do in England to help these people. You've got to go and speak at meetings and tell them what you've seen here. Nurses are always the ones who draw the crowds and raise the most funds. We need money desperately, and we have to make the public aware of what's going on and get them to put pressure on the government to let more Spanish refugees into Britain. We're trying to sort out the paperwork for the evacuation of these people and we're hoping to move the sick ones into French hospitals as fast as we can. It looks to me as if you would soon become a patient yourself anyway if you stay much longer.'

Addie could tell that Constance was wavering a little. Recognition of the truth in Addie's words, combined with exhaustion, was taking effect.

'The adjutant said you hadn't got your passport, but anyway, I can arrange for you to go back, though it will take a few days. While I sort things out I'll try to get some medicines to you for these men.' Addie attempted a smile as she added, 'Just give me a list as usual.'

'I have got my passport,' Constance confessed, 'I hid it. And I'll certainly give you that list, but what about Aurora? I'm not leaving without her - she's been with us through it all. She can't possibly go back to Spain and risk being put in prison.' Addie suddenly realised that the diminutive figure helping the doctor was, in fact, Aurora, almost unrecognisable with her close cropped hair and wearing a pair of men's trousers that were yards too big. Constance's face had now taken on an air of determination that Addie preferred not to challenge.

'I'll start straight away,' Addie replied, hoping that she would be able to pull enough strings to get an entry permit for Aurora from the Home Office without all the usual prevarications and delays. When she eventually waved goodbye, loath to leave them in such distressing conditions, she was thinking frantically, 'Now who do I know with friends at Whitehall?'

It was Addie's father who saved the day by contacting colleagues he knew through his work at the University. Some of the professors were not as firmly entrenched in their ivory towers as others, and were equally at ease casting their pearls of wisdom in government circles as they were when lecturing the nation's elite in hallowed college precincts. Expedited by the old boy network, the application for entry was given official approval on the understanding that Addie's parents would act as Aurora's sponsors for as long as she stayed in England. Once Constance and Aurora were safely dispatched, Addie tried to find other sponsors for refugees and pestered the Home Office as much as she dared to speed things up, but the right channels were so constricted that only a trickle of permits issued forth. She felt ashamed and angry when each day she had to say 'mañana' to the soulful group of waiting refugees who always asked her, 'When shall we go?'

Allocating places on board the ship bound for Mexico

was a task that was not as easy as it seemed, bringing agonies of indecision. 'How can I choose?' Addie would cry, 'it's like playing God to say this one should go and that one shouldn't.' Guidelines were issued; so many places for people from each political group within the Republic, and priority for families with young children. But many refugees had feared to give their political affiliation, and the lists she had to work with didn't have the ages of the children, only their names. Another member of the relief team pointed out to her that the children born before the war had names of the saints or episodes in the life of the Virgin, such as Concepción or Asunción, whereas the younger ones born since the war began, were named after the political leaders of the Left, or with slogans like 'Libertad' or 'Solidaridad'. Addie was not at all at ease with the idea of basing so important a decision on such flimsy criteria, but in some cases there was no alternative. The women and children were scattered over a wide area and there wasn't time to visit them all.

Slowly, the great day of the sailing of the SS Sinaia inched closer. Addie was filled with excitement at the prospect of so many refugees setting off to begin new lives. It had been all shoulders to the wheel for weeks to get everything ready. The Quakers had turned up trumps as usual, and a smattering of writers had arrived to lend a hand, Nancy Mitford amongst them. Addie wondered if she would write them all up as characters in her next novel, and hoped that Nancy wouldn't find her interesting enough to caricature in any recognisable way. 'There's certainly plenty of scope for a mocking pen here. Anyone inclined towards literary cruelty could have a field day,' Addie wryly observed as she looked around at the motley collection of relief workers and visitors. Several people that Addie had encountered in Spain reappeared. Phyllis, now in tweeds instead of the floral frocks that Addie remembered from Murcia, greeted her enthusiastically and made her promise to keep in touch.

'There's always a call for stalwart refugee workers,' she had said breezily, a fact that Addie found extremely depressing, even apart from having been classified rather unappealingly as 'stalwart'. Geraldine Rees Jones and Vivien Errol turned up again. It seemed as if years had passed since Addie had last seen them at the Writers' Congress in Madrid. The tension between them was still almost palpable at times, arousing Addie's curiosity about whether or not it would be any easier to be in love with someone of the same sex. She sighed deeply. It certainly seemed that she and Byron had understood very little about each other, despite all the hours they had spent talking. He would probably be back in the States by now. She was glad that there wasn't much time to think of him with such a lot going on at the camps, but she feared there might come a day when the sad little whimpers that she had to suppress when she remembered him would burst forth like screaming harpies.

The Duchess of Atholl was among the dignitaries who came to the harbour in Sète to see the Sinaia steam away, loaded with a cargo of hopeful refugees. The sun blazed down on a blue sea and Addie could feel its warmth radiating from the cobbles on the quay-side through the soles of her shoes. Emotions jostled within her as she listened to the speeches; sadness that these poor souls were leaving their own country far behind them, relief that this part of her job was done, pride that a project requiring the co-operation of English, French, Spanish and Mexicans had actually come to fruition, though this meant suffering a surfeit of national anthems in the farewell ceremony. The refugees, clustered together in a solid mass, stood on the deck silently when the gangway steps were heaved away and the sirens sounded. Mopping their eyes, they looked mournfully at the shore. But then the band began to play again, the flags started to flutter in the sea breeze, and the crowd on the quay waved and shouted with immense gusto 'Viva Mejico!', till the departing refugees responded with cries of 'Viva la

Libertad!' that could be heard until the ship was well on its way out into the open sea.

After the exhilaration of seeing the sailing of the Sinaia, Addie wanted to weep when she saw the camp at Gurs. Bleak rows of flimsy huts housed the remnants of the International Brigades, unable to return to their own countries. It was a dismal purgatory. Addie had volunteered to drive a woman from the Red Cross to the camp to deliver parcels to the men, but the guards wouldn't let the small truck in at all, or even allow them to leave the packages. It seemed that one of the official stamps was missing from their paperwork.

'Are we allowed to talk to a representative from the men here, or am I to report back that your camp is every bit as bad as those in Germany?' Addie asked the guard indignantly, with as much of an authoritarian manner as she could muster.

They were told to wait in the guard house, and were left standing there for an hour, gazing out onto the bare earth within the compound, the tattered huts and the formidable fence. At last the guard reappeared with two of the interned men, an Austrian and an Italian. Addie thought her heart would break when the Brigaders presented them with gifts, for despite all her arguing, they had not been allowed to bring anything into the camp at all. The gifts showed that at least some of the parcels from aid workers had got through, and that arts and crafts materials had been amongst the contents. The Austrian gave Addie a handmade album with a soldier's head stencilled in one corner. Inside were a series of minute photographs taken with a pin-hole camera. The roughly cut prints, glued to the small black pages, showed details of an art exhibition the men had put on in one of the huts. A sailing ship rigged with string, a model house complete with picket fence, painted portraits and landscapes, were displayed alongside the most popular artistic endeavor - political montage.

'We know the things we make are simple,' said the Austrian, 'but it helps keep up morale.'

The Italian gave Addie something she knew she would treasure. He had obviously decided that the large blocks of soap included in the aid parcels could be put to a much better use than just washing. He had shaped his featureless cube into a crucifix, but instead of the figure of Christ, a Republican soldier had been carved hanging on the cross. Addie managed to remember the Italian for 'beautiful', and 'thank you', but the man had seemed pleased enough just to see the appreciation of his craftsmanship in her eyes.

Promising to return soon, Addie drove away to the cheerful sound of whistles and compliments from a group of Italians by the fence. The tears in her eyes prevented her from noticing another Italian who had rushed over to the fence, his handsome features still with a youthful charm despite all he had endured. Rafael had hoped that he would have the chance to speak to the visitors before they left. He had heard they were British and he desperately wanted to ask them about his English Rose. She had never answered his letters and then someone had told him she had been badly wounded and sent home. He didn't even know if she was alive or dead. Next time a visitor came to the camp he would be better prepared. Tonight he would barter his supper for a scrap of notepaper.

II

England 1939

Rose could see that Constance disapproved of the doilies. At first she had thought it was the butterfly buns that had provoked a barely perceptible scornful sniff, but Constance had accepted the proffered cake, wings painstakingly cut and iced by Rose, with alacrity. However, the lift of Constance's eyebrow at the sight of the paper doily beneath it was enough to let her know that she had made the wrong choice. She hadn't been sure whether to use one or not and now regretted having done so, even though the delicate filigree pattern made the plate look so pretty.

'Silly,' she thought, gazing with irritation at the offending doily, 'these class things didn't seem to matter so much in Spain, not when you were surrounded by death and destruction, but now we're back in England, they're just as important as ever. There are so many stupid rules about what the 'done' thing is and isn't, I don't know how I'll ever learn them all.'

Rose had been rather dreading this meeting. She had been tense since the moment she had heard Constance's voice on the telephone. Now she felt considerably worse. She had so wanted to make a good impression, arranging flowers in the room and laying out the bone china tea set that she loved so much. It had pink roses entwined round each piece, and fluted rims edged in gold. But even though she had felt a few moments of pleasure when her preparations were complete and everything looked so nice, the minute Constance had come into the room it all seemed to change. The pretty things just became frivolous, pointless trifles. So much of Spain still clung to Constance, the room suddenly felt unreal. Its comforting air of affluence was overshadowed by the aura Constance radiated, a mixture of terrible sadness and fierce pride that Rose found most disconcerting.

'She knows she's been part of something important,' Rose realised with a flash of intuition, 'it's like an elite club only for people who went to Spain in the war.' Although she knew that she too had every right to be a member of the club, and part of her longed to join, she had a much stronger urge to leave it all behind, to cut Spain out of her life completely. These disturbing thoughts created an unwelcome turmoil in her head, so she attempted to calm herself by pouring tea and chatting about her luck in having found such an ideal job - private nurse to an elderly, bedridden gentleman whose wife had died.

Constance wished Rose would stop fluttering about. She had no idea why Rose was in such a flap, and was totally unaware that she had added to the problem by her unwitting condemnation of the doily. She would have been horrified if she had known that her reflex reaction had been noted so attentively and had caused distress. It was, after all, bad manners to offend one's hostess. It had taken considerable effort on Constance's part to track Rose down. The Medical Aid Committee had told her the name of the hospital where Rose had been treated on her return, and the hospital had given her the name of the doctor concerned, Dr. Edward Morris. He had told her that Rose was now nursing one of his patients, a frail old chap who needed a full-time nurse to care for him in his own home. He had given her a phone number to call. Rose had seemed rather reluctant to meet, but Constance had insisted. She had something to give to Rose, sent from Addie in France, and she wanted to deliver it in person as soon as possible.

'Well Rose, you seem very comfortable here,' Constance remarked when Rose finally sat down, 'are you quite recovered from your surgery now?'

'I'm much better, but they told me I may need another op in the future because they're not sure if they got all the shrapnel out. The work here isn't too hard fortunately. My old gentleman doesn't weigh much, he's no trouble really, and he told me I could invite friends here if I liked, and the woman who comes to clean the house helps me with any lifting, and then there's the doctor too of course, he visits often.' Rose cast her eyes downwards as she spoke, mumbling the last words into her tea cup. Constance could see a pink flush rising to her cheeks and knew she must hurry up and get to the point of her visit without further delay, before Rose imparted any confidences she might regret.

'I had a letter from Addie the other day,' Constance began quickly, 'you know she's working with the refugees in the internment camps in France.' Rose nodded, a sharp little flick of the head that allowed her to turn a little to look out of the window and gaze distantly at the trees at the far end the garden, leafless and stark, standing forlornly amongst the dank green shrubbery.

'She's been several times to the camp at Gurs to see the International Brigaders who can't return home. One of them gave her this note. It's from Rafael.'

Constance held out the small grubby piece of lined paper, folded in half. Rose didn't look at it for a moment. She went on looking out of the window, saying almost inaudibly, 'I thought he was dead. Nobody knew where he was and I didn't get any letters from him.' When she accepted the note and opened it, she merely stared at the writing rather than reading it, and asked, 'Did Addie say if he looked well?'

'She didn't see him herself, the guards don't allow her in, but they let a representative of the Garibaldis speak to her for a few minutes and he slipped her the note.' Constance knew what the note said, it had been impossible to resist reading it. When she had unfolded the copious pages of Addie's letter, it had fallen into her lap. Rafael's English was much improved – he'd been learning as much as he could from a comrade in the battalion - and had a rather romantic, poetic character that was very moving. He had written of his sadness at hearing Rose had been injured and the pain of not knowing if she still lived. He was longing to hear from her and loved her more than ever.

'He just wants to know how I am, really,' said Rose in a toneless voice after glancing at the note. 'I'll write to him, of course, but it all seems so far away from life in England - and Franco has won the war, so there's nothing much more we can do.'

Constance put down her tea carefully and drew a very deep breath. She didn't shout at all, but her words were as hard and fast as machine gun bullets.

'That's not true, Rose, there's plenty to do and you know it. You must have heard what Franco is doing now. He's executing thousands of people who fought against him; they don't even get a proper trial. Others are dying in Spanish prisons, some of them are Brigaders, our friends. Do you remember Max? He's just been released from a concentration camp called San Pedro where he was beaten and half-starved and nearly froze to death. There are still Republicans in there now being taken out and shot each day. And what about Rafael and all the others in the camps in France? If Karl was still alive and being held in Gurs I would move heaven and earth to get him out. How can you say there's nothing to be done? Surely we have to try to do something?'

Rose looked at Constance's face, white with tightly suppressed rage, and understood that she would never feel such a passionate commitment to anything, or for that matter, to any person. It seemed to her that Constance was binding herself to a lost cause and a dead hero. Rose wanted nothing more than to leave the past behind and concentrate her attention firmly on the future.

She shifted uncomfortably on the edge of the soft arm chair.

'I'm really sorry, Constance. I didn't know that Karl had been killed, and I'm sorry that Max had a terrible time in prison.' The ring of the doorbell allowed her to escape Constance's contemptuous stare. She said 'Excuse me,' and hurriedly left the room. When she returned, she looked, if possible, even more ill at ease. A personable looking young man accompanied her.

'Constance,' this is Dr. Morris,' Rose said, inwardly cursing the Fates that had ordained he should arrive early on this particular day.

'We needn't be so formal Rose, I'm sure. I've already spoken to Constance on the telephone, and I feel I already know her anyway, after hearing you talk about her so much. Please call me Edward,' he said stretching out his hand to Constance in a friendly way, 'or Ted if you prefer. That's what Rose usually calls me.'

Softly spoken, gentle mannered and intelligent, under other circumstances Constance would have taken to him immediately. He smiled and moved closer to Rose, putting his arm round her lightly, saying, 'Has Rose told you yet that we are engaged to be married? She was put in my care when she came back from Spain and I intend to hold on to the post permanently.'

This time, Rose blushed an unmistakeable scarlet, tumbling out her next words in confusion.

'Edward, Constance brought news of Rafael, you know, I told you about him - my Italian friend in the Garibaldis - when I was in Villamalea. Now he's in one of those horrible internment camps in France.'

'Poor chap,' said Edward, with what appeared to be genuine concern. 'Perhaps we can send him some things, Rose - cigarettes, food - anything you like.'

Constance had been stunned into silence when she heard that Rose had acquired a fiancé, only murmuring 'How do you do,' as they shook hands. Of course, she could see immediately that Dr Morris was all that Rose could have ever hoped for. He could offer to fulfil any dreams she may have had for a safe and secure future.

'She certainly moved fast,' thought Constance, wondering how Rose could have turned her back so quickly on Rafael. Not so long ago, she had declared that Rafael was her husband, and now that he had lost almost everything, she was about to finish him off by marrying someone else. Would that make Rose a bigamist? Constance remembered that Rose had described some sort of wedding in Villamalea, but wasn't sure of the legal standing of such ceremonies. The best thing to do, Constance decided, would be to write to tell Addie all about it. She might know more about such things. Right at that moment, Constance wished to escape as quickly as possible, and fervently hoped that she would never set eyes on Rose again.

'I must be going,' she said abruptly, rising to her feet.

'I'll write to Rafael,' Rose said with a beseeching look in her eye. Constance knew she was silently asking her to say nothing more to Edward about Rafael.

'I'll see you out,' Edward held the door open for her to walk out into the hall, 'I'd like to ask your advice about a couple of surprises I'm planning for my bride to be.' He closed the door behind him, leaving Rose alone and anxious. 'What would they say to each other?' she wondered uneasily.

As she put on her coat and hat, Edward addressed Constance in a low voice, 'I hope you won't mind if I speak frankly. I want you to know that I'm already aware that Rose had an affair with this young man, Rafael, although she didn't tell me in so many words. I could see from your face that our engagement came as rather a shock to you. But please have no fear that I will put pressure on Rose to go ahead with our marriage if she has any doubts, now that Rafael has turned up again. I'll try to talk to her about it and help if I can.' His pleasant features suddenly became more wistful. 'She's not strong and she needs someone to care for her, you know. She's been so brave, especially when she found out that she will never be able to have children. The shrapnel damage was very extensive.'

A shaft of pity passed through the dark disgust that Constance was feeling towards Rose. It was despicable of her to have abandoned not only Rafael, but all that the war in

Spain had signified. To be childless however, was not a fate that Constance would ever have wished on her.

'Well,' she said in her usual brisk manner, having no desire to leave this kind young man with nothing but a frosty silence, 'Rose is very lucky to have you to look after her.'

A few weeks after Edward had helped Rose carefully compose a long letter to Rafael, enclosing it within a large package addressed to him at Gurs, Rose went to the door and found there was a letter for her amongst the usual mail. It had been forwarded to her from Gurs by the National Joint Committee. Writing to Rafael had been so difficult, especially when she came to the part explaining how her feelings towards him had changed, and the reasons why she was going to marry Ted. She had told him that she did still love him in a way, but it was like loving a dream that was fading in the morning light. She remembered clearly writing how everything that had happened in Spain seemed to have no connection at all with her life in England. 'Two different worlds,' she had said. For a few moments more, she held his unopened letter in her hand, reluctant to open it in case he had not understood and was filled with bitterness at her behaviour.

'Dearest Rosa,' she read,

> To see the envelope with your writing made my heart beat faster. Then to read your words and know that you are alive and in England again gave me great joy. I feared you dead because the news of your wounding had reached me.
>
> You write that you have met a good man who wishes to take care of you. I am happy for you Rosa, and lay no blame at your door. Our lives have not taken the path we hoped for and we can not be together. I say this with sorrow, but we must look at our situation with no illusions. I see the barbed wire around me and

know that my future is uncertain. The Fascists have won in Spain and I can not return to my homeland. If one day I am free, I will still be fighting because the capitalists must be overthrown and there is much to do to bring the revolution. I will meet persecution and imprisonment and perhaps death in this struggle.

I still love you Rosa, as I did when we were in Spain, but I do not want to bring you more danger. Marry this man and be proud to be his wife. Do not spoil your happiness in thinking of me often, for I do not want to be the cause of any pain for you. It will give strength to my soul to know that you are safe and that you will do your work as a nurse to help those that are oppressed.

Several hours passed before Rose was able to read the remaining pages of the letter that described the camp and the cultural activities of the men. She cried till her throat was sore with sobbing and her eyes were so puffy and red she looked like a prize fighter.

'I did love you, Rafael,' she said to her reflection in the bathroom mirror, squeezing out the flannel in the sink of cold water to bathe her swollen eyes.

But she knew his love for her was far more unselfish than hers had ever been. She dabbed ineffectively at her hot, tender eyelids with the dripping flannel and thought, 'God, I'll look a mess for ages.'

III

Nothing had changed as far as Constance could see. The neat gravel of the long drive still stretched into the distance, making the manor house at the far end appear quite small. Its impressive size only became apparent as one drew closer.

'It's all just the same, it's me that has changed,' Constance decided. Since she had visited the house with her mother to see Lady Cunningham and Diana, so much had happened to her in all the turmoil of war; it was strange to think that here life had gone on in exactly the same manner, basking contentedly in wealth and tradition, without even a hiccup. Constance had discovered rather to her annoyance, that she could no longer fully enjoy the pleasant walk between stately trees and landscaped grounds in the soft English sun of early summer. Now, every way she turned she saw symbols of privilege. Socialist ideas of equality had apparently sunk deep into her psyche.

'Pah,' she snorted in disgust, thinking of the hymn, 'All Things Bright and Beautiful', and of the one verse in particular that she used to sing so innocently. 'The rich man in his castle, the poor man at his gate, He made them, high or lowly, and ordered their estate.'

'Poppycock!' she muttered as she strode up the drive.

She had postponed seeing Diana for several weeks, unsure of how well she could handle talking to her face to face. But the niggling voice in her conscience had insisted that she do so, and at last she had reluctantly given in, promising herself that the next time she visited her parents she would call at the Cunningham's without fail. She had to tell Diana that Freddy had been a patient in the cave. She wanted to make sure Diana knew he had been given treatment and had been alive when the medical unit had pulled out, though she had no idea what had happened to him afterwards. Exactly what was impelling her to tell Diana about her encounter with Freddy was not entirely clear. Was it out of duty to Diana as an old friend? Freddy could have died and Diana might be longing to know what had happened to him. Perhaps it was partly because Constance wanted to make sure that, in this case at least, the image of the medical services in the Republic was untarnished regarding the treatment of wounded prisoners. She had come so very close to denying Freddy his chance for survival.

She laughed inwardly as she rang the brass bell on the door, remembering how she and Diana used to read 'The Water Babies' over and over again when they were little. Now she felt almost as out of place here as the poor little sweep Tom had done when he arrived so spectacularly down the chimney, covered in soot, in Ellie's wonderful clean, white bedroom. As she waited for the door to open, she vividly remembered the sisters that Tom met in the world under the water. Both she and Diana had been spellbound with delicious dismay at the stern punishments handed out by Mrs Bedonebyasyoudid, and had longed to turn the pages for the arrival of the kindly Mrs. Doasyouwouldbedoneby. 'One can do worse than emulate one's childhood heroines, I suppose,' thought Constance with a wry smile. If it had been the other way round, and Diana had nursed Karl, she knew she would have been grateful if Diana had come to see her, thankful for any scrap of information about him, however small.

The servant who opened the door was about to ask Constance to go round to the back. Such shabby clothes were not often found on the front step, after all. Fortunately, Constance began to speak, giving her name and asking if Diana were at home, before the servant's initial doubts had time to be put into words.

'Please wait here in the hall, Miss, and I'll see if she's available,' he replied, still slightly uncertain as to the correct form of treatment for an impecunious visitor who spoke as if to the manor born. Constance remained standing in centre of the spacious hall. Even though her appearance was more disreputable than on her last visit she was no longer at all embarrassed by the fact. She was wondering how many refugees could be housed comfortably at the manor. Emerging from the drawing room with none of her former languor, Diana seemed genuinely pleased to see her.

'Diana has certainly changed, even if the house hasn't,'

Constance thought as they briefly shook hands. Diana seemed somehow brittle, as if she could snap at any moment like a twig dried through and through by the Spanish sun. Her every movement betrayed her restlessness. She greeted Constance with a taut smile, saying immediately, 'Let's go for a walk. I feel like a caged beast in this mausoleum.' Although doubtful that there could actually be any corpses interred in the house, Constance was eager to escape the dead weight of tradition that the house had come to represent.

Once outside, Diana set off at the pace of a forced march, passing straight through the formal gardens to reach the wooded slopes beyond.

'I haven't been back long,' she began, 'and I shan't stay in England. I'll die of boredom if I do. I'm just here to get a basic nursing certificate at St Thomas's, then I shall be ready to go abroad to nurse in a field hospital if war breaks out. But it's so mortifying! Yesterday I spent all day being shown how to make beds, when a few months ago in Spain I was looking after a ward with eighty patients! How about you? Did you enjoy nursing the Reds?'

'I wouldn't say that "enjoy" would be quite the correct word, nor that all the patients were "Reds".'

Diana shot her an apologetic look. 'I'm sorry,' she said hastily, 'that was terribly rude of me, I'm just a bit strung up. The war has played hell on my nerves, and of course, it must have been much tougher for you than it was for me. And I haven't heard from Freddy for ages. I think I showed you his photograph, do you remember? I only hear the tiniest bits of news from his mother – she doesn't approve of my relationship with Freddy, you know. She has her heart set on him marrying a princess since his elder brother was killed. I'm not good enough any more. All I know is that he was shot down towards the end of the war. I've heard he's alive but he hasn't written to me at all.'

'His plane was shot down and he was badly injured,' Constance said quietly, 'I know that because he was brought to the hospital where I was nursing.'

Diana gave a gasp of surprise, exclaiming 'How wonderful that you should be the one to care for him. Do tell me everything, every detail you can remember.'

They soon became engrossed in lesions, operations and transfusions. Diana was particularly fascinated by the preserved blood that had almost certainly saved Freddy's life. She had only seen transfusions very rarely, and they had always been arm to arm.

'I take my hat off to your lot for new treatments. And fancy having to work in a cave or a tunnel, how dreadful for you. I remember sometimes in the operating theatre, the red and white tiles on the floor were so covered with gore that you couldn't tell which were which, but at least there was always electric light and running water.'

'We had a spring in the cave,' Constance protested, 'and an old truck engine as a generator. Sometimes it worked. All mod cons.' They smiled at each other tentatively, each knowing that the other was well aware of the true horrors of wartime nursing, ruined bodies, pain, death. Few people in England really understood that at the moment, and what was worse, only a few really cared.

'Can't you go back to Spain and see Freddy?' Constance asked, seeing Diana's expression grow sombre.

'I can't go chasing him, it would be very bad form, though there's nothing I would like more than to be in Spain. I love it so. But now they're talking of war again, only this time it will be terrible because I will have to support Britain, and Freddy and Spain will be on the other side. I've lost him really, one way or another.'

There was a sad despair in Diana's words that made Constance feel a stab of pity for her. Compassion was not restricted to allies it seemed. Although they were enemies in political terms, they also had much in common, not least in that they both were feeling the pain of loss in different ways. In the cave, she had hated Freddy for surviving, but the anger she had directed against him was now dissipating. To her surprise, she found another rage still burned, even deeper, a white hot fire of fury. All at once, she knew that Freddy's survival hadn't been the main cause of her anger. It was Karl; Karl who had died and deserted her, leaving her to face the world alone.

'Bastard!' she longed to shout, 'Why did you have to go and get yourself killed?' but instead she compressed her lips together and turned away. She could feel the pressure of unshed tears building up within her, as if all the snows of Teruel had melted and streamed down from the mountains in a single day, and only a flimsy dam of rapidly weakening will power still held them back. Perhaps there were enough tears to wash away the anger, but Constance certainly didn't want to find out in the presence of someone else.

Diana, for once rather more sensitive than usual, looked closely at Constance's face, so clearly full of suffering.

'Have you lost someone, Constance?'

'I'd rather not talk about it just at the moment, if you don't mind.' Constance focused all her attention on a speckled thrush in the branches of a nearby tree. It was singing as if its chest would burst with the beauty of the day.

Diana knew better than to press for confidences. Reserve was one quality for which the British were rightly famous. They had honed it to perfection over generations. To have a stiff upper lip was considered admirable, it would get you through. 'And,' Diana thought silently with a shiver of dread despite the sunshine, 'with another world war in the offing we're probably all going to need to be as plucky as Constance before long.'

'Come on,' she said cheerily to Constance, 'let's go back to the house for tea - Earl Grey or Darjeeling?'

IV

The Blitz, London, 1941

They had finally plumped for the Lyon's Corner House in Coventry Street. It was conveniently near Leicester Square tube station and not far from the hall where the International Brigade Association was holding a meeting later on. Constance chose a seat near the door where she would be able to see Addie's arrival clearly. The atmosphere was one of convivial activity; constant comings and goings, chinking of cutlery and crockery, friends chatting, and the Nippies, neat and tidy in their black dresses and little white aprons, bustling round between the customers with a degree of efficiency that Constance found most satisfying.

It was so long since she'd seen Addie. Their telephone conversation had been hurried, but soon they would have plenty of time to catch up on each other's news. The last she'd heard until the day before was that Addie had been rounded up in Paris with other foreigners when the Germans entered the city and had been interned in France. The news of her dramatic escape from the camp after months of incarceration had appeared in the late edition of the Evening Standard, together with a photograph showing her arrival in London from Lisbon, 'hatless' as the reporter was at pains to point out. 'It's quite amazing,' Constance thought as she read the article, 'even when a woman has escaped from the Nazis by crawling through barbed wire, has crossed occupied territory and returned to a city bombarded for months by the Luftwaffe, the newspapers still comment on her lack of headwear.'

'What is there to eat?' was the first question Addie asked when they were seated together a short while later. 'The food was awful in the camp, and I'm still gorging to make up for hundreds of missed meals. What luxury! Decent food and a waitress too.'

'It's good to see you. I thought about you so often,' Constance said watching Addie consuming crumpets with gusto. 'Being cooped up like that must have been terrible. I knew you'd try to escape. But what will you do now? Are you staying here in England or going home to America? It's been pretty grim here you know, what with the Blitz and one thing and another, and I suppose your family would prefer you be safe in the States.'

'Oh, I shall stay,' Addie replied without hesitation. 'I've already been offered a job here in London with the Free French.'

'How on earth did you manage that? You only arrived two days ago.'

'I had to go immediately to the Free French HQ at Carlton Gardens and find General De Gaulle. It was thanks to the French Resistance that I managed to get back here – they took me to the border, and gave me contacts to help me sneak through Spain and Portugal. I carried a message from them for De Gaulle, rolled up inside a cigarette. They insisted that I should give it to him personally. It was the least I could do after they had risked their necks for me. Anyway, De Gaulle was pleased and offered me a job. The 'Call to Honour' speech that he broadcast last June didn't bring quite as many French volunteers as he wanted, and my French isn't bad, so I can be useful for the war effort in a small way, thank goodness.'

Addie paused for a moment while Constance ordered more tea.

'And what about all our old friends?' she asked when the waitress had whisked the empty teapot away.

'Well,' replied Constance, 'Max will be at the meeting tonight, and Aurora too. They married as soon as he was released from that dreadful Spanish prison. He's been working non-stop for the association that the Brigaders have set up since they got home. That's what the meeting is about tonight – it's part of the campaign we're running for the release of political prisoners in Spain. The Army won't accept Max of course, although he tried to enlist. His health's not up to much, months in a damp prison didn't do him any good at all, not surprisingly. He kept his sense of humour though, goodness knows how. Sam joined up as soon as he could. He writes to me from abroad whenever he can, and I write back, keeping him in touch with news about the Association campaigns, and discussing books. He likes that.'

Talking of friends reminded Addie of someone else they had known in Spain.

'Here's a bit of news about an old acquaintance,' she said to Constance. 'Guess who I saw with a group of Whitehall mandarins when I was at Carlton Gardens?' Without giving Constance a chance to reply, she went on to answer her own question. 'María! She was very thick with these British Government types. They're secret service according to one of De Gaulle's officers. He told me he had dealt with them personally in the past, but he wouldn't give me the details. Too "hush, hush". María was probably working for them all along in Spain. No wonder she could get away with so much.'

An expression of irritation passed across Addie's face at the memory of all the trouble María had caused.

'We've got more important things than María to worry about now,' said Constance sorrowfully, and Addie had to agree she was right. The fact that María had probably been spying on them and undermining their work in Spain would always rankle, but there was nothing that could be done about it now. Perhaps in this war she would exonerate herself completely by some brave act of espionage, though Addie somehow doubted it.

'I haven't asked what you're doing yet, Constance. Are you working as a midwife again?'

'No,' Constance replied, 'apparently someone in Whitehall thinks I can be useful too. They're employing me to train nurses in the treatment of war-related casualties.'

'That's wonderful, Constance, there's so much you can teach them.'

'I hope so, but none of them can know what it's really like till they actually arrive at the front. Sometimes I don't think they believe half of what I tell them about conditions in Spain. You'll soon find out, now you're back. Hardly anyone is interested in helping the Spaniards, even though they were fighting Hitler and Mussolini as well as Franco for ages before we went to war. When I first came back from Spain I felt as if I'd arrived on another planet and was speaking a different language. That's partly why I joined the Communist Party – they cared more about Spain than all the others put together. Will you join?'

'I don't think so,' Addie replied thoughtfully. 'All that business of the Nazi-Soviet Pact was very distressing. How could Stalin sign any agreement with Hitler? None of the excuses the communists gave seemed to ring true to me. And there are other things that worry me – things they say are happening in the Soviet Union. Perhaps some of them are not proven yet but still.....' Addie saw Constance's frown deepening, so she hurriedly tried to explain her feelings a little more clearly.

'Perhaps I just think that a communist dictator is every bit as likely to be as bad as a fascist one,' she said finally.

The moment the words were uttered, she felt overwhelmed by guilt. 'What a traitor I am.' she thought with a sickening lurch of her stomach, 'am I being disloyal to all the comrades who died in Spain? I was once pretty convinced that communism was the best way forward, just like they were, and now, when they're not here any more to argue their case, I've abandoned them and their cause with a few glib words.'

'I'm sorry, Constance,' Addie said when she saw her friend's distressed expression. 'I know there couldn't be finer men in the world than those like Karl who were so deeply committed to communism. But sometimes things don't turn out the way you hoped.'

Constance bristled, 'You of all people should know that it would be ridiculous to write off something as wonderful as Beethoven's Ninth Symphony just because it was badly played. We may not have got communism right in the Soviet Union, but that just means we will have to try again, and try harder.'

Addie agreed, wishing to diffuse the tension as quickly as possible. 'You're right there, without a doubt. I've ruined enough splendid violin concertos in my time to know the truth of that argument.' She laughed lightly, but Constance wasn't quite ready to change the subject.

'Some of the chaps who were in the Brigades are thinking of going to China as soon as they can. I was talking to them about it last week. There's so much work to do there and the communists are trying to organise and change things. Perhaps I'll go there after the war. I'm sure Karl would have tried to help them.'

Addie had been trying to think of a way to introduce Karl's name into the conversation, but hadn't wanted to ask outright if time had made his death any easier to bear.

'I'm sure you still think of Karl often,' she said sadly, then ventured to ask, 'do you feel very bitter about his death, Constance?'

'Not so much now as before,' Constance replied, remembering the night after her meeting with Diana. Hours of cathartic sobbing had left her exhausted but purged of the anger that had been building up within her ever since Karl's death. To begin with, she had held Karl's photograph in her hand and raged at his image, about to rip the picture to shreds. But she couldn't bring herself to destroy the one thing he had given her, and when the tears eventually stopped, she carefully put the photograph into her handbag again. Her anger was gone, but the pain of loss, sharp as a hypodermic needle, had not. It could still pierce her heart without warning, sometimes when she was least expecting it, and with an intensity that could make her gasp with surprise.

Sitting at the table in the busy and cheerful restaurant, once again she experienced the jolt of remembering she would never see him again.

'I sometimes think of La Pasionaria's speech that day in Barcelona,' said Constance, a far away anguish in her eyes. 'She said "Better to be the widow of a dead hero, than the wife of a coward", do you remember that part?'

Addie nodded as Constance continued, her words laboured and painful.

'I'm not so sure she was right. I wish Karl had hidden behind a rock instead of rushing into the attack on the slopes of that hill. It wouldn't have made the slightest difference if he had, the hill was never taken anyway.'

'Oh, Constance,' Addie said softly, 'you would never have fallen in love with Karl in the first place if he had been the sort to hang back, would you? His courage was one of the things you loved about him. You wouldn't have changed that, would you?'

'No,' Constance replied, managing to twist her lips into something resembling a smile, 'I wouldn't have changed anything about him at all.'

After a few moments silence, Constance had recovered her composure enough to ask, 'And you, have you heard anything from Byron?'

'Well, in a manner of speaking, yes, but actually, no,' Addie said, leaving Constance puzzled as to what on earth she meant.

'Mother told me yesterday that Byron had tried to contact me before Christmas. He wrote to father at the University - I suppose I had mentioned he was working there - enclosing a letter for me. In the note to father he said he would soon be leaving the States. He had found a way to enlist and fight for the Allies.' Addie paused and took a breath before she went on. 'He also said that he intended to marry a Spanish refugee before he left, but that was all. No more details. My parents forwarded his letter to me in the camp, unopened of course but, along with quite a few others they sent, it never reached me. Mother and father didn't know that the letters weren't getting through, they were doing what they thought best. It's a pity really. I would have liked to know what he wrote.'

'Aren't you going to write to him now?' Constance asked, realising that Addie was putting a brave face on the fact that this letter, of all letters, had gone astray.

'I haven't got his address,' Addie said lamely.

'We can find out through the Association,' Constance said triumphantly, 'the Lincolns will have some organisation set up, I'm sure.'

'No,' said Addie with resignation, 'It would be too late now. I'd rather not.'

There didn't seem much more to say if he had married already, though she wondered yet again if he had written anything in the letter about the deserter. Had he explained how he had really felt about having to do such a terrible thing? The boredom of internment had given her plenty of opportunity to think over their last meeting, and in retrospect, she feared that perhaps she had condemned him out of hand for failing to meet up to her own expectations of perfection. It was a pity they had parted on such bad terms.

'And Rose?' Addie asked, wanting to change the subject. 'Have you seen much of her?'

'Oh, no,' Constance replied, 'Not since I took her the note from Rafael. I wrote to you about that. She and Dr Morris are married now. She sent me an invitation to her wedding but I didn't go. There's no news of Rafael at all. Goodness knows what happened to him and the others in Gurs when the occupation began. The Germans had lots of Republicans and Brigaders shot immediately, and sent some to labour camps in Germany and elsewhere. A few managed to escape and join the French Resistance, I believe.'

Both knew that the chances of Rafael's survival were slim. Even if he had been amongst those who had escaped the camps, as an experienced fighter he would probably be in the forefront of any guerrilla action and the risks would be inordinately high. Although neither Constance nor Addie had ever actually met him, they recalled the boyish, smiling face they had seen in the photograph that Rose had shown them. Like him, they had all been full of bright hopes. Defeat is such a cruel teacher, thought Addie. Only the most fortunate and resilient students can survive the course and come out stronger.

'It must be time to go to the meeting,' Addie said suddenly, 'I'm so looking forward to seeing everyone again, and I want to find out what I can do to help now I'm back.'

'Let's hope there isn't an air raid,' Constance said as they paid the bill. 'There've been lots lately. If there is, just hang on to me, I know the ropes.'

Whenever the sirens sounded, Constance wondered if Freddy might be amongst the German pilots flying over Britain. Each time the bombs began to fall, she couldn't help asking herself if she should have let him die in the cave. The choice she had made in a moment was one that was bound to have consequences, whatever she had decided. She always thought of Freddy in his plane as a particularly persistent and aggressive pigeon that insisted on coming home to roost.

The street outside was busy as they set off at a smart walk to arrive at the meeting in good time. Addie still wasn't accustomed to all the changes that had taken place in London since she had last been there; blackouts, sandbags, men in uniform. It pained her to see the destruction that she had been so familiar with in Spanish cities, now so clearly evident in London streets. Suddenly she saw a face in the crowd that she recognised.

'It's Rose!' she exclaimed to Constance, 'Rose, Rose,' she called.

Rose had apparently not noticed them. She was heading in the opposite direction, loaded with shopping bags. She stopped and turned, giving them a nervous smile of greeting.

'Rose,' said Addie warmly, 'You look so well. It's nice to see you.'

Addie had received Constance's letter about Rose while she was still working in the refugee camps. She had immediately tried to get permission to see Rafael, but it had proved impossible. In truth, she hadn't really been surprised to learn that Rose wanted to make an advantageous marriage in England. Her tactful enquiries had given her to understand that the legality of battalion marriages carried out in the Republican Army was highly questionable. How binding they were in moral terms was a different matter altogether. It was a matter for Rose's own conscience. Although Spain had been a dramatic experience for Rose, and had proved traumatic in many ways, it had been no more than a deviation from her original path, one to which she had now returned with relief.

In her smartly tailored suit, Rose looked very different, though somehow she had failed to attain the sophisticated elegance to which she aspired.

'I'm very well, thank you,' Rose replied politely to Addie's greeting. 'Did Constance tell you I got married? You must meet Ted sometime, he's so nice, isn't he Constance? I'm sure you'll like him.'

Constance mumbled her agreement and glanced at her watch.

Addie decided to offer an olive branch. 'We're just going to a meeting – it's the International Brigade Association. We could all go together. We've got to plan how we can help political prisoners in Spain.'

'Oh, I'm sorry,' Rose replied after a brief but significant pause. 'I have to meet Ted at Charing Cross Hospital. He's working there one day a week in the Poor Ward. We're moving into a new flat soon and there's so much to do. Perhaps we can meet up again another day.'

She rushed off with a wave of her gloved hand, her small figure disappearing into the crowd within seconds. Constance and Addie looked at each other wordlessly for several seconds.

'I think we may have seen the last of her,' Constance said as they walked on, 'and she never even mentioned Rafael.'

'She may not have said anything about him,' Addie said sagely, 'but I don't think she will ever be able to forget him. And if she never finds out what has happened to him, it'll be worse. He'll be like a restless spirit, haunting her for years.'

Constance never uttered the words she was thinking, and later she was glad they remained unspoken. 'Serve her right!' would have sounded harsher than she really felt. 'Temperamentally never very sound,' thought Constance, 'always inclined to histrionics.' Rose definitely needed a firm anchor.

The wail of sirens washed over one familiar reality - that of individuals quietly going about their business, and replaced it with another which Addie remembered well from Spain - the urgent need to take cover from the planes that dropped death from the skies. But just as in Madrid, she could see that the raids had occurred too often to cause complete panic. Constance took Addie's arm and shouted above the sirens, 'Come on, we're not far from Leicester Square, we can shelter in the Tube Station.'

They entered the tunnels, arms linked tightly together, impelled onwards by the rush of the crowd. Echoes of falling bombs penetrated deep underground and the sea of unknown faces around them became indistinct as the lights flickered and dimmed.

CHAPTER 9

Twilight Fires

I

Madrid 1996

'It's almost like being back in the Blitz!' Addie shouted to Constance as they were rushed along the tunnel under the Sports Palace in Madrid. But instead of the muffled sound of falling bombs they had heard in the passages leading down to the Tube Station, this time a strange rolling thundering noise echoed in the distance. It was growing louder and louder as they drew nearer the far end of the tunnel. Two enthusiastic young men noticed Addie was finding it difficult to keep up, and each then took an arm to help her along, almost whisking her from her feet. They talked loudly to her in Spanish. She'd no idea who they were, students probably. She caught glimpses of a few familiar faces in the gloomy light, but most were strangers, albeit of the most friendly sort imaginable.

Constance, much to her disgust, was in a wheelchair. Lately, she had begun to find that walking even for a short distance made her feel dizzy, and she certainly couldn't dash about as she used to do. 'How stupid of me,' she would say in annoyance, 'I really must pull myself together.' Increasingly, she was finding that she had to suffer the indignities of dependency for the sake of expedience. On this occasion, she had resigned herself to being propelled along by Angela, perhaps not a good choice after all. Judging from her performance, Angela had probably never pushed anything larger than a baby buggy. As they raced along at top speed, they could hear the rattle of a battalion of other wheelchairs bringing up the rear. Angela smiled at Addie excitedly, sensing the tension in the air that permeates history in the making.

Constance and Addie had both grown rather fond of Angela during the past year. They had spent hours together, Angela with a video camera recording their memories of Spain. She had contacted them initially because she was carrying out research for a thesis on the role women had played in the Spanish civil war.

'I suppose you consider us "Living History", is that it?' Addie had said at their first meeting.

'Rather than "hallow'd relics that should be hid" you mean,' Constance had added with a dry laugh, as fond as ever of finding an apt quotation - Milton this time. Angela's broad smile accentuated all the pointy facets of her features, 'Possibly more like lights trying to hide under bushels,' she had replied. It had taken her quite a while to persuade them that their lives really were worthy subjects for historical investigation.

In the eyes of Addie and Constance, now both over eighty, Angela still seemed young, even though she was well into middle age. She was a late starter, revelling in the newfound joys of academia as a mature student at university. Constance and Addie both found the eagerness with which she listened to their recollections most gratifying. As elderly women, they were accustomed to having to fight hard just to be visible, let alone heard, in a society that considered grey hair tantamount to non-existence. Though the interviews were completed, the visits continued. Angela, they noted with approval, could fight her own corner in an argument and like them, was inclined to be forthright; a nascent feisty old lady. When the invitation had arrived asking Brigaders to return to Spain for the sixtieth anniversary, they were pleased to hear that she would be coming along too. An extra pair of helping hands would be more than welcome now they were not as spry as they used to be, and she spoke Spanish. Theirs was undoubtedly a little rusty.

For Angela, the experience of meeting two such indomitable characters had been a revelation. Constance and Addie were still full of indignation at what was wrong with the world, and still actively campaigning for causes rather than moaning at what was lacking in the meals-on-wheels menu. She had tried to analyse exactly why her friendship with them had blossomed despite the difference in their ages, eventually coming to the conclusion that it was most likely due to a generational affinity. When young, they had all believed in the possibility of changing the world for the better; but whereas Constance and Addie had put their faith in a new political order, she had trusted in love and flower power, a hippy in spirit if not in practice. Their sense of disillusionment at their failure to revolutionise society was something else they shared, though the melioristic dream had merely been postponed for a few centuries rather than abandoned completely.

Light burst upon their faces as they entered the vast stadium. The crowd roared, greeting them as if they were champion footballers arriving for a cup final. The noise was deafening. Rising from their seats, people cheered and applauded, waving banners and stamping their feet. A chant spread through the audience reaching high into the rafters, '¡No Pasarán! ¡No Pasarán!', 'They shall not pass,' the defining cry of resistance to fascism used so often during the civil war. Constance, taken aback at first by the warmth of the welcome, blinked in surprise and then began to smile. Addie held on to her friend's chair for support, breathless from the exertion and emotion. She could see that most of the International Brigaders were below, already in the seats that had been reserved for them in front of the stage. All had been awaiting the arrival of the veterans in wheelchairs who had been taken to a different entrance. Eager hands now guided them down the steep ramp descending into the arena to join their companions for the concert that was about to begin.

Angela was certain this would prove to be one of the

most memorable occasions in the week of events that had been planned to commemorate the sixtieth anniversary of the war. Since then, Spain had passed through thirty five years of Franco's dictatorship, followed by an unspoken pact of silence lasting twenty five years. But the fear of re-opening the deep wounds left by the war was receding, and there were many Spaniards who now felt the time had come to show their gratitude to the Brigaders for having fought beside them so many years ago. Such outpourings of emotion in public were very alien to Angela. She had never been a screamer at rock concerts. Even the choice of the word 'Homage' that the Spanish used to describe the commemoration seemed overly obsequious to her. Nevertheless, she could feel the pull of this backwash from other people's lives sweeping her along in a current of emotions.

She parked Constance at the end of the row next to Addie and the British contingent. Sam was there, and Max, who was missing Aurora more than usual on this particular day. It had been years since she died, but he knew she would have been overjoyed to see the welcome they were getting. Janet and Florence were long dead too. The only other person Addie could see from the medical units was Reggie Aston, now asthmatic and a little absent minded. 'Although Rose is present too, in a bizarre way,' Addie thought, clutching the dilapidated large handbag on her knee. Inside, tightly wrapped in the rustly sort of supermarket carrier bag, was an unprepossessing brown plastic jar containing approximately half of Rose's ashes. It had been a problem for Addie to decide whether or not to declare them when checking in on the plane. In the end, she had kept quiet, hoping that she wouldn't be searched and the ashes pronounced 'a suspicious substance'. With all the excitement of lunches and speeches, she had forgotten to take them out of her bag before leaving the hotel room. Now she was rather glad that she had brought Rose along, even if only in the form of symbolic dusty remains.

A few weeks earlier, Addie had been very surprised when a solicitor had contacted her, saying he was carrying out instructions according to Rose's will. She had never seen Rose again, or heard anything from her, since the time their paths had crossed in the Blitz. According to the solicitor, Rose had recently added a strange little codicil to the passage in her will relating to the disposal of her ashes. Previously, she had wanted them all to be scattered on her husband's grave, but now she had requested that the ashes be divided. She wished half to be taken to Spain. Apparently, Addie learned to her amazement, Rose had been making substantial annual donations to the International Brigade Association for years. She had become a wealthy woman, helping Ted run his successful Harley Street practice. Their marriage had been a good one, but when he had died, having no children or surviving close relatives, Rose had made a will leaving everything to various institutions and charities, and a considerable bequest to the Brigaders. She had also left a letter for Addie. In a childish hand, she explained how she had tried to find out what had happened to Rafael after the end of the Second World War, but could find no record of him anywhere. Recently, she had written to the Brigaders' Association in Italy, but they hadn't been able to help her either. She had been hoping to join them on the trip back to Madrid, but as the date drew near her health had begun to fail. In the case of her death, she asked Addie if she would scatter some of her ashes in Spain at a 'suitable' spot. Quite how to interpret 'suitable', Addie was unsure. She intended to talk to Constance and Angela about the choice of site as soon as they had a moment. She felt a little sorry for Rose. It was a pity she'd died too soon to be with them in Madrid. 'I knew she could never forget Spain,' thought Addie. 'None of us can. It's engraved on our hearts.'

The concert was long. There was no shortage of famous actors and musicians who considered it an honour to perform on this particular occasion. Probably very few of the

International Brigaders fully appreciated the authentic Flamenco singer, whose veins swelled to such enormous proportions with the effort of producing 'Cante Jondo' that Reggie's medical instincts were alerted. After the folk songs and the recitations of poetry, a well known actress gave a moving rendition of La Pasionaria's farewell speech to the Brigaders. There was as much mopping of eyes in the audience filling the galleries as there was amongst the phalanx of veterans sitting in the arena below them. Finally, the Brigaders were asked to come up onto the stage. This manoeuvre presented some difficulty as the steep steps at either end of the stage were a daunting obstacle, but many Brigaders rose to the challenge. Angela looked up at the stage and saw to her dismay that not a single woman had appeared amongst the dozens of veterans.

'Come on, Addie,' she said firmly, 'there should be at least one woman up there to represent all the nurses. I'll help you up the steps.'

'But I wasn't a nurse,' Addie protested, 'and I wasn't really actually a member of the Brigades.'

'Oh, never mind that,' Constance snapped impatiently, 'you did your bit. We'll both go.'

Constance was extremely frail, but very determined. As she made her stately progress towards the stage along a cordoned aisle, leaning heavily on a shiny black walking-stick, video cameras followed her closely, recording the rush of well-wishers to the ropes. They leaned over to pat her arms, to shout 'Gracias'. One even managed to give her a kiss. 'People always like to make a fuss of nurses,' Constance said resignedly to Addie, though her delight was evident. Addie was embarrassed to be receiving her share of attention too, cameras flashing, reporters thrusting microphones at her asking, 'How does it feel to be back at last?' 'Wonderful,' she replied every time. Angela helped them up the steps to take their place with the others, then stepped into the wings to wait for them.

The veterans, on their best gentlemanly behaviour, insisted that Constance and Addie should move to the front. Television cameras zoomed high overhead, the cheering went on and on. Then the music began again. This time, the old songs were played, scratchy versions recorded in the thirties. As the well-remembered tunes boomed forth from the speakers, Addie found herself leaning for support on the arm of a gaunt figure next to her. There was something familiar in the brown eyes that met hers, though the wild silvery hair and deeply lined features confused her for a few moments. Now deaf as a post from machine-gun fire, Byron bent down low to hear the few words of greeting Addie shouted into his hearing aid, several times. He looked at her in surprise. Addie was even tinier than he remembered, and her face had changed considerably with the years. It was the glint of the vibrant light in her eyes that he recognised. His smile broadened as memories of the past flooded into his mind. Rather than a whispered sentimental endearment after so many years apart, he boomed into her ear, 'How's the research coming along?' But Addie saw his eyes beginning to shine more brightly. 'Old men shed tears so easily,' she thought, 'perhaps the glare from the footlights is bothering him.' There was, however, also the distinct possibility that he was really very pleased to see her. She took his arm and he put his hand on hers, enveloping her fragile fingers.

The audience was happily joining in the old war time songs. Constance was amazed that so many young people actually knew the words. Then, as she heard the first notes of the favourite melody of the German Brigaders, she felt a tremendous weight lift from her heart. The strong German voices filled the air. Karl had loved to sing. For a moment, she felt the gossamer-winged touch of a hovering ghost. The television cameras relayed pictures of her, standing as immobile as a statue, a slightly bemused smile of blissful contentment on her face. Constance was remembering Karl: the sunlit day when they had swum at the pool, the moment when he had given her his photograph. She had never spoken a word about those days since his death. Only Addie really knew how much she and Karl had loved each other. She thought of her unhappy marriage to Charles' father. It had been a mistake to marry someone she had seen more as a Party comrade than as a lover. But she had been so lonely, and Harold had asked her to come to China with him. She had believed she could find a new cause there in which to drown her sorrows. It hadn't worked at all. After Charles was born, they had separated.

'Perhaps I wasn't kind enough to Charles,' she thought with a pang of guilt, remembering his squalling cries when the Chinese doctors had eventually, and incompetently in her opinion, finished helping her give birth. 'I wonder, did I resent the poor little thing for not being Karl's son? I shall write to Charles as soon as I get back to the hotel. Perhaps I ought to tell him about Karl. He might understand after all.'

To the strains of the 'Red Flag', the Brigaders were helped down from the stage. 'Well, that was a pretty memorable experience,' Angela said to Constance, still slightly reeling from the emotional overload, 'and I'm only a historian. Goodness knows what it must have been like for you.'

Constance didn't reply. She seemed very far away.

II

Byron didn't let go of Addie as they left the stage. His hand still enclosed hers as it rested comfortably in the crook of his arm. When they eventually came out into the street, groups of Madrileños were waiting for them, their clapping sounding clear and crisp in the chill night air.

'Let's go for a drink somewhere,' Byron said as soon as the noise level allowed.

Addie hesitated, looking round for Constance.

'You're not still mad at me?' Byron asked her in dismay, misinterpreting her silence and thinking she was searching for a means to escape.

'No, I'm not,' Addie replied, 'and I would like to go for that drink. I just want to make sure Constance is alright. Can you see her?'

'Would I recognise her if I did?' he asked with a hint of the ironic humour that Addie remembered so well. 'Will she still be the one getting everyone to jump to it?'

'Usually, I'd say yes, but I'm worried about her tonight, she seemed so distracted.'

'Too many ghosts for most of us here,' said Byron, who understood as well as anyone the sway the dead could hold over the living.

Just then, Addie saw Constance and Angela as they emerged from the stadium.

'Hello there,' said Angela as they approached, 'I see you found an old friend.'

'Yes, indeed,' replied Addie, 'Constance, Byron's here. We're just off for a drink together somewhere quiet.'

Constance gave Byron a piercing look. 'Good,' she said at last, a hint of sarcasm creeping into her voice, 'it's about time you two made it up.' Addie was relieved to see she seemed almost back to her usual self.

'We'll see you later then,' said Addie. Byron took Constance's hand for a moment.

'Watch out for the ghosts,' he told her with a sad smile, but whether he meant they were to be avoided or welcomed, he didn't say. Constance nodded slowly, her eyes fixed on his, an understanding of some kind passing between them.

Neither Addie nor Byron wanted to go back to the Hotel Convención where all the Brigaders and their families were staying. Apart from being as impersonal and boring as the name implied, the hotel lobby and bar were usually full of journalists, all trying to grab a veteran for an emotive sound bite. Eager to be useful, one of the young helpers leapt into the road to get them a taxi.

'Hotel Gran Via,' Byron said to the driver, turning to Addie to say 'Is that OK? First place I could think of.'

'That will be fine,' said Addie, curious to see the changes that would have taken place in their old haunt.

It was a bizarre experience to be back in the hotel after so many years, especially to be sitting in the Hemingway Bar on the first floor, surrounded by images of him in framed photographs on the walls. The decor was presumably supposed to reflect the macho nature of his character, copious wood panelling and strong colours in the carpets and furnishings. Addie remembered the times she had seen him in this very hotel in Madrid, the centre of attention in a less upholstered setting. He had seemed a larger than life character then, a quality that was not much evident in the collection of black and white faded pictures.

'I don't think he ever stayed in this hotel,' Byron said in astonishment. 'He used the Florida over the road. He only wrote a few articles in the bar here, that's all. They sure have capitalised on their assets.'

He continued in a more sombre tone. 'I expect you read what Hemingway wrote about Spain in *For Whom the Bell Tolls*? I didn't see much of him after that was published. I was pretty mad when I read some of the things he'd written and ripped off a letter telling him exactly what I thought about it. I could stand the Hollywood treatment he gave the hero, artistic license and all that, but there were other things that I just couldn't stomach, the stuff against La Pasionaria for instance. He did write a good piece later, a eulogy for the American dead in Spain, and I spoke to him then, but we were never what you could call friends again.'

By now their drinks had arrived and they had found somewhere to sit, Byron finding it difficult to sprawl in the compact bucket-style chairs that were all that the bar offered apart from stools.

'Talking of books,' Addie said, 'I read yours - the novel

about the war, I mean. There were certain episodes that seemed clearly autobiographical. It explained a great deal, especially about the difficult decisions commanders have to make sometimes. I wish I had known how you felt before.'

Byron knew instantly what she meant. 'About that deserter you mean. I wrote to you about that, years ago.' He couldn't recall exactly what he had written, only that he had done his best to put into words why he had shot the man, why he had felt at the time it was the only thing to do, and how much he regretted having been so unwilling to talk to her about it in Marsá. He also remembered writing something about marrying a Spanish girl. She was one of the refugees who had gone to Mexico. He'd agreed to marry her so she could stay in the States, but at the last minute, she'd changed her mind and married her Mexican boyfriend instead. Then he'd headed straight off to fight in World War II.

'I never got the letter.' Addie told him, a slightly wistful note in her voice. 'I was in an internment camp in France and the letter went astray. By the time I got home and heard you had written to me, you would have been married and away fighting somewhere.'

Byron smiled wryly, 'But I never did marry her.'

A short stunned silence followed as both of them glimpsed a rapid sequence of scenes from an alternative past, one in which they might have spent their lives together after Spain.

'Did you marry?' Byron asked, hoping Addie's life had been good, that one missed opportunity had not had dire results.

'Oh, yes.' Addie replied, 'after the war was over. He was a biologist. We had four children. He died about twenty years ago.'

'I was married twice,' Byron told her, 'It seems a long time ago. I see the kids sometimes.' For a moment, they felt old and tired, two pensioners reviewing their lives, counting regrets. Just as Addie was thinking, 'This won't do at all,' a young couple on their way out of the bar stopped hesitantly by their table. They seemed to epitomise the changes in modern Spain. From their manner and appearance, they could have been from any major European city.

'You are Brigadistas?' the smartly dressed young Spanish woman asked in English.

'Sure we are,' replied Byron. Having endured the harrowing years of McCarthyism, he was half expecting the couple to hiss some anti-Red insult at them. There were still plenty of people left in Spain who believed that Franco had done a great job.

'Could you sign your names here for us, please?' asked the girl, her gold bracelets glinting as she thrust the paper napkin, printed with the words, 'Hemingway Bar', in front of Byron. 'My grandfather was a Republican. He died in the Battle of the Ebro. We don't know where he is buried.'

Byron signed the napkin with a flourish, and decided to elaborate a little. 'I knew Hemingway in Spain. He was always generous with the whisky, but don't believe what he says in that book about La Pasionaria. She was great!'

Addie sensed an ongoing contest between Byron and his old rival, despite Hemingway's suicide. Hemingway's fame had given him a distinct advantage, but Byron was retaliating with longevity. His face took on a softer expression as he added, 'She inspired us all, you know. I danced with her once, at a dinner after the Farewell Parade in Barcelona.'

It had been one of the few moments that day when the remorse of leaving Spain whilst the war still raged had diminished a little. 'Not that those of us who were left weren't glad to have got out alive,' Byron admitted to himself sadly.

The delighted couple left the bar and Byron turned to Addie once more, suddenly feeling guilty that he had hogged the limelight and hadn't noticed till too late that she hadn't given the couple her autograph too. He was pretty certain that spending so much time on his own was turning him into a self-centred old dinosaur.

'Well,' he said, determined to make amends, bony elbows perched on the arms of the narrow chair and long fingers pressed together, 'tell me what you've been doing.'

Addie thought of all the years of committees and campaigns, the hundreds of marches for everything from nuclear disarmament to 'Hands Off Cuba'.

'How many hours have you got?' she asked him.

'I've got all night,' Byron replied, 'How about you? You look as if you've brought an overnight bag with you. We could get a room here.'

It was very strange. A few minutes ago she had been feeling as old as the hills. Now a frisson of excitement ran through her. The idea of spending the night together, if that was what he had meant, still seemed deliciously risqué.

Addie chuckled, looking at her undeniably large handbag, and saying, 'No, I didn't actually come prepared for a night of passion. It isn't a nightie, it's Rose.'

She produced the jar from the depths of her bag, unwrapped it from its carrier, and deposited it on the table before them. Byron laughed out loud.

'An unusual ménage à trois, not the way I envisaged it at all,' he said, looking at the jar with amusement. 'What do you intend to do with her?' The business of scattering the ashes of old comrades in arms was nothing new to him. As Battalion Commander he'd been asked to do the job quite a few times. The trick was testing the way the wind was blowing before you started, though you always seemed to end up with ashes on your shoes however hard you tried.

'I'll ring Angela in the morning and get her to round up a few of the others. We can all go together and hold a small ceremony somewhere.' Remembering her visit to the front she added, 'Perhaps we can find a garden in University City, or near the river.'

'Puente de los Franceses,' said Byron, 'it crosses the Manzanares and it was a key point in the battle for the defence of Madrid.'

Addie agreed, 'I'll sort it out with Angela tomorrow.'

The room was certainly very different from the one they had last shared in Falset. The double bed was extra large and didn't have springs that sagged in the middle. There was air conditioning and an 'en suite' bathroom. Outside the window, instead of distant mountain ranges, the Madrid traffic snarled continuously, interrupted by the random whistles of policemen on traffic duty and the impatient hootings of car horns. When Addie shut the double-glazed window, everything went so quiet Byron thought the batteries had run out in his hearing aid. It took them quite a while to settle in; sorting through the basket of impossible-to-open cellophane packets to find the things they needed, struggling with the tiny toothbrushes and soaps, searching for more pillows and plumping them up in the right places. They chatted while they undressed, almost like an old married couple.

Then the conversation gradually faltered, words falling away with the clothes they removed. Such a strange combination of old familiarity and shock at the changes in each other left no room for any other thoughts. Very little about their bodies remained recognisable, an angle here and there, perhaps a subconscious gesture or two, but the rounded curves had all been obliterated by time and gravity.

'We look very different now, don't we?' said Addie, once they were comfortably side by side, leaning against the pillows. Their bare arms outside the covers reminded Addie of the Twiglets her children had loved to eat at parties; bumpy sticks, blotched with brown. But even so, perhaps there was a certain quality of beauty in aged limbs and bodies. Like gnarled and ancient trees, though they had been shaped and weathered by time, they were still able to contribute something to the landscape. Byron moved his arm closer to hers. He closed his eyes with pleasure as they touched. There had been other women since his second wife had died, considerably younger than he was, but the pressure to perform well had made these episodes increasingly stressful. It had been longer than he cared to remember since the last time. Addie was comparing the maps of their veins. His ran like prominent trunk roads just beneath a faded yellow tan from the California sun. Hers were like a network of rivers, meandering bluely under a translucent paper-thin skin.

'All these wrinkles are amazing,' she said, after considering the assortment of crêpey folds that had appeared since their youth. 'Do you think they are intrinsically ugly or is it just the way we are conditioned to think of them? After all, rhinoceroses are wrinkly and they find each other attractive.'

'I'm not sure,' Byron replied, opening his eyes hopefully, 'but I think it's a subject worth investigating.' The feeling of warmth radiating from another body in the bed was far more sensuous than that of an electric blanket, and being together again felt as good as arriving home after a long journey. With great tenderness, they began to discover each other all over again.

III

Habitual night wanderings to the bathroom would be better if synchronized, concluded Addie, waking yet again as Byron swung himself to his feet. She had lost count of the number of times they had woken each other up, but old bladders brook no denial. She opened her eyes just enough to see the glimmer of a bright November morning creeping round the curtain. A variety of interesting atonal compositions were erupting from the vicinity of the toilet, which Addie duly baptized, 'Duet for Bowel and Bowl'. Though there was no denying that things were different, not everything had changed for the worse. They could still find an inordinate amount of pleasure from sharing something they found beautiful or interesting, just as they had sixty years ago. Now, this shared enjoyment could be gleaned from things so small and trivial that they would have gone unnoticed before. When Addie had commented on this to Byron, he had laughed and replied, 'Are you saying size doesn't matter any more?'

Returning to their room after breakfast, they lay together on the bed, Byron on his back stretched out at full length, Addie curled beside him. The last few days had been hectic for them both. 'Just for a few minutes,' they agreed, neither of them in a hurry to rejoin the heavy schedule of organised events. Addie was thinking she must ring Angela before it got any later and let her know where they were, but sleep drifted over her as soon as her eyelids closed. The shrill ringing of the telephone startled them. Confused at being woken so abruptly and wondering who on earth could be ringing, Addie answered. Angela's voice sounded strained.

'I've been trying to find you, then I remembered you told me how you used to go to the Hotel Gran Via. Are you alright?' she asked anxiously, but Addie knew that she wasn't ringing just to check on their whereabouts.

'We're fine,' she answered hurriedly, 'what's wrong?'

'I'm ringing from the hospital. It's Constance. We don't know exactly what's the matter with her, they're still doing tests. You know I was sharing a room with her in the hotel? When I got back last night she was already in bed and she didn't wake up, but then in the early hours of the morning, I realised her breathing sounded odd. I tried to rouse her but I couldn't, she was unconscious. She still is. Sam and Max are on the way here – it's the Hospital de la Princesa.'

'I know it, we'll meet you there,' Addie had replied, replacing the receiver and rising shakily to her feet.

As with all sad little groups of anxious friends or relatives hanging around in hospital corridors, each member had to deal with the protracted periods of waiting in their own way. Sam paced. He would try to sit down but moments later would set off again, over to the window, back again to the door of Constance's room. The doctor was with her. They had all been told to wait outside, that they would be able to go in one at a time afterwards, but Angela had insisted on staying with Constance. She wasn't going to leave her with strangers, just in case she regained consciousness. Max went off down the corridor to find cups of coffee for everyone. Nobody really wanted one, but they hadn't liked to say no. He so obviously wanted to be doing something. Addie sat next to Byron, deep in thought. The doctor had asked if she knew the family's wishes regarding resuscitation. At first, she hadn't known what to say. Until then, she hadn't realised that Constance might actually be dying. They'd known each other for so many years, it was hard to imagine what it would be like without her.

'I'm not sure about the family, but I'm certain Constance wouldn't want it,' she had answered finally.

Byron patted Addie's arm from time to time and glowered at the bare pastel walls, hating hospitals and the whole damned business that usually surrounded the act of dying these days. A quick bullet was, after all, distinctly preferable to having your life prolonged when your time was up, just because some young medic wanted to prove he could pull out all the stops.

When the doctor came out Angela was besieging him with questions; diagnosis, prognosis, treatment? She knew she had to telephone Constance's son and wanted to be able to explain what was happening, but the doctor was reluctant to give anything more than vague reassurances that they were doing everything they could. It didn't seem to be much. Whilst Angela struggled to make sense of Spanish medical jargon, Addie went in to see Constance.

Exactly how much of Constance lingered in the pallid figure lying so passively on the bed, Addie was unable to judge. Her heart skipped a beat at the shock of seeing

Constance, not so much peaceful as absent. An oxygen mask covered her nose and mouth and the hiss of the gas was the only sound in the room apart from the occasional rattling, irregular breath. Addie sat by the bed, holding Constance's hand, the one without the needle for the drip, and talked to her, telling her that Byron was waiting outside with Sam and Max, that they were hoping to come in to see her soon. She was unsure whether she felt a fleeting response from the cold fingers, the slight squeeze of acknowledgement, or if it was no more than the random firing of disengaging nerves, or even her imagination. Then, there was a gap in her breathing that didn't end, it turned silently into forever. Addie didn't want to move, didn't wish to relinquish her hold on Constance's hand, knowing that it would be for the last time. She removed the oxygen mask and looked at her friend's face, though now it seemed only the mask of a lifeless waxen effigy. They'd been through so much together – only Addie would remember now. Some memories had been of awful things, like the fire in the Barcelona flat when the nurses died. Some had been dramatic but had made them laugh later, such as the time Constance had come to visit Addie when she was expecting a baby for the first time. Addie was complaining of a very painful indigestion that was making it difficult for her to concentrate on the book she was writing on the French Resistance. Constance had delivered her baby about half an hour later. Despite all their differences of opinion over the years, it had been a wonderful friendship.

'Well done, Constance,' Addie said quietly, aware that soon, the inevitable rituals of death would begin, 'I'm sure you died just as you would have wanted. No fuss.'

When Addie came out, they all knew immediately that it was over. Angela called for the nurse. Sam shook his head when they asked him if he wanted to see Constance. His lips trembled a little as he replied, 'No thanks, I'd rather not.' He preferred to remember her alive. He never had told her he loved her, knowing that it wouldn't have worked out between them. Sam had never wanted to play second fiddle to Karl's ghost.

'What now?' asked Addie, 'We can't all stay sitting in this corridor, moping around.'

'I'd better ring Charles,' replied Angela, desperately concentrating on practicalities, 'then I'll try to sort out what's to be done here.' She fished in her bag for the programme. 'All the others will be just arriving at a lunch now, the one put on for you by the Trades Unions.'

'Oh, hell,' Byron groaned, 'I'm supposed to give a speech at that one.'

'We'll all go,' Addie said determinedly, 'we were invited to come here for these events, and we shouldn't let them down. Anyway, it's what Constance would want us to do, we all know that.'

They all nodded in agreement. Constance would have been the first to tell them that they hadn't come along just for a free trip. It was another opportunity to make sure people understood about fascism. That was why many of the Brigaders still went to meetings and made speeches and visited schools. It was to warn people that fascism wasn't dead. It had other names but it still flourished, always a danger that must be resisted. Constance had always been determined to spread the message of the International Brigades, that people must unite to fight for freedom.

They'd all had plenty of practice at postponing grief in the war. There would be time for mourning when they got home again. Only Angela was new at it. She'd had no idea that historical research could be so painful. What she would have really liked to do was to go home and have a good cry, but she knew she had to try to be pragmatic.

'Tomorrow morning you'll be at the Spanish parliament for the ceremony offering you citizenship, then afterwards, groups of you go off to different towns where events have been planned for the afternoon. The next day you all travel to Barcelona for a farewell parade. It's a heavy schedule.'

Angela looked at them, wondering if they were up to it. Despite their resilience, they all suddenly seemed so frail.

'I've forgotten all about Rose,' said Addie, clutching at her handbag. 'We've got to do something about her ashes. I can't just tip them out anywhere, she particularly requested somewhere suitable.'

After a brief discussion, all agreed that Byron's suggestion of the Puente de los Franceses would be appropriate.

'I'll ring some friends who run the 'Women's Bookshop' here in Madrid, they'll help us fix something up,' promised Angela. 'You go on to the lunch now, and I'll meet you there later.'

When the meal and the speeches were over, dozens of Madrid women, exuberant and noisy, piled onto the coach with a handful of Brigaders to set off for the Puente de los Franceses. After Angela's phone call, the word had spread like wildfire amongst the women who frequented the book shop that there was to be a ceremony to scatter the ashes of a 'Brigadista' - a nurse from the civil war. They were not going to allow the occasion to pass unnoticed. Most of them were far too young to remember the war, thought Addie, as they sang verse after verse of the songs their mothers or grandmothers must have taught them. They sang of the Puente de los Franceses, of how it had been so well defended by the people of Madrid that the fascists couldn't enter. Their voices rose to a crescendo when they reached the verse describing how well their city had withstood the bombardments. Addie looked out of the window and saw the new Madrid passing by; no houses in ruins, no bomb craters in the streets. The buildings of University City were no longer empty, hollow shells. She joined in the singing, remembering the words as if it were yesterday:

Madrid ¡que bien resistes!
Madrid ¡que bien resistes!
Madrid ¡que bien resistes!
Mamita mía, los bombardeos, los bombardeos.

Another surprise awaited them at the bridge. A large crowd had gathered there too, mainly of elderly people, waving Republican flags resurrected from almost forgotten hidden places. Even though Franco had been dead for years, there were many eyes still filling with tears at the joy of being able to flourish the flags in public without fear of retribution. They advanced along the path by the side of the river Manzanares to the bridge, a slow and colourful procession, especially if compared to the lone joggers who regularly ran the distance in seconds. The afternoon sun had begun to slip behind the apartment blocks but it was still warm. Angela had found some ribbons in the violet, yellow and red of the Republican flag to tie round the jar in an attempt to make it a little more ceremonially acceptable. Addie made sure she could unscrew the lid before she began to say a few words in Spanish about Rose; how she had been wounded when working as a nurse at the front, how much Spain had meant to her, how she had never forgotten it – clichés, Addie knew, but true nevertheless. She tipped the contents of the jar onto the grassy bank of the river at the foot of the bridge. The breeze was so slight that only the finest film of dust was blown towards her feet. The ashes that didn't disappear in the grass were soon covered with red carnations brought by the women from bookshop and others.

Angela said guiltily, 'We forgot all about bringing flowers, what with one thing and another. We should have brought some roses, you said everyone called her English Rose.'

'Never mind,' Max replied, 'there's plenty anyway, and carnations look pretty much like roses.'

'You're right, Max,' Addie said, smiling as the singing

began again, 'it really doesn't matter. Rose would just be pleased we'd had a bit of a party for her.'

She was sure that was true. Rose, quite unlike Constance, had always liked a fuss being made of her. The two of them had been so different, thought Addie, particularly in the lessons they had learned from the war in Spain. Constance had never lost faith in the beliefs they had held then. Her image of Karl was changeless, a petrified ideal that she had embraced with all her heart. His crusade remained hers until she died. Rose had tried so hard to forget, to leave everything that had happened in Spain behind her, but it had followed her like a shadow. In the end she had turned to face it, to accept that it had been a part of her life.

'And what did Spain teach me, I wonder?' Addie went on to ask herself. The question, stirring into sentience, set off to quietly rummage round in her mind like a determined mother looking for a child's lost teddy in an overflowing toy box.

It had been a very Spanish affair, not a bit like an English funeral, thought Angela when they were on the way back to the centre of Madrid. Normally, she tried to avoid going to the so-called 'chapels', where groaning conveyor belts carried chipboard coffins off to the incinerator to the strains of piped music. Rose's farewell had been infinitely preferable, though after so much hugging, crying, and kissing, all following on so soon after Constance dying, she wasn't surprised that she felt exhausted. She had to go back to the hospital later to sign more papers relating to the disposal of Constance's body. She was dreading it. Such matters were not as straightforward as she had supposed. It might take days to sort everything out.

'I remember a good bar near here,' said Byron suddenly, 'stop the bus.' He didn't usually drink much these days, but they all could do with one now.

The bus driver pulled in to the side of the road, ignoring the angry hootings from other vehicles. The Bar Chicote hadn't changed much. It was a bit like stepping back in time - Art Deco furnishings, discreetly curtained windows and high sided booths. Sam, Max and Angela joined Addie and Byron in one of them. Angela had noticed with amusement that when Addie and Byron had walked down the street together they had seemed to be propping each other up, occasionally having to make directional adjustments when their steps had veered off track. Now they had chosen to sit closely together on the bench seat, Byron hunching down low because he was so much taller and both of them leaning towards each other till their heads were almost touching. Neither wanted to miss what the other was saying.

'At least these events give old friends the chance to meet up again occasionally.' Angela was forming presumptions that reflected the usual slightly patronising attitude of younger people towards the elderly.

'I expect you'll be keeping in touch now,' she said to them, 'when this week's over I mean?' The idea of elegantly scripted letters crossing the Atlantic between them had a romantic appeal.

'Oh, very close touch,' Addie replied, an unmistakable twist of humour playing impishly across her lips, 'we've already talked about that. Byron's coming back to England with me so I can collect a few things, then I'll be going to the States to move in with him. I haven't been back for years and I feel like a bit of a change. The children should be old enough to manage without me, after all, they are all middle aged.' She was beginning to think that it might be rather enjoyable to tell them she was leaving home to go and live with a man. It had certainly startled Angela.

'There sure as hell's no point in wasting any more time,' said Byron cheerfully, 'we're all dropping like flies, but you never know, there might be a few good years left.'

They talked for a while about what life was like in the USA and debated the iniquities of the government's foreign policy but, inevitably, their thoughts gravitated towards the absence of Constance. Angela took the single sheet of a letter from her bag and gave it to Addie.

'Constance must have been writing this letter to her son before she went to bed. I found it when I went back to the hotel today. I thought you might like to send it to him. Perhaps it would be better coming from you than from a total stranger like me.'

Addie scanned the few lines written in Constance's familiar hand on hotel notepaper.

> Dear Charles,
> There are several things that I would like to say to you and I would rather write than telephone. It will be easier for me to explain things in a letter.
>
> Firstly, I want to thank you for all the concern you showed towards me before this trip. I know you were worried about my health and advised against travelling, but I am very glad that finally, despite the risks you so carefully pointed out, I decided to come. I have just returned to the hotel after attending the most wonderful concert here in Madrid. The welcome the people gave us was overwhelming. I shall never forget it and have no regrets whatsoever about my decision to come back. Please don't worry any more on my account.

Addie looked up, the last stilted words wavered slightly, then there was no more. Whatever else Constance had intended to say would remain unspoken. 'I wonder if she was going to tell him about Karl?' thought Addie, as perceptive as always, 'how hard it is for children to understand their parents, probably even harder than it is for parents to understand their children.'

The barman approached them with a newspaper in his hand. He beamed at them, 'Los Internacionales, ¿Sí?' He placed the evening edition on the table in front of them, folded back to the inside pages. Constance's obituary bore the headline, MORIR EN MADRID - 'To Die in Madrid', the title of one of the most famous documentary films made during the war. Below was a large photograph of Constance taken at the concert. Wisps of white hair escaped from the plait wound round her head and formed a frame for her striking features – the slightly deviated nose, the peaceful smile and the sad eyes that seem to be looking into a distant past. It captured her exactly as they remembered. The text told the story of the death of an English nurse who had returned to Spain for the first time since the civil war.

'Poor old Connie,' said Max, 'what a trooper. We're going to miss her.'

Sam pulled on his moustache and cleared his throat noisily.

'That's for sure,' said Byron, 'but she was ready to go. When I saw her after the concert, she'd decided it was time. She wasn't afraid at all. It was perfect timing.'

Angela felt the tears prickling in her eyes. She hadn't known Constance for long but she was already missing the times they had spent together in the basement flat, always comfortably warm on the coldest days with the Aga at full blast. Constance had liked to talk about the birds that came for the food she put out by the window. A wren had been her favourite, Angela remembered. It had been obvious that Constance was no longer strong; she'd never really recovered after the boating accident. But somehow Angela had not really appreciated the fact that indomitable did not mean indestructible. She'd come on the trip in order to understand the significance of the Brigaders' return to Spain, but as she looked at the picture of Constance spread out on the table before her, she realised that the weight of symbolism could lie very heavily on the heart. Addie watched her as the tears fell silently and plopped onto the paper.

'What remarkable lives you've had,' Angela eventually managed to say to Addie, blowing her nose on the tissue Addie passed to her. 'I hope my thesis does you all justice.'

Although there were thousands of books on the Spanish civil war, they were mostly about politicians and battles. Very little had been written about women. Angela didn't want their stories to disappear leaving barely a trace, yet she doubted her own abilities. If only, she thought enviously, I had one of those analytical minds that can draw incisive conclusions from a mass of historical data and a stack of weighty tomes. Only the fact that nobody else was carrying out the research needed to do the job had persuaded her to begin.

Addie fixed her with an intense, unwavering stare and tapped the hand holding the crumpled tissue sharply with a rather bony finger.

'You,' she said slowly and carefully, 'must write a novel when your research is done. You want to write about women and the war? That's the best way to do it. There's often far more truth in a novel than in history books.'

Angela turned to look at Addie in surprise.

'I don't think I could. I've never written one before.'

Byron gave a loud laugh, 'I'm just an uneducated kid from Brooklyn and if I can do it, so can you.'

Addie became aware that she now had found the answer to the question that had been bothering her earlier. She knew that even though they had lost the war in Spain, some things had been learned despite their defeat. The International Brigades had certainly shown people that it was possible to fight together in a just cause, and the lesson hadn't been forgotten. Why, the very fact that they were here in Spain for these events proved that.

'You must try,' she said to Angela, 'it's important to try, even if you fail. That's what the war in Spain taught me.

Even though we lost, just trying was valuable, much better than having done nothing at all.'

Angela hesitated. Just as surely as the war in Spain had drawn all these people together, she was now being caught in the wake of their lives.

'I'm sure you can do it,' Addie said with conviction, 'if you really care enough'. Her eyes took on a look that Angela already knew well, a sort of steely confidence that you would choose to do the right thing, that you would undertake some long and arduous task. All in a good cause, of course. Angela knew that the promise, once made, would have to be fulfilled even though it might take years. She took a deep breath and said, 'I'll do my best.'

POSTSCRIPT

My thanks to all the women whose stories of the Spanish civil war, told to me over many cups of tea, were the inspiration for this novel. Readers who have enjoyed this book may wish to know more about the lives of real women who went to Spain during the civil war. Published memoirs and diaries include the following:

Penelope Fyvel, *English Penny*, Arthur Stockwell, Ilfracombe, 1992.

Nan Green, *A Chronicle of Small Beer: The Memoirs of Nan Green*, Trent Editions, Nottingham, 2005.

Molly Murphy, *Molly Murphy: Suffragette and Socialist* (ed.Ralph Darlington) Institute of Social Research, University of Salford, 1998.

Priscilla Scott-Ellis, *The Chances of Death: A Diary of the Spanish Civil War* (ed. Raymond Carr) Michael Russell Ltd., Norwich, 1995.

A collection of women's letters from Spain together with extracts from interviews and memoirs was published as *Women's Voices from the Spanish Civil War* by Jim Fyrth and Sally Alexander, (eds), Lawrence & Wishart, London, 1991.

Of particular interest and quality amongst the unpublished memoirs on this subject are those of Frida Knight.

The Imperial War Museum Sound Archive, London, hold recordings of interviews with many volunteers, both men and women, who served in Spain. Patience Edney describes her experiences there as a nurse with exceptional clarity and detail.

Books relating to the role of women in the civil war include *British Women and the Spanish Civil War* by Angela Jackson, published by Routledge/Cañada Blanch Studies on Contemporary Spain, London, 2002 (soon to be published in paperback), and Paul Preston, *Doves of War: Four Women of Spain*, HarperCollins, London, 2002. For more on the war and Spanish women, see Shirley Mangini, *Memories of Resistance: Women's Voices from the Spanish Civil War*, Yale University Press, 1995.

There are numerous memoirs written by men of different nationalities who fought in the International Brigades. Many are listed in the bibliography of *British Volunteers in the Spanish Civil War: The British Battalion in the International Brigades, 1936-39*, by Richard Baxell, Routledge/Cañada Blanch Studies on Contemporary Spain, London, 2004, recently published in paperback by Warren & Pell Publishing. The atmosphere of the times is well-captured in the autobiographical novels of the veteran Brigader, Milton Wolff, *Another Hill*, University of Illinois, 1994, and *Member of the Working Class,* iUniverse, New York, 2005.